Praise for Book Four, *The*

"Another spellbinding dive i... This time very local and very relevant to the time we now live in. We see another side to Tammy, juggling mother-hood (who would have thought), with crime fighting. Andrew Segal's style and authenticity make this as usual a 'must read' that will have you on the edge of your seat."
— Charles Shiplee, avid Crime Thriller reader

"Wow, this one left me gasping for air! Fast pace and hits you straight from the very first page. The prologue really brings the cover to life, too. You can hear the car tyres squealing. The various timelines the story brought past books into play too, very clever! Fantastic writing and in this one Tammy although still a badass super woman, shows a softer side to her. I loved it, my favourite one so far!"
— Lisa Hamer, Bookstagram Reviewer

"What a read! Another outstanding book from Andrew Segal. Once I started I just couldn't put it down. The storyline is compelling with so many unexpected twists and turns making you think that they're on the way to resolving the murders, but then finding a dead end and having to virtually start again. Segal's imagination and ability to introduce such interesting characters is stunning with Tammy such an outstanding heroine. She really does delve into the case in such unexpected ways. I look forward to the next one."
— Mike Wylie, Trustee, MidasPlus

"I really enjoyed the darkness and shock! Tammy's relationship with Dov is heartbreaking for them both. It is so real but in the craziest of circumstances. The hook to go on to the next book is intense."
— Kate Edmondson

"A gripping and emotionally resonant crime thriller that keeps you turning pages late into the night. Following investigator Tammy Pierre as she navigates a chilling series of murders across the nightclub scene, the story balances sharp investigative detail with genuine heart. The author handles complex relationship and identity themes with sensitivity and urgency, creating a narrative that is both suspenseful and socially aware. Tammy Pierre is a compelling, believable lead whose determination anchors the novel, making this a powerful and memorable read for fans of modern crime fiction."

— Emily Tout, Flexible Resourcing, NHS

"I really enjoyed this book. The story is strong, and a pleasure to read! The book is in third person and is in multiple points of view. Including the killer which was a great addition. The continued building of Tammy's London is brilliant. The descriptions and attention to detail are exquisite. The characters are a joy and very well thought out. Tammy is a strong female main character and is very well written. I definitely recommend the book and the series."

— Nicola Doyle, ARC Reviewer

"Absolutely loved it, another fast-paced Tammy Pierre novel, every scene a surprise, and this time the heroine is also a loving mother. We see her in context, and the other characters, too: Segal makes us understand even the most wicked creatures, gets into their heads, gives them a heart, shows their brokenness with compassion. Which makes them no less terrifying! I did not suspect the killer until very late. Word of caution: it is way too interesting to put down, gave me a proper jetlag!"

— Zsuzsanna Pataki, artist, uni lecturer, choosy thriller addict and Segal fan

Praise for Book One, *The Lyme Regis Murders*:

"*The Lyme Regis Murders* was a really great read. A riveting murder mystery with a modern feel. It was fast paced with lots of twists and turns even to the end. The author is a superb writer and I shall be buying more of his books."
— Mrs. H. Bate, UK reviewer

"Dead bodies, suffering children, multiple suspects, and everyone hiding skeletons in their cupboards. It's a heady mix and leads to an appropriately tortuous investigation, blending dramatic characters, complex background stories, convoluted action-adventure, and a pleasing sense of time and place. *The Lyme Regis Murders* is not cozy or sweet, but it's the sort of read that becomes hard to put down because you want to see the ending."
— Sheila Deeth, US reviewer

"Grab your copy if you like crime thrillers with strong female protagonists with LGBTQIA+ representation!"
—Booky Charm, Bookstagram Reviewer (audiobook)

"I liked the in depth descriptors of characters, places and attention to detail. This book will please those who enjoy language as it's first rate. Damn good read."
— Gail Pearson, UK reviewer

"A great read with an ending made to shock — it's got me hooked and I'm ready to dive into Book Two!"
—Book-a-holic, Bookstagram Reviewer (audiobook)

"Great read! I would definitely recommend and have already bought his next book *The Black Candle Killings*.
— J. Walsh, UK reviewer

Praise for Book Two, *The Black Candle Killings*:

"I loved the writing style and the story. I love Tammy. ... I was definitely surprised a few times. It certainly wasn't who I thought it was. I'm looking forward to the next book. Definitely recommend!"
— Sue Wallace, #Bookstagrammer

"A book with an unconventional female heroine, an abundance of complex characters and settings as diverse as London, Trinidad and Aleppo. Add a little voodoo to the mix and you have a thrilling detective page turner. ... A fast-paced thriller tied together with a descriptive narrative that transports the reader across continents. A compelling protagonist, intricate plotting, global settings, and unique cultural elements, Segal offers readers an unconventional thriller. If you're tired of the same old, same old, and want a thriller that truly stands out, check this one out."
— Sue Oxley

Praise for Book Three, *The Politician's Wife*:

"Gripping latest edition to the Tammy Pierre series. I was immediately sucked in by the complex female protagonist and found myself flying through the pages, eager to learn how this 'who-dun-it' tale would unfold."
— Shana Sexton, Luxury Travel Consultant

"*The Politician's Wife* is a real page-turner and the twist at the end was really unexpected. It was an intriguing tale and well plotted; I became invested in the characters and what was driving them. I don't normally read crime fiction but Tammy Pierre is a credible hero and I am keen to follow her further Runyonesque escapades and Jilly Cooper had best look to her laurels if she wants to stay ahead of the game."
— Lynne Brooke (Mr), Solicitor, The Brooke Law Group LLP

"Andrew Segal's *The Politician's Wife* is a masterclass in weaving intrigue, emotion, and raw human experience. Every page pulls you deeper into the intricate lives of its characters and leaves you both pondering and eagerly turning to the next chapter. A truly gripping read that resonates long after the final page is turned."

— Kenneth Kufeji, B.Sc. Computer Science & Accounting; MBA

"A gripping, witty tale that kept me on the edge of my seat throughout. Interesting and challenging — indeed at times disturbing — the characters are fascinating. Particularly Andrew Segal's heroine, Tammy, is brought to life, as are all the characters that interact to deliver an exciting plot. Takes the reader on a journey through the complexity of extremism, relationships, and human emotions — with a number of surprises along the way. A great read!"

— Jasper de Q Adams, Retired Army Officer / Security Consultant

THE CLUBHOUSE SLAUGHTERS

ANDREW SEGAL

The Clubhouse Slaughters
Copyright © 2026 by Andrew Segal

ISBN: 978-1-917626-06-4 (paperback)
        978-1-917626-07-1 (ebook)

Cover design: Mike Dewey
Interior layout & design: Tom Collins

All rights reserved.

No part of this book may be reproduced in any form or by any electronic or mechanical means, including information storage and retrieval systems, without written permision from the author, except for the use of brief quotations in a book review.

The moral right of the author has been asserted.

This is a work of fiction. Names, characters, businesses, places, events, locales, and incidents are either the products of the author's imagination or used in a fictitious manner. Any resemblance to actual persons, living or dead, or actual events is purely coincidental.

THE TAMMY PIERRE SERIES

Book One: *The Lyme Regis Murders*
Author's Edition - April 2025

Book Two: *The Black Candle Killings*
Author's Edition - August 2025

Book Three: *The Politician's Wife*
January 2025

Book Four: *The Clubhouse Slaughters*
February 2026

And . . .
Coming in Spring 2026
Book Five: *A Corridor of Mirrors*

Don't miss the preview chapters
at the end of this book!

.

DEDICATION

For Roberta
Best Beloved

THE CLUBHOUSE SLAUGHTERS

Little boy blue, explosions at dawn
As ye sew so ye'll reap,
It's not you that they'll mourn?

But where is he now, who treats life so cheap?
Why, he's setting those timers to wipe out more sheep.

R.A.

PROLOGUE

RECENTLY

3:00 AM

THE SCREAM OF TWO MONSTER MOTORS bellowing their challenge to duel; a pair of night-time predators.

A freezing night of deserted roads in Oxford's town centre. A white-faced full moon reflecting eerily on the shining surface of icy puddles in the city's many potholes; spectral blind eyes, making motoring treacherous. A sparkle of hoarfrost sugar-coating parked vehicles in streets too narrow for the two racing supercars to squeeze through unscathed. Insane driving, inviting catastrophe.

Empty pavements, apart from a few late-night-wandering pedestrians, partygoers, nightshift workers, breathing vapour, staring speechless as the two vehicles raged past them.

The two-seater, 6.5 litre, 789 bhp Ferrari 812 Superfast, a flash of elegant red, weighing 3362 lbs, swooped past. Emerging from a side street, Private Investigator Tammy Pierre's brand-new, supercharged, 621 bhp Porsche Panamera Turbo S in a typhoon hail of gravel.

With a top speed of 211 mph or more, the Ferrari could climb from nought to sixty in 3.0 seconds. She'd seen this car before. Only recently, she'd duelled with it. The same car? Had to be. Not too many of these supercars around.

Tammy's more practical 4.8 litre, heavier at 5290 lbs, four-door, four-seater silver car would reach sixty unofficially in about 2.6 to 2.9 seconds, but it's top speed at

196 mph would fall short of the Ferrari's by some 15 miles per hour, her car's smaller engine carrying the greater kerb weight.

Overtaking the Ferrari would require all of Tammy's skills. She was accompanied on this chase by long-term colleague Detective Chief Superintendent Bob Walker, her ex Met boss and mentor. Her vehicle's heavier payload might yet prove useful.

On Israeli Secret Service Mossad's discreet advice, having kept a low profile throughout the investigation which was not their brief, Mossad had tracked the Superfast through ANPR and CCTV images over a number of weeks, never getting anything other than blurred images of the man they were trailing. Even when he was out of the car, he was still too far distant to secure a clear picture.

All they knew was that he was probably Middle Eastern, as evidenced, if nothing else, by the company he kept and the clothes he wore. Sort of loose, cropped harem trousers with collarless placket cotton tops, usually in khaki, but sometimes in plain white. And always with a black taqiyah, or skullcap. His only other distinguishing feature was his height, which was slightly greater than those with whom he mixed, so that he usually stood out in a group.

Also, worth noting, a man answering Eckstein's description had been seen looking into the Ferrari, talking to the driver. Again, the positions had occasionally been reversed with the Eckstein lookalike being the driver. Impossible to know who owned the luxury car. Unsurprisingly it carried false number plates.

Today, neither Tammy nor Bob could clearly discern who the passenger might be; at a guess, the tall Middle Eastern gentleman spotted by Mossad.

But both Bob and Tammy knew full well who the other man was, the driver. After all, hadn't he recently fled their presence? The balloon of white hair distinctive. Dexie. But if this was his car, how could he possibly afford it on his presumed wage?

Swerving at breakneck speed through the town centre, the red car, slamming into a power glide and ignoring the 40 mph limit, roared onto the A34 outer ring road heading north, from where they'd almost certainly be aiming for the M40 at Junction 9, the Wendlebury interchange. A distance of no more than eight miles. They'd be there in bare minutes, that is if Tammy's instinct still held good.

At sixty-eight miles to their next main junction off the M40, the M42 would lead them to the M6 thence into Birmingham, barring accidents. At the speeds they were travelling, they'd cover the distance to Birmingham in about thirty minutes. Another one hundred and ten miles to Blackburn would take no more than forty-five minutes.

Eckstein, who lived in Blackburn, had mentioned he had a lock-up in Birmingham, but Eckstein wasn't in the car in front. And while the driver might be seeking to shake them in Birmingham, if he didn't succeed, Blackburn was, she felt sure, his only final option. But then if she was wrong, did this pair even know where Eckstein might be right now? Or was this all a blind alley?

"They will be making for Blackburn," Tammy observed quietly. "Sure of it. Somehow Eckstein is involved and these two will be looking to him for help."

"It's a long way to their destination, Tammy." Bob sounded doubtful.

"Yep." She shrugged. "And with their speed they'll ultimately be leaving us behind."

"Do you think you can catch them before they hit the M40? You've hardly got the time."

"We'll have a problem if I don't." She didn't sound optimistic, neither did she feel it. But she was geared up for the hunt. Taut as a bowstring. Despite her earlier exhaustion, she felt a renewed adrenalin rush and smiled to herself as she urged the engine towards its capacity, her palms clasping the wheel light as a lover's caress. Realistically it was unlikely they'd overhaul the Ferrari, but for her, not entirely professionally, it was all about accepting the challenge. Too exciting to ignore. She felt the back of her neck prickle; onward, she decided, whatever the consequences.

The Ferrari, taking a bend too quickly, crashed its nearside flank into a row of illegally parked cars, producing a hollow crackle. Tammy took the same corner using better judgement and gained on the car ahead. There was still ground to make up. Bob breathed a sigh and reached forward, bracing himself with a hand on the dash as Tammy squeezed through the mercifully thin, slow-moving local traffic, slaloming left and right like a speeding skier, trying not to lose sight of her prey.

She flicked on the wipers as a thin smattering of rain spattered the windscreen. "That's all we need," she said. "It'll make the roads treacherous."

Bob remained mute, his fists clenched.

The direction of the pursuit had been based on no more than a hunch. A hunch that the driver would be making for what he considered to be safe ground. Bob Walker had agreed with her. Blackburn, the city. Eckstein, the man. She'd been positive she was right, and they were on a trail now, the right one, the individual motoring ahead at a rate suggesting something close to panic. They'd lost him when he'd first raced from them but had made up time with her driving skills and his ignorance of how close she was. He was no longer ignorant, as reflected in his lunatic manoeuvring.

One thing was certain, however: he was their target, Eckstein's plant. The driver. Had to be, or else they were back to square one.

"You know you'll never overtake him, Tammy," Bob advised quietly.

"I don't intend to. He's got the speed. I've got the acceleration. Anyway, I've got something else in mind." Bob looked perplexed but made no further comment.

"M40 junction ahead," said Bob. "What next?"

"I'm thinking," she muttered, watching the red car gain distance, the gap between them widening as the two made the M40.

"We're being outrun," Bob muttered. "He's too fleet."

The wipers smeared the screen as they settled into their rhythm, and Bob asked tentatively, "Should we, maybe, ease up a bit?"

Pressing her foot harder on the gas, she said, "We need traffic now. There's not enough here for us," she added, pushing the Porsche to 140 mph, the howling of wind in the vehicle's slipstream more pronounced in response to the Ferrari's burst of speed.

"Traffic?" Bob glanced at Tammy, alarmed.

"If there's nothing in front of him, there's nothing to slow him down. That's how he'll escape us."

"Wow!" breathed Bob as the car ahead made for the tightest of channels between two cars, straddling the middle and overtaking lane, getting it wrong again.

"He's mad," murmured Bob, as the Ferrari was hammered on both its sides, sustaining further damage as the carbon fibre bodywork showed fine but visible cracks. But it was through the gap, barely slowed, and now surging to 170 mph.

"Not good," said Tammy, her heavier car momentarily matching the lighter Ferrari's speed, like a lion chasing a gazelle. The chase would be limited if the bigger beast failed to quickly capitalise on its short-term advantage.

"A single car in front of us now, Tammy, then it's all open road ahead," Bob said, agitated.

"Don't panic," she said quietly.

The car immediately ahead of them, a lumbering black SUV, seeing the menacing red motor in its rear-view mirror shifted from the centre lane to the nearside, gifting the Ferrari access to a clear and uncluttered road.

"Damn! We're losing him," said Bob, shaking his head in frustration as Tammy floored the accelerator, pushing the silver car to 180 mph.

"Maybe," she said, her palms dry, focus sharp.

The two cars were past the black SUV, engines roaring, exhausts billowing, the red car having barely slowed, but still, allowing Tammy the briefest instant when her greater acceleration brought her alongside it, her nose actually in front.

"You're easing up, Tammy? Why?" Bob stared at her. "Empty road in front. We might have had him."

She saw the flashing image of a crumpled wreck, an explosion and ball of flame. Her car? A premonition? The truth, seconds away. Then she'd know.

"You could be right." She sounded angry. "We just needed a moment, that was all."

"Do you think ...?" Bob started but was cut off as the red car, using its greater speed, eased forward, its nearside rear wheel dangerously levelling with the Porsche's offside front, rim to rim, the two vehicles practically touching.

What happened next happened very fast.

"Last chance. No! We're gonna be too late. Dammit. You were right, Bob," she breathed, gripping the wheel hard. Knuckles white. Glancing to her left and right, a final futile check. All clear.

"NOW!" she shouted, as Bob looked on aghast while she deliberately rammed the Porsche's offside front end into the Ferrari's nearside rear, wheels crunching against wheels, the ominous sound of carbon fibre breaking up, coupled with a metallic screeching of her own car's aluminium bodywork as it was torn into.

"Christ!" called Bob, sounding alarmed for the first time. "You'll destroy us all."

The two cars were momentarily trapped together, rearing like stampeding horses that might topple at any moment, before scraping untidily apart.

"Watch what's going down now," she said softly, slowing the silver car further, while the red car, its rear end forced to the right, its nose to the left by Tammy's gambit, careered forward out of control, heading straight for the safety barrier on the hard shoulder, unimpeded by any stray motors.

The shriek was jagged, terrified. Sounded clear. But, a woman? A man? Someone beyond the edge of reason?

"They're going to crash. My Christ, Tammy, they're going to crash. What've you done? They'll be killed at that speed," Bob cried out, anguished. "Madness! Madness!"

"Not necessarily," she replied softly, continuing to brake, the Porsche now completely under her control.

"Although no great loss if they were." This last said under her breath.

A second of silence. A lull. Unnatural.

Endgame beckoning.

They both heard the thunderclap as the Ferrari hit the barricade, collapsed and broke up, with bits of eggshell bodywork flying off in all directions, the vehicle still retaining something of its overall integrity.

Moments later the silver car, skidding in a cloud of dust and pebbles, was brought to a stop by Tammy on the hard shoulder, three hundred yards further on.

"Where the hell did you learn how to do that?" Bob whispered, clearly shaken.

"US cops. It's safer than trying to overhaul a car ahead. Our weight gave us a slight advantage." She sounded as though she did this sort of thing on a regular basis.

"Their car looks like bits of jagged Bakelite. How can you sound so relaxed? Do you think they've survived the crash? Not possible, surely." He was registering confusion. Unusual for someone generally as cool as Bob Walker. But then, it wasn't every day he enjoyed the benefits of Tammy's reckless risk-taking.

"Let's take a look," replied Tammy, as if it were of little consequence either way, leaning back to see through the rear-view window and reversing the Porsche, until they were parked in front of the ruined Ferrari. Parallel black skid marks traced the vehicle's path from the motorway impact to the safety barrier. The red car's doors had burst open, whether at the behest of the pair inside or as a result of the collision, couldn't be clear.

Otherwise, there were splinters of red carbon fibre all over the hard shoulder looking like sprays of blood. Maybe it was blood.

Bob frowned, distinctly uneasy, as he heaved himself out of the Porsche and made for the red car. "I dread to think what we've got here, Tammy. God willing, no corpses."

She was close behind him, a considered expression on her face. Time to assess the damage.

Two bodies. Both men. That scream? A conversation with death.

The passenger was slumped forward, his head sideways against the steering wheel, his eyes wide open. Something about the man struck a chord. Couldn't put a finger on it. It would come back to her. But still, alive, just.

He caught Tammy's gaze and spat, "Infidel!"

On the other side of the car, Bob, gazing in, had gone deathly white. "Oh no! My God, Tammy. My God. It's horrific. It looks as though the man is decapitated."

"What?" she replied.

"Decapitated. Decapitated. Do you not hear me, Tammy?"

CHAPTER 1

PRESENT DAY

THE PERMANENT UNDER-SECRETARY to the Ministry of Defence, Norman Cutler, a dynamic, pink-cheeked, besuited little man, who seldom seemed to sit still, faced his auburn-haired wife, Phoebe, in the dining car of the Northern Region train as it sped towards Edinburgh for the family's first holiday together in five years.

Phoebe, wearing her usual travel outfit, a grey two-piece suit and white blouse, looked happy. Happy and contented, as well she might, having finally persuaded her workaholic husband through a cocktail of bullying, cajoling, and the promise of an excess of sexual favours, to take the break he so badly needed.

The vacation had been further encouraged by his friend and parliamentary colleague, the erstwhile MP and 'Chancellor for a day', now astonishingly a convicted murderer, Oscar Mountford. They say, still waters run deep. But who would have believed it of a fabulously wealthy highflyer like Oscar? He'd even been tapped as a future PM, but at the trial had been revealed as a mover and shaker involved in a number of extremist far right groups, characterised by the term, alt.right. It would be some time before Oscar would be able to enjoy a furlough with such of his friends, if any, that still existed.

Next to Cutler was his five-year-old daughter, curly-haired Milly, in her new frilly pink birthday dress, giggling with every opportunity at anything and everything. On the table in front of her, thoughtfully prepared by an accommodating rail company, was a small cake with five candles just waiting to be lit.

The train rumbled on, its rhythm gently accompanying the family's festive mood.

Opposite Cutler and next to his wife sat their older daughter, Poppy, in her Paddington party dress. At seven years of age, she'd largely taken over responsibility for Milly, berating the little one when she didn't use her knife and fork properly, and generally finding every possible excuse to otherwise boss her adored younger sister.

Reaching forward with the gold Dunhill lighter his wife wished he'd ditch, along with the twenty-a day-habit, Cutler applied the flame to each wick till the circle of five candles flickered together like a group of medieval country dancers.

"Norman," said Phoebe, suddenly fretful, "I've just thought. Did I pack my sponge bag?"

"Check your case after we've eaten, my dear. All up there on the rack. I'm sure I saw you pack it, though."

"Okay, darling." She smiled, reassured.

A family of three, that is parents and a young son no older than Milly, at the table on the opposite side of the gangway, looked over and smiled indulgently. They had that 'going on holiday' look about them too. Casually dressed and relaxed. The boy, a tousle-haired lad in shorts, a check shirt and a cowboy hat, whispered, "Can I talk to the little girl, Mum?"

"Yes, Jimmy," replied his mother softly. "As soon as they've finished with their birthday song, coming up about now, I should think."

As if on cue, and turning his attention to his youngest, Cutler announced, "Why don't we all sing Happy Birthday to our Millicins."

"I've got my case, Daddy," interrupted Milly, looking up at her father. "See here," she said, eagerly pointing down with a chubby pink finger to her khaki rucksack on the floor in the gangway.

"So you have, little one." Then glancing over his daughter's head, he added, looking interested, "Are you sure that's yours Millicins? It looks a bit big to me. I wonder if you picked up the wrong one when we were getting our tickets."

"It was heavy," said Poppy. "I know, 'cos I picked it up for Milly."

The Cutlers had married late, and at age forty-five doubted they'd ever have children. Norman's commitment to what was amounting to a highly successful Civil Service career meant there was little time or energy to think about family. So, they'd been overjoyed when Phoebe conceived and Poppy was born, and were, they knew, now doubly blessed with the arrival of the talkative and cuddly little Milly.

An undemonstrative man, Cutler nonetheless viewed his family with enormous pride and affection. Sitting in that train carriage with the three women in his life, he felt his heart being squeezed with love for them.

Winking at his wife and taking her soft, extended hand in his own, Cutler said to his youngest, "I wonder what could possibly be in it, Mills. Not birthday presents. Surely?" Milly was squealing with delight. "Come on now." He grinned. "About time. All of us, let's sing Happy Birthday before the candles burn down and set the place ablaze."

Still the train rumbled on, its rhythmic pounding lulling the family into a delicious state of soporific apathy.

But Milly couldn't wait for the song to end, and, unzipping the bag, went, "Weeeee!!! All for me?"

"All for you, darling Millicins."

Then, "Phoebe," Cutler added, peeping into the bag before turning to his wife. "My dear, weren't you looking for your travelling clock?"

"No, I found it before we left," she replied, relaxed and smiling as the sun blazed through the windows of the carriage, accompanied by a volcanic explosion and the white heat of a blast that blew the carriage and two families to shreds.

CHAPTER 2

SOME MONTHS AGO

THE HAMMERING AT HER APARTMENT DOOR was insistent, becoming thunderous, echoing in her ears and throughout the first-floor corridor of the compact, modern, Queen's Park block of flats.

Tammy's black Siamese, Risky, looked up at her mistress quizzically, as if expecting an explanation, wagging her tail agitatedly.

Whoever it was clearly had no problem with the front door to the block. Her own apartment entrance was secured by a Banham lock and two safety chains. How long before her visitor, viewed by the unclear CCTV images, broke through those too? she wondered. Mere moments, judging by his success so far.

She could hear soft laughter, "Heh, heh, heh," and her heart hammered in her chest like a snare drum. A shuffling of feet. The man had already gained silent entry to her home, her sanctuary. Of course, fool that she was, she'd forgotten to apply the security chains at the entrance to her property. What sort of PI was she? He was now pausing on the other side of the twin living room doors, a thin wood screen separating them, an instant from confronting her.

She'd forced herself awake, despite having earlier taken a couple of tranquillisers. The cat, nervous and sensing trouble, had scratched her mistress's hand. The effect had galvanised Tammy, who now, properly in control of herself, smiled at the prospect of a meeting with her guest.

There'd be insufficient time for her to get to the nightstand by her bed where she kept the gun her boyfriend had somehow smuggled in from Israel. Replacing the hitherto preferred Walther P99, now in a lower drawer, a Mark XIX Desert Eagle semi-automatic pistol, manufactured by Magnum Research, sat in the top drawer. Chambering the largest centrefire cartridge of any magazine-fed, self-loading pistol, a single shot with a soft-nosed .44 magnum shell could blow a hole in a man the breadth and depth of the Grand Canyon.

Glancing up at the CCTV screen moments ago, she'd seen a tall guy in grey tracksuit trousers and a hoodie, partially obscuring his cadaverous features. Then she'd recognised him.

It could only be one person. A hired killer outside in the corridor. The man who'd fired a gun at her a few short weeks ago when she was jogging in Queen's Park. The knife she'd stuck into his leg during that savage attack, a small Gerber 06 automatic with the barely legal 3.6-inch blade that she always carried on her person, if she carried no other weapon, enjoyed a significance which seemed to have been lost on her assailant at the time. He was a man without a sense of humour, or indeed a sense of the inevitable. She'd expected he'd one day return to try to redress the balance. What paid male assassin would wish to admit failure, and that to a woman, after all?

Ephraim Loughty. Of course. Who else?

She felt cold with the realisation. Not a good time to make his reacquaintance.

But then she'd just recognised a second smaller figure behind the leading visitor on the CCTV screen. A little man in denim jeans and leather jacket, wearing wire spectacles. The same man who'd warned her off when she was searching for the missing wife of MP Oscar Mountford.

Jailed for murder, MP Oscar Mountford, the ultra-right winger, had retained Loughty, who'd now gained entrance to the apartment, to do away with Tammy. Involved with

CHAPTER 2 • SOME MONTHS AGO • 15

extremist groups around the world, who firmly believed a woman's place was in the home, Mountford cannot have been too impressed with his man's recent performance in Queen's Park against an injured and pregnant target.

She took several deep breaths and let herself be calm as she got to her feet. Concentrated her mind on the job in hand. Closing and opening her eyes for just a moment, she smiled inwardly.

Then she grinned down at Risky, whispering, "Don't worry, sweetie. We'll soon have this under control."

From outside her door an effeminate voice she knew all too well. "I know you're in there. No escape this time, butch lady."

Her throat still tight, she made her voice sound as casual as she could. "Why, it's Mr Loughty, I do believe. To what do I owe the pleasure? Do please wait a moment and let me unhook and open the doors for you."

She had bare moments to assess her situation.

A 2010 study of dozens of boxers, weighing in at a required minimum of 200 lbs, found the best could punch with an almost unbelievable 1300 lbs of force.

The heavyweight world champion Rocky Marciano, a mere five feet ten, tipped the scales at just 185 lbs, his drive and commitment making him unstoppable. After forty-nine fights he'd retired, unbeaten.

Tammy, at six feet plus and pregnant, weighed 185 lbs.

Immediately outside her living room doors, presumably pausing for effect, her visitor, she reckoned, despite his lack of bulk but with his height, would be close on 200 lbs, leaving her at somewhat of a weight disadvantage. But then, years of training with the help of her coach and sometime lover, Dov Jordan, had given her one of the finest weapons in the compendium of martial arts: Krav Maga.

The Israeli system of self-defence had ensured Tammy was well able to account for herself on a significant number of occasions. But to be effective it required the proponent to be reasonably fit and fresh. Tammy was neither fit nor fresh. In fact she was exhausted, wounded and heavily pregnant. She was going to be encountering problems, she realised. But then, if you don't show fear, you don't feel it. This was something she could handle. Of that much she was certain.

"There now," she said, flinging open the double doors. First rule for anyone facing attack, do whatever you can to defuse a situation. And now, echoing Oscar Wilde's view of second marriage, since it applied to her present situation, that being one of hope over experience, Tammy stood back. And hoped. But the hope evaporated in the nanosecond it took for Ephraim Loughty to shoulder the door aside and storm in.

She was prepared, of course. But she was also unprepared. In her present condition she was sluggish and slow. Too slow. Loughty rushed her and, before she could respond, lashed out, landing a heavy punch on her shoulder, despite her swaying sideways to ride the blow. The jolt felt like a steel ramrod, and the crunch of her bones left her wondering at the damage.

The little man, who'd followed Loughty, looked on with arms folded, and giggled.

The cat screamed, momentarily distracting Tammy, and a second punch landed flat on her chest, throwing her backwards against the wall. If there'd been a plan, this wasn't going according to any known schedule.

She could smell the man's sour breath, the stink of an unwashed body. He grinned insanely, revealing the pointed rodent teeth she remembered from their last encounter.

She was already panting and gasping with effort, though she'd hardly moved, the man sneering at her aware he had the advantage. At least he was unarmed. The noise of a gun would have alerted the world. A knife would be messy. And the individual was clearly intent on finishing her off as cleanly as possible.

The cat had distracted him too, though.

CHAPTER 2 • SOME MONTHS AGO • 17

Locking into the discipline of Krav Maga, Tammy aimed a front kick hard at the man's chest. It barely registered. A second, round kick landing her shin against his thigh, the injured one, brought forth a grunt of pain from him.

The fight quickly developed into a duel of his brute force against her martial art skills, with the two of them grappling untidily. She was sweating freely now, droplets spraying over her assailant, who just laughed at her efforts.

The wound in her side from the New York knifing was dragging, as though it might open up at any moment, hampering her freedom to move as she would have wanted.

She was already weakening fast, knew she'd have to do something quickly or she'd go down. In which case she'd be finished. He wouldn't be as charitable to her as she'd been to him in Queen's Park that time. In her present state she was struggling, fighting to maintain her stance; yet unable to, her head spinning, the room tilting crazily, she finally went down, fell to her knees, watched helplessly as he aimed a kick at her head, moving aside just too slowly so that the toe of his boot scraped her forehead, leaving a trail of blood.

From where she crouched, gathering what reserves she had left, she aimed a knee kick at his shins, swung her leg in a horizontal arc with the grace of a hip hop dancer, connected with a muffled thud, and saw him stagger before regaining his own balance. It gave her enough time to regain her feet, agonisingly hauling herself up through pain and weariness, before squaring up to him, elbows bent, fists bunched. He laughed at her again, not realising her residual strength and plain bloody-mindedness. Not 1300 lbs, but enough power wielded in that 185 lb frame of hers to make a Krav Maga straight left to the face count. He was confident. Too confident, he advanced menacingly and walked right on to the punch which burst his nose.

"Fucking bitch," he muttered, producing a long-bladed knife, seemingly from nowhere as a curtain of blood drenched his mouth and chin.

"Enough of this shit, lady. I'll finish what I came here to do, mess or no mess."

Her adrenalin exhausted, she wouldn't plan a counter-attack. With bent legs spread while leaning forward in a semi-squat, one fist on the floor as a prop, she anticipated her own end. Blood seeping into her eyes from the wound in her forehead. Only moments of consciousness left, her vision beginning to blacken and close in, she turned sideways on to the man, heard him snigger again.

"Gotcha now, haven't I."

Hopeless, she realised. Everything slipping away from her. She inhaled deeply. Fists clasped together under her chin in an attitude of supplication, and glancing at the leering individual with the raised knife from the corner of her eye, she shook her head to clear it and regained some fragile semblance of control, stating defiantly, "Don't think so. Not just yet."

She smiled, a struggle. But then, a queen about to checkmate the king she faced. Raising her bent leg as high as her shoulder, a monumental struggle in her present state, she brought it down, kicking out smartly at Loughty's knee. Hit it hard, between the femur and tibia. Heard the sickening crack of the joint, like a breaking branch, as the leg bent horrifically. Witnessed the man fall, shrieking, to the ground, grasping the knee with both hands and writhing in agony.

She stood over him now, hands on her hips, gasping with the exertion, sweat and blood running down her face. She was feeling better again, but angry too. She contemplated snapping the other leg but denied herself the questionable luxury. Just.

He saw the mobile in her hands and muttered through clenched teeth, "What the fuck're you doing?"

"Calling an ambulance, Mr Loughty," she said, her voice icy cold.

He held up a restraining hand, whined, "No. Don't."

"Don't? Don't, Mr Loughty? Really? How were you proposing to get home then? With that leg under your arm? And you certainly can't stay here. I'm sure you'll understand when I say I've already gone beyond the bounds of extended hospitality."

Lying on his side grasping the smashed leg, his face distorted in a tangled spaghetti of agony, he whispered, "This isn't over, lady. Not by a long shot."

"Oh, I think it probably is, sir. The time for silly games is really well and truly over. Next time I might not be so gallant, Mr Loughty. Next time I might just take that leg away from you altogether."

The small, white-faced man was no longer laughing, his hands dangled by his sides.

"I know we've not been properly introduced, despite our brief meetings in Wapping, sir," said Tammy. "But whoever you are, don't you think it might be an idea if you helped your comrade home?"

Then glancing down at her hands, the palms horrifically scarred during her involvement in what the press had labelled 'The Black Candle Killings', she muttered under breath, "Bugger. I've broken another bloody nail."

CHAPTER 3

SIX WEEKS AGO

THE AREA WAS BARREN, a moon surface littered with rubble and rocks. A picture of desolation by Dalí or Magritte. There was no sound. No sound at all. Just an all-enveloping silence.

To one side lay an avocado-green wheelie bin, tipped over, rubbish spilling out. Torn black bags, their contents scattered. Newspapers, old packaging, food waste, broken toys. From the depths of the bin, through all the detritus, the glow of a jewel could just be seen. That was all. Still, not a sound.

Then sudden, unexpected activity. A hubbub of noise. Voices cut through the illusion, interrupted the dream, the hallucination.

"You'll have to do better than that, you know. It's been six hours since you became fully dilated. I'm well aware you're tired. But you've got to try harder." It might have been a schoolteacher admonishing her.

"I'm doing all I can." The response was firm, rebellious even.

"Come on now, push, sweetheart. Harder. Your hips are too narrow. Sorry about that. You know what I mean."

Reaching up to the man, she said, "Hold my hand, darling. But please don't look down there, it's horrible."

"No it's not, it's beautiful," he said, beaming at her.

"Ugh! You'll never want to make love to me again."

"You want to bet?"

Sweat was pouring off her, and she seemed to be drifting in and out of consciousness.

The senior midwife, a buxom woman in her fifties, looked worried. "She's bleeding from the vagina." Looking at the man, she added, "It's usual after the birth has taken place. But not generally to this extent during the process of giving birth."

"Is she at risk?"

The nurse frowned, and muttered, half to herself, "It's starting to look that way."

"What do you recommend, nurse?"

"She needs a caesarean section. And she needs it now."

"Otherwise?"

"Otherwise, we could lose her. The mother. Not the baby."

"Tammy." He looked down at her pleadingly. "Please?"

"No, Dov. No way. I'm having this baby as a normal birth."

"For God's sake, Tammy," he protested once more. But she'd lapsed into unconsciousness again.

The dream resumed, but this time the jewel was not so apparent. It had receded from view. The wheelie bin was covered in a filigree of fine lines, a spider's web of cracks that started to widen as the bin began to fall apart. The jewel was barely visible now amid the piles of waste.

A muffled voice filtered through, "We're losing her."

But she'd heard it clearly. "No. No. No you're not," she raged, but they could barely hear her.

"We have to operate. For God's sake. The wound in your side is starting to rupture. We can't deal with that too. You can't go on."

"Je dois. Je vais," she murmured. *I must. I will.*

CHAPTER 3 • SIX WEEKS AGO

The staff midwife addressed the young midwife assisting, "Mary. Quick now. Get Mr Trevelyan. Tell him it's very urgent. We're going to lose her."

The pain which had been diminishing as she lay dying, now returned with a vengeance, so she knew she was coming back. Going to survive. But the pain was overwhelming and the screaming she heard was her own.

Dov had her hand in his, her nails biting into his palm.

The consultant, a balding, harried-looking little man, rushed in and took one look, shook his head, and said, "This will not do. This will not do."

But she was fully awake now, and shouted at him, "It'll just bloody have to do. There'll be no caesarean. You hear me? No bloody caesarean."

Looking over at the staff midwife, Trevelyan said quietly, "Carry on, Staff. I'll keep a watching brief."

Two more hours passed, with Tammy visibly weakening. Staff kept herself under control despite showing tears.

Dov remained mute, merely gripped her hand, tried to ignore the massively blood-soaked sheets, while willing her to survive.

Then Staff nodded at Trevelyan, who said, "I see. The head's engaged. Ms Pierre," he said softly to Tammy. "Could we manage just one final push?"

"No we bloody couldn't," shouted Tammy, heaving with all she had.

"I have it," said Staff. "I have the baby's head, it's clear and the shoulders are coming out now."

She lay back utterly wasted, like a blooded wet rag stuck to the bed. She just wanted to sleep, and to sleep forever.

Sounds all around her. A baby crying softly. Water splashing. A voice saying, "He's all cleaned up now. Ready for his mother. Isn't he a beauty? Going to break a lot of hearts that one, when he's all grown up."

Another voice, younger. "Breaking my heart already, Staff. He's gorgeous."

And now, she was being cleaned up by two new nurses, sponged down, a fresh nightdress and sheets, before she was allowed to settle back against the plumped-up pillows.

"Lucky, she won't be needing sutures," said Staff.

Then she thought of the jewel in her dream, and her vision began to clear as did the conscious thought, the actual realisation, and she spoke aloud, as though utterly disbelieving. Unaccustomed tears flooded her face, drenching her fresh nightdress. "I'm a mother."

They put the baby to her breast. "Matty," she breathed. And she understood for the first time why a mother would be willing to die to protect her little one. She cradled the tiny bundle of softness and warmth in her arms as he fed from her, and she thought her heart would burst with love.

Dov, who'd been shooed out of the room while Tammy was being attended to, was allowed back. He towered over everyone yet didn't seem an overwhelming presence. "My son. My son," he intoned, beaming hugely.

The senior midwife smiled down at Tammy. "We'll need to check that wound in your side, my dear. It looked to be opening up. And there'll be a bit more stitching to do where you've torn slightly. But it'll wait till after your visitors have gone and should heal up fine. You're very fit and look to be good and strong, despite whatever it is you've clearly been through recently. Not many would have lasted the pace you have without some sort of sedation."

She watched the baby feed for a few moments more, before adding, "You're doing beautifully, my dear. Baby's very hungry, and you may find he needs more milk than you have. That's not going to be a problem. There's plenty of milk substitutes we can supply."

"But?" Tammy started to protest.

"No buts, my dear. I know what it means to want to feed your own, on your own, and it's no disgrace if you need a bit to supplement. We don't want a hungry little lad, do we."

Then Dov said, "Darling, Matthew's here. Shall I bring him in?"

"Mmm." She smiled.

A few moments later the old man shuffled in, still tall despite a stoop, his advancing Parkinson's clearly slowing his progress a little more each day. Immaculate as ever, shoes with a mirror gloss, a smart brown tweed jacket with tie to match, his cropped white hair magnificent against his ebony complexion.

"Papa," said Tammy, holding up the swaddled baby. "Say hello to your grandson, Matty."

Matthew took the baby in his arms, and with tears streaming down his cheeks said simply, "Your Maman would be so proud."

It was then that something about the baby caught Dov's attention, and he squinted down at the tiny mite. Tammy noticed the look, but avoided his gaze, said nothing, and prayed that Dov would make no comment.

CHAPTER 4

PRESENT DAY

"I WANT THE BLACK BITCH TAKEN OUT." The voice was middle-aged, cultured, hoarse, seething with venom.

"You want her killed?" The respondent could hear the sound of jagged breathing at the other end of the line. It was some time before the question was answered.

"No," came the reply, carrying a note of regret, or maybe one of reluctant submission. "On reflection, perhaps not this time. I've tried that. My man Loughty…"

"Ephraim?"

"I've mentioned him in the past, I know. Made a complete fool of by the woman."

"Really? I thought Loughty was your absolute failsafe. Skilled with guns, knives, hand to hand. You name it. Not sure I could better him if you want this person, whoever she is, got rid of." The man spoke with an accent, with an abrupt emphasis on consonants. He might have been Greek? Greek Cypriot? The line was subject to interference.

"I said no, not what I have in mind any more, Mario. The more time I spend in this stinking rat-hole the more time I have to think of ways to get back at her. In the months since the trial I've been shifted from one top security prison to another. Friends, that is, those I still have, don't visit because they don't know where I am at any one time, and they find it bloody impossible to get any details from the authorities."

"Where are you calling from now, Oscar?"

"HMP Frankland."

"Where's that?"

"County Durham, nearly three hundred miles from London. Much further north and they'd have had me in the North Sea."

"Aren't you appealing? I thought you said you were planning to last time we spoke."

"Not so easy. My lawyer effectively consigned me to prison, committing judicial hari-kari himself. Damn fool panicked, made a confession that implicated me in everything he'd been involved in. If I ever get my hands on him." His voice had become an almost animal growl. "Still, he'll never see the light of day again."

"Which prison is he in?"

"God knows. I certainly don't."

"So what is it you want me to do, Oscar? If I'm not to organise her death, then what? Capture and physical torture? I do know the people."

"No, no. Better than that. I want you to contrive to humiliate Ms Goody Two Shoes. Bring her to her knees. She knows the high-ups in the police. People like Chief Superintendent Bob Walker. He thinks the sun shines out of her backside. He was with her when I was arrested in the House of Commons. Smug bastard that he is.

"Everyone has their weak spots, their Achilles heels. Follow her. Get others to follow her. Find her vulnerabilities and then play on them."

"It'd help if I knew her name and something about her, Oscar. Where she lives, works, what she looks like."

"You can't miss her. She's all of six feet tall. Black. Well, mixed race. Dresses like she's just walked out of a Paris fashion house, no expense spared. Short black hair, sometimes curly, sometimes pixie fashion. She lives in Queen's Park, North West London. A small but flash modern block of flats. Expensive.

"Her father, who's black and a retired architect from Trinidad, lives in the same area in a Victorian conversion. Mother was a white Parisian Jew. Rich banking family. Damn them. Now dead. Don't know what of. Heil Hitler! The old man had his points with the Jews. Recognised the threat. Just over-reached himself. If I ever get out of here…"

"You've done your homework."

"Had it done for me. There's more. Lots more."

"Now we're getting there."

"The woman. Got offices in Bruton Street, Mayfair. Small unit. Up-to-date interior in a smart period building. Just her and a PA, one Mrs Gilchrist. Florence Gilchrist. Know nothing about her, other than she's a chartered accountant."

"You still haven't told me this character's name."

"Tamsin Pierre, calls herself Tammy. And she's a private investigator. Business is called Pierre Search and Security. Incidentally, for what it's worth, she speaks with a slight French accent. Also, she sounds a bit like a male baritone. Some might say sexy. I know what I'd say… Bitch."

"Okay. We'll look around for something to cast aspersions on her character. Maybe one of my boys could entertain themselves by breaking one of her arms or legs?"

"If it'll amuse you, Mario. I don't want her killed. You understand? She's to be kept alive."

"Sure, Oscar. A little softening up perhaps?"

"Perhaps," Oscar replied, sounding almost absent-minded. "One thing though, Mario. Like I said, she's big and she is formidable. Beat the hell out of Loughty. And he was, till now, my best."

"I'll bear it in mind. Warn the boys to keep alert."

"Listen, Mario, you should know she's an expert at Krav Maga."

"The Israeli martial arts skill?"

"Right. Taught by her occasional squeeze, Dov Jordan."

"Who's he then?"

"Not absolutely certain. He may be, or has been, a member of Mossad at some point. Served time in the army. Now deals in antiques and objets d'art. Got a place off the Edgware Road. Divides his time between here and Israel. He's bigger than her. Teaches Krav Maga. Her coach, in fact. Really, best left alone. You'll have your work cut out with her."

"Maybe. The boys love a challenge."

"Up to you, Mario. Don't forget, I'm paying for results. Don't blow it."

"Don't worry, my friend. We won't."

CHAPTER 5

SEVERAL MONTHS AGO

THE KNIFE WAS UNIQUE, untraceable to any known manufacturer. That's because it had been made specially and to order by a New York bladesmith located in the cramped basement of a block of craft studios off a main thoroughfare in Greenwich Village.

Tiny the place may have been, but it was equipped with all the tools necessary to ply the trade. That is, a traditional coke-burning forge, a smith's hammer and anvil, as well as other smithing tools. Furthermore, an impressive system of ducts ensured proper ventilation. Despite that, the place smelled of sour sweat, metal shavings, burning coke and wood.

Blade smithing is an art thousands of years old, possibly originating in China and Japan, but later to be found all over Europe and the British Isles. It differs a little from sword making, insofar as the longer sword blade requires carbon spring steel, which is less liable to bending or shattering, while the shorter knives can be better fashioned from a steel classified as A2, known for its toughness and wear resistance, and which is used in custom-made fighting knives.

The client wanted a curved, six-inch retractable blade, serrated on one side, fluted on the other. Not a unique request, and anyway the smith wasn't inclined to make enquiries, however much he might wonder about the planned use.

Apparently, the handle was to be in the medieval dragon design: black iron backed with mother of pearl and a gold pommel, or crossbar with dragon's teeth. The whole was to be governed by a simple push button which would allow the blade to snap open. Because of the knife's dual sharp edges, in order to allow the user to avoid touching the steel, the same button when pushed would allow a clever contra spring to have the blade retract. The completed weapon was as much a work of art as it was an implement of death.

There are innumerable choices of knives available at comparatively low cost for purchase online. Many, perhaps not as uniquely sharp but still every bit as lethal as the one now being ordered. What made this one special was the nod to an antique design, coupled with that retractable blade.

The customer was evidently an individual of refinement and taste. Whatever he had in mind, the bladesmith wouldn't dwell on it. This item was clearly not an ornament to be put on display. It was designed for someone to relish the ritual of killing.

It was ready in two weeks, and despite the asking price the client made no argument, merely handing over the sum in dollar bills.

"One of the finest blades I've made in a while, my friend," said the craftsman, a short thickset man in his sixties, with skin like wrinkled leather matching his bib-fronted apron, a shiny bald pate and powerful forearms beneath rolled up shirtsleeves. "Yours," he announced, handing the knife to the client.

"Press the button and see if you're satisfied with the mechanism. Whatever you do though, don't even think of touching the edge. It's sharper'n a razor, sir, and it'll draw blood with just a touch."

Glancing at the client as he spoke, the old man witnessed a moment of misgiving as he locked eyes with a pair of grey irises, cold as the steel the craftsman worked with.

Wanting to break the sudden silence, he added, "Don't get that many really unusual requests these days."

"No?" The voice was low, betraying little interest.

"Just sometimes," he offered, as though to avoid a further awkward silence. "A while back we had a lady here who wanted me to make her several shuriken."

"Shuriken? What's that?"

"Not that. Them. Ancient Far-Eastern weapon, Japanese actually, used to soften up your opponent before the swords came out. Your order reminded me of hers. Hers were to be bigger than the average and designed to fly flat like a frisbee rather than vertically as otherwise. I made her a belt to hold several of them at one time."

"Did you get a name?"

"She never said. Tall lady, had an accent. Could've been French?"

"Thanks," said the client. "All I need to know."

CHAPTER 6 DAY MINUS 2

MOST OF THE GIRLS were in miniskirts. Skirts so short you could practically see what they'd eaten for breakfast the day before.

One of them, a voluptuous tease, conspicuously pulled up the back of hers, briefly revealing tight rounded buttocks cleft by the mere hint of a thong. Laughing uproariously, she cocked a snook at some gob-smacked young guy who couldn't take his eyes off her, before pulling the skirt down again.

"None for you, darling." She giggled, before turning back to her friends.

But someone else had seen the action, felt himself respond as his black chinos became constricting in the area of his crotch. Nice, he thought. She's really good-looking. He was middle height with short sandy-coloured hair, and the shoulders and neck of a US all-in wrestler. But his face was gentle, even kindly, despite the apparent broken nose. A boxing or rugby injury?

He might perhaps approach the feisty young lady, maybe she'd give him a dance? This was his first time at a venue like this. He was a bricklayer by day, but was shy to the point of timidity where it came to girls. A protected childhood, virtually smothered by his mother, meant that the man was inexperienced, innocent, naïve.

But he knew what he liked. Even if, at his age, he'd never enjoyed any of it.

The place was crowded with probably more than fifteen hundred people in what was a vast converted warehouse close to the Thames in Tilbury, where the docks were situated. Youngsters all heaving in a friendly communal fashion to the wall of sound produced by massive speakers strategically placed.

Strobe lights flashed in a variety of colours casting beams up and down the walls and along the floor, illuminating the undulating mass making the place a riot of incandescent colour. The effect was spellbinding.

The unmistakeable bouquet of hash lined the nostrils and despite the ubiquitous no smoking signs, a clouding fug of tobacco smoke swirled lazily about. The spark of a lighter here and there, and the glowing tips of innumerable cigarettes punctuated the darkness between the strobes, adding some indefinable jeopardy to the atmosphere. Something resembling a sense of undeclared hazard.

Situated close to one of the walls, and placed higher than the bouncing throng behind a bank of equipment, the principal DJ, a gorgeous Afro with a balloon of dyed white-blond hair that would have done Hendrix proud, her matching white lipstick against an ebony complexion, switched casually and competently from one turntable to another, jigging up and down in time with the music, mainly the insistent four-on-the-floor beat characteristic of house. At a repetitive one hundred and twenty beats per minute the effect produced by artists like Frankie Knuckles, Zedd, and Afrojack was hypnotic. Adding to the risqué atmosphere, several scantily clad dancers on raised pedestals or podiums were bumping and grinding in time with the music, in a nod to stunning drag queens like Lucy Fizz and TeTe Bang.

If the aim of the club owner was to produce a Glitterbox effect of inclusion, adding in disco and classic dance anthems, the numbers on the floor bore testament to the success of her objective.

Lining an adjacent wall a long bar, backlit, with several bar staff, mainly red-uniformed youngsters, serving an endless procession of drinks, provided an oasis of glowing white in the otherwise darkened interior. Single pedestal round tables with bar stools were dotted around for those who needed to take a weight off their feet.

Finally plucking up courage, the man approached the girl. "Hey," he said.

"Hey, yourself." She immediately grinned back at him.

Angling his head questioningly towards the crowd, she nodded eagerly, and they were soon jumping up and down in harmony with the rest. It was fun. It was so easy. All he'd had to do was ask.

She was a good dancer, moved with feline grace, her blond curls framing elfin features. He could hardly fail to notice the enticing décolletage, her braless breasts practically bursting from the white open blouse, knotted above the navel.

He had no idea how to progress things, so he said simply, "You're very sexy." Then wondered if he'd been too forward.

"Yes, darling," she responded. "I know that, don't I?"

"Can I see you again?"

Her friends clustered around giggling, laughing, whooping. Tiny skirts, bouncing busts, blood-red lipsticks, constantly moving, gyrating, bumping, grinding.

"Go, Julie," said one with a long black ponytail.

"You can see me now, can't you," she said coyly; the one called Julie who he was dancing with.

"Yes but, you know. Another time?" he stammered, dazed at all the noise, the attention, the brazen display.

"How about now?" she whispered invitingly. "Why not right now? Hmm, muscleman?"

"Now?" he asked blankly. "I'm not with you. I don't follow. How do you mean, now?"

"Come on, you idiot," she laughed. And taking him by the hand, started threading her way through the crowd, her friends' garbled voices receding into the distance. He's weird, she thought. But cute. Good for a laugh.

"Where are we going?"

"You'll see, darling. Just be patient."

She led him down a corridor off to one side of the venue until they were faced by two doors. One was marked M/f and the other F/m. The toilets.

"I don't understand," he said. "What's...?"

"Oh, for Chrissake." She sounded exasperated. Then smiled indulgently. "Now what do you think?"

"You're taking me to...to...?"

"Yes, lover boy. I'm taking you to...to..."

Two girls emerged from the F/m door, clutching each other, laughing and jostling.

"Your choice, honey. M/f, mainly male, or F/m, mainly female?" said Julie.

"Well." He sounded unsure of himself. "M/f I suppose. Will it be private, though?"

"Let's try F/m," she countered, without enlarging. "Private enough, sweetie. Not that it'll make any difference. Everyone's used to it these days. Where you been anyway? Still, we'll use a cubicle if it makes you feel less self-conscious. You are a strange one, though."

At first the place seemed empty, no-one around. Then the sound of murmured endearments could be picked up in one or two of the cubicles. Down one side of the facility was a row of a dozen booths, and on the opposite side the same number of mirrors and handbasins.

The décor was very much all black, matching the main dance area, apart from the relief given by individual lights over each handbasin.

It all smelled of air freshener and the unmistakeable aroma of semen. The man curled his nose in faint disgust. The floor was littered with spent lipstick cases and balled up used tissues, many with blood-red traces of lipstick.

"Come on, love," she said, opening one of the doors, panting slightly, and ushering him in.

Squeezing in behind her into the tight space available, the man angled himself around the door, which he then proceeded to lock. He'd barely finished when she had her arms around him, her lips on his, her tongue exploring his mouth. Feeling himself becoming aroused, he put his hands on her buttocks, sampling their ample firmness. Then he pulled her skirt up, and shoved a hand in the back of her knickers, what there was of them. She groaned and said, "Hang on, big boy. Not too fast. Keep it nice and slow. Spin it out. Better that way."

But his breath was coming faster as he found it harder to hold back the rush of desire. The surge of want.

She still had her back to him as she took hold of his erection, one arm bent behind her back, rubbing her hand up and down the length of him.

"Now!" he practically begged. "Come on then. Now! For Christ's sake, I'm bursting."

"Okay, lover," she relented. "Do it here." And dragging her tiny skirt above her hips, she bent over the chipped lavatory bowl and spread her legs. "In my back pussy, sweetheart. Shove it in now."

"No. Not there. Come on, love, turn round. I want it up the front. Not interested in arse."

She twisted round to look up at him. "You're not?" She sounded surprised. Disappointed even.

He couldn't read her. Was puzzled by her attitude, but reached down anyway to fumble with the front of the tiny thong.

That's when the shock wave hit him in the face, a hammer blow.

"What's that?" he snarled. "What the fuck are you?"

"Come on, darling. I'm a chick with a dick. Don't say you wasn't aware. This is trans night."

"But you're a fucking bloke."

"I'm a trans, love. Had the hormones, got the tits. Just need the op'. Tell you what? I might not bother. Got the best of all worlds this way, 'aven't I. Come on now, be nice to me. That's it, darling," she said as he, seeming to relent, let his hands gently caress her shoulders.

"No?" she asked, uncertainly. Timidly.

Looking up into his eyes, she could see him smiling benignly, a look of love and affection creasing his face as he, with a sound like a breaking branch, casually snapped her neck and left her limp body where it fell.

CHAPTER 7 DAY ZERO

"I'M FRIGHTENED, MS PIERRE." The woman in her office, sitting opposite Tammy, was tall and elegantly turned out in a pale blue turtle-neck sweater and mid-blue trousers. Having introduced herself as Hester Lamont, she now nervously primped her blond hair, constantly tucking it behind her ears.

Next to Tammy's Art Deco rosewood desk in a pink cot, and wearing a pink Babygro, was Tammy's baby, Matty, gurgling happily and waving chubby hands at the mobiles tinkling above his head. She kept him with her at all times in the office, and as often as possible when not. Whatever business or life threw at her, Tammy had only to look at her son, see his grin, smell his talcum powder freshness, to find all her stresses melt away, like butter on hot toast.

Since the baby, Tammy's curls had become softer and more manageable. This morning she'd blow waved her hair into a pixie bob and chosen to wear a blouson tartan jacket with plain dark blue culottes. Her scoop-neck white guipure blouse was low enough to reveal the twin triangle, gold amulet, given to her by her father, with its protective Hebrew inscription.

She felt happy. But not smug. Life was too unpredictable for that.

On the desktop sat a tray thoughtfully provided by Tammy's PA, Mrs Gilchrist, with a choice of tea or coffee in Wedgwood bone china, plain and sparkling water and a selection of biscuits. That is, Hobnobs, custard creams and Tammy's favourite, Garibaldi.

There were also several stacked plastic shelves of paperwork, carefully sorted, for Tammy's attention, and the prized, large glass dolphin ashtray, sans its usual panatella. No smoking would be strictly observed now that Matty was in attendance. The stash had been flushed away and the bison grass vodka was being kept strictly within limits. At least, most of the time.

"Your daughter?" the woman enquired, looking down at the cot and sipping from the tea Tammy had poured.

"My son," returned Tammy, pouring herself a coffee. "We showed him pink and blue to get a reaction. He gravitated towards the pink, so pink it is. And anyway, it goes with his colouring."

"He's beautiful. That stunning café au lait complexion." She hesitated, as though uncertain, then continued, "Like his mother, if that's okay with you?"

"Thank you. You're very kind."

The woman leaned forward to get a closer look at the child. "Goodness," she said. "He has the most astonishing blue eyes. I never realised…"

"That he might be blue-eyed?"

"I don't mean. I didn't mean…"

"Please." Tammy held her hands up reassuringly. "I'm not in the least offended. It's not generally realised that where there is some Caucasian in the family a black or mixed heritage person may have blue eyes. It's rarer for a purely black couple to have a blue-eyed child, but certainly not unique. Matty's father is Israeli."

She paused, despite herself. Matty's pedigree was an issue to be dealt with at a later date. But only if she was forced to. She carried on, "He's fair-skinned with ginger to copper-coloured hair. Hence, Matty has more au lait in the coffee than I do."

The woman seemed to relax for the first time. "And, and you're French? Your accent?"

"Maman was. She was white, adding to the mix. Papa is Trinidadian. Black. Hence my complexion. I was born in France. French was my first language. The intonation lingers."

"You said 'was', when referring to your mother?"

"Maman died of breast cancer ten or more years ago." She'd never once complained, recalled Tammy. Indeed, the only time Tammy had ever seen her mother upset was on the occasion when, collecting her from school, she'd been asked by her six-year-old daughter what it had meant when a bully had called her 'un cochon brun', a brown pig. Pascale had cried then, and Tammy had comforted her, having experienced her first lesson in racism.

Leaning back in her swivel chair, Tammy steepled her fingers. "Now, Ms Lamont, you say you're frightened. What are you frightened of and how may I help? Talk to me."

The woman shifted her position slightly as if the move might help marshal her thoughts. "I own a club, well three clubs really, but all under the one banner, the Clubhouse banner. The main one is near Tilbury docks. The other two are located at Dagenham and Dartford, the last one south of the river. They each get a mixed crowd. All ages, races, and genders."

"Isn't Clubhouse a social media site?"

"It is. But we've been around longer than they have, and so far, no objections have been raised."

"Understood. Tell me then, what type of clubs are these?"

"Sort of discos. The Tilbury club is in an old converted warehouse close to the docks. I spent a lot of money on the place. On all three actually. Top hi-fi equipment, experienced DJs. Clean toilets. At least at the start of each evening's session. A bit grubby by the time we close. All sorts of detritus. We turn a blind eye to some of what goes on, as far as we can." She shrugged.

"Drug taking, I suppose," offered Tammy.

"Inevitably. But what can one do? I've got a couple of private nurses on hand all evening, just in case anything happens. You know, overdosing. That sort of thing."

"And sex, presumably."

"For better or worse. Our loos offer a choice. M/f or F/m."

Tammy was distracted for a moment when the baby started to cough and snuffled, then he murmured softly before resettling, allowing her to turn back to her client. "Not sure I follow."

"Well, we run regular LGBTQ sessions, and clubbers have a choice; the M and the F are obvious, for cisgender people."

"I understand. Those who choose to maintain their birth gender."

"Right. So, the lower case suggests previous gender, if it's relevant. So, a trans male to female might want to use the F/m and vice versa."

"Neat."

"My idea, and it seems popular with the youngsters."

"I might like to visit your clubs sometime," said Tammy, considering its possibilities. "Do you just cater to the youngsters? Teens and twenties, that is?"

"Not at all," the woman replied, distractedly taking a nibble on a Hobnob, then brushing crumbs from her lap. "We have dual thirty and forty age-group evenings and older too. Straight, gay. Young, even elderly. What sort of event would you be thinking might suit you?"

What indeed? thought Tammy, smiling. "You seem to offer quite a choice."

"I must say, when I first saw you…"

"You wondered if I might be trans?" Tammy suggested.

"Your height, that baritone voice. But then I saw the little one."

"The baby defines me," said Tammy. Then, allowing herself to become more intimate, "Like most mothers I'm besotted with my child. If anything ever threatened him… Well, you know what I mean. So, you will understand, more than anything else, I am a woman with, of course, the usual female blessings and curses and more."

"Curses?"

"Irregular cycle, endometriosis, high testosterone levels. You name it. Look, I'm getting a bit too personal here." Tammy felt her neck flush, shook her head imperceptibly. She was being unprofessional. A moment of weakness?

"No really," the woman replied. "I see what you mean."

"We all have issues. I live with mine. In the end we all do."

"But you are straight?" the woman asked, then reddened. "Oh dear, I… I seem to be straying somewhat…"

"Don't worry, Ms Lamont. Frankly, any one of your evenings might suit. "For the record, I'm bi, uninhibited and totally amoral. I crave variety and excitement. Much to my boyfriend's chagrin. As long as you're not hurting anyone." She shrugged.

"Refreshing," said the other. "I seem to have picked the ideal private investigator. And I love these offices, small enough not to be intimidating, modern enough, the glass partitions, to be reassuring. And Bruton Street, Mayfair. Impressive."

"How did you find me then, Ms Lamont? Providence?"

"Actually, I googled private investigators and spotted you, among others. I liked your website, and everything on it, the testimonials, the wealth of experience, the Met links. And the legend on the glass outer wall of your offices: 'Pierre Search and Security. Discreet investigations, forensic accounting, personal security'. Also, if I may say, you look somewhat impressive yourself."

"I'm flattered," Tammy said, chomping on a Garibaldi. "So, about the drugs, if you're worried about drugs, the taking or the dealing, you could install CCTV in the loos?"

"No." The woman shook her head firmly. "Far too intrusive. We cope with what we have in the best way we can. CCTV within the main club and bar areas, of course, and at the street entrances of each venue. And I've got internal security people as you would expect, not specialised like yourself, really just there to keep an eye on things. But they can't be everywhere all the time."

"So, Ms Lamont, talk to me. What is the problem, and why are you frightened?"

The woman, who had started to look relaxed, more at ease, began to appear agitated again, fidgeting with her hair, pushing it behind her ears. The see-saw echo of an emergency vehicle trailing down Bond Street lanced into the office, crowding the space. The blue flash strobe effect sweeping the room. A police car? An ambulance? The siren soon after faded but left behind it a sense of something portentous.

Hester Lamont drew breath. "We've recently had an incident at the club."

"What sort of incident?"

Replacing her cup and saucer on Tammy's desk, Ms Lamont then sat back and clasped her hands nervously together and paused, as though preparing herself for what she was about to say. "A couple of nights ago we had a murder in the premises."

Tammy frowned. "Go on."

"A young woman. A trans was found in the M/f loos with her neck broken."

"The M/f loos? You said, young woman? A trans male?"

"Well, that's just it, you see. The victim was trans, but male to female."

Stroking her jaw pensively, Tammy said, "She was in the wrong loo?"

"Is that what you think?"

"Unless, of course, her assailant was male. That is cisgender male. If he accompanied the victim, at her behest, perhaps? He'd have probably chosen the M/f loos, I'm guessing. The victim was trans, you say. Anything else relevant?"

"Yes. She hadn't yet had surgery."

"Ah," Tammy said, gazing straight at Hester as though waiting for a reaction. "I could be wrong, but I think I can surmise what might have happened."

"Yes. And it is likely we agree. He went with her for sex, presumably not realising she was trans, and then on discovering she'd not yet had surgery, got angry."

"Murderously so," Tammy added.

"Exactly."

"And I suppose it's affected the club's takings?"

"Of course. We've tried to be discreet, but of course, the police have been all over the place. So people are understandably staying away."

"As you say, understandably. What about the other two venues? Any drop in business there?"

"Not so far, but as they all trade under the same Clubhouse banner... I know it sounds heartless, but any more incidents and the business will need to close. I need takings to pay staff and cover club running costs."

The baby snuffled again, attracting the attention of both women.

"I wish I could..." Hester began, then stopped abruptly. She looked so acutely sad that Tammy wanted to reach out to her. Then, as one woman to another, she said in a moment of clarity, "You'd like to have a baby."

Hester nodded, looked down, avoiding Tammy's gaze.

"But you can't." It was a statement, not a question.

"You know," she whispered.

"You're trans."

Hester shrugged, but said nothing.

"You've had the surgery?"

"I'm booked for it."

Tammy sat for several moments studying the backs of her hands. There could be a way. Then she looked up and said, "Why not store your own semen, while you can, then when you find a partner, if you're lucky enough to find a cis female, she could carry your child." She noted the woman looked doubtful.

"I considered that, but…"

"But? Whatever doubts you might have, shelve them. Just do it, then you can have the surgery and worry about babies later."

"Do you really think—?"

"Yes, I really think," Tammy interrupted her.

"Now I'll want to visit the club and start talking to people. I assume the police have been and are conducting their own investigations?" Tammy reached forward and brought an A4 notepad towards her, picked up a Cross ballpoint and made to start taking notes.

"Of course, and they are," said Hester. "But I'm encountering some resistance. They mean well enough, but I get the feeling they're somewhat out of their depth with this particular sort of thing."

"Hester," said Tammy. "I meant to ask. What about further security? The physical, I mean, rather than simply the observational that you've already mentioned? Do you have any? What if there were a ruckus? How would you cope?"

"On the doors at each venue we have maybe half a dozen men." She smiled for a moment, as though realising what she'd said.

"Like real men, as it were?" offered Tammy, amused.

Pinking slightly, Hester ventured hesitantly, "I s'pose. Yes. I mean, that's what you'd call them. Men. Cisgender, that is," she quickly added as though in justification.

Their conversation was interrupted as the baby hacked and spluttered again. A sharp sound unlike the earlier coughing. For a moment Tammy felt as though she'd been dropped naked into Arctic waters. Leaning over the cradle she watched, horrified, as Matty gradually went bright pink, with arms flailing, his breathing becoming increasingly laboured.

"Dieu! Non! Non! L'hôpital. Immédiatement," she exclaimed, and jumping up, her heart scrabbling in her chest, she scooped her son from his cot, clutched him to her and dashed from the room without another word.

CHAPTER 8 DAY 1

JUDGE ROLAND JEFFREYS, or as he was known among his enemies, 'Hanging Judge Jeffreys', in a nod to his namesake the notorious seventeenth-century George Jeffreys (who once sentenced two hundred and fifty-one rebels to death), or else known to his peers and friends as simply Jeffreys, or even 'Jeffles', surveyed the prisoner in the dock. The judge, a wan, soft-spoken man whose outward demeanour was entirely at odds with his reputation, made up for his apparent passivity by the severity of his sentencing.

Whatever the jury's views, Jeffreys would form his own assessment based initially, and simply, on whether the defendant looked him in the eye when reciting the oath. The successful Lebanese-Brazilian Jewish banker, Joseph Safra, counselled, 'Always look the customer in the eye. For eyes tell more than balance sheets.'

Then too there was the individual's reaction to the judge's habit of incessantly tapping his nails on the desk in front of him during the trial. The guilty always seemed unmoved by the mild eccentricity, the innocent, entirely abashed. Hardly what one would describe as a scientific way of making an assessment.

Still, he'd never yet been wrong.

A man of fifty-five, he'd had a successful career as a criminal QC, both as defence lawyer and, more frequently, as prosecutor. Born into a middle-class family with a huge pile in Gloucester, Jeffreys, an only child set to follow his burly and somewhat intimidating father into the law, had been educated at Eton where, as a bookish non-sporting type, and on the short side like his mother, he'd been endlessly bullied.

Not least among his tormentors, and to his mother's distress, was his father, who refused to be impressed by anything his wimp of a son could achieve. Jeffreys had learned to cope early, through a quicksilver mind, an ability to divert verbal or physical attacks via humour or plain dogged courage, both of which earned him the respect, if somewhat grudgingly, of his fellow students. Again, his father failed to be convinced, not even when Jeffreys, following a successful university career, began to shine in his chosen profession.

And it was with a sense of overwhelming relief when one day, after a particularly harrowing trial involving rumours of jury intimidation, back home in his luxury rooms in The Albany, an exclusive residence near Piccadilly, and over a large single malt, that Jeffreys learned of the death of his father from a heart attack. He noted during the call from his mother her singular lack of emotion. She was probably as relieved as Jeffreys, although her class and upbringing would preclude her ever admitting as much.

"Are you alright, Ma?" Jeffreys had asked solicitously, taking a further sip of the whisky.

"Perfectly, my dear. And Henry has left me well provided for."

Jeffreys pondered for several moments before admitting, "Never saw eye to eye with him, y'know. Bit too brutal for my liking. Real old-fashioned patriarch."

"Yes, darling. But not a real old-fashioned male."

"You've lost me, Ma?"

"Have you never wondered why you have no siblings?"

"Presumably because you didn't want or couldn't have more?" He sounded puzzled.

"Why do you ask? Something I should know? You're not ill, are you? Something prevented you from having more children?"

"No, darling, I'm not ill. The reason there were no siblings is because your father made it clear, once you were born there'd be no more children. Having you was simply to prove a point."

"I'm at sea, Ma. What point?"

"Darling, your father was a closet homosexual. It was illegal when he started in legal practice. Any whiff of it and he could have been disbarred. Possibly imprisoned. Did you not know? Had you not guessed?"

Jeffreys shook his head as though to rid it of an unbidden notion.

"It never once dawned on me," he said, shocked.

"There was never any affection in our marriage," his mother added sadly. "His fine features took in a lot of women. I was the unfortunate one he married. Of course, he lost the looks quite early. Not a happy man; he was also a secret alcoholic. Hence the florid complexion."

"I can think of nothing sensible to say, Ma. I'm just amazed."

"And you, darling. Are you happy?"

"Perfectly."

"Tell me again, what do you call yourself when you visit those clubs?"

"I'm Rolande, Ma. Easy enough to use and remember. No surname. It's not required where I go."

"And are you fully recovered from the operations?"

"Totally."

"Did you really have to go that far?"

"Yes, Ma. I'm a woman. I always was. It just needed the surgery to complete everything. I think Pa may have guessed something."

"What about your colleagues at work?"

"Nobody knows. Nobody need guess. It's simpler that way, and I prefer it. I dress as a male for court. Voluminous shirts and gowns hide the bust more than adequately. When I'm in chambers or in court, I'm still Roland Jeffreys, Ma."

"Yes, darling. And you're still Roly to me, my love. You always will be."

Jeffreys sighed and turned his thoughts back to the case before him, tried to assess the prisoner in the dock. A man who had just been adjudged guilty of the crime of embezzling some £1,000,000 from his partners in an accountancy practice. A tall, smart-suited man, about his own age, with side-parted dark hair, tanned complexion, a hawk nose and an attitude of supercilious confidence.

With a hand in his pocket, he looked at the judge as though it were the latter who had just been found guilty of a crime by a jury of his peers. He was about to be comprehensively disabused of his arrogance, a trait Jeffreys could not abide, but not before he'd be given a chance to speak for himself in these august surroundings.

During the trial Jeffreys noted the defendant had played scant regard to the constant tapping of his fingernails on the desktop. A likely sign of guilt, at least in the judge's intuitive opinion. Apparently correctly so, as was now borne out by the jury's verdict.

"Prisoner in the dock, you have been found guilty of the most egregious crime of embezzling sums amounting to a minimum of £1,000,000 from the four partners in your joint accountancy practice. As a result, two of your partners have now been forced into bankruptcy, have lost their licences to practice their chosen profession, and are presently divorced. The other two have had to resort to five years of individual voluntary arrangements in order to avoid bankruptcy themselves and retain their practising licences."

Jeffreys sat stock still, his eyes boring into those of the defendant. "Would the defendant please stand."

The man brushed down his lap, straightened his tie and got slowly to his feet, as though granting the court the benefit of his undivided attention.

Behaviour that did not go unnoticed by Jeffreys, who managed with effort to disguise his mounting impatience. "Do you have anything to say in mitigation of your crime before I pass sentence?"

"Come on, judge," the man smirked, his arms folded defiantly across his chest. "We're both men of the world. Don't tell me the other four didn't know what was going on. If they didn't, they shouldn't be in practice. If they did, how come they did nothing to stop it? If you ask me, they all had their sticky mitts in the till from time to time."

"I would remind you I am not here to respond to your questioning." Jeffreys now displaying his annoyance, tapped his nails ever more impatiently on the desktop.

"Okay, okay," the defendant protested, holding up his palms in surrender. "You win. I'll take whatever's coming to me. But not too harsh, hey, judge?"

"And I'm not judge, young man. You address me as My Lord."

"Fine, fine. Have it your way."

"This is quite insufferable." Jeffreys peevishly stacked the papers on the desk in front of him, making a neat edge of them.

"I will ask you one final time, before I pass sentence. Do you have anything to say in mitigation of your crime? Are you proposing to repay any of the embezzled funds, and if so over what period."

"No can do, judge. Oops, My Lord. All spent," the man said, grinning.

"And what of the hardship you've caused your partners? All of them likely to lose their homes, their marriages already lost or otherwise in jeopardy." Jeffreys looked hard at the man, tried to perceive some shred of regret, apology, or even embarrassment in the defendant's demeanour, but could find nothing. It was like peering into the shell of a hermit crab and finding it empty of its occupant.

"Listen, it's a hard world out there," the defendant responded, with the first trace of animation in his voice. He shifted about in the dock edgily, irritated. Could no-one understand him?

"You know, ju— sorry, My Lord, it's dog eat dog. I stuck with the whole partnership business for as long as I could but got bored eventually. I wanted to expand, make a lot more money, have some real fun, but the others said it was too risky, held me back. They said we're accountants, not Musk or Branson."

A typical sociopath? Jeffreys asked himself. The puzzling thing was, however did a man so unstable ever get to be accepted into a partnership of professionals, and at what stage did he decide he was sufficiently confident, capable, or simply arrogant to start helping himself to the business's funds? And for how long did he imagine his crime would go unnoticed with his fellow accountants? A million pounds, for heaven's sake.

Still, he sighed to himself, 'Stranger things' and all that. He was fast wearying of trying to understand or evaluate the defendant who seemed to be a man quite beyond redemption.

He'd unwind tonight at the club, Jeffreys comforted himself. Hopefully there wouldn't be too much of that blasted music they insisted on playing. At least the smaller side bar there was quiet. He'd look for Algernon, Algy. His heart quickened a moment, before he returned to the present agenda.

"Very well," Jeffreys continued. "I am bound to say you have treated these proceedings with disdain bordering on contempt."

"Oh, now please," the man interrupted.

"You will refrain from talking while I pass sentence."

The defendant merely shrugged disinterestedly.

"I will continue. You have offered no mitigating circumstances, you have even chosen to plead innocent, on the flimsiest of grounds. Of course your partners were not informed the cash taken was a mere short-term loan, and more than you had realised, with your claim you had thought it was only half that sum. As though embezzling half a million pounds is an acceptable oversight, when the actual figure was twice that. Having regard to the court sentencing guidelines we're looking at a range of five to eight years for this crime."

At this, the defendant went white, then quickly recovered and, addressing the judge, said, "I suppose, if we're looking at the lower end of that scale, My Lord, with part of the term suspended, I could be out in a couple of years."

"I am utterly confounded by your presumption. Let me make it clear, if I had my way I would create a precedent and impose a longer tariff. As it is, your attitude compels me to impose the maximum sentence allowed. You will go to prison for eight years."

"What the fuck," he spat.

To the defendant Jeffreys said, "Anything further from you and I'll hold you in contempt."

And to the court officials, with a peremptory sweep of the arm: "Take him down."

People in the public gallery could be heard murmuring among themselves, debating the case and the defendant's attitude as they rose to leave.

Turning away, the judge sighed. The court quickly emptied now, the shuffling of feet giving way to a moody silence. Drama over. End of the day.

Peculiarly deflated, he dialled his mother and hoped she'd be pleased to hear from him. "Ma?"

"Yes, darling," she replied, almost immediately. "You sound tired."

Relieved she was in, he said, "I'll be over tonight."

"Lovely. I shall look forward to it."

"I miss you." Unaccountably, he felt desperately sad. Didn't know why. He was as one who'd suddenly woken up to the falseness of their position in court, the given semblance of power that quite belied the actual timidity of the judge.

"Come, Roland. I'm here. I'm always here for you. You know that."

"Yes, Ma. I do know," he whispered. "I love you."

CHAPTER 9

RECENTLY

A press of the button and the blade snapped out with an emphatic click. The knife had become part of his individuality, as though it were welded to him, an extension of his persona. It might have been spawned with him. It performed his every wish just as he had planned it would. This iron and steel dragon with its gold pommel was his totem, his talisman.

Grasped in the palm of his hand he was invincible.

Guns were too noisy and there was no sense of community with the new friend. For that's how he regarded them. All, as new friends. But then, friends he was angry with. Friends who'd let him down. Friends he'd have to deal with in his own unique fashion

He'd followed her into and later out of the club wearing silent rubber soles, but she'd spotted him and got nervous. She shouldn't have been on her own. Very unwise, and with the light rain, in those high heels she'd be unable to run too far or too fast. Her skirt was no help either, being over tight and constricting.

The station was a good ten-minute walk away, and the alley was dark, a single lamp post casting a balloon of light into one of the puddles. He'd easily caught up with her. She'd heard him coming and spun round to face him, putting on a bold front, tossing back blond curls. Her denim jacket was already dark with epaulettes of damp at the shoulders, and she shivered slightly, whether with cold or fear, he didn't know.

Didn't care.

It was enough that he had her.

"What do you want?" She sounded strong, sure of herself, as though she'd been coached in how to deal with unwanted attention. It wasn't what she felt.

"I want you to be my friend," he replied softly. "That's all. Only to be my friend."

"Weren't you just in the club. Didn't I see you drinking by the bar? On your own?" Make conversation, she told herself. Keep him occupied. Engage the man to keep his mind away from whatever it was he might have been contemplating. He was probably harmless, anyway. But one didn't take chances, nor make optimistic assumptions. Her mother had always said, assume the worst in any given situation, that way you can plan your best route out.

"My day off. Nice place, the club. I was in the bar. I was looking for a friend," he breathed. "Will you be my friend?"

She hesitated a moment, saw him frown, realised it would have been better to have answered sooner. Couldn't make out the rest of his face shrouded as it was by the hoodie. He was about her height. Slim. There was something like sour sweat mixed with the aroma of aftershave or possibly perfume. Then she recognised it. Unmistakably. Chanel No 5. What would a man be doing wearing a woman's perfume?

Glancing down she noticed he had something in his hand. Something that looked like a dragon. She saw the flash of the streetlight reflected in the curved blade. She glanced behind her. Safety was barely a hundred metres away. If she discarded her shoes, she might just make it.

"Thinking of going someplace?" he enquired politely, moving so he stood between her and her escape route.

"What's that?" she shouted in a moment of inspiration, pointing to an imaginary spot behind the man to distract him. It worked and in that instant, she kicked off her shoes and ran for her life.

Ran blindly as she had never run before, slipping and sliding on the wet pavement, heart hammering in her chest, splashing through puddles to freedom, to hope, and to life. And she was practically there, so that she was entirely unaware of the man overtaking her and sliding the blade clumsily across her throat.

As she fell, she heard him say sadly, "I only wanted her to be my friend."

* * * * *

IT HAD BECOME UNEXPECTEDLY OVERCAST and was starting to spot with rain. The surface of the road was already a sheen of black, with motorists' headlamps piercing the gloom like theatrical spotlights.

Holding Matty with one arm, while keeping him tucked under her blouson, Tammy dashed out of the office building and hailed a black cab, waving aloft the clutch she was holding. The pavement-widening schemes in London, designed to get people out of their cars, had merely had the effect of slowing everything down to a snail's pace. New Bond Street, now reduced in part to a single lane, moved with the speed of slowly setting volcanic lava.

Watching the cab as it crawled towards her, Tammy felt she'd explode with the tension of witnessing her baby's life ebbing away. Matty's breath was increasingly laboured, ever more patchily inconsistent. The little one's hoarse struggle to inhale impacted Tammy as though it were she who was being smothered.

Maybe she should have called an ambulance, she berated herself. At least there would have been paramedics on hand. Oxygen. Medications. But with the narrower roads all emergency vehicles were finding it a nightmare to get through when needed. Quicker, she judged, to grab a taxi. Black cabs could use the bus lanes, giving them a minor advantage over the ubiquitous Uber drivers.

Without waiting for him to reach her, Tammy ran for the cab, almost slipping on the oily pavement. "St Mary's, Paddington. Please," she begged. "A&E. My baby's choking."

The driver, a grey-haired old boy, with a prominent mole at the side of his nose, simply said, "In, darlin'. See what we can do."

Then to Tammy's amazement the driver reached out of his window and affixed a magnetised flashing blue light onto the roof of his vehicle.

Slamming the door behind her, Tammy shouted, "Mount the pavements if you have to. Anything. There's five hundred pounds in my purse if you get us there in time." She brandished the bag for him to see, but he said nothing, instead concentrating all his attention on the roads.

Turning immediate right on Bruton Street the driver made for Berkeley Square, which he had no choice but to circle clockwise most of the way around. There was traffic at every juncture, with some vehicles slowing to try to get a glimpse of the interior of the famous Annabel's club, named originally after the founder, Mark Birley's wife. The flashing blue light and sounding the cab's horn helped, but only marginally.

Meanwhile the baby's breathing seemed to have stopped. Pressing her hands against Matty's chest, tears streaming down her face, Tammy did what she could to try to get a response. Breathing into the baby's mouth helped fill his lungs but she couldn't be certain whether or not he'd be able to breath unaided.

Past the club the driver motored up Davies Street, hung a left at Grosvenor Street, and then ran into more clogged hold ups. Now he mounted the pavement, the motor rocking crazily, narrowly dodging pedestrians who gazed at the vehicle in astonishment. A few waved fists at him, despite the flashing blue light.

He was making for Park Lane where there had once been a forty-mile-per-hour speed limit, now reduced to twenty. Jumping an amber light at the junction to the dual carriageway he pulled onto the Lane going north, and roared ahead at over fifty miles per hour, reaching the big Marble Arch gyratory system moments later. There he swung round clockwise, picking up the northbound Edgware Road.

Only minutes from St Mary's, the cabbie, leaning over his shoulder, called into the back of his vehicle, "Nearly there darlin'. 'Ang on."

But he could hear his passenger crying, see her in his rear-view mirror, hiccupping in between trying to keep the baby alive, pressing his chest, exhaling into his mouth.

The tiny thing was blue.

It was over. She'd lost her second child. There wouldn't be another. Her world was falling apart, yet she would carry on until Matty was pronounced dead.

They were alongside the ambulances at the hospital's Accident and Emergency entrance.

Jumping out of the taxi, she reached into the driver's window, thrusting the clutch with the money in it. "Here," she said. "Take it. Take it. Thanks so much for trying."

"Don't be daft," said the driver, pushing the bag back at Tammy. "Orf with yer. Get the kiddie seen to. Be quick nah. Be quick."

She stopped for the merest instant and caught the driver's eye. "I love you," she called, and ran into the hospital with her son, knowing in her heart she was too late.

"Course yer do, darlin'," said the cabbie as he drove off.

CHAPTER 10 DAY 1

RECENTLY

That first one was easy. Neat. Quick. Plunge into the solar plexus. Nice sharp blade, dragged up to the heart. No genitals to remove. Shame. We'll have them, though. Maybe next time. It'll happen.

Then there was another one reported happened before mine. A slit throat, botched job, I read. Died in hospital, not at the scene. Someone tall and white, she managed to say before she snuffed it. Nasty. Not me, guv'nor. Someone anticipating my tricks, are they?

Surprised the police let the club stay open. Still, only one's actually happened inside the place. Maybe that's why. Lovely. Great hunting ground.

There'll be more in there to look for. I'm just wanting to meet someone who wants to understand me. Someone to talk to, to be nice to me.

But the bastards don't always follow. So I deal with things. In my own way of course.

Love it.

* * * * *

DAY 1

SHE'D LOST TRACK OF TIME, time spent pacing up and down outside the A&E entrance to the hospital, chain smoking panatellas, despite her resolve to cut back. The roof of her mouth was tobacco sticky, her tongue felt like a piece of damp carpet and her head throbbed. She hadn't done a line in months but ached for one right now. Even if the lift was only temporary; any diversion, any boost however artificial would have been welcome.

Echoing her mood, the sky remained menacingly black and overcast, although the rain had let up somewhat. Not normally given to self-deprecating introspection, Tammy found herself critically analysing her failure to attend to the baby the moment he'd started to show signs of distress. She should have dropped everything the moment Matty first coughed and snuffled. The time lost while she'd been dealing with the client would very likely prove to be fatal for her baby.

There'd be no-one to blame but herself. She wasn't fit to be a mother.

As the day wore on she was barely aware of the constant ebb and flow of people, ambulances, doctors, nurses, and even at one time four uniformed police who piled out of their vehicle, its blue lights flashing, and hurried into the hospital. Several times she'd gone to the reception to enquire about Matty only to be told there was no news as yet, and that as soon as there was, she'd be the first to know.

About a third of children will develop bronchiolitis in their first year, but only 6 percent require hospital treatment, and intensive care. It's a viral infection affecting the small airways in the lungs. Symptoms include a cough, runny nose and difficulty breathing, and treatment: fluid and nutrition given intravenously, oxygen therapy, and suctioning out mucus from the nose and mouth. Then, all being well, it's generally two to five days before the child can go home.

Tammy was back at the reception desk yet again, and saw it was still occupied from the time she'd first entered A&E by the middle-aged Caribbean woman in nursing blues, whose proportions and obvious kindness seemed to fill the whole area.

"Anything yet?" begged Tammy, realising she'd never felt so totally powerless in her life.

"Honey, you looked so distressed when you brought your baby in, I follered you downstairs to see you how you was gettin' on and I watched you outside, pacin' up and down, smokin' them damn things. Ain't gonna do you nor your baby no good you make yourself sick.

"Listen, darlin', go sit down over there." She pointed to a bank of four vacant linked chairs by the wall. "You need some sugar. Give you a boost. Tea? Coffee? I'll get it."

"Coffee, please," said Tammy. "Black. No sugar."

"Uh! Uh! You'll have sugar and like it. One cup ain't gonna spoil that pretty figure none. Coupla chocolate biscuits too. Gotta have something to sustain you, sweetheart. Staff nurse Garcia insists."

The coffee when it arrived was scalding hot and if it was sweet, Tammy hardly noticed. She sat, absently eating the chocolate biscuits while nurse Garcia kept a watchful eye on her. No telling what sort of foolishness people might get up to if they were really stressed, as this woman clearly was.

It must have been mid-afternoon, with the area now crowded, when a harassed-looking young Asian doctor came running into the reception area. "Matty Pierre's mother?" she called out. "Is Matty Pierre's mother here?"

It was clear from the concern on the doctor's face that all was not well, and Tammy felt nauseous with fear as she got unsteadily to her feet.

"I'm Matty's mother." She sounded hoarse, tried to keep the tremor from her voice.

"Ms Pierre?" she asked, looking up at Tammy.

"That's right."

"I'm Doctor Kapadia. I have the charge of your baby." She shoved her hands into the pockets of her hospital white coat.

"How is Matty?" As she waited for a response, it was then that Tammy realised her dreams of motherhood were burning into ashes.

"Touch and go," said the doctor.

"Touch and go? He's ... he's still alive?"

"What I meant to say is, it *was* touch and go. We've used suction to draw blocking mucus from his nose and lungs and he's stable for the moment."

"Dieu merci," she whispered. "What was it? Why couldn't he breathe?"

"He'd contracted bronchiolitis. It's a virus, not uncommon in babies under the age of twenty-four months. But only serious, like Matty's, in a tiny minority of cases. How soon after you noticed he was having problems breathing did you bring him in?"

"We were in my office. I was with a client. Matty was in his cot next to my desk. Once or twice he snuffled. I should have brought him here immediately."

"No, you should not, Ms Pierre. If parents brought their children to A&E every time they coughed we'd be unable to cope. We can barely cope as it is. I presume you made the decision as soon as you perceived real difficulties with his breathing?"

"That's right." The doctor's apparent calm seemed to have the same gentling effect on Tammy. "As soon as I realised he was choking I ran out and grabbed a cab."

"You didn't think to call an ambulance, then?"

"No. Tell me, doctor, did I put my son's life at risk? Would it have been better to call emergency services?"

"Again, absolutely not. By grabbing a taxi, you did the right thing. Any delays and the boy wouldn't have survived. Ambulances are having major and increasing problems getting through London's ever-narrower roads."

"What happens next, then? Can I see my baby?"

"We'll keep him in for a couple of nights, under observation, and then if he's settled, we'll consider letting you take him home at about this time the day after tomorrow. And yes, of course you can see your baby." Doctor Kapadia smiled for the first time. "Follow me."

He was in a tiny side room, off the main ward. A tiny, defenceless little thing surrounded by bleeping monitors, with a spaghetti tangle of lines and drips.

Seating herself in a chair by his cot, Tammy looked up at Doctor Kapadia, who said, "I'll leave you with him. Stay as long as you like, Ms Pierre."

"Thank you so much, doctor. For everything." Then turning back to Matty, she thought, Touch and go, the doctor had said. The baby seemed restless, unsettled. Far from home and dry, she realised. The doctor's apparent optimism clearly designed to allay Tammy's own fears.

But how realistic was that confidence? Again, she felt her spirits sink.

Leaning over the cot, the baby seemingly unaware of his mother's presence, Tammy extended a hand. "Hello, little man," she said sadly. "Maman is here."

Matty, reaching out one chubby palm, took hold of his mother's finger, and as she held her breath, her baby cracked an enormous smile.

CHAPTER 11 DAY 2

"SO, OSCAR WANTS the black lady discredited." Mario Kerkut lifted the wine glass to his lips and sipped, then rolled the taster of the Kolias Shiraz, a Cypriot wine, around his tongue, before nodding to the sommelier who proceeded to fill both Mario's and his companion's glasses.

"I'd say tame, if you ask me. Be better to go to town on her," said his brother.

"I don't think so," replied Mario, categorically.

In their early forties, the two men were seated on a circular cushioned bench at one of the round tables along one mirrored wall of the Savoy Grill. Brothers with a lot in common, they'd each opted for the roast of the day, which was beef, done rare. Middle height and powerfully built, both men in immaculate dark suits and ties, with their groomed thick black hair, were the picture of business respectability.

Nothing in their appearance could have been more misleading. Shrewd transactions in drug dealing, money laundering and people trafficking had made them wealthy, with neither having sustained the inconvenience or ignominy of a police record. So far.

Their hero was the glamorous Italian criminal Alessandro de Gourcy, a man, unrelated to the Kerkuts, whose family, originating in France, had found themselves in Naples in the 1920s without means of support when a planned business venture by the father in their adopted city had failed. The boy, Alessandro, a beautiful tow-haired urchin, at seven years of age, had quickly learned to pick the pockets of gullible tourists from whom he'd initially begged a coin, eventually in his teens graduating to gaining the confidence of apparently well-to-do matrons staying at some of the city's smarter hotels.

He had big plans, though no idea, just yet, how to go about achieving what he wanted.

On the day the boy had witnessed a daylight bank robbery on Spaccanapoli, the narrow main street that divides the old city, his life changed for ever. What Alessandro remembered was the noise, the screams, the shots and the shriek of tyres of the getaway vehicle, a magnificent Alfa Romeo 6C 2500. The year was 1938 and Italy, under Mussolini, was preparing to support Germany in what became World War II.

In the robbery Alessandro spotted, dropped by one of the robbers, and partially hidden by a windblown newspaper, a Luger P08 semi-automatic pistol. Nobody noticed as Alessandro casually slipped the weapon into the inside pocket of his jacket before calmly walking away.

It was the beginning of a lucrative career. He sold the gun, and bought two more with the proceeds, continuing from there. A natural businessman, he was able to do mental calculations with astonishing speed, the buying and selling becoming increasingly profitable.

Eventually Alessandro aimed to talk to any government who'd be looking for ordnance. Germany, where his Aryan looks served his purpose perfectly. And Italy would be no problem. He was, after all, Italian. Simpler than he'd imagined it would be, by eating at the city's top restaurants every day, he'd eventually recognised a government minister at the man's favourite haunt and found engaging the man in conversation no problem.

So his main focus began. Comprising deals with both Italy and Germany, Alessandro started by supplying orders as placed: major arms, including tanks, troop carriers, aircraft and artillery. Then he moved on to short-changing his customers, until eventually he was taking payments for orders that would never be delivered.

It was astonishing how long it took ministers of procurement to spot what was happening. By the time they did, the War was all but over.

MI6 had been following his activities with interest, noting how useful he'd been to the allies. He was a wanted man, probably rich to the tune of hundreds of millions of dollars.

But he'd gone to ground. Rumour had it he'd changed his appearance surgically, or was living modestly on a farm in Tuscany, or perhaps had been killed by the Mafia.

He was never found.

Alessandro differed from the Kerkuts in one significant way. He never chose, nor needed, to use violence. His wealth was based solely on his wits. His genius. And he was Mario and Jason's hero, in all their dealings, and particularly in those with their MP principal.

And Oscar Mountford had proved to be a most lucrative source of work. If they got this one right, which Mario had no doubt they would, Oscar wouldn't be turning off the tap.

The temptation to break the lady's arms or legs was there; women were getting too uppity these days. In time, Oscar's far right pals would be addressing that issue. But, for now, Oscar wanted her kept alive. No point in jeopardising the goods. Jason's temper might be an issue, it had been on one or two memorable occasions in the past, but Mario was comfortable he could persuade his brother to keep it in check.

"What do we know about her?" asked Jason, the older of the two by one year.

"Only what Oscar's told us. Plus, I've been doing a bit of nosing around myself," said Mario.

"We need to know her weak spots. Where she's going to be most vulnerable."

"Of course."

"Any ideas?"

"A couple. She's got a kid. Just got out of hospital. Breathing problems. Might be an avenue there," said Mario, and took a long draught of wine, gazing contemplatively across the expanse of the restaurant.

"Anything else?"

"Yeah. Her old man lives near her in Queen's Park. Retired architect. Got Parkinson's. Might be diabetic too. I'll give it some thought."

"Done your homework." Jason smiled.

"Don't I always?"

CHAPTER 12 DAY 3

THE MIST HAD LIFTED, and sunshine beamed through the windows. A promising start to the day.

Tammy had slept longer than planned but she felt refreshed. Risky was lying on her chest, as usual, and started licking her face as soon as she stirred. She could hear Maria bustling around the apartment, humming to herself and chatting to a chortling little boy whom she would have by now given a milk feed.

Her phone buzzed twice only, before she picked up.

With the mobile to her ear, she stated, "Tammy Pierre. Who's calling?"

"Ms Pierre, you won't know me but I'm DCI John Manus." There was nothing distinctive about the voice. Well spoken, it might belong to a man in his mid-forties, she surmised. A strong, self-assured tone, though.

"What can I do for you?" Tammy asked, hauling herself up on elbow while wrestling with a small black cat insistent on her undivided attention.

"You've probably read or heard about the murders that have taken place in or around the Clubhouse venues?"

"I have. In fact, I've already been approached by Hester Lamont—"

"The owner?" he cut in.

"That's right. I think she'd had the vague notion that a private investigator might be able to act with more discretion than the police who'd inevitably be called upon to give press statements and interviews."

"Well, clearly that was never going to happen. You can't simply hush up a murder. Even if you planned to, when they become several." He let the comment hang in the air.

"So, Mr Manus—"

"John, please," he interrupted.

"John," said Tammy, apparently trying out the name for size. "How may I help you then?"

"You understand the nature of the clubs, of course?"

"Of course. Hester was very clear."

Manus hesitated for a moment as though uncertain how to proceed. "I'm phoning because your old boss Bob Walker suggested I call you."

"I see," said Tammy, guessing where this was going, but deciding not to help John Manus just yet. Slightly amused, she'd see how he'd handle things.

"Well, er, Bob said. That is, he advised me. Or, in fact, all of us on the team…"

Now she was beaming, hadn't smiled as much in months, and deciding to help him off the hook, Tammy rescued him. "Let me help you out, John."

"I wish you would, Tammy. I'm floundering a bit here."

"Aren't you just. Okay, Bob will have told you I lean both ways. I was in a relationship with my PA, Ginny Jones, while still seeing my sometime current, or ex, depending on anyone's view, Dov Jordan."

"Thanks for that. I must admit the team were unsure how best to approach this whole thing. Gay clubs are something that don't attract opposition the way they used to, thank heavens. People are growing up at last."

"Try telling that to my far right friend, Oscar Mountford."

"I read how you put the bastard away. Everyone back at the nick was talking about it."

"Oscar Mountford brings a whole new construct to the term far right. He hates people of colour and Jews, and by the way, I'm both. Then there's gays and the disabled, God knows what else. The latter with the odd exception of his autistic son, Davie."

"Now dead," said Manus thoughtfully.

"Now dead. Clearly you know. Very sadly. Killed pointlessly by his mother, in what seems to have been an unplanned fit of pique. Then the daughter, provoked beyond reason by the mother, killed her in the same way the mother had killed Davie, in the bath, by hauling up her feet pulling her head underwater."

"It was all a buzz back at the Yard. Terrible affair."

"The judge was amazing. Involuntary manslaughter due to sudden and temporary loss of control, allied to extreme provocation, so she got three years suspended for two. Allowed to leave the court and go straight home."

"A perceptive decision. Another judge might not have been so prescient," added Manus.

"Getting back to the present situation, John, the Tilbury Clubhouse of the trio of premises has experienced a number of killings inside or close by, I understand. Hester only mentioned the one when we met recently. But I'm aware there've been more in the past few days. And I've no doubt I'll be hearing from Hester again. The news last night brought me up to date, without giving away much detail. They're all three, unremarkable places," said Tammy.

"But otherwise very well-appointed dance venues with a couple of bars in each. One large one looking on to where the dancing goes on and a smaller, quieter one where people can chat in relative peace. Regularly twice a week they have LGBTQ nights, so that with the usual crowd of straights, there'll be others that fit the categories mentioned.

"From what Hester told me, for the most part, with the exception of some drug taking in the loos and inevitable sexual activity in the cubicles, the places offer havens of safety for some fun and meet-ups. The trans crowd have come in for a lot of vile abuse on social media and elsewhere, and until now they've felt well-looked-after in the Clubhouse venues."

"Okay, we're with you on all this. Our own current chats. People are slow to learn, aren't they," put in Manus. "That is, to take up any new ideas. My team have been okay, but I'll be honest, they've been uncertain how to proceed. They need to ask a lot more questions but have to take care not to inadvertently offend."

"And that's where Bob felt I might be able to help?" She was sitting up now, the cat in her lap purring with satisfaction as she scratched her gently under the chin. Maria had looked in, and seeing Tammy on the phone, made hot drinks gestures which were met with a smile and nod from Tammy.

"Exactly," agreed John Manus.

"Might be an idea if I meet your team?"

"Of course. And asap."

"How about tomorrow at the Yard, say 10.00 am?"

"Suits me. I'll check you in with the doorman and reception."

"Okay. Obviously with different resources and different approaches we'll need to feed each other info as it all moves along."

"What do you have in mind?"

"I'm going to start talking to club employees, see how many of them know current attendees, members, if any, and or knew any of those killed. I appreciate your team have spoken to staff at the clubs already, but I may have a different take on things. Also, I'll find it easier to get some people into my confidence. They'll see me as one of them. Come to think of it, I am one of them."

"That's exactly what Bob had in mind."

"What have we got so far? Apart from Sky News, I've read the newspapers, albeit skimmed them, but have been tied up with my own issues the last few days. You can give me a fuller briefing tomorrow, but so far?"

"Well, so far we've got two victims with broken necks, both found inside the Tilbury club, some CCTV evidence, but nothing more at this stage. Those are Julie Crosbie and Liz Armstrong.

"Then one with her throat cut," Manus went on. "Karen Richardson, a messed-up job that, and another with a knife in the belly, Anna Proby. Both in the street close to the Tilbury club.

"Then there's two more," he continued, "I'll go into the last one in a moment, as it brings a whole new dimension to the word murder." Manus sounded almost surgical in his recounting of events.

"That first victim," he enlarged, "was found in the men's toilets of the Tilbury club. Julie Crosbie. A partially transitioned male to female. Liz Armstrong, number two, was fully transitioned. Found in the female toilets. Possibly linked to the first killing, CCTV suggests, and the killer of similar description to the Crosbie killer."

"Julie is the one Hester talked to me about in my office," offered Tammy.

"Okay," Manus acknowledged. "Next death, I'll enlarge, number three, Karen Richardson. A fully transitioned male to female. Her throat was cut in what amounted to a botched job. Knife, sharp as a razor and likely curved, should have done the job, but she must have moved or else somehow disturbed her killer. Died in hospital without being able to say much about her assailant, obviously. Whispered, mouthed, he was tall and white, least, that's how it sounded.

"Then we've got Anna Proby. Also a fully transitioned female. An ultra-sharp but straight-edged blade, thrust into her stomach and forced up to her heart. Apparently, from behind, according to the pathologist. Killer must have been a contortionist. Different weapon. Different killer to Karen Richardson? The only knifing so far apparently not delivered from behind. Will have died instantly. There'd have been a lot of blood there. Certainly in the street there was.

"Teresa Finch was next, throat cut," he said, sounding some emotion for the first time. "Horrible.

"And now," Manus continued, "we've got an Old Bailey judge, believe it or not, killed, or more appropriately, slaughtered. The one I said I was leaving till last. Judge Roland or, if you will, Rolande Jeffreys. A case of genital removal. He'd been fully transitioned, so the mutilation was largely internal. The most horrific of the lot, so far. It doesn't bear thinking about. God knows what our killer has lined up next."

"The degree of violence in the case of the two mutilations might be suggestive of revenge killings?" Tammy suggested. Maybe your people could look at some of the more severe sentencing carried out by the judge in recent times that might have prompted retaliation. What do you think?"

"I think you could be right, Tammy."

"Okay, so we need to be thinking about someone with a real score to settle. Also, we might be looking at as many as three different killers. I'll do some digging around."

"Good. Anything you uncover that points us in the right direction."

"Any more?" said Tammy.

"I'm gold commander, which means from the police point of view I run the whole show. But be assured, I'll support you with as free a hand as you need in this, Tammy. We need to move as quickly as possible. Prevent any more of these sick killings. Ten am tomorrow, then?"

"I'll be there," she said and rang off.

In the next moment her mobile rang again. "Tammy Pierre," she said.

All she could hear was the sound of someone crying.

"Who is it?" she implored. "Who are you? Can I help you? Can I help?"

But the line went dead.

CHAPTER 13 DAY 4

"I KNOW OSCAR WANTS HER HAMMERED, but it may not be so easy. I've snooped around some more, a lot more, and she looks clean to me."

The two men sat opposite each other at a table in The Foyer, Claridge's brightly lit Art Deco restaurant. At the back, tall, mirrored arches gazed down on the place. A colossal vase of white flowers adorned a spot just in the front of them and a pair of squared columns either side of the eating area completed a picture of genteel elegance. The breath-taking Dale Chihuly glass sculpture hanging from the ceiling like a giant chandelier of white and grey swirls and curls was an added attraction.

The brothers wore their customary dark suits and ties, with white shirts. Their hair and shoes were polished to a matching black sheen. They occupied their places at the table with the casual confidence of those accustomed to dining at only the finest eating establishments.

Grammar school boys, living in Acton, whose family hailed from Greece, they'd been fostered out when their parents, a quiet law-abiding couple who owned a kebab restaurant in West London, died together in a car crash.

Both unusually bright, the boys had never settled with their surrogate parents and, becoming increasingly troubled in their new home and unmanageable at school, Jason had almost killed another boy over some trivial argument. They'd dropped out of school without ever sitting their GCSEs. A criminal waste, decided their headmaster with unintended prescience.

Displaying true university potential in maths and sciences, and still in their mid to late teens, they'd walked out of their temporary home and, having lived rough or in squats for a while, turned their considerable talents to trade. Trade being initially, drug dealing. Easy to get hold of and easy to negotiate.

They quickly built up a small empire and a big reputation. A reputation, that is, for uncompromising violence. Jason had a unique talent for collecting debts, the trail of broken bones left in his wake bearing testimony to his temper and his immense natural strength.

The offices they occupied in Baker Street, with a staff of six, bore the legend on the brass name plate at the entrance: 'Kerkut Brothers & Co. Import & Export'. The employees were well paid and if they ever suspected their generous employers of anything untoward, they'd been politely persuaded to consider their futures and those of their families.

Comfortable in the restaurant's upright pale blue and white armchairs, they surveyed their starters: beluga caviar with buckwheat blinis, at nearly £200 a dish, for Mario, and Rock oysters for Jason, who slurped them down unselfconsciously while his brother tried not to wince too obviously. They might be brothers, but Mario had learned early in life never so much as to raise a critical eyebrow in Jason's direction; both the older and slightly taller of the two, Jason would one day see his temper get him in the sort of trouble, thus far miraculously avoided, from which Mario would be unable to extricate him.

If asked to classify the men, one might have called Jason the thug and Mario much more the elegant Raffles-type criminal. Despite that, it was Mario who packed the gun. A Ruger SR40c recoil-operated, locked-breech handgun, carrying a total of sixteen rounds, and reckoned to be one of the most powerful of its type on the market. A weapon that few would choose to argue with.

The gentle bulge in his jacket from the discreet shoulder holster added rather than detracted from the younger brother's sartorial symmetry. Mario didn't need to display temper, he merely explained the semi-automatic's capacity, and recalcitrant business associates could normally be encouraged to his way of thinking.

Jason relied rather more on brute strength, which he possessed in spades. He worked out at home and in the gym with the fanaticism of an Olympic contender, and had been known to demonstrate his physical prowess at family and business gatherings by bending a 2 p piece in half with his bare hands. If that didn't convince, he'd do the same with an iron horseshoe. It was a wonderful way of swaying an argument. Jason favoured the more intimate approach to violence, getting to know his victim, no matter how brief the acquaintanceship, and having recently returned from New York with an artisan-created piece of self-opening cutlery, planned to employ it with that in mind.

He'd already used it once, recently, for the first time, when a person he'd met by chance at a club he frequented refused his sincere offer of friendship. Mario would be astonished to learn of his brother's profligate sexuality, always having imagined him to be a cold-hearted, mean-spirited heterosexual psychopath.

"So? What do you think?"

"About?" asked Jason, looking blank.

"What do you mean, about? About the girl. Woman. Oscar wants her hurt."

"Good. Suits me."

"Come on, Jay. He said to leave her alive."

"I can manage that," he said, pausing. Then, smiling, "With an effort."

"He wants her humiliated, my brother. Not physically damaged. Wake up, Jay, for crying out loud."

"Okay! Okay!" He held his hands up defensively as Mario chewed contemplatively on the delicious caviar dish.

"Come on then, man. Come up with an idea for once. You can't rely on me to plan every deal we get into. You've seen what she looks like on her flash website. She's big and she's black. And she can handle herself."

"Can she?"

"Jay. Jay. Where the hell are you? Pierre Search and Security. She's into one-on-one security. She's a Private Investigator. Ex DI in the Met. Website says she's also an expert in Krav Maga."

"What the hell's that?"

"Israeli martial art."

"Oh yeah, I forgot," responded Jason, slurping back another oyster.

"So, do we go for the brat? Or her old man? If we're looking to blackmail her somehow?"

Wiping his hands on his napkin, Jason finally concentrated on what Mario was asking. "No. We don't."

"We don't what?"

"Go for the kid. Or her old man."

"Good. A response at last. What do you suggest, then?"

"You've seen the news on the Clubhouse murders?"

"Sure, I have. What's that got to do with anything?"

"Been two inside the Tilbury club, and others outside it."

"How many of these clubs are there? Do you know?"

"There's three. Tilbury, Dagenham and Dartford."

"Any idea who owns them?" Mario drank from his glass of Blanc de Noirs, noting the way it caressed the tongue. Glancing at Jason, he indicated his empty glass and at his brother's nod, beckoned a somewhat put-out-looking sommelier to freshen it.

"Hester Lamont."

"Who's she? Never heard of her."

"A businesswoman. Came into a packet of money after her father died. Spent most of it on fitting out the clubs."

"Is she someone we can lean on?"

"Maybe. Coupla things here we can use."

"Go on."

"First, and you won't believe this."

"Try me."

"I've found out that Ms Lamont is really Mr Lamont."

"Whut?"

"Yeah. The clubs have LGBTQ nights, and it seems our Ms Lamont hasn't had the surgery yet."

"Christ! You have been busy."

"There's more."

"I'm listening."

"Well, I know the black bitch."

"News to me. How do you know her?"

"Not personally, but she stands out. You don't forget her. I've seen her in the past in one or two Soho clubs."

"What sort of clubs, Jay?"

"Mixed, you know."

"No, I don't know."

"Look, just leave it. I know the Clubhouse clubs, too."

"So?"

"The Lamont woman was seen going to Pierre's offices a few days ago."

"By who?"

"After Oscar spoke to us I had someone start keeping an eye on her."

"Okay. And?"

"She might have been retained by the Lamont woman to poke around a bit."

"Aren't the police on to it?"

"Sure. They closed all the clubs briefly. But so far, they haven't a clue. Clubs were all reopened on a promise to install more CCTV. Lamont must've been afraid of seeing all Daddy's hard-earned legacy slide down the drain if they stayed closed. The kids don't seem too bothered by what's happened. You'd have thought..."

"Bloody hell, Jason," Mario interrupted. "Why've you kept this from me?"

"I wanted something definite before we made any sort of move."

"Fair enough."

Mario finished his wine and beckoned an increasingly irritated-looking sommelier to top up his glass. "You said you'd seen the Pierre woman at some Soho clubs?"

"Yeah. I saw her, more than once. Watched her chatting to some of the people in them. She sure looked interested. You ask, I'd say she's bi."

"What were you doing there, Jay? Not your sort of places, I'd have thought." Mario looked for a sign, any sign of discomfiture on his brother's face, but saw none.

"I think we can get Pierre on something she won't find easy to wriggle out of."

"What d'you have in mind?"

"What say, we try and pin a murder on her?"

"Whose murder, Jay? Can't produce murders to order, you know."

Changing the subject, which didn't escape Mario's attention, Jay said, "We need to scope her out properly."

"Of course."

"I know where she lives."

"How?"

"Followed her home from the office one day. That easy. She lives in Queen's Park. North West London. Smart modern block. She's not short. Business must be booming."

"Christ, man! You've been a lot busier than I realised. Good work."

"I don't need you to tell me good work, Mario," said Jason, suddenly flared. "Just stop acting like a fucking mother hen all the time."

"Fair enough, fair enough," replied a chastened Mario.

"And I don't just rough 'em up."

"Okay, sure. I understand," he said, noting the flush rising from his brother's neck to his cheeks. A familiar sign Jason was getting dangerously edgy.

Seeking to pacify him, Mario offered, "But we need to let her know we're around and that we mean business. That is, before we start setting her up for whatever we have in mind."

"Fine," responded Jason, smiling happily as he reassured his brother. "I might just lean on her a bit. Bend an arm or a leg. You know. Let her know who's in charge."

"Jay?" asked Mario. "Is there anything else here?"

"What do you mean?"

"You disappear for days at a time. Just recently. Where were you?"

"I had business to attend to."

"Why do I have this feeling you're holding out on me?"

Jason just shrugged and didn't reply.

"I've had another idea." Mario smiled. "Could be lucrative."

"Go on."

"Two birds with one stone."

"Get on with it, then," said Jay irritably.

"The clubs are in trouble, so we rough up a couple more of their patrons, not too many or too much though, just enough to see the places closed down properly, but as briefly as possible, then we offer to buy out Ms Lamont."

"Mm, that's a thought. Say, tell you what, if the clubs belonged to us, we could use 'em for our laundry as well."

"In one, brother. Lotta money for us to clean up. Ideal venues with over a thousand a night attending each of the three."

"Tell you what," added Jay, as though suddenly inspired. "Oscar's into trafficking."

"So, what's new? Aren't we too?"

"Yeah, sure we are. But listen. We could bring in some girls. You know, young ones, not too young, teens maybe. Scrubbers."

Jay closed his eyes, looking contented at the thought.

"Haven't we been doing that anyway?" asked Mario, perplexed.

Jason went on as though Mario hadn't spoken, "Have them mix in with the crowd. Generally upset things at all three venues, make a nuisance of themselves. It'll lower the value even further. That Hester woman will beg us to take the places off her hands. Hell! She'll end up paying us."

"You know, Jay, you're leading me into mentioning another brilliant idea I've been working on."

Jay yawned, reached for his glass and finished his drink, before beckoning a thoroughly nettled sommelier to freshen his glass once more.

"Okay, what is it now, Mario?"

"Don't sound so bloody patronising, Jay."

"Alright, alright. For Chrissake, will you just get on with it, then?"

"I've thought some more about it, the trafficking. I've got a whole new angle. We'll bring in our young tarts. But, and here's the thing, if we bring in some who are pregnant, maybe let others get pregnant when they're here, we've got another source of revenue?"

"You've lost me."

"Baby sales, my man. There's people willing to pay big money."

"Where?"

"Christ, Jay. Everywhere. Here. Europe. The States. You name it."

"And who's going to organise all this, Mario?"

"I am."

"Really? Just like that, you've got it organised. You'll be telling me next you've got a boatload of girls on the way."

"That's right, bro. I have. Coupla days from now."

"You bought a boat?"

"I never said that. Got a guy from the Middle East to finance his own boat. So, no financial risk for us."

"Chancy, Mario. What if the bloody thing capsizes? We're always hearing about that sort of thing in the Channel. Up to now we've used safer ways to bring in the people."

"If it sinks, no problem. We'll find another boatman."

"And another load of girls." Jay grinned. "You bastard!"

"You've got the idea."

"You're something else you know, Mario. But hey! Forget the girls working the clubs. Too chancy. They could just run off. Better we hire them by the night. Tell the punters, we'll select only high class, they don't need to use condoms."

"Got it. That way we get an income, then when the tarts get pregnant, we sell the kids."

The two men sat contemplating the other for several moments, then touched knuckles. "Partners." They grinned in unison.

"And what about the girl?" asked Mario.

"The black?"

"Who else?"

"I'll do what needs doing."

"Alright, Jay. But keep it gentle, for God's sake."

"I'll try. You know me, brother," he said, leaning across the table to put an avuncular hand on the other's forearm. "I always try."

CHAPTER 14 DAYS 2 & 5

DAY 2

In a narrow alley some two hundred yards from the Dagenham Clubhouse, a woman struggled with her assailant. He'd ripped open her blouse to reveal small braless breasts. There were shallow cuts to her neck and shoulders as though her valiant fight had thwarted his immediate attempt to kill her.

Though her palms displayed deep defence cuts, she hadn't given up yet. She couldn't see him, and because she was cloaked in the surrounding mist and there were few residential properties in the immediate vicinity, she too could neither be seen, nor her screams be heard.

"What've I done to you, you fucking creep?" She was strong, but no match for the man or the knife he wielded. One last effort and she thought she might just be able to free herself, before the blade, easily slicing through the waistband of her mini skirt, opened her up from pubic bone to breastbone.

She screamed in a prolonged caterwauling wail before falling unconscious with shock, but still alive. Then the man quickly set about dragging up the skirt, tearing off the tiny knickers, slicing expertly through flesh, removing the remodelled genitalia before delving deep into the false uterus, all of which he slipped into a polythene bag.

"Fuck you, Judge Jeffreys, Rolande, with your girly voice," said the killer.

"Two years for importuning? Bullshit. Ten years ago. I don't forget that easily. Not nice, jail. Had a hard time. Think I'd forgotten about it? My turn to pass sentence," he muttered, before escaping the area on silent, rubber-soled trainers.

It wouldn't be long, but Rolande was fully awake and aware when her executioner ran.

* * * * *

DAY 5

AS THE RAIN LASHED THEIR FACES, drenching hair and clothing, one of the girls screamed, prompting others to follow suit.

The heavily bearded man handling the inadequate and greatly overworked outboard motor, leaned all of his considerable bulk against the tiller, forcing the craft to face the oncoming wave to avoid capsizing and losing his valuable cargo and possibly his own life at the same time. A non-swimmer, he'd done this trip dozens of times before, earning sufficient to take care of his wife and children in Damascus. But he was greedy, wanted more, and hadn't been prepared to invest in a larger, safer boat. This time, he was aware the trip might be his last as he faced the several hours' sluggish voyage in increasingly threatening conditions with trepidation.

The two dozen young women crammed aboard the flimsy wooden open vessel had been neither properly briefed nor prepared and were mostly attired in skirts and blouses. One or two wore jeans and had had the precautionary sense to don jackets or coats before they'd set off. On close inspection several of the young girls might have been in the early stages of pregnancy.

The language they spoke among themselves sounded like Romanian. They frequently turned to one of their number, a young woman in jeans with a long ponytail, and apparently more self-possessed than the others, who looked to be offering advice, or solace, to the girls closest to her, whom she hugged as reassuringly as was possible in those conditions.

The girl with the ponytail, Daria Florescu, had been promised work in London. Some of her friends had taken a similar route, although not this one, and despite the absurd risks, had nevertheless met with some success.

Daria, however, was now under no illusions as to what this trip was all about and what type of work the girls, and inevitably she, were going to be forced into. A simple conclusion she'd reached as soon as she'd set eyes on the crowd of anxious faces on the side of the Channel they'd left behind. Her boyfriend, back in Bucharest, had said he would try to join her as soon as he could, but his problems of immigration would match hers. Namely, neither could fulfil the criteria required in the UK points-based system of entry.

Even as she'd boarded the flimsy boat on the French coast, she'd suspected the folly of her position, dithered about whether to climb aboard or not, considered the money she'd laid out for the journey, and decided to take her chances. Now, with her clothes soaking and the taste of saltwater on her tongue, it was a decision she was coming to regret more with every lurch of the boat.

Seated among the women were four heavyset bearded men. They could have been brothers of the man at the tiller. The only distinguishing feature among them, a tic on the face of the tallest of the four. Only they weren't his brothers. They were here with the object of making themselves known to attendees at a number of London's larger mosques. What they had planned would become apparent in due course.

Better prepared for the trip than the girls, instead of the more traditional tunic-style thobes, all four wore baggy, shapeless clothes, with high-neck sweaters under now soaking jackets. Like the man at the tiller, they all had floppily wound dun-coloured turbans, each with a loosely hanging tail of cloth at their backs. Muttering quietly among themselves, they chewed absent-mindedly on what looked like black-bread sandwiches and drank from clear plastic bottled water, while the girls looked on hungrily.

The sea was rougher than had been anticipated. The boat owner, as usual, had neglected to check weather forecasts before setting off, and while he'd been fortunate on previous trips, it looked as though both his luck and that of his passengers was running out. The heavy wave he'd just steered into crashed over the boat which came through it seemingly unscathed, although there was an ominous creaking of timber as though the craft might be about to break up. The four males in the boat glanced up at the owner enquiringly, but he shrugged and otherwise ignored them as another wave, which this time he failed to anticipate, hit the boat broadside, causing it to tilt at an angle of forty-five degrees.

It was now the turn of the four men to look alarmed as they clung on to whatever they could find to avoid falling in. And the girls were screaming again, some of them becoming hysterical as it looked as though they'd never make it to safety.

Small bits of timber floated away from the boat. From where they'd broken off wasn't immediately apparent to the occupants.

Daria wondered about her boyfriend. He'd never know what had happened to her. Then she thought about her family. About the hopes Mama and Tata had had for her future. Tata had counselled against the trip. A cautious man, he'd have been horrified if he'd been aware of the manner in which she planned to gain entry to the UK.

As for Mama. She couldn't bear to think what her mother's reaction would be if, as was now increasingly likely, she drowned. A degree from the University of Bucharest in the faculty of veterinary medicine where she'd met her boyfriend, had opened up their joint ambitions to work in London. It now looked like what it was: total madness.

The boat had somehow righted itself but was now becoming even more sluggish as seawater seeped through planking at the base of the craft, with the rain lashing them all, especially the man at the tiller. Standing higher than his passengers, he seemed to be trying to make a call on his mobile while hanging on to the tiller. Some of what he had to say could just be heard, "Double this time... Want double... I take risk you got girls. Double. No argument. Try to make it. Maybe sink. No take risk again. Fuck you."

The storm lashing them ever more powerfully howled in their ears, drenching them as much as if they were in the water instead of in a boat.

Through the curtain of rain, she could just see the shore now. Had no idea what depth of water they were in, nor how many of the girls could swim, and, if so, whether they'd make it in such uncertain seas, albeit now becoming calmer. She herself was a weak swimmer. At this distance she'd not get to the shore.

As instructed, the tillerman had made for one of those secluded, hidden beaches that aren't that well known to tourists. Being mainly frequented by locals, the Warren Beach near Folkestone, Kent, a sandy beach, features rocks and rock pools, and is popular with fossil hunters.

Inland, the Warren Country Park has been formed by centuries of land slippage. Steep paths wind through this woodland and the chalk cliffs. The Country Park is home to a wide variety of rare animal and plant life, including some one hundred and fifty species of bird.

The clifftops offer spectacular views out to sea.

None of this was likely to be appreciated by the five men, nor the group of girls, as their terror expressed itself ever more volubly against the shrieking of the gale.

For the most part the area was deserted. It was a spot picked by the Kerkut brothers, in particular Mario with his plans for baby sales, to collect their latest shipment of human merchandise.

Finally, the boat gave up, breaking apart with a shriek and a groan, flinging them all into the sea, a gasping clot of humanity floundering about helplessly. But they were closer in than Daria realised, her feet touching the bottom as she stood up in water that swirled around her chest. The terrified crowd dragged themselves wearily to the shore where two men in black hooded parkas awaited them, the five males making for the beach and attending to themselves while pointedly ignoring the struggles of the women.

They'd made it. All of them. Most of the girls falling to the ground in exhaustion, Daria included. She felt the bliss of sand and shingle beneath her palms, the blessed pungency of the banks of seaweed all around.

Their tillerman now made for the two who'd turned out to meet the boat, berating them and shouting, "Double. You give me double..."

Against the high wind the twin thumps of the suppressed semi-automatic could barely be discerned as the boatman coughed once, twice, gushing blood from his broken mouth, and fell on his face in the wet sand where two shredded exit wounds gaped blackly in the back of his neck.

CHAPTER 15 DAY 5

"DOV JORDAN, WHO'S CALLING?"

"Shalom, Dov."

"Reuben?" he said, sounding pleased. "Shalom, Reuben. Vas tut zikh?"

"You know what's happening."

"I do? Well tell me, then."

"We're chasing terrorists. Remember? It's a full-time occupation, Dov. You don't become part of Mossad for the pottery classes or the evenings in spent knitting."

"Okay," sighed Dov. "But then I didn't exactly volunteer, Reuben. I was co-opted as an occasional agent."

"Well, this is an occasion, my friend."

"So, what can I do for you?"

"Where are you?"

"You know where I am. I'm in London."

"I meant, at this precise moment. We don't have eyes on you twenty-four seven."

"I'm in the apartment, off the Edgware Road, sorting out some pictures and jewellery for a couple of clients."

"Esther?"

"Divorce is still not finalised. She's being impossible."

"She had the baby yet?"

"Not yet."

"Your baby?"

"God knows."

"You know she's been playing away."

"You've got time to check up on her, then?"

"Not really. But word gets around. How about your London girlfriend? She got herself into any more trouble?"

"Not as far as I know."

"She's quite something. We can't decide whether trouble stalks her, or she stalks trouble."

"Probably a bit of both. She's a risk taker. It's what makes her tick."

"See if you can get her to join us, Dov. We could use someone with her talents."

"Funny."

"What's so funny?"

"She told me her CIA contact who calls himself Felix, after his Bond hero, told her the same thing. They could use her in the field."

"Would she be interested?"

"No way," replied Dov emphatically.

"How can you be so sure. I mean, if she's looking for excitement. If she wants challenges…"

"She's an independent. A maverick. Lone wolf. Call it what you will. She takes orders from no-one."

"Understood. I won't raise it again."

"And, she's got enough risks in her line of work without volunteering for the firing line. She's a mother now too. Got to think of the baby's welfare."

"Your baby, Dov?"

"Of course," he said quickly. Perhaps, too quickly.

"She was in Syria recently."

"Back safe. Baruch Hashem."

"You're right, thank God. She nearly died out there."

"Don't remind me."

"Lunatic mission. Ill advised. Bound to fail."

"But she succeeded. Like I said. Back safe."

"Was she pregnant when she left for Syria?"

"Must have been, judging by the timing of the birth."

"Any chance she could have met someone while she was in Aleppo?"

"What, between the bullets? Don't be absurd."

"Well, we may have something for you. It'll involve her, not necessarily directly."

"I'm listening."

"She was very recently approached by two brothers, family originally from Northern Cyprus, Mario and Jason Kerkut. Introduced, if you will, by Oscar Mountford."

"That reprobate. I thought she'd put him away for good," said Dov.

"She did. But he's not prevented from contact with the outside world."

"So, what do we know of these two? And why was she approached?"

"Why she was approached we don't know as yet. We're working on it. What we do know of these two is that they're into drugs, prostitution, people trafficking and money laundering."

"Go on," said Dov, his interest aroused.

"Your girlfriend—"

"She's not my girlfriend, Reuben," Dov corrected him, feeling and sounding irritated.

"Very well then, Dov, Tammy Pierre. We both know who I'm talking about, whatever she is or isn't to you."

"Okay, so what's the problem here?"

"It's not a problem yet. But we're fairly sure it's going to become one. Tammy has been retained by the owner of several dance clubs, that is, clubs with bars, to look into a number of murders of clients that have happened either within or else close to club premises."

"How many clubs are we talking about?" Dov enquired.

"Three, they're situated in East London."

"Where in East London?"

"Hang on, I'm getting there. We're talking Dagenham, Dartford and Tilbury."

"Tell me about the killings, Reuben. And who's the club owner?"

"The owner is Hester Lamont. Clever businesswoman, business person," he corrected himself. "Knows how to run a successful club, or clubs. But here's the thing. She's a transsexual."

"How do you know?"

"Oh, come on, Dov. Do I need to spell it out? We make our own enquiries." He paused. "So, Hester has regular LGBTQ nights. They're very popular and the crowd is good-natured. She seldom has trouble. Or she seldom had until now."

"Very well. Why does she want to employ Tammy? Isn't this a police matter?"

"Of course. Initially, when Hester employed Tammy there'd been a single killing. In the few days after, when Tammy was occupied with the baby in hospital, several further murders took place."

"Are they linked? Do you have a motive? I guess you got all this from the UK police?"

"The Met. Bob Walker, among others. Bob has a nose for these things. He's looking at the bridge between the Kerkut boys, Tammy and the clubs. Working a hunch, no more than that, he wonders if the brothers might be planning to take over the clubs to use them for money laundering. It's plausible. A couple of killings arranged to soften up the owner and then buy the places for next to nothing."

CHAPTER 15 • DAY 5 • 101

"Tell me about the killings," he asked again.

"The problem is, so far we can't see a link. No common ties, apart from, that is, the LGBTQ angle. The first, a young girl who worked at Tesco, called Julie Crosbie, had her neck broken. Possibly unplanned. Spur of the moment murder. Done in anger? She wasn't fully transitioned.

"Then a girl called Liz Armstrong. Something in IT. Broken neck.

"After her, Karen Richardson, trainee chef. Fully transitioned, slit throat. But she survived until they got her to hospital. Basically, a messed-up job. Possible revenge killing? Just a feeling, nothing more.

"The next, Anna Proby, a knife in the gut, pushed up into the heart. Worked in IT. Pause for thought here."

"I see, so why are you so interested in Anna Proby?" Dov asked, puzzled.

"Because we can't see any sort of motive. No spite, like Karen Richardson. No apparent anger, like the broken necks? No sexual motive. Just a neat stab to the belly. What you might call an execution. If this is the Kerkut boys seeking to close and buy up the clubs, expect more of the same."

"Two knifed to death," said Dov. "They do look like professional executions, don't they?"

"Except that the blades were different. One was curved, the other straight, according to the pathologist," explained Reuben.

"So, possibly different killers? With different motives?" he mused.

"Could be," Reuben agreed. "Or maybe one copycatting another to confuse."

"Any more?" Dov asked.

"Teresa Finch. Butchered from behind, no less. Nothing known about her at present. But we're working on it."

"That it?" asked Dov.

"Wait for it. Next, we have Judge Roland Jeffreys."

"Really? A judge?"

"A judge by day. A transitioned female going by the name of Rolande at night. No-one in his chambers was aware. He was very discreet. Obviously dressed as a male during the day. Clothing sufficient to mask the small bust.

"At the top of his profession, but known as 'Hanging Judge Jeffreys'."

"Someone with a real grudge, then?"

"Could be."

"Nasty."

"Very. We want Tammy to be involved beyond merely assisting the police in looking for a murderer or murderers."

"I don't see where she figures in all this, Reuben."

"Then let me enlighten you. The Kerkuts come from Northern Cyprus and we think they have links with some of the extremist communities in the Middle East. We've been nosing around and are picking up hints that amongst the illegal immigrants they're ferrying into the UK there might be some fanatics hoping to infiltrate several of the mosques in and around London."

"Does Bob Walker know about this?"

"Yes, very much so. He's police, of course, not counter terrorist, but he approached me after some of your boys in MI6 expressed concerns to him about intel they'd picked up."

"Like what, Reuben?"

"Like a flimsy wooden boat, broken up and partially sunk, found at Warren Beach, near Folkestone a couple of days ago, with a dead body close by on the shore. Judging by his appearance we're looking at an Arab. MI6 are fairly sure the boat would have been used to ferry in either or both the girls and maybe terrorists. This is hot off the press and MI6 are investigating."

"What do you expect Tammy to do."

"Her visit to Syria, Dov. It could have given her an edge. A feel for what might indicate an agitator type in the club. To be honest, Dov, we can't be sure. Can't pretend to know. We just want her to be our eyes and ears in the club, or clubs for a while. Nose around a bit.

"To be honest, the terrorist aspect is more immediate than the money laundering and the girls. She's all we've got. Far from ideal, of course, but let's see what we, or rather, she can find."

They were interrupted by a loud hammering at Dov's door and a voice screaming, "Let me in. Let me in!"

CHAPTER 16 DAY 6

SHE HADN'T IMMEDIATELY SPOTTED the two individuals across the road, or she might have driven on before doubling back once she thought they'd gone. Big men, she'd see them soon enough if it couldn't be avoided.

There was a heavy mist and cloying damp in the air, so she'd had the windscreen wipers working overtime. The hospital staff had been brilliant. Staff nurse Garcia had plied her with sweet drinks and food really meant to be for patients, which she'd insisted was surplus to requirements.

"Gotta eat, honey. Keep that gorgeous figure in shape. No matter you just had a kiddie. Wish I had a body like that. Lucky lady."

After the first night, she'd stopped smoking. She was out of panatellas, anyway. A vodka would have been a lifesaver, chilled, in an iced tumbler, but unfortunately hospital sales machines don't usually extend to the vending of spirits.

She'd kept Papa informed of the baby's progress. Not wanting to frighten him she'd made light of the issue. She'd not meant Dov to find out, but Papa had let him know, and bless him, he'd spent two whole nights with her and the baby, and after that, returning for hours at a time both day and night once his own most urgent matters pending had been attended to. The little one was after all Dov's son. So she hoped and fervently believed.

They'd kept Matty in for treatment and then observation for five nights and now the baby was back bouncing and gorgeous, lungs and airways all clear, while Tammy was leaden with exhaustion. But relieved and exhilarated at the same time.

Parking the Lexus outside her block, she depressed the ignition to kill the engine and looked over at her boy who, catching Tammy's eye, held out a tiny hand and grasped her extended forefinger.

"You gave us a scare, little man," she murmured and, leaning over him, planted a kiss on his forehead. Then another on his cheek, then the other cheek, only to hear him giggling so she felt her heart would burst with love for him. I'm a mother, she thought, as though a whole world of understanding had made itself known to her for the first time.

It was then she spotted them again, the two besuited men across the street, both looking at her, at least she presumed it was her, with apparent interest. The taller of the two was carrying an expensive-looking brown briefcase Tammy recognised as a Maxwell-Scott luxury item, the Buroni model. Its distinguishing features being its capped corners and the simple grooved picture frame lines joining the caps. Even with her tendency to profligacy, she eschewed the temptation to splash out the best part of £800 to buy one, opting for the less costly Samsonite.

Climbing wearily out of the SUV, she clicked the door shut. Desperate for a proper shower and a change of clothes, even though the hospital, or specifically Staff Nurse Garcia, had allowed her the use of some patient facilities, she wandered around to the passenger door and was about to open it to haul out the baby's strapped-in carrycot when her two visitors presented themselves.

She could see them weighing her up, noticed smiles that didn't extend to their eyes. Both had a casual hand in a trouser pocket, the taller of the two held a gold-tipped, liquorice-black cigarette between the index and middle finger of his free hand. The Buroni was deposited at his feet.

Leaving the vehicle's passenger door unopened, she straightened up to face the men. If you don't want to appear threatening never look at a stranger directly. On the other hand, if you do want to assert yourself look your interlocutor straight on the eye. All really basic stuff for which Tammy needed no schooling.

She experienced a ripple of adrenalin. They were big. She was bigger. At least, she was taller. Whatever they might have in mind she could deal with. No issues there. She resisted the desire to smile. Not necessary to be deliberately provocative.

"Is your name Tamsin Pierre?" The shorter of the two spoke almost too softly to be heard.

Spreading her feet slightly, one hand on a hip, she asked, "Who wants to know, gentlemen?"

"We do," said the taller, drawing on his cigarette, oddly exhaling smoke from the mouth then inhaling it back up his nostrils, while drawing his jacket away from his side like a cowboy going for his gun, to reveal a curved scabbard, presumably securing a curved blade.

She glanced up as there came a distant rumble of thunder followed by a flicker of lightning. Almost immediately the first few drops of rain splashed around her head and shoulders. She'd need to pull the cover of the carrycot well around to stop the baby getting wet. She sighed, glanced at the men and thought, here we go, then.

"Any more party tricks?" she asked, viewing the performance with interest.

"I said, are you Tamsin Pierre?" repeated the shorter of the two.

"And I seem to recall only recently enquiring, Who's asking?"

The man with the cigarette spoke: "Lady, we're asking the questions here. You're doing the answering."

"The Kray twins," she said like one who had just discovered the answer to a particularly difficult cryptic crossword clue. "Of course. I should have realised immediately."

"What?" he responded, stubbing out the remains of the practically unsmoked cigarette with his foot.

"Or, maybe, Tweedledum and Tweedledee?" She was grinning outwardly now, but continuing to assess the two. Looking for any movement, however slight, that might suggest an imminent attack. Instinctively she felt at her leather belt for the shuriken she carried when on a dangerous assignment. And generally, when not. Of course, they weren't there. She'd left the belt off, unusually, when she'd left for work the day Matty got ill.

Their legality was debatable, despite her blades being barely longer than the three inches permitted in law. New discs. Deadlier than her previous. Artisan-fashioned recently in New York and brought surreptitiously back to the UK. They'd saved her life, or ones like them, twice recently, but she'd manage perfectly well without them today.

"Jay, don't," said the shorter man, reaching out to hold the other's forearm as his brother moved menacingly towards Tammy.

"Forgotten something, lady?" the one called Jay asked, glancing towards where the belt would normally have been.

He knows something, she thought, quickly dismissing the notion. But still, that look of triumph?

Then unbidden, something else, the shadow of a memory came back to her. Comments made by ex-boss, friend and mentor from her time as a DI, Detective Chief Superintendent Bob Walker of the Met. She cast her mind back. He'd mentioned them some time ago. The two men. The memory wasn't there. Lost. Grasped at. Then gradually beginning to emerge, it came into focus.

These men were known to the police. Money launderers. What else was there? People traffickers. So-called sex workers, some as young as ten being brought into the country from places like Romania, Poland and Albania. Drug dealing on a grand scale. Shrewd operators never yet convicted of any crime. Nor yet even charged. All and any opposition ruthlessly suppressed.

"I know who you are," she announced. "You're the Kerkut brothers, aren't you. Mario and Jason."

"So what if we are?" said Mario.

"So, gentlemen; let me ask you a question. Please, what do you want with me?"

"Your friend Oscar Mountford suggested we introduce ourselves to you."

So that was it. Intimidation? Revenge? "He's no friend of mine."

"That's right. He's not keen on the inferior races," said Mario, looking at her with an expression of smug superiority.

"You mean vermin like you?"

Jason paled at the insult and moved a step closer to her. "Who're you calling vermin, lady?"

Glancing pointedly to her left and her right, Tammy offered, "I think it must be you, Mr Kerkut. There doesn't seem to be anyone else in the immediate vicinity to whom the appellation might pertinently be applied."

"Why, you fucking black…"

She was starting to weary of the exchange and at the same time sense her simmering temper beginning to approach boiling point. "Enough!" she snapped. "You've said your piece. Now go. Bugger off."

Jason's visage changed visibly while she watched, fascinated. As he paled, his cheeks seemed to become hollowed out. His pupils were tiny black dots while webs of red threaded the whites of his eyes. A vein stood out at his temple, another throbbed in his neck. His shoulders slumped and his arms hung loose like a primate about to rampage.

A silverback gorilla, she thought, though not as beautiful. She'd never witnessed such a complete and total metamorphosis in a human being. It was like witnessing Computer Generated Imagery in action in an X-rated movie.

It was apparent the time for debate was fast coming to an end, but Jason had to have one parting shot. Glancing through the SUV's passenger window, his lips drew back in a sneer. "You or the kid, lady. When the time comes. Makes no difference to us."

Believed by some to be the deadliest form of self-defence, the essence of Krav Maga, the Israeli martial arts skill, is to think quickly, make assessments and keep a cool head. If you lost your temper you lost the game. Tammy was an advanced exponent of the art, having had much additional coaching from occasional boyfriend, Dov Jordan. Don't aim to kill unless you're faced with no other alternative. Above all, remain calm.

By now Tammy's head was on fire with rage, her pulse thudding like a bass drum in her chest, but still, she spoke slowly and deliberately, albeit with immense effort. "Hear this, Messrs Kerkut. If either of you so much as lays a finger on my son I will personally remove your genitals and force them down your miserable gullets."

Too much for Jason to accept, he rushed Tammy with fists bunched, roaring at her, but she was ready for him, and spinning three hundred and sixty degrees till she faced him again with one raised arm bent, cracked an elbow hard, as hard as she could, into the side of his face. Swiftly repeating the manoeuvre, she pirouetted in the opposite direction, striking the other elbow with all the force she could muster into his other cheek. Both elbows would be bruised, but the action had the desired effect.

It all happened so quickly that stopped in his tracks, Jason paused, gasping for breath, and stared at Tammy in something resembling disbelief, before his brother said, "Come on, Jay. We've wasted enough time on her. There're better ways."

"Your time will come," snarled Jay, retrieving his briefcase and pointing a finger at her. "This isn't over yet."

"Where've I heard that before?" she muttered.

* * * * *

CHAPTER 16 • DAY 6 • 111

Back in her flat, she changed Matty's nappy, prepared his bottle of milk, watched as he sucked greedily at the teat, and after that fed Risky. Then she poured herself a stiff vodka, taken from the freezer, kicked off her shoes and sat back in the living room, with the cat contentedly purring on her lap, to watch her baby, to revel in him, every moment of him, and to unwind.

In the morning her au pair, Maria, a marvellous young bright-eyed Albanian girl, who'd taken to Matty from the first time she'd set eyes on him, would arrive at 8.00 am to help. She'd remain in residence thereafter as a live-in help.

Then her mobile rang. She wasn't expecting anyone but answered immediately with an odd sense of foreboding as she recognised the caller's number. She'd seen him several times in the past few days, and he'd been amazing, supportive, loving, but still…

"Tammy," said the voice. "We really need to talk."

"Hello, Dov," she said quietly.

CHAPTER 17 DAY 7

ANOTHER OVERCAST DAY with a bite in the air, as she drove towards Scotland Yard on the embankment.

She'd chosen to wear low heels and a sober two-piece clerical grey trouser suit, offset by a lavender and navy silk scarf. She'd found time to stop off at her favourite hairdresser, Girligig, in Ladbroke Grove and had the unruly curls softened into her current favourite pixie bob. Eschewing perfume and selecting the pale, satin rouge Hermès lipstick, she would present as stylish, but deliberately understated at what was after all a murder enquiry.

Her mobile rang out. "Tammy?"

"Bob, my dear. How are you?"

"I'm fine. Sorry I've not been in touch directly, but it's been hectic."

"I can imagine."

"You're seeing John? John Manus?"

"On my way."

"Good man, John. You'll like him."

"What can I do for you, Bob?"

"We know Hester Lamont has asked you to look into these ghastly killings, in or near her clubs."

"I know this is really a police matter, Bob. I'm just going to give John Manus my two pennorth where I feel there's something I can contribute."

"That's perfect. What we're really concerned about is the terrorism threat looming large in London. MI6 have reported a vessel beached at Warren Beach near Folkestone.

We've reason to believe that girls were being brought in for the purposes of prostitution, possibly working the Clubhouse angle, and further that a number of Middle Eastern men, maybe three or four, were on the same boat. One was left shot dead on the beach they arrived at. Not sure whether or not there is or may be a link with the Clubhouse situation here as well."

"Where's the intel from, Bob?"

"It seems Mossad have been tracking these men all the way from Iraq, and with your friendship with Dov Jordan, and your experiences in Syria, it occurred to us that you might be able to see if there's any way you can add to what we do, or more likely don't, know about them."

"I'll need to get a handle on these four and where they might have got to." She paused for a moment, then added, "Might be an idea if I have a meet with some of the guys at MI6 and SO15, your counter-terrorist people."

"I was going to suggest the same thing, Tammy. I'll set it up in COBRA."

"Cabinet Office Briefing Room A," she offered.

"Exactly," he replied. "Let you know when."

"Talk soon, Bob," and she rang off.

With a mere twenty reserved spaces available at the police nerve centre, she was required to leave the Lexus at a car park as close as she could get to the building, itself on the Victoria Embankment near the Houses of Parliament.

So she walked the five minutes to the showpiece, Art Deco, curved glass entrance of the New Scotland Yard headquarters. Designed by William Curtis Green, and first opened in 1940, the recent lavishly expensive refurbishment had seen the building reopened in 2016. Very much resembling a luxury hotel, it sported an Eames lounge on the penthouse floor and a reflecting pool with a permanent flame commemorating officers who had died on duty. All both highly dramatic and impressive, to say the least.

CHAPTER 17 • DAY 7 • 115

Arriving at reception, Tammy wasn't sure what she'd expected to find, but it certainly wasn't what confronted her when she entered the building.

Approaching her was a portly middle-aged gentleman, no more than five feet four or five inches tall. Dressed in a tight-fitting dark two-piece suit, he had the sort of pinkish to red complexion normally suggestive of blood pressure issues. Added to that, his lips had a purplish tinge to them. She stared at him, fascinated. He reminded her of a little bird, with his hooked and pointed beak for a nose.

"Tammy Pierre?" he enquired, extending a hand and looking up at her.

"That's right." She smiled, taking the proffered broad palm and noting its strength and dryness.

"I'm John Manus, John, as you of course know. Well now, I won't beat about the bush," he said in a business-like manner.

What's coming next? she wondered.

"Bob told me what to expect, but I can see you're a bit surprised."

"Oh dear. I am sorry. That obvious, is it?"

"Of course not," he reassured her. "Only, you had no idea how short I am. And I'd no idea how tall you are."

"Abject apologies, John. I didn't mean to seem —"

"Not at all. Not at all," he interrupted, deliberately catching her eye. "I just couldn't help thinking we'd make a fine couple walking down the aisle."

At that she burst out laughing. Absolutely no doubt, she realised, they'd work well together.

"Incidentally," he added. "Everyone calls me Robin, or Robbo."

Tammy stared at him, puzzled.

"Well, just look at me." He indicated his face and physique with a careless flap of the hands. "What else do you think I look like?"

"Really?" she asked, astonished.

"Truly. That is, unless any of them steps out of line. That's when I cease being a robin and resemble instead a cassowary." He smiled.

"Sorry?" she enquired.

"The most dangerous bird known to man. If you'll forgive the sexism. Google it. At nearly six feet tall and weighing in at around forty-five kilograms, that's one hundred pounds, they've been known to kill. No-one argues with them. That's when I also become Mr Manus and the bonhomie stops."

"Got it," she said. "Loud and clear. Just the same, I think I'll stick with John, if you don't mind?"

"Not in the least." He smiled.

They took the lift and emerged on the fifth floor to be confronted by largely the same team she'd met when working with DCI Rosemary Sharpe on the matter of the Black Candle Killings. An event that now seemed to have occurred light years ago, rather than just a few months.

The place was as she recalled it, mainly white-painted, open plan with regular desks in use, accompanied by staff on stools at a hot-desking bar. Highbacked sofas for officers gave the feeling of private meeting rooms.

The team, a dozen or more individuals, mostly milling around, glanced in the direction of the couple as they came in, and to Tammy's delight she was greeted by several she recognised from her last sojourn here.

Walking to one end of the room, Manus addressed those present, introducing Tammy and explaining, in his own discreet manner, in what way it was felt she might be of assistance.

Tammy made no comment beyond saying, "Hello again. I think I met most of you last time I was here. As John has just said we'll share information as we go along and hope we can prevent any more of these horrific killings."

She glanced around at everyone and noted acquiescing nods. Only one, head and shoulders above the rest, floppy red hair, immaculate suit and a grey complexion, shook his head despairingly, as though he'd just been condemned to hang for a crime he'd not committed. There's always one, she sighed inwardly. Let's hope he doesn't prove too difficult.

There were seven sets of pictures, each in its own neat separate square on the TV screen. The first showed a cute young girl with shortish, centre-parted fair hair and slight pout in a cheeky smile, but no other distinguishing features.

"Okay, so I'm going to recap to an extent, for all our benefits. We start with Julie Crosbie," said Manus pointing up at the picture. "First of our victims, happened in the club. Aged nineteen, very petite. A partial transsexual. A cashier at a local Tesco. Enquiries indicate she was happy to have hormonal treatment but was reluctant to go for the full surgical procedure as yet. We know she flat-shared with a couple of others in Walthamstow, East London. Still checking this out. She was found in the mixed loos, specifically what the club delineate as F/m which is..."

"I know." Tammy nodded. "Hester explained to me the choice offered. In this case male transitioning to female, whether or not complete."

"That's right," agreed Manus. "So Hester will have advised you the girl had her neck broken."

"It'd need a strong pair of hands. Male?"

"Insofar as one can clearly attribute gender, we've got blurred CCTV images that suggest a mid-height, muscular-looking male accompanied her from the dance area, presumably to the loos. The only feature seems to be a cleft chin if these images are to be relied on. Has to be unplanned, we believe. Hester thinks a cisgender male might have felt angered when he found this dishy girl to not be what he'd hoped for."

"That's what we surmised when she came to my office."

"Not too far out an assumption," said Manus.

"Any touch DNA traces on her skin? Should be, if, as you point out, she was strangled."

"It's being checked out now. A bit too early yet for results. Only of any use if her killer already has a record with samples on file we can use for comparisons. Otherwise, it won't be of any use until we locate the man she was seen with on the CCTV." Manus touched the screen by the square with Julie's picture and the view changed to show the corpse from different angles. Then they moved on.

"Liz Armstrong, shop girl. Fully transitioned. Another broken neck, again found in the toilets at the club. This time, female loos."

Tammy passed on to the next of the several pictures, a photograph of a young woman in a hospital bed. "Karen Richardson," explained Manus. "Fully transitioned. Trainee chef. Respectable background. Shared a flat in Islington. This was the fouled-up job I mentioned. Throat cut, but they got her to hospital before she died. Sadly, unable to communicate anything to us."

"This one?" Tammy asked, looking at a photograph of a dark-haired woman of about thirty. The ghastly wound down her front was open like a bloodied crack in the surface of the earth, her viscera clearly visible. She had, what on closer inspection looked like facial hair on the upper lip, possibly bleached. A method preferred by some, as facial hair if shaven tended to promote thicker growth.

"Anna Proby. Age thirty-two. Worked in IT at a firm in Beaconsfield, Kent, where she lived with her parents, who are understandably devastated. Fairly regularly travelled up to the club. No known current partners. Hester thinks she came for casual meet-ups. Found several streets away from the Tilbury club. She was a fully transitioned female."

"How do you know this much? I mean the club could accommodate around two thousand people at any one time."

"That's right. But over a period, Hester's got to know some of the regulars. She's bright, got an excellent memory. A talented businesswoman. And some of the clubbers seem to have cultivated her, for whatever personal reasons they might have had."

"Loneliness?" Tammy suggested.

"Could be. There's still massive prejudice and ignorance out there. So, a sympathetic ear from a like type person…" Manus touched the screen again to show alternative views of the victim and the surroundings.

"So, we've got no signatures here. No clear idea of whether we're looking at one or more killers. Three different types of murder," he said.

"Exactly. Looks like three different murderers, John. Two random. A botched, possible professional job. And a Jack the Ripper style killing."

"We're agreed on all that," Manus said, looking closely at the two pictures again.

"Then there's this fifth victim," she said, moving to a different part of the screen and trying not to wince at the corpse on display. "Teresa Finch. Also butchered. Don't have much on her at this stage."

"Any opinions, Tammy?"

"Well, looking at this victim, the genital mutilation carries the signature of a very sick sexual deviant. That, or else a raging revenge killing."

"That's right," Manus agreed. Then indicating the last picture, commented, "And this is the last of our victims."

"Another horror story, like the previous one," said Tammy. Adding, "Only, worse. If that's possible. An older woman? Any ID?"

"Oh yes. This is the respected Judge Roland Jeffreys."

"Good heavens. And butchered like Teresa Finch, only far, far worse. But, John, you said Roland?"

"That's right," agreed Manus. "A fully transitioned female who was Roland by day, and a practising judge, but Rolande at night, when he was able to be the woman he clearly wanted to be.

"We thought about the possibility of as many as three murderers," Manus continued. "But really, to all be happening at the same time? Seems too much of a coincidence."

"Unless our killer is set to confuse us."

"Wouldn't be the first time we've seen disguised killings like these."

"So again, for now, we've little if anything to go on."

"'Fraid not. It's still very early days, of course," added Manus. "I've got some of the crew looking at all the CCTV images from both inside and outside the clubs, unfortunately no images from the street or streets where the Tilbury club is located, and when they've finished, we'll start on the Dagenham and Dartford venues, although till now it's all been quiet there."

"CCTV images are going to be really copious, John."

"They are, but apart from talking to staff and attendees there's no evidence, no signature, no obvious motive."

"You'll be taking things up with next of kin?"

"Already underway. Again, we'll be looking for motive. Likely enemies? Persons with a grudge? You name it."

Glancing at her watch Tammy said, "I'll make a start. Keep you in the loop with anything relevant."

"Good, likewise. Oh and, Tammy."

"Yup?"

"Bob tells me you're a risk taker."

"Maybe. Not reckless though, I would say."

"Be careful."

"Okay, I will." She paused for a moment, then asked, "By the way, how's Rosemary getting on? I feel very guilty not having had the chance, baby and all, to visit her."

"Out of hospital. Chemo ongoing. But seems to be working. Tumour or tumours shrinking."

"That's really good news. Tell me, John, is she still smoking?"

"I'm afraid so. Can't see her ever giving up."

"Her own worst enemy. If you see her before I do, give her my love."

"Of course," he replied.

Well that went well, she thought as she waited for the lift to arrive. Then the atmosphere subtly changed. The tall detective, the one with the red hair and grey complexion, came out from the meeting room and approached Tammy, looking her up and down as though she were something the cat had brought in.

She saw he'd removed his jacket, but kept his tie on, still neatly knotted. His shirt was crisply ironed, the creases along the arms clearly visible, and she noted beyond the cufflinked sleeve what might have been an expensive watch. Rolex have been copied over and over, but from what she could perceive this one had a look that suggested the genuine article. But on police pay? Maybe not. Still, the man had style, but then he also had attitude as she correctly surmised.

"Think you're so clever, do you?" he hissed.

"I beg your pardon?" Tammy frowned.

"With your fancy clothes. And your cocksure ways." He hesitated, sneering at her. "Your butch voice, and that accent? You can't hide it, lady. You're a frog, aren't you? Fucking Frenchie."

"What's your problem, officer?" she asked, turning to face him head on, looking him right in the eyes.

"Who needs you? Fucking trans shit getting what they deserve. Look at you. All bloke, aren'tcha? Have you had the op' yet, mister? Or have you still got your meat and two veg?"

"What the devil are you talking about?"

"Your cock and balls. Still gottem down there, have you?" He pointed an outstretched arm at her crotch.

"I think you should go back to your room, young man, and we'll forget this ever happened." She stood with her arms folded across her chest, legs slightly spread. Ready for, whatever. Certainly ready for whatever this man might have in mind. Her pulse slowed and she viewed the individual, calmly appraising him. When facing a possible assault, the exponent of a martial art assesses the situation, doing everything in their power to avoid a physical altercation. But there are limits, and Tammy was fast approaching hers.

"What if I don't want to drop it? How about I grab you by the balls, you fucking imposter." So saying, he advanced towards Tammy and shoved her on the shoulder.

Lurching back, slightly under the weight of the push, she said firmly, "Enough. I said, enough."

In Krav Maga, the minute you get attacked, you are no longer the victim. You become the assailant. It is, strictly speaking, not a martial art but a self-defence system designed to give the physically inferior an advantage over their aggressor. You become practised in the art of quick thinking and instinctive response, as this individual would shortly be learning.

As the man came at her again, about to push her other shoulder, she moved, grabbed his wrist before he realised what was happening and brought her knee up with some force into his solar plexus. A soft target, it could be attacked with minimal damage to the individual, beyond generally stopping them in their tracks.

Which is precisely what now happened. He grunted and doubled up with pain, falling to one knee. "Fucking bitch," he muttered.

"You seem to be getting your genders confused, young man. But thanks anyway for acknowledging my female pedigree. Any more of your nonsense and I'll leave your masculinity, what there might be of it, in some state of disarray."

CHAPTER 18 DAY 7

"WHAT'S SHE LIKE, ROBBO?"

"Hmm?"

John Manus was at home, a small detached cottage in Buckhurst Hill, Essex, not far from the Central Line underground, with his wife, Meg. The green views of the Roding valley visible from the large picture window in their living room were a constant stress buster in the summer months on those rare occasions he was home before dark.

The late evening news was showing on Sky, with reports on the Clubhouse murders. A press conference was anticipated shortly.

John was sipping from a large gin and tonic and reclining in his favourite battered armchair opposite the TV in his slippers and shirtsleeves, his collar open. His wife sat next to him in her equally ancient armchair with a cup of tea perched precariously in her lap, wearing an old, flowered frock and likewise her slippers.

"This private investigator Bob wanted you to work with?" Meg was of a similar height and build to her husband, and was affectionately known among their friends as Pigeon. John called her Pidge for short.

"Where does one start?" he wondered.

Meg smiled, her head tipped to one side enquiringly. "How about first impressions, then?"

"Well let's see now," John pondered. "Right, then. She's very tall, at least six feet, exotic, fashionable to say the least, charismatic, slight French accent, deep voice, mixed heritage."

"Attractive?"

"What does that mean these days? I'd say, outstandingly striking. Not everyone's choice. But really, from where I was standing, very presentable."

He hesitated, then scratching his head, he added thoughtfully, "No. Beautiful, actually."

"What about her credentials?" asked Meg, sipping from her cup of tea.

"Highly recommended by Bob Walker, who was once her Super. She was fast-tracked to DI, before leaving the Met five or so years ago to open her own agency, Pierre Search and Security in Mayfair. She can be unpredictable, he said. Volatile, unmanageable. In fact, to use his precise words, 'a force of nature'. He absolutely thinks the world of her and her talents. Wishes she'd stayed in the force.

He mentioned scarring to her hands. Told me not to ask about it. Happened when she was investigating a case not that long ago. Although she kept her palms closed most of the time we were together, I spotted it. Nasty."

They both looked up as the twin chimes of the front doorbell sounded.

"Bit late, isn't it?" said John, looking puzzled.

"I'll go," offered Meg.

"Don't worry," replied John, already on his feet. "I'll get it."

A moment later John ushered the tall officer with whom Tammy had had the altercation into the living room. He was still in his working suit, and as he came in, he slightly self-consciously shot his cuffs.

Meg, who missed nothing, spotted the Rolex and involuntarily raised her eyebrows slightly.

"Darling, this is DC Harry Ricks."

"DC Ricks," she welcomed, getting to her feet and shaking hands with him. "Can I get you anything, young man? Tea? Coffee? Something stronger?"

"No, that won't be necessary," he replied.

"Do sit down then," offered Meg.

"No really, I'm fine. Thanks. I'm only here for a moment or two."

"Of course." Then turning to her husband, "Rob, you okay with your G&T?"

"I'm alright for the moment, Pidge. Now," he said, addressing Ricks. "What is it that's so urgent it couldn't have waited till the morning?"

Ricks looked uncomfortable, shifted from one foot to the other. Looked at Meg as though she might be able to assist, and she smiled back encouragingly. Then he spoke.

"It's the woman," he said.

"The woman?" asked John, though he knew perfectly well who Ricks was referring to. Only, he saw no reason to help the DC.

"The big black one you brought in today to lecture us on how to do our job."

John frowned for a moment, trying to guess where this was going. "After she left us, Ricks," he said eventually, "I saw you follow her out to the elevators. You came back shortly afterwards looking a bit the worse for wear. Anything happen that I should know about?"

Ricks shrugged noncommittally and said, "I asked her how she thought she might be able to help us."

"Did you now, lad? I wonder how you put it to her. Forcibly, I'd hazard a guess. What you won't have been aware of is that I've heard she handles herself as well if not better than any man I know."

"Boss," Ricks pleaded. "We don't need her or the likes of her. No-one on our floor likes her or wants her. That type, I mean."

"That type, Ricks? You specifically mean black? Female? Or French origin? Out with it, lad. And who says no-one likes her? She worked with the team before, assisting Rose. Believe me, son, she earned their affection and respect. You saw everyone's reaction when she came in today. She got a big welcome. So I'd say, this is all about you. Tell me, what is your problem?"

"I've got a bad feeling about her, boss. My gut tells me…"

"Your gut, Ricks? Your gut? My gut tells me you don't have a clue. We work on facts in our profession, laddie. The gut comes later when you've got years of experience. Which you don't have. And when you've risen up the ranks. Which you haven't, Ricks. How many times have you failed your sergeant's exams?"

"Twice, boss. But—"

"No buts, my boy. You're not here to lecture me on who I do and who I don't work with."

"Boss."

"Yes, Harry," John responded patiently.

"Does the Chief Super know you're using her?"

"Which Chief Super did you have in mind? We've more than forty in the Met."

"Bob Walker, gov. He's the one we seem to have most contact with." Ricks again shifted uneasily on his feet.

Meg just looked up at him bemused but added nothing.

John, regarding Ricks seriously, said, "As Rosemary Sharpe had it, Bob Walker was the one who actually recommended her to work with."

"Does he know she's working with you now, boss? I mean, shouldn't someone tell him?"

"I've not asked his permission. I don't need to, laddie. Were you by any chance intending to put your two pennorth in there?" John studied the other man's face for several moments, then said, "Look, this is beginning to trouble me, Ricks…"

"Have you seen the gold amulet she wears round her neck?" he interrupted urgently.

CHAPTER 18 • DAY 7 • 127

"Yes. Rose mentioned it. I'd have spotted it anyway, a beautiful piece like that. The one her father apparently gave her with the Hebrew inscription on it."

"Mumbo jumbo, sir. Not Hebrew. Voodoo. All voodoo. Means she's a Jew as well."

At that, John's face became redder, almost purple, while he tried to control his rising temper. "Go home, Harry. Go to bed and rethink things in the morning, as will I.

"Might be an idea — might be a necessity — I have you transferred to another unit. Maybe a course in diversity training would help? Though I rather doubt it. You're obviously an ambitious young man, judging by your general appearance and the jewellery." John glanced down at the Rolex without actually commenting on it.

Then he added pertinently, "Albeit with no apparent talent yet displayed for policing. Business perhaps? Or are you already engaged in business on the side? Either way, goodnight," he said and ushered a protesting Harry Ricks to the door.

When he returned to his armchair and picked up his gin, he was visibly panting and Meg looked over at him, worried. "Rob, love, don't let him get to you. Think of your blood pressure."

"I was, sweetheart. It's only that that stopped me from hitting him."

CHAPTER 19 DAY 8

"YOU IDIOT! What the fuck did you think you were doing, Jay?" Mario took a deep drag of his cigarette, the same type with the black liquorice paper his brother favoured, before blowing the smoke ceilingward in a long looping coil of grey.

"She saw me coming," protested his brother. "I hadn't realised. She moved suddenly as I swept the blade across her neck. Left only a surface cut. Too bad, Mario. Not my fault. She shouldn't have moved."

"Surface cut? For Chrissake, Jay. She's dead. Dead, man. And whaddaya mean, 'she shouldn't have moved'? Did you expect to have her stand still for you while you cut her fucking throat?" It was the first time Mario had ever berated his brother so positively without fearing a devastating reprisal, and Jason stood with shoulders slumped, looking humbly contrite but clearly unprepared to apologise.

"I just wanted to talk to her, Mario. I've only ever got you for company. I thought I could have someone to talk to. She walked away from me when I tried to chat outside the club. I just wanted a buddy for sometimes. You know."

"With a fucking custom-made scythe you want to make a buddy? Are you really out of your fucking mind, Jason?" Mario was heaving with rage and frustration, Jason looking both embarrassed and annoyed. Never a good sign with his unpredictable temperament.

The two men were seated in Jay's apartment in a Georgian terraced property in Grosvenor Square. The place had set him back thirty-three million pounds and he'd spent a further five million on renovations and decorations. Festooned with antique furniture, and objets d'art, the place was cluttered where it should have been genteel. But then business was profitable, although the upkeep of such a property, even with the brothers' apparently limitless resources, still needed a constant flow of income.

Oscar's contribution was not the fee they'd earn for dealing with Tammy, but more importantly the stream of introductions from all over the world, so-called business people and out and out crooks who needed money laundering.

Then Mario's mobile beeped. He could see the caller. "Hi, Oscar."

"You sound harassed, Mario. Everything in order?"

"Yeah, everything is fine."

"What about the black bitch, Mario? What have you done, or what do you plan to do? I want her humiliated. I've told you. See her lose her PI licence. Do whatever you have to. Only, as I've made clear, don't kill her. You hear me? Killing's too good."

Mario paused for a moment, looked at his brother. "You heard him, Jay. You're the man with the big ideas. Tell him what you have in mind."

"I'm gonna have her done for murder, Oscar."

The sound of Oscar's contemplative breathing drifted from the mobile. "Now there's a thought, Jay," he said. "But tell me, how do you envisage doing that? She's a PI, for God's sake. What possible motive could she have for killing anyone?"

"Jay's working on a few ideas, Oscar," suggested Mario, attempting to calm the other.

"Ideas? A few ideas? I want more than ideas, you and your psycho brother, two birdbrains. With what I'm paying you, I want to see progress. If you can't do the job there's plenty more out there can do it instead."

Mario said quietly, "Don't worry, Oscar. It's all in hand."

But Oscar wasn't listening any more because the line was dead.

CHAPTER 20 DAY 9

"WE'VE GOT A PROBLEM here, Tammy. Can I call you Tammy?" The man sitting opposite her was the one she'd first spotted in charge of the music. Tall and stick-thin as she remembered him from her first visit to the Tilbury club, close up he had the duskiest, coal-black complexion she'd ever come across. That and the quite astonishing cloud of white-blond hair made for an outstanding contrast. It was, perhaps, the eyes she found most arresting. They were a generous, dark, dark brown.

Tammy felt an immediate affinity with the individual, whom she judged to be hiding a more timid personality than he might care to admit. Decked out in the regulation red jacket and trousers, the man, his brow a pleated frown, was more stressed than his cool demeanour was intended to suggest.

He smelled of a perfume she couldn't identify. Subtle aroma. Expensive. Exclusive. She smiled. He'd make a fabulous catwalk model, but as a woman, not a man. Who knows? she thought. Maybe...

Occupying a seat in front of the individual, at Hester Lamont's desk in her office at the club, Tammy had been interviewing club staff and some members who'd responded to an email requesting their presence if they felt they had anything at all to offer.

It was mid-afternoon on another overcast day, when rain threatened but hadn't yet materialised. The office itself was furnished with a modern glass-top desk facing a couple of bright red swivel recliners, in one of which the young man lounged. A black lacquered cabinet hugged one wall and supported an enormous vase of mixed black and white trumpet-shaped calla lilies. A woman's touch, Tammy smiled. Unlikely you'd find the same in a male office, unless placed there by a woman.

She'd brought her Mac laptop with her and a black and red notepad and pen to jot notes and focus thoughts. She was dressed soberly in one of her dark blue jackets and skirts. White high-neck blouse. Low heels. Minimal make-up and no perfume.

"So talk to me, Mr…? Sorry, I didn't get your name?" She smiled at him encouragingly.

"Call me Dexie, everyone does."

"Unusual," she noted. "Short for something I suppose?"

"Short for Decimus. Catholic parents from Martinique, Black mum, Portuguese dad. So, mixed me. See?" he said, pointing to his aquiline nose. "Afro skin, but white man's beak. Had a large family. I'm their tenth. Hence the name." He gestured expansively with white leather-gloved palms outstretched.

"No accent," Tammy observed.

"I came to the UK with an aunt, Mom's sister, a midwife who ironically couldn't have children. I was two years old. Mom donated me, as it were. It wasn't too difficult to do with what she had on her hands."

"Okay. So what have you got to tell me?"

"What do you want to hear?" He sighed, sounding almost hopeless.

"Anything. Anything at all. Just thoughts and observations as they come into your head."

"The police have already been here," he said. "Tall one stuck out. Not a nice person to know."

"Yes, I know."

"I've met the DCI, John Manus. He's good. I liked him as soon as we started to talk. And I've come across the tall one you mention. Not a wow when it comes to diplomacy."

"Manus is okay," she agreed. "I'm working with him to see if we can stop any more of these killings."

"But really, they didn't have a clue, the cops, none of them. Mostly looked lost or else embarrassed. Tried to do it by the book. But there isn't a book yet on what we are here. That tall guy. Flash suit and tie. Quite belligerent. Questioned staff here, and I heard at the other two venues, as if they were the bloody murderers. He achieved absolutely nothing, except to put people's backs up. And what about that watch? Bloody Rolex. On a copper's pay? I mean, come on. He didn't even try to hide it."

Folding her hands together on the surface of the desk, Tammy offered, "Mm! I hear what you say. So far there's only been two incidents actually inside any of the three clubs, namely this one. I say single incidents, although they were, of course, both killings."

"Two's already two too many."

"Of course. But I'm looking for a link, as will the police be too. The only obvious tie-in is the fact that all those attacked so far have been members or else visitors at one or more of the clubs. Each of the killings has taken place generally close to this venue, and at neither of the other two. Does that strike you as odd?"

"Local person? I don't know. You're the expert."

"Believe me, when it comes to this sort of thing, no-one is an expert."

Changing his focus, he asked, "What about the trans thing, Tammy?"

"Nothing consistent there. It's been all females, it seems. That is male to female, with five fully transitioned and one partial not yet fully transitioned. We're not aware of any female to male trans people as yet. But forensics and the pathologist are keeping an open mind on all possible permutations in case anything has been overlooked."

"Hester must be really worried," said Dexie. "She sure looked it to me, though she's kept her thoughts to herself."

"Worried? I'll say. You know about her, then? Her condition, that is?"

"Yeah. We don't keep secrets from each other. We've become a sort of community, everyone boosting everyone else's morale."

"The police didn't close you down for long, did they?"

"Hester begged them not to. The clubs need to operate to stay solvent. Hester probably told you she spent a fortune on renovations and decorations. You can see it for yourself. Soon as you walk in. Fabulous place. Other two the same. Can't afford to lose all that."

"What about the kids behind the bar? Are they happy to keep coming to work?"

"Not happy, but we all need the money. Rents, mortgages in some cases. Living expenses. You know."

"And how is business? It must have been affected to some extent by what's happened?"

"Well now, there's the thing. You see, the places have been gaining traction. Despite the killings. Maybe because of them? People are unpredictable. Ghoulish perhaps. All three venues. Getting more successful by the month. If someone wanted to take them over. You know, buy 'em up for a song? A bit of interruption in trade might have made the owner more willing to consider a sale. But there's been none of that."

"And Hester? Concerns, beyond the obvious?"

"Lots on her plate. The clubs. Our safety. Her own safety, come to think of it. She would have closed, I reckon. We pleaded with her to stay open. So she begged the police."

"Understood."

"For all the worried regulars who stayed away, enough other ghouls showed up to bolster the numbers. But that won't last if there are any more incidents. But there's more."

"Tell me," said Tammy.

"I'm pretty sure we've got a number of girls touting for business in the clubs."

"You mean, sex workers?"

"I wouldn't put it so delicately. But they're unsubtle, young and clearly inexperienced. Judging by what I've heard from patrons their English isn't too good either."

"You think they're recent illegal immigrants?"

"Could be," he said.

Tammy nodded. "My sources suggested as much. But whether they've just been put to work, or whether they're planted to discredit the clubs further, I couldn't say."

"Really!"

"Yup. Something else to think about," she added. "And what about you?"

"What about me?"

"Are you transitioned? Transitioning? Okay if I ask?"

"No, it's no problem. I'm going female to male. We few seem to be out of the picture, for the moment at any rate. Safe, it would seem. But who knows for how long?"

"But your name? Decimus? Isn't that a man's name? Sounds like one."

"Actually no. As I said, it's a name, a sort of nickname for a tenth child of either sex. I was actually christened Grace. Grace Mathura. But Decimus sounds masculine, so I was always fine with it."

"Understood. So if I'm not prying, although in light of what's been happening I think I should know. Surgery?" she enquired bluntly.

"That's fine. So, for your information, I've had a double mastectomy, with lots more surgery planned. I've been on testosterone supplements for a while. Lower voice, some chest hair, and so on. And I'm tall, you know, so that helps. Penis construction to follow."

"Oh! I see." Tammy leaned back and folded her arms, looked and felt expectant.

"Do you?"

"Not entirely," she admitted.

"Shall I explain?"

"Do I really want to hear this?" She paused a second. Then, "Okay, I'm listening."

"Well, as I said, I've had the mastectomy. I'm now due a hysterectomy, which includes removal of the uterus, ovaries and fallopian tubes. Then, vaginal removal and finally penis construction."

"Doesn't sound like a barrel of laughs." Then looking contrite she added, "Sorry, that was uncalled for."

"No, you're right. Going to be a long haul. The last part will be something called a metoidioplasty."

"Which is?"

"Surgery changing the clitoris into a penis. Hormonal therapy will enlarge the clitoris, then the urethra will be lengthened using tissues from the cheek, vagina or labia minora to direct urine through the penis so that urination may take place standing up."

"Christ. It sure needs commitment. While we're on the subject, what about sex?"

"Different results for everyone. The metoidioplasty allows a small erection, but not enough for penetrative sex."

"And the alternative?"

"Is a phalloplasty. A bigger penis results, but no unassisted erection."

"Any other worries?"

"Just one."

"And that is?"

"Men go bald. Not all of them. But I've seen some trans males lose their hair." He indicated his own luxuriant white coiffure. "It'd break my heart to lose this."

"Doesn't always happen?"

"All my decisions. I won't change my mind."

"Difficult choices," said Tammy, looking sympathetically at him. "I wouldn't want to be in your place."

"Thanks. But while we're discussing me, how about you? Are you a trans? Looking at your height and voice?"

"Nope. I'm all woman. Just had a baby. But, as we're being open, I have high levels of testosterone which gives a boost to my skeletal foundation and muscular strength. Handy in my profession."

"I can see that. And the voice is beautiful."

"Thanks. Some men find it a bit intimidating."

"I don't. Won't," he corrected himself.

"And are you scared?"

"Of?"

"The prospect of surgery?"

"I am. But what choice do I have? What sort of male would I make otherwise?"

"And the killings?"

"Of course I am scared. Like everyone else. We're all just hoping you or the police will be able to put a stop to this bloody nightmare before anyone else…" He shrugged.

"Lastly, for the moment, can you think of anyone who might have a motive, however bizarre, for the killings? I know, I know." She held up her hands as though he'd been about to interrupt her. "They're all different, no real consistency. But still, does anything, however trivial, tenuous or unlikely come to mind?"

"Nope. Not a thing. You read about this sort of horror, but it's never this close to home."

"One other thing."

"Shoot."

"What's with the white leather gloves?" She'd noticed the way he moved his hands, emphasising anything he had to say that was particularly relevant. "Very smart, but do you wear them all the time? A fashion statement? If so, that's pretty cool."

"These?" He grinned, holding his hands up and studying the backs as though he'd noticed them for the first time. "Truth be told, I've got something called allergic eczema.

Itchy, and looks ugly. Really wouldn't be appropriate to be seen serving food and drink with red scabby hands."

"Okay. Point taken. Thanks for that. No offence intended."

"None taken. Anything more?"

"That should cover it for now. Oh and, if you don't mind, may I call you from time to time? You know, the occasional comment, opinion, awareness of anything noteworthy. My card," she added, pushing it across the desk.

"Any time," he agreed, looking more settled than he had at the start of the interview.

CHAPTER 21 DAY 10

The bitches are causing problems. Clients don't like it. I like it, though. A bunch of tarts touting in an LGBTQ atmosphere. Lowers the tone.

Barman doesn't like it. Plain to see on his scowling black face. Ridiculous white hair. Man's a bloody clown. That's fine. They think no-one knows what I've seen, but I do.

Hee hee.

They're pregnant. Not all of them. Just some. Hmm. Gives me an idea. The occasional caesarean? By little me?

Of course, if they want to talk first. All I really want is someone to talk to. Before I operate, that is.

Love it. Love it all.

* * * * *

"I WANT TO MARRY YOU, TAMMY."

"No, you don't."

Sun streamed into the apartment. As always, the place was dotted with a neat clutter of towers of books, both new and first editions, spread all over the carpet, pictures by a variety of upcoming and established artists leaning against walls, and small statuary in an assortment of mediums, including wood, iron, bronze and marble. The whole, representing the stock-in-trade of Dov Jordan's business, comprised an eclectic mix valued at a small fortune.

Both of them wore jeans and T-shirts. Dov was reclining on his leather sofa, baby Matty cradled in his arms as he fed him a bottle. Looking down at the little one, Dov felt he might explode with love for his son. Every little swallowing noise he could hear from the babe wrenched at his heart.

"I'm a father." He beamed, more to himself than anyone else. Then, pensively, "You know, his hair's not as gingery as mine. I noticed that when I first saw him. More, a sort of darkish brown."

Ignoring his delighted comments, Tammy said, "This place is like a mini museum, Dov. I could spend ages simply looking around and rooting through things. Business must be good?"

"You just changed the subject, Tammy. I asked you if you'd..."

She interrupted him, easily anticipating what was coming next. Hard to know how not to hurt him, whom she adored. Plus, there was a secret in all this she could never reveal, no matter who the father might turn out to be. She spoke as gently as she could. "I know what you asked, Dov. And the answer's the same. Anyway, your divorce isn't finalised, you told me. How is Esther? What's happening?"

Dov had put the bottle down by his feet and was busily winding Matty, holding him over his shoulder. "She came to the apartment recently. Started hammering on the door to be let in. Screaming, in fact, like a banshee. Flew in from Israel, despite her advanced state of pregnancy."

"You never said. What did she want?"

"To harass me?" He shrugged. "She's meshuga. Drives me mad. Wants a divorce but still wants to keep an eye on me. Wants to know what I'm up to all the time."

"What's she afraid of? Me? My influence on you?"

"Probably." Dov smiled. Then swiftly altering tack. "Matty needs a father, Tammy."

"The boy has a father."

"That's right. Me."

"You," she agreed, pausing for a micro-second too long, and Dov picked it up immediately.

"Tammy?"

"Yes, Dov." She sighed, dreading what was coming next. Leaning forward to look at the little one, she avoided Dov's gaze.

"He is mine? Yes, Tammy? He is mine, isn't he?"

"Why, who else's do you think he might be?"

"You're not answering the question."

"Dov," she sighed, "of course Matty is yours. We made love just before I left for Syria. Remember?"

"Of course I remember." He sounded slightly testy.

"Well, when do you think I might have had time for anyone else before leaving for the Middle East? Hmm?"

"Alright," he accepted.

Then, apparently giving the matter more thought, "How about while you were away?"

"In Syria? Are you being serious, Dov? I practically died out there." He looked so crestfallen she wanted to take him in her arms to comfort him. But she was well aware she wouldn't be able to fool him, so she added nothing further.

"Tammy, I have to ask you for something. It's the only way I can get peace of mind."

"Well?"

"Will you have Matty do a DNA test? It's the only way," he repeated.

The flat seemed to become eerily quiet, save for the murmur of traffic on the Edgware Road, a muffled car horn, the tinkle of a biker's bell.

"Yes, Dov," she agreed quietly. "If that's what you want. Of course I will."

"If you'll take the baby," he said, holding Matty towards her, "I'll do us a coffee."

"No. Don't disturb him while he's sleeping now. He looks so peaceful. I'll go."

Watching the coffee machine as it oozed black liquid she wondered, What have I agreed to? God, she thought. It hardly bears thinking about. But then he'd have to know sometime. And so, in fact, would she. Probably the sooner the better. Would he believe she'd been raped? How would she feel if the baby were Nabil's and not his? Shaking her head, she dismissed the worry for now and settled back in the living room with Dov and Matty.

"What's happening on the case?" Dov asked, Tammy having placed the little one in his cot.

"The Clubhouse killings?"

"Right."

"No clues. No evidence. No consistency. No pattern. Police have drawn a blank so far."

"Door to door?"

"Zilch."

"All transsexuals?"

"Yup. And so far, all male to female in various stages of transition. Innocent, vulnerable kids. At least, mostly kids." She breathed in quietly, the subject of the baby's paternity dropped for now. But for how long again?

"That's a pattern," said Dov. "Isn't it?"

"Mm! Quite thin though. And if there are more murders they could just as easily go the other way."

"Female to male, you mean?"

"Exactly."

Dov sipped at the scalding coffee. "Any way I can help? You know about the girls working the clubs?"

"I do. I've been told by Dexie, the DJ who largely manages things at the clubs, particularly the Tilbury venue."

"My people are keeping an eye on things."

"Your people?"

"Mossad, alright?" He sighed. "We're aware of the recent landing of a number of mainly young girls in a boat that capsized close to the Folkestone coast. Four large beturbaned gentlemen accompanying have decamped to East London. A fifth was shot without preamble and left on the beach. The welcoming committee, comprising a pair of brothers…"

"The Kerkuts, by chance?"

"The same. You've come across them?"

"I have, although it wasn't what you'd call a formal introduction."

Dov took another sip of the scalding coffee. "Any way I can help?"

"Not at the moment." She too drank from her mug. Then, half thinking aloud, "I remember one early morning, ages ago, I was taking a walk in Bushy Park."

"Hampton Court?" he asked.

"Yes. Hardly anyone about. Fresh breeze, sun spreading warmth. Bliss. Then I spotted a small bird, maybe a thrush? Not sure. It was clearly in distress. Cheeping plaintively and seemingly trying to hide behind the trunk of a tree, clinging on to the bark. From what? I wondered. Then I saw two large crows, evil, black, circling menacingly. The smaller bird clung quietly to the trunk of the tree out of sight of the two larger birds, until it looked as though the coast was clear, then the smaller bird made a quick break for it. There was nothing in sight that I could see. But suddenly from nowhere, the two black crows re-emerged. The smaller bird saw it had made its move too soon and frantically tried to run or more correctly fly to ground in the long grass, thinking it would be hidden. Then I saw the two big birds, homing in on the smaller, like a pair of helicopter gunships. I saw no more. I heard no more. It was chilling."

"The law of the wild," said Dov.

"Mm! That's what our victims are facing, isn't it. No escape. It's probably no more than a single killer. That is, a single killer each time rather than a pair. But is it the same killer, or are we looking at a bizarre situation of more than one killer using a copied modus operandi..."

"Tammy? Tammy? What is it?"

She was doubled over, coffee spilled from the mug which fell to the floor and broke.

"It's not possible. Christ, you look as though you've been shot," he said, looking up wildly at the open window, half expecting to see a gunman staring at them from the building opposite.

CHAPTER 22 DAY 10

RECENTLY

Two down, lots to go. You'd think they'd learn. How dumb can people be? Leaving the clubs on their own, half of them. Darkened streets. So dangerous.

Saw a little cherub there a night or two ago. Tilbury, that is. Ivory complexion, innocent Bambi eyes. Legs to die for.

And she will. When I get the chance. Maybe I'll hug her as she dies. Get real close to her. A new experience. Blood splashes may be a problem.

Someone needs to warn them. Not little me. Hee, hee.

Love it all.

* * * * *

DAY 10

SHE LOOKED GREY under the normal olive complexion. Grey and weary, as though she were close to shutting down completely.

Dov was aghast. "What's happened? For God's sake, Tammy! Let me call an ambulance," he practically begged, starting to dial 999 on his mobile.

"No don't," she said, holding up a restraining hand. "I'll be okay in a minute," she added, straightening up and sitting back in the armchair, her eyes closed, taking deep breaths as she quietly composed herself.

"What happened, Tammy. For God's sake, I thought you were dying. You looked as though you'd been shot. I was even checking outside the window to see if I'd missed something. It seems ridiculous now, but, a sniper?"

"Dov, I suffer with endometriosis. You know I do," she said, exasperated.

"Yeah, but I've never seen you with an attack like this one. You had me really worried."

His concerned frown had her heart squeezed, but she quickly pulled herself together, sounded business-like once more. "Yes, well it's passed now. So there's nothing to worry about. I'll clear up the mess," she offered, gingerly getting to her feet as though preparing for another possible episode.

A few moments later she returned with a long-handled dustpan and brush and began clearing up the broken pieces of mug. As she swept, to the chink of broken crockery being shovelled into the pan, she chatted, thinking aloud.

"So far the police have drawn a blank," she commented. "We've got two deaths with broken necks; Julie Crosbie, suggesting someone with the strength to carry out that sort of killing. The second broken neck, Liz Armstrong. Could be the same killer as the first. Only grainy CCTV. Useless, but neither likely to be a female killer.

"One with a slit throat, Karen Richardson, a curved blade and a botched job, died in hospital. One victim slit frontally with the heart pierced, that was Anna Proby; killed with a straight blade. Teresa Finch, terrifyingly butchered. And finally, the judge, Rolande Jeffreys, with horrific genital mutilation; also a straight blade.

"All these killings, several different modi operandi, at least two different weapons. If you ask me, I think different killers too. Though, don't ask me how many. As for motive," she pondered, shaking her head. "I'm lost. I have to admit it."

"I've already had some briefings, so I'm more or less up to date with you, Tammy. So where next?" asked Dov.

"On top of everything else, we've got no witnesses. Inadequate CCTV images. No items forgotten at any of the scenes. No clearly identifiable DNA, at least at this stage, of a potential murderer on any of the corpses, except perhaps the strangled ones, Julie and Liz. And there, we've nothing to match it with. So she wasn't killed by anyone with a police record." Tammy shrugged. "Until we get something more, something definite, we're flying blind, in the middle of a whiteout."

"But, Tammy, you can't just wait for another murder to happen."

She stood straight-backed, a hand on one hip and regarded Dov. "Might have to. I know it's totally unpalatable. But what other choice do we have?"

"I mean, how many more are you going to need before you get a lead. Before you've got something to follow up. Basically, you and the police are impotent."

"No, we're not."

"Really?" he said, surprised. "How can you say that? You've got no plan of…"

"But I have, Dov." This time she smiled.

"Well? Tell me."

"Hester put out notices in the clubs and sent emails to members asking them to help if they had any info. I spent some time at the Tilbury club in Hester's office questioning any who chose to come forward. Few did. The barman, the Afro you'll see with the cloud of white hair if you go to the place, tried to help. But he's also in the dark. And as frightened as the rest of them."

"So? Don't keep me in suspense."

"We need bait. Tease the psycho out into the open."

Dov's face fell. "Please, Tammy, don't tell me what I think you've got in mind."

"There's no other way, Dov."

"But you've been seen at the club," he protested. "They, or he, will know you're an investigator. The investigator, for God's sake. It'll never work. You'll be courting trouble. Disaster. If you ask me."

"You're wrong. Think about it. There's over fifteen hundred to two thousand people a night turn up at each venue. A handful of staff only saw or spoke to me. I'll wear a short dress and heels. Whoever it is, when they see me, will assume I'm a transitioned female."

"Crazy, Tammy."

"It's all trans females who've been the victims so far. Could be one clue. Remember, whatever the motive or motives, and however many killers there are, the one common denominator is the clubs themselves. They form the magnet for the murders."

"So when were you proposing to go on this little jaunt, Tammy."

"Tomorrow evening."

"God in heaven, Tammy!"

"I doubt he'll help, Dov. Face it, he didn't help any of the victims, did he."

"Please don't," he practically begged. "It's not the first time I've pleaded with you, Tammy. I told you before, months ago, Oscar Mountford was dangerous and you should steer clear, but you wouldn't listen. I know he's in jail right now, but that never stopped him, or any other criminal with outside contacts to do their bidding. I'm just asking you to give it some serious thought."

"I'm seeing John Manus tomorrow for a chat." Then changing the subject, she asked, "Did you see Manus's press conference on Sky News yesterday?"

"No. Was it bad?"

"You might say that," she pondered. "With anyone else it would've been a disaster, but Manus seems to have handled it like the professional he is. Trouble is, as we've seen, we've got a series of killings, but apparently not a serial killer."

"My people have been in touch, Tammy."

"Mossad, of course?"

He went on, as though she'd not asked, "They've an interest in what's going on here. Those illegals I mentioned, shipped in a day or two ago in rough seas were lucky they made it at all. Some of them were pregnant."

"Not too difficult to spot in the clubs," offered Tammy.

"Really? Where do they fit into the picture?"

"Dexie, who runs the bar at the Tilbury club and checks things out at the other two, told me there's a crop of new girls with poor English, working the clubs, who I'm thinking are probably your illegals."

"You mean touting for business?"

"Yup."

"Prostitutes?"

"You said it."

"I wonder who's pimping them."

"Obviously, whoever brought them over."

Climbing out of the armchair Dov started restlessly pacing the room. "Not going to do much for business at the club, is it?"

Sipping at her fresh mug of coffee speculatively Tammy suggested, "Maybe that's the whole idea. Lower the tone to lower the value then buy the clubs on the cheap."

Dov stopped pacing and faced Tammy, his arms folded across his chest, offering the thought, "While earning some cash through the pimping on the way."

Replacing her cup on a side table, Tammy murmured, "Poor kids."

Changing tack slightly, Dov debated, "What piqued my people's interest though, was the fact that the four gentlemen in that boat have been followed to various mosques in London. They were found on CCTV wandering around Folkestone looking lost. Then they were picked up in a black Ford Transit. Tracking was easy after that."

"Your people are thinking, terrorists?"

"Could be," Dov agreed. "The reason they called me is because they think that with your recent Syria experience you might have a slight gain in finding out what's going on here."

"Doubtful." She shook her head. "Anyway, I'm supposed to be looking for what the press, according to Manus and the news, are now calling the killer: the LGBTQ executioner. Probably a wrong assumption here. Should be executioners."

"Yeah, I've seen. Poor kids," he said, echoing Tammy. "As if they didn't have enough flak to put up with."

CHAPTER 23 DAY 11

THEY MET ON THE TERRACE of the Hyde Park Serpentine Bar & Kitchen overlooking the lake on a sunny if somewhat brisk early morning. At that time of day the air had a clean, traffic-free smell, coupled with that of newly mown grass. John Manus had a steaming coffee in front of him; Tammy, a double vodka, neat.

"A bit early for that, isn't it?" Manus grinned.

"Never too early for a bison grass," said Tammy, fashionable in a deep burgundy silk satin V-neck blouse, worn under a black Aviator Flight leather jacket, with black pants and black Nikki Reed trainers. She'd noted Manus's unspoken but appreciative glance as he joined her.

The bar was comparatively empty, with only one other young couple at a table nearby chatting animatedly over hot drinks. In the distance by the lake, a tall man in a brown bomber jacket strode purposefully, a Rottweiler at the end of a lead, the dog straining to be let go.

"Thanks for agreeing to see me at short notice, Tammy."

"No problem, John. Any reason why we're here and not back at the Yard?" She took a long slug from her tumbler, feeling that satisfying nip at the back of the throat and warmth spreading around her stomach while awaiting Manus's response.

"To tell the truth I just wanted a break away from the claustrophobia. The team are doing everything possible to nail this, but we've so little to go on. I thought a change of air might spark some inspiration."

"What have you got from SOCO?"

"Next to nothing beyond what could actually have been viewed by any casual observer."

"Pathologist reports?"

"Still awaiting a full complement. But it doesn't look too probable we'll find much there, beyond the obvious causes of death. Worth noting though, the pathologist commented that Karen Richardson was killed with what looks like a highly sophisticated curved blade. A specialist item, despite the killing nearly failing. And, importantly, the killer was almost certainly right-handed.

"The other killings, Teresa Finch, Anna Proby and the judge, whether slit throat or mutilation, seem to have been carried out with a straight-edge knife. In these two cases, the killer is likely to have been left-handed."

"Okay. Again, the botched job might have been the reason for the change of weapon. Might still be the same killer."

"It's possible. But then what, an ambidextrous murderer?"

"Stranger things."

"True," agreed Manus. "At this stage nothing is being ruled out."

"You've chased up phone records?"

"Of course. But there's nothing indicating any foreknowledge or relationship with any potential perpetrator." Manus gazed thoughtfully across the expanse of water as though it might provide inspiration. He blew on the surface of his drink, then sipped tentatively from the cup. One or two swimmers were in view in the lido area. It was still early, their time finishing at 9.30 am, and a number of rowers plied the calm waters.

Manus cut back to attention as Tammy asked, "Instagram? Facebook? Twitter? Maybe even LinkedIn?"

He leaned forward, elbows on his knees, and rubbed his temples with his forefingers. "Same thing. No leads at all."

"So, we're looking at random killings? Spur of the moment attacks?" she offered.

"Looks like it, so far," he replied, self-consciously adjusting his tie and shifting ever so slightly in his too-tight suit.

Why would a man in John Manus's position wear an ill-fitting suit? she wondered. Unless, that is, he'd gained weight recently and not had the time to arrange alterations. That, and the florid features? High blood pressure? She'd noted it when she first met him. Unfortunately, all too possible.

"What about next of kin? Housemates? Flatmates?" she asked, keeping her concerns to herself for the moment.

"Karen's two flatmates were Perdita Prentice, PA to the boss of a Mayfair art gallery, and Tiffany Pugh, head of PR at a big firm of jewellers. Seems Karen and Tiffany had something going between them. Tiffany was quite shocked when she learned Karen was a transitioned bi-sexual. She found it hard to take in. Felt she'd been let down. Lied to."

"Any other names come up in questioning?"

"Well, possibly. The flatmate Perdita Prentice came up with an Amyra and a Pattie, mentioned once or twice in conversations in the flat. She thought they might have been known to Karen but could provide nothing further."

"That's all? No surnames?"

"Unfortunately, not. And nothing else to go on here. At least for now. But we're keeping an open mind."

"Hmm." Tammy sighed. "Not going to be easy, is it."

"I'm afraid not. And with the press baying for an early arrest… They behave as though it should be as simple as picking out the ace of diamonds from the backs of a fanned pack of cards." Manus sounded exasperated.

"So, what we've got is: Julie Crosbie was a broken neck. Ditto, Liz Armstrong, Karen a cut throat. Different killers, do you think?"

"Likely." Manus paused. "I don't know. Possibly. But then, if the killer, assuming it was the same person, and whether male or female, was maybe finding it too hard to break a victim's neck, they might have resorted to the knife as the easier option."

"We've talked about the only other probable link being the attack on the trans community."

"That's right."

"Anything turned up on the Sex Offenders' Register?"

Reaching into his jacket pocket, Manus extracted a foil strip from which he snapped out a couple of tablets and swallowed easily without needing to drink anything.

Tammy looked at him doubtfully. "Blood pressure?" she asked tentatively, having recognised the obvious signs the first time they'd met, finally posing the question.

"Best to be on the safe side," said Manus, offering nothing further.

She finished off the last of her vodka, then indicated a waiter to bring her another. Nodding when he mouthed, "A double?"

"So, if there was nothing from any of the families of the deceased, we're left with only two first names," offered Tammy.

"That's right. I've got the team going through all three clubs' registers of attendance, insofar as they were kept, and membership lists."

"Members of some clubs wanting to remain anonymous will occasionally adopt an alias, won't they?"

"They will. It doesn't make the job or the task any easier."

"Have you made any progress with Judge Jeffreys yet?"

"No, we'll be visiting his mother to see what, if anything, she can add. So far, she's been visited by family liaison, but not yet questioned."

"How did she take it?"

"Badly. She tried to maintain the old British stiff upper. She's of that sort. Her generation, I suppose. But then she broke down."

"You're going to have to talk to her."

"Of course."

"Let me do that, John. I've a feeling she could do with some non-police, female input. Not suggesting your team couldn't do the job, but just a sense I might make some progress there."

"Fine by me. I'll text you the address."

A high-altitude plane rumbled lazily overhead trailing twin vapour trails. And there were more boats on the lake now. It was all a picture of tranquillity; how very at odds with what lay just beneath the surface of so many lives. The man with the dog had disappeared, but there were several other walkers out for the early morning.

"Tell me, John; what do you know about the Kerkut brothers?"

"We know them. Know them well," Manus said as the area erupted in an explosion of sound. Principally that of a woman shrieking and the hoarse roar of something rocketing towards them, now in their midst. The glimpse of an open jaw, shark's teeth, and dripping saliva.

CHAPTER 24 DAY 11

THE NAKED CHILD, for she was little more than that, screamed hysterically, her throat rasping as though it were being torn to shreds. Her thighs parted, knees drawn back in the attitude of one attempting to give birth, the child begged, "Please, please. Is hurt so much. Help me."

Seated next to the bed, holding the little girl's hand in a vain attempt to bring her some sort of comfort, Daria Florescu reached over, and with her free hand mopped the child's brow.

The place smelled of old leather, rotting garbage and sweat. The retired midwife, a frail old lady in her eighties with curly white hair, was dressed in a shabby, nondescript dress. She looked as though she was at her wits' end, with hands and arms covered in the child's blood.

There were rusting kettles and chipped bowls of heated water together with threadbare greying towels cluttering the place. Paint peeled from the walls and what little furniture there was comprised ancient wood tables and ladder-back chairs.

Turning to look up at the man behind her, the old lady pleaded, "The child needs a caesarean section. Can't you see that? She's been like this for hours. Much too long. The head still isn't engaged. And it looks like a breech to me. And I can't do that," she added. "I don't have the tools necessary for a caesar, and anyway, I'm not qualified."

Blood, its metallic stench all too apparent, soaked the insides of the girl's legs and flooded the frayed sheets on the filthy iron bedstead. As she screamed again, the midwife winced as though she herself were the one barely able to cope with the pain.

"I'll say when she needs opening up," snarled Jason Kerkut, standing over the woman, arms crossed over his chest, legs apart like some ancient Greek god. "You just get on with the fucking job. We want this kid. We've got a customer already."

At the door to the gloomy, darkened room, the only light that from a rag-curtained window barely supplemented by a single unshaded bulb hanging from the ceiling, a cluster of young women and girls, heads strained forward, tried to see what was going on. Chatting animatedly and clearly confused, they also looked very frightened, particularly those among them who were showing signs of advanced pregnancy.

With an arm now cradling some of the terrified girls who'd crowded up next to her, Daria Florescu muttered under her breath, "We'll see. We'll see about this."

But with no access to mobile phones, any and all confiscated at the start of their sea-trip, and the doors to the Dagenham squat securely locked, unless the girls were being taken to the clubs or else to paying clients, she was forced to bide her time. There'd been no obvious or immediate chances of escape.

Furthermore, the turbaned men who'd accompanied them on their perilous crossing of the Channel were in constant attendance. Large, forbidding presences.

The child twisted on the bed, her face running with sweat, the sheets caught up in her writhing body. The midwife turned again to Jason imploringly, but before she could say anything further, the girl screamed once more, a strangled wail of desperation, a cough, and then she lay still, her eyes wide open, staring at the ceiling.

"What's going on?" growled Jason. "Why isn't she moving? Answer me, you stupid cow. What the fuck's going on here?"

The old lady took the girl's wrist in her hand and shook her head, tears coursing down her cheeks. Then standing to face Jason she said simply, "I'm afraid the child is dead. I really should never have agreed to help."

"Dead? Dead? You stupid bitch. Whaddaya mean, dead? You were supposed to keep her alive." He stopped a moment, then looked from the girl to the old woman, his eyebrows raised as though a brilliant idea had just occurred to him. "Can we rescue the kid, then? Can you open her up and get the kid out?"

"For heaven's sake," said the old lady. "For your information there is no heartbeat detectable from the foetus. Hardly surprising when the mite would have been nearly four months premature. Periviable births stand less than a fifty percent chance of survival."

"What does that mean?"

"It means," she repeated slowly, "to repeat, that this baby is dead. As such I've no intentions of extracting the corpse of a foetus to satisfy your morbid curiosity. I propose calling the police without more ado."

Sounding like the bursting of a balloon, the flat of Jason's hand connected with the midwife's cheek, sending her flying across the room where she fell, hitting her head against one of the fire dogs of the ancient grate. Blood oozed from her temple as she twitched once or twice before remaining still.

On his mobile almost immediately, Jason was heard to shout, "Ricks? Ricks? That you, Harry? Yeah? Good. Gotta situation here. Two dead. You deal with it? Good. I'll be here waiting."

CHAPTER 25 DAY 11

THE DOG LOOKED TO BE about the size of a small horse. At the next table the woman cowered away, screaming. The man stood up, looking at a loss as to what to do as the dog spun around, ears and tail flapping like a mad thing, seemingly unsure of where it wanted to be.

His owner, whom Tammy recognised as the man she'd previously seen walking in the park, seemed equally nonplussed. "Tyson!!" he shouted. "Down boy. Down."

At Tammy's table, John Manus, looking concerned, instinctively drew back. "Tammy, no. Leave it," he urged as Tammy appeared to lean towards the animal. "It's not safe. You can't be sure with those dogs…"

"Here, boy," she said, reaching towards the ground and showing the dog the back of her closed hand.

"Sorry about that," the man said as he came running up panting, a lead in one hand and a muzzle in the other. "My fault. He slipped the lead. Can be a bit temperamental at times. Here, I'll put this back on him, though he hates it," he offered, wielding the muzzle.

Then, his eyes wide in alarm, he said to Tammy, "Oh really. I wouldn't if I were you. You never know with…"

But it was too late, and Tammy had the dog's head between her palms as Tyson, tail wagging madly, eagerly licked her face, while she then took to scratching him behind the ears.

"Hello, Tyson," she said quietly. "Helluva champ, aren't you, hmm? But just a great softy, really."

"I'll be blowed," said the man. "Never seen that before." He was a big man, probably in his mid-forties, decked out in bomber jacket and trousers with brown walking boots.

At the next table the couple had resumed their seats, but the young man, clearly nettled, pointed and snapped, "That dog should be kept on a lead."

His companion, a good looking girl, smoothed her floral summer frock and shushed her partner. "It's alright, Terry, no harm done. Just gave us a bit of a scare, that's all."

"I'm sorry if you were frightened by him," said Tyson's owner, sounding contrite.

"Oh, I wasn't frightened." The young man appeared offended. "Just concerned for my girlfriend here, that's all."

Then addressing Tammy who was still occupied with the creature, he added, "I'd take care if I were you, miss. He'd as soon take you apart. Dogs like that. Bloody menace, if you ask me."

Resisting the desire to advise the young man that she wasn't asking him, Tammy merely smiled back, then watched as the owner, squatting down, replaced the muzzle and lead.

"Tom Volkan," he said, standing up again. He extended a hand which Tammy took in her own.

"Tammy Pierre, glad to make your acquaintance."

"You like dogs," Tom observed.

"I like animals." Tammy smiled. "There aren't too many that will attack if they feel safe with you."

"I'm impressed," he replied.

His hair was tousled, giving him the look of a small boy. "You live around here?" she enquired.

"Brondesbury Park, near Tiverton Green. You?"

"Queen's Park."

"Okay. Not far. I know the Black Swan in Salusbury Road. They do a decent pint."

"You go there a lot?"

"Time to time. More so since my wife died."

"Oh!" She seemed stumped for something to say; he looked suddenly so glum.

"I pop in there too. They do a decent vodka."

It brought a smile to his face. The dog was now tugging at the leash, impatient to be off. "I'll look out for you," Tom said. "Nice to have met."

"Likewise," she said and turned back to Manus.

"So," he said, pausing while he indicated to the waiter for another coffee at the same time as Tammy pointed at her vodka. Manus's eyebrows raised slightly, but he eschewed any comment.

"You were asking about the Kerkut brothers."

"I presume you know them?"

"Very well. They've never been convicted of anything. How, I've no idea."

"Slippery customers. My friend Dov Jordan knows a lot of useful people. Tells me he thinks they may have recently brought in a small boatload of illegals. Possibly some prostitutes. Oddly, a number seem to be pregnant. I'm wondering whether we're going to find some of them at Hester's clubs trying to disrupt things even further. The Kerkuts might be interested in taking over the clubs."

"Money laundering?" suggested Manus.

"Could be."

"And, pregnant. I wonder…"

"Let me guess what's on your mind, John."

"Go on."

"Baby sales?"

"Exactly. Very lucrative."

"I'm going to need to get into the clubs again. This time as a patron. Nose around a bit. I may go as a male. Not too difficult with my height. Or maybe I'll try to entice our killer if I dress provocatively. You know, short skirt, heels."

Manus looked worried. "Be careful, Tammy. This killer, or is it killers, is skilled and maniacal."

"I'll start with Mrs Jeffreys. See what if anything she can provide. Then I'll do the clubs. But first," she said, finishing off the last of her third double vodka, "I need to get into the office to catch up with calls and emails. My PA, Mrs Gilchrist, will be furious if I don't show my face."

Ignoring the humour, John Manus got to his feet and shook hands with Tammy. And in an echo of Dov's concern added, "For God's sake be careful, Tammy. Look, let me know if you need backup. Any time at all, as many as you need, you'll get it."

"I work best alone."

"You could be putting yourself in the lion's jaws. No unnecessary risks, please."

"Come on, John, you know me," she said, smiling broadly.

"I'm beginning to," he said ruefully. "That's what worries me."

CHAPTER 26 DAY 11

THERE WAS A CLATTERING of noise, the sound of shouting, screaming, a hysterical tone, a banging of fists on a desk surface, papers being thrown around.

A voice raised in protest, Tammy's PA, the usually imperturbable Mrs Gilchrist: "Please, please. I must ask you to stop that now. You must make an appointme..."

"What the hell?" Tammy muttered, getting out from behind her desk.

She'd come to the office right after leaving Manus, to be faced with the expected mountain of hard copy correspondence, trail of emails, and calls to get back to.

After the calm and the clear air of Hyde Park, Bond Street had presented a hubbub of scowling traffic and cloying fumes. Back to work, she thought. Then smiled.

Whatever the pressures, she loved it. Loved London with all its busy self-absorption. This street in Mayfair in particular. A centre of fashion and fashionable innovation, together with its wealth and colour, from its shops to its stylish people. From upmarket jewellers like Boodles and De Beers displaying the crafts of skilled artisans, to art galleries like the Halcyon with its stock of mixed modern, traditional and impressionist works.

Now she found her door being slammed open as a beautiful young blond in a white track top and joggers came crashing into her room. The woman was panting, whether in rage or exhaustion was impossible to tell. Tammy recognised her immediately, knew who she was from Dov's descriptions of her, although they'd never met face to face. But the wavy hair, retroussé nose, full bosom, and petulant expression said it all.

"Good day, Esther," she said. "What can I do for you? Why not take a seat and tell me what's on your mind."

"I want him back," she shouted at Tammy.

"Esther," said Tammy quietly, noticing the woman's obvious advanced state of pregnancy. "Please sit down."

Leaning over Tammy's desk, her face inches from Tammy's, her cheeks showing beads of sweat, she yelled, "Give him to back me. He's mine, not yours."

"Esther," said Tammy, still on her feet and finding herself becoming irritated. "If you don't stop shouting I shall have to ask you to leave."

The young woman suddenly flopped into one of the two chairs facing Tammy's desk and, putting her face in her hands, burst into tears.

"Now then, Esther. What is this all about?"

"I want you to give him back to me," she sobbed. From charging in like a bull in a china shop, the woman now looked as fragile as a porcelain cup. As though she'd crack and fall apart at the slightest touch.

"Esther," said Tammy, resuming her seat. "Dov isn't mine to give back. He is his own man. The choices he makes are all his."

Looking up at Tammy, her face streaked with tears, Esther said, "But he told me he wants to marry you. Doesn't he? Hmm? Answer me. Please."

"In the first place, he can't marry me until his divorce with you is complete."

"But I don't want to divorce him," the other woman wailed. "I love him and I want him to come home."

"Well, you must realise I can't make him go back to you, Esther. And yes, he has asked me to marry him when he is free to."

"I knew it. I just knew he had."

"But I've turned him down."

"What? You've what? But why? Why? Why would you do that?"

"Come on now. Make up your mind. You can't have it both ways."

Wiping her eyes with a tissue she'd taken from the box on Tammy's desk, she said again, "But why would you? Why would you turn him down? He's beautiful."

"Yes, he's good-looking."

"Good-looking?" she said, raising her voice nce again in protest.

"Look, Esther. I've turned him down because I'm not the marrying kind."

"He already told me. About the other woman in your life. Are you lesbian?"

"What I am is really none of your business. But, insofar as you ask, let me reassure you that I'm not ready at this stage in my life to commit to anyone. And there is no other woman in my life. That was all sometime ago. Furthermore, I'm concentrating, when not at work, on my young baby."

Esther sat saying nothing for several moments, then, after blowing her nose again, asked, "Is your baby his? Is he the father? I have to know."

Hedging her answer, why was it so hard to tell an outright lie, Tammy said, "I've no reason to suppose he's anyone else's."

Esther waited several moments, then responded, "That's no kind of answer. Is he yours or not? The baby. Do you even know?"

On the point of asking the other woman the same question, Tammy, deciding against further argument, got to her feet and said, "If there's nothing further, I've a very full schedule today."

"Alright, alright I'm leaving. You can busy yourself away," she said.

Then she turned back from the door and pointed an accusing finger at Tammy. "But you won't get him. One way or another, I'll have him back."

CHAPTER 27 DAY 11

"THEY WATCH OVER US day and night. Oh, my love, will you ever get here to rescue me, to rescue us, from this nightmare? How can I tell you what it is like? I've stolen this phone from a policeman, a man called Ricks who works with those in control, so I'll have to get it back to him. Please don't answer this text because he'll realise what I've done.

"What do you dial to get the police in this country? 911? 111?

"I wonder, will you still want me when you find out how we've been used and abused? I feel unclean. One of us has died in childbirth. They shot the midwife dead, in front of us all, when she threatened to report them for what they were doing.

"They've groomed others and sold them to rich buyers from the Middle East as children for sex. But they're not children, they just have to pretend to be. Others who bore babies had their little ones taken away to be sold to couples who are barren. If there's a place called hell, we're in it now.

"They feed us starvation rations, except for those being groomed for sale. The house here is filthy, I've seen cleaner in a cowshed.

"There are two brothers, Mario and Jason, both ruthless, from Greece, or Cyprus, perhaps. They control everything. They're working with the police; this man Ricks. He wears expensive clothes, has a Rolex watch. I didn't realise such evil existed. What chance do we have if we can't trust the police?

"From what I hear, the little snippets, it was they, the brothers, who organised our trip across the Channel. The boat, it was ancient and the weather terrible. I thought we'd capsize and drown. Maybe it would have been better if we had.

"The girls look to me for guidance, for support. But there is nothing I can do to help them. All I say is, be patient. It cannot last forever. I feel as though I shall go mad. But I have to appear strong for the others.

"My darling, when I think of what we planned and hoped for.

"I have to hurry now; he'll be back soon.

"If you find the money to pay the gangsters who organise these trips across the Channel, look for a boat that doesn't seem too overloaded. If such a thing exists. We were naïve and allowed ourselves to be coerced into boarding a wooden vessel. The inflatables are probably more reliable.

"We're in East London, 38 Naseby Street.

"That's all I know."

But before Daria could replace the phone on the wooden chair where Ricks had forgotten it, one of the girls, a wan, frail, exhausted child, grabbed the mobile from Daria and scrolled through recent calls. Finding nothing, she started to look through the address book.

"What are you doing," hissed Daria. "Elena, give me the phone. Now!"

"I look for something. Anything. Maybe private detective use by police. I don't know. Ricks not have me again when you not here. He pig, animal. I die before carry his child," cried the girl, terrified tears coursing down her cheeks.

"Can't trust police."

"You're pregnant, Elena? When did he...? Tell me you're not expecting his child."

"Don't know. He pig, animal," she repeated.

The sound of a heavy tread on the stairs made them both look up, afraid.

"I hear him, Elena." Daria was frantic. "Have to be quick. Quick. Quick. Quick."

"Look, here." Elena pointed at the screen, unable to stem the tears. "Is here. Priva—" she gasped as she pressed the dial button.

"Tammy Pierre," came the immediate response.

But all that was heard was the sound of sobbing as the phone was snatched from the girl and the call cut.

CHAPTER 28 DAY 12

HURRYING FROM THE FOUR-DOOR PORSCHE saloon to avoid the rain, Tammy strode up the path, through the tidy little garden, to the front door of the Islington Georgian town house, straightening her jacket as she went.

The car had been a recent impulse purchase made sometime after she'd hired one similar with the object of bringing a couple of Israeli mediators securely from Blackthorne Airport to a safehouse in Surrey. They'd been chased by several sinister-looking SUVs and were thankful for the car's turbo-assisted speed and run-flat tyres which had seen Tammy, Dov and the couple with them escape with their lives. The Lexus was parked at the moment in a mews lock-up off the Kilburn High Road.

She knew she was being followed. Harry Ricks was too tall to miss, too amateurish to be able to conceal himself properly. Though she'd no idea what he hoped to gain by watching her entering the home of Judge Jeffrey's mother.

He'd parked away from the house and made the last few hundred yards on foot, ostensibly with the object of keeping Tammy in view while maintaining his vehicle out of sight. Was he proposing to stand around outside the house and wait till she emerged? If so, then what?

Pathetic, she thought, shaking her head. He'd be soaked in no time. Nothing really thought out. Not hard to see why he'd failed his sergeant's exams. Manus wouldn't be happy when he learned of Ricks' behaviour. Quite impossible to know what the man had in mind, beyond, that is, disrupting Tammy's investigation in any way he might. He'd already presented her with his credentials outside the elevators in Scotland Yard and received her firm response.

At the sound of her knocking, and after a brief pause during which padded footsteps could be heard, the door was opened by an elderly lady, behind her, a narrow hallway furnished mainly with antiques. A demilune table in walnut surmounted by a large, bevelled-edge mirror and beautiful Hepplewhite chair were the first things Tammy noticed. The place had an aroma of air freshener and furniture polish. The sound of a vacuum cleaner could be heard coming from the floor above.

The old lady's neat white hair was lank, as though it somehow reflected her mood. Pulling her cardigan close about her shoulders she smiled at Tammy. Mrs Jeffreys was quite petite, and despite what she must have been going through held her head erect, her steel-grey eyes trained directly on Tammy's.

She looked tired despite the aristocratic bearing. She was of a type, thought Tammy. The sort that bears up no matter what the challenges.

"Thank you for agreeing to see me, Mrs Jeffreys. I know it can't be easy for you right now."

"Come in, my dear. Do come in." She sounded as she appeared. Brisk and polite, with a cut-glass accent.

The living room was furnished with expensive-looking rugs and comfortable chintzy sofas arranged in a U-shape in front of an antique fireplace filled with faux logs. There was a mixture of sketches and oil paintings on the walls. One picture particularly catching Tammy's attention was the drawing of an old man, jowly, with shoulder-length curly hair, a neat moustache and beard, topped by a broad-brimmed hat. "Wonderful," she murmured. "A Rembrandt print, perhaps?"

"No, my dear. Not a print. It is an actual Rembrandt sketch. My Roland bought it for me as a special celebration after he was first appointed a judge."

She paused. "You like it?"

"It's magnificent," said Tammy. "But..."

"Yes. Let me guess. Was it expensive, you were wondering?"

"I..." Tammy felt disconcerted, shifted uncomfortably on the lush sofa, self-consciously smoothed her skirt. Was she really that transparent?

"No need to be embarrassed," said Mrs Jeffreys, correctly reading Tammy's mind. "The answer is yes, very. But then we don't become a judge every day of the week, do we."

"I love it," said Tammy. "Love all Rembrandt's work. The Night Watch, The Storm on the Sea at Galilee, wherever it is today after its theft, all the self-portraits—"

"Now, my dear," said Mrs Jeffreys, interrupting, again putting Tammy in her place. "You didn't come to discuss art with an old lady. You want information about my Roly, and how it may help you solve these ghastly murders that have been happening in East London."

"Of course," said Tammy, mildly chastened. "Could you tell me anything you know about your son, specifically his lifestyle, associates, and so on? Was he ever threatened by anyone you can think of?"

"Of course, I do understand what you need to know. But look at me. I'm forgetting my manners. Can I offer you anything? Tea? Coffee? Something stronger? I know it's early, but..."

"Coffee would be good, Mrs Jeffreys."

"Oh please, Tammy. May I call you Tammy? Well of course I must," she said, answering her own question. "And I'm Elizabeth. But Beth will be perfectly suitable," she insisted, getting up to prepare the coffee.

"Can I help you with anything?" Tammy offered.

"No, you just sit there and make yourself comfortable, I shan't be more than a trice."

While Elizabeth prepared the coffee, Tammy walked around the room admiring the pictures. An eclectic mix of drawings, etchings, oils and watercolours. But no prints; she smiled. The old lady returned quickly, trundling a wheeled mahogany trolly whose shiny top surface and bottom shelf cleverly swung out on cantilevered arms to form a single tabletop. There was a Queen Anne teapot and matching coffee pot in the Summer Rose design of white china patterned with red flowers and green leaves. Next to those were two large plates of neatly squared sandwiches with crusts removed. On display was a choice of white bread or brown, filled with smoked salmon and cucumber, tomato and cucumber, and radish cream cheese.

It all looked eminently civilised. And to complete the ensemble, a plate of Garibaldi biscuits. The old lady's casual offer of refreshment had obviously been preceded by a lot of preparation.

"You've gone to far too much trouble, Beth. You really shouldn't have."

"It's really no trouble at all, my dear. Just so nice to have someone to entertain. And to talk to," she added sadly.

Looking to try to brighten the mood, Tammy commented, "You've laid my favourite biscuits too."

"Oh the Garibaldi, you mean," said Beth, smiling and pouring Tammy's coffee, before seating herself on the adjoining sofa. "My preferred choice too. Black? Sugar?"

"Black without will be fine, thank you."

As they both sipped from their respective drinks, Beth said, "And so, you're looking into these brutal killings?"

"As I said when I called you, Beth."

"I have already been visited by the police, you know."

"They'll be working their way around all the known contacts of murder victims."

"Of course. He was here only yesterday. A policeman. Quite a striking-looking young man."

"Very tall, smartly turned-out detective constable, by any chance?" Tammy asked. "Reddish hair?"

"That's right. I forget his name. Oh dear," she said. "I am becoming so absent-minded these days. You know him?"

"We have met," said Tammy, studying the steaming surface of her coffee. "I recall an expensive watch."

"A Rolex, from what I could see," suggested Beth.

"On a DC's salary?"

The old lady picked up one of the biscuits and chewed it absently. "He seemed distracted, disinterested. Kept checking the time."

"Anything else?"

"Only one thing." She paused, reaching for a sandwich. "His telephone rang, and he walked away towards the window, to speak in private, I presumed."

"Did you hear much? Anything at all?"

"He seemed agitated, as though trying to justify himself? I couldn't be sure, but I thought I heard him say Jay several times. Whatever that meant."

"Jay?" said Tammy softly. "Well, well. I wonder if our DC Harry Ricks is involved with Jason Kerkut and—"

"Ricks, that was him, I remember now you mention it," put in Beth. "And do you mean the Kerkut brothers?" she asked.

"You've heard of them?"

"Only what Roly told me. A couple of utter reprobates. Never yet been brought to justice."

"Hmm," pondered Tammy. "Sounds as though our Mr Ricks might be involved with some fairly unpleasant people. I am sure he's followed me here, you know."

"Oh dear. Really? Doesn't that worry you?"

"Not in the least. So, shall we make a start?"

"Well, my dear, I suggest you ask away. Anything at all I can do to help. You do know, of course, that Roland was a transsexual."

"Yes, of course. The police are all well aware of the nature of these killings and the targeted victims."

"He'd had hormonal treatment and the surgery too. Although, revealing nothing to his work colleagues, he chose to continue appearing in court as a man."

"No-one suspected anything?"

"Apparently not. A loose white shirt covered a modest bosom, helped no doubt by his judge's formal robes. Socially and out of hours he kept clear of the City, not that he would have been likely to be recognised as a woman. He called himself Rolande, you know. Fairly obvious, I suppose, but, as he said, it kept things from getting too complicated. He even hinted at a relationship among those who only knew him as a woman, presumably with another man?" Beth sighed, paused for a long moment.

"Why did he have to be butchered in that way? What sort of madman…? Why couldn't he have simply been satisfied with a homosexual relationship?"

"I'm afraid there are no easy answers, Beth."

"His father was a closet gay, you know; isn't that the term they use today? It was a loveless marriage. The one child to establish his heterosexual bona fides, and no more. It was illegal when we wed. Henry's legal career could have been compromised. He might even have had to face jail had it been discovered.

"Still," she pondered, "he left me well provided for. Our place in Gloucester fetched a small fortune. I'm sorry, I'm blathering on. How can I help you, Tammy?"

"Let me open with the obvious question: is there anyone you can think of who'd want to hurt your son? Did he, or is it she, have enemies?"

Beth nodded sadly. "I'm afraid so, Tammy. You see my Roly was a fair-minded man, believe me. I'm sorry, but I could never think of him as a woman.

"He was one who believed society should be protected from its rogues and vagabonds. Not for nothing was he called 'Hanging Judge Jeffreys'."

"Does anyone in particular come to mind?"

"Well, there was one. Let me see," she said, glancing up and recalling the memory. "Ah yes. Dominic Pope."

"Deceptive, isn't it?"

"The name, you mean?"

Chewing contemplatively on a biscuit, Tammy offered, "That's right. So often one finds the most evil of people have the most inoffensive of names. Dominic Pope," she mused. "Could almost fit a pontiff. So, what can you tell me about this individual?"

"In appearance, nondescript. Could be your average family man from his pictures in the press. But that's where the resemblance ended. The police know of a family of five, that is parents and three sons, all slaughtered. Two of the boys were horrifically emasculated, the other youngster killed but left intact. The irony is that those last two I referred to were in their mid-teens and planning transsexual surgery. Had he picked on them for that reason? If so, how had he found out about them? Did he have a particular issue with that sort of thing? Also, it is believed there are more as yet undiscovered bodies. He refused to say where, or how many. Roly sentenced him to forty years with no parole before at least thirty. He's in Belmarsh prison. They say it's really awful there. Just as well, I suppose."

She paused. "But hardly a consolation for the victims or their next of kin."

"Pope could be a really important lead," said Tammy, feeling a frisson of excitement at the revelation. "I've not come across murders of this type before. I wonder if Pope could be persuaded to reveal anything? Might the East London murders be copycat, carried out by someone who's read the numerous press reports?"

"As he was taken down he screamed abuse and threats at Roly. Said he had friends outside and Roly would never feel safe walking the streets again. Not him nor any of his family. It's had an effect of course, as he intended. I'm not sure I ever feel entirely secure, you know. More so since my

Roly..." She stopped short, like a horse being pulled up; her eyes filled with tears which she brushed away impatiently.

"That's terrible for you, Beth," said Tammy, seeing the old lady bow her head as though she was in pain.

In the quiet moments that followed, the rain could be heard coming down harder than ever. The flashing blue lights of a passing emergency vehicle cast their pattern on the walls of the room as the sounds of its siren and splashing wheels could be heard offering a cryptically appropriate backdrop to their conversation. The vacuum cleaner had been moved to another room, but still hummed on.

She waited until Mrs Jeffreys had composed herself, then asked, "Anyone else, apart from this man Pope?"

"Too many to try to recall. I'm afraid that is the fate of many judges presiding over criminal cases. Something to live with, I suppose. But really, Pope is the one I feel Roly would have had the most to fear. I've read that some psychopaths publish boasts and even pictures of their crimes online. As though comparing notes. My son speculated there might actually be a loose fraternity of these people. One wonders what could be found if Pope were to be forthcoming. But why would he?"

"He might, you know. If he could be convinced he was talking to a like-minded individual. A killer, that is."

"Wouldn't that be terribly dangerous? Assuming, that is, that such a thing could be organised. After all, who would you ask? Who would be willing to take such a risk? I've heard that sexual offenders are frequently set upon by other inmates."

"That's true, but then they and other high-risk prisoners are generally kept in a specialist high-security facility. Ironically, Pope will probably be quite safe inside. He'll be mixing with his own types."

There was nothing further she could think of for the moment, and so getting up to leave, Tammy said, "I've taken up far too much of your time, Beth."

"I hope I've been of some use, my dear."

"Oh you have. If this man Pope is a link to be explored, I'll see what I can do about gaining entrance myself to Belmarsh. As a prisoner, that is."

Looking worried, Beth asked, "Really? To try to speak with him? But how will you manage that? I understand it's an all-male prison."

"I'll go in as a man," said Tammy simply. "My ex-boss Detective Chief Superintendent Bob Walker will probably be able to organise it. He knows I've done something like it before."

"As a man, Tammy? But how would you do that?"

"I'll have my hair cropped to the skull, and obviously be wearing the appropriate prison clothing. I'm just over six feet tall. I'll manage to look the part. As I said, it won't be the first time."

Beth's next remark left Tammy shocked. "My dear, you're not a man. In fact, I think you're one of the most beautiful women I've ever come across."

"Good heavens," whispered Tammy, quite taken aback, her eyes suddenly welling up. "Beth, you're so kind."

"Not at all. You make me feel, how shall I put it, protected, my dear."

Tammy gazed distractedly out of the window. "Oh, now I can't think what to say."

"There's no need to say anything." Then, facing Tammy, Beth abruptly flung her arms wide and asked, "Would you hold me, Tammy? A moment. Please?"

"Of course, Beth. Of course, I will," she responded, stooping to take Mrs Jeffreys gently in her arms.

And as Tammy held her, the old lady's heart beating against her own, she was struck by how Beth's physical frailty was entirely at odds with the contrasting strength of her personality.

"Thank you, Tammy," she said falteringly as she pulled away. "I wasn't sure whether…"

"Nonsense, Beth. Look, here are my contact details," she said, offering her business card. "Call me any time. Day or night. I'll be there for you."

"What do I say?"

"You say nothing at all," responded Tammy, walking towards the door.

"Tammy, do be wary," counselled Beth. "Roly said Belmarsh was the worst prison he'd ever known for inmate attacks. And now I recall it, he told me they don't have a separate wing for sexual offenders."

It had stopped raining, but there were puddles and pools everywhere, reflecting the emerging sun. Steam rose off the parked vehicles. No sign of Ricks.

But it looked as though someone had spat on the windscreen of Tammy's car. Her lip curling in disgust, she wiped the mess off with a tissue, which she then slipped into a plastic evidence bag. Small wonder he'd failed his exams, she thought once more.

CHAPTER 29 DAY 13

"I NEED TO SEE YOU, TAMMY. I mean right now. It's a bloody emergency."

The pitch of the voice more than adequately conveyed the need for immediate action.

The buzz of the mobile had Matty stirring and snuffling in his cot next to the queen-size bed occupied by Tammy, but the little one, a thumb comfortingly in his mouth, went back to sleeping peacefully.

It was 4.30 am as Tammy turned over, her sleep brutally interrupted, and a mewing Risky immediately seizing the opportunity to gain a little attention from her mistress as she pulled the duvet ever further over her head in a half-hearted attempt to shut out the joint intrusion.

"Merde," she muttered under her breath as she reluctantly answered the call. "Who the hell is this? Don't you know the bloody time?"

"It's me," came the hurriedly whispered response, delivered as though someone might overhear.

"And who's me?" Then the dawn of realisation. "Juliet? Juliet Mountford?"

"Yes. That's right. I've been meaning to get in touch after all you did for us."

"I'm a private investigator, Juliet. It's what I do."

"Still, you went far beyond."

"Juliet, it's not yet five in the morning. What do you want?"

There was a long drawn-out sigh, then, "I think Pa's going off the rails."

"Going off? Tell me something I don't already know. I thought he'd gone there a long time ago."

"Tammy, please; this is serious."

Despite her irritation at the hour, Tammy found herself recalling images of Juliet's arrogantly brazen behaviour, the absurdly short miniskirts she made no attempt to correct as they rode tantalisingly up her thighs when she was seated. She shivered slightly at the thought, pulling the duvet open to cool herself down a bit, her white nightie having tangled itself round her waist as she slept. She also remembered that of all the family, the sole sibling not taken in for one second by their father was Juliet.

"Very well, talk to me, Juliet," she sighed, sitting up and settling a warm and furry Risky in her naked lap. "I'm listening."

"You know he wants to humiliate you." It was a statement, not a question. "Any way he can."

"Well, that's a relief." Tammy smiled.

"It is?" Juliet sounded nonplussed. "I mean to say, is it? Tammy, for God's sake. How can it possibly be a relief?"

"At this time of the morning, at the very least, I'd have expected you to be warning me your father was attempting to plan my murder."

"Knowing Pa, that's almost certainly the next thing on his agenda."

"He's locked up tight, Juliet. He's going nowhere for a very long time. Even his telephone calls are limited. Not much time for him to be debating with any of his goons how to deal with me."

"You know perfectly well he doesn't need time. All it needs is a word. And the word is out. Do you know the Kerkut brothers?"

"I've had the dubious pleasure. We engaged in a little light banter recently."

"Please, Tammy. Hear me out, just for a moment."

"Very well, Juliet," she sighed again. "I'm all ears. How is your father going to go about all this?"

"He wants to see if a murder can be laid at your door."

"Really?" said Tammy, in a tone suggesting a clear lack of conviction in the notion. "Whose murder, Juliet? With what for a motive? What for a means? And, come to think of it, what sort of opportunity? You know it's nonsense. Does your father seriously think the police, with whom I've been involved for years both during and since the time I was a DI, are going to be taken in by anything that anyone else has in mind?"

The woman paused, then added, "I don't know. But when I spoke to him last, a day or so ago, he sounded deranged."

"So, what else is new, Juliet? You know, it wouldn't be the first time I've had something like this," she said, recalling the incident when one DS Susan Thompson had tried to frame her for murder during her investigation into the Black Candle Killings.

"It's happened before?"

"'Fraid so."

"But who would try such a thing? How could they hope to get away with it?"

"Precisely, Juliet. Who? The answer? It was a detective sergeant who didn't like me very much. And they, or she, to be precise, is presently residing at His Majesty's pleasure. So, no. They didn't get away with it."

"Another member of the force," she breathed.

"Another member of the force?"

"You know, Pa has some sort of contact with a DC."

Tammy turned over possibilities in her mind. There was only one. "Would that be a DC Harry Ricks, by any chance?"

"I don't know."

"And, Juliet, why are you calling me at this unearthly hour? Couldn't it have waited until a bit later?"

"I got a call at midnight last night."

"From whom?"

"He said he was Kerkut and that Pa had told him I might be able to help him get close to you."

"Never!" she exclaimed. "Kerkut, you say? Well, I can tell you there are two brothers, utter reprobates. I've already met them. So introductions are hardly necessary. And there's no way your father can imagine you'd be either willing or able to assist on that front."

"So why?"

"It's your father's own warped way of laying on the intimidation."

"I don't understand."

"Juliet, he just wants to use every means at his disposal to soften me up. Hopefully to frighten me by having an alarmed you contacting me with news of what he's supposedly planning. As has clearly happened. I'll expect more calls from various other sources as time goes on."

"You don't sound alarmed."

"Your father doesn't frighten me, my dear."

"What about the Kerkuts, then? Pa seems to think they live charmed lives."

"Hmm!" Tammy responded dubiously. "Depends on your definition of charmed. They'll slip up one day. And if I have anything to do with it..."

Then hearing Matty stirring awake, she said, "Hang on a moment, I think the baby's waking up. Probably hungry. My beautiful boy has an appetite like a horse."

"Baby?" Juliet sounded astonished. "You have a baby? I had no idea."

"It does happen, Juliet. You know, women, sex, and that sort of thing?"

"Oh, oh. Sorry. So sorry, I didn't mean to offend. It's just that..."

"Yes I know. And, don't worry, I'm not in the least offended. I well understand that somehow it doesn't seem to fit my image."

"Is it what you wanted? Are you happy? The father?"

"Juliet, for heaven's sake. Okay," she said patiently. "In the order you've asked. Yes, it's what I wanted. And yes, I'm deliriously happy. We'll leave the last question unanswered for now."

"I'd love to meet up for coffee some time, Tammy." Juliet sounded uncharacteristically hesitant. "You know, see the baby. See you again. I thought we were... You know..."

"Yes, I do know. And sure, why not. You've got the office number. Call Mrs Gilchrist and fix a date. If I've time we might do a lunch too. Spend some time..." She left the rest unsaid.

"I'd love that, Tammy."

She'd clambered out of bed and retrieved Matty from his cot while she was talking, the telephone jammed between her shoulder and her ear, Risky scooped up with the other hand. "Gotta go, Juliet. The man of the house is demanding his breakfast."

"I'll call," she whispered.

They ended the call and now Tammy wandered out of the bedroom towards the kitchen and the wonderful smell of morning coffee brewing. Thankfully Maria was an early riser.

"Good morning, Miss Tammy," said Maria, still in her pyjamas, glancing wide-eyed at Tammy's near nakedness, the girl's short blond hair tousled from sleep. The nightie, Tammy's that is, was tiny and very much transparent.

Not wanting to embarrass the au pair, having overlooked the need for a dressing gown, she ignored the remark and simply said, "Tammy, please, Maria. I've already told you. Not Miss Tammy."

Glancing down at Matty, Maria said, "You are hold the baby and Frisky."

"No, Maria. The cat is called Risky. I'm the one that's frisky. Generally," she added, smiling.

"I don't understand."

"Don't worry, my dear. It's not important."

The mobile in the bedroom, the private one, bleeped the arrival of a text on WhatsApp and Tammy let the cat go, handing her son to Maria, after first giving the precious bundle of talcum powdered joy a quick cuddle.

"Matty first, please," she said. "I'll nurse him later, if I've enough milk. But for now, his bottle. Then coffee, next priority, while I see who's texting me."

She frowned slightly. "Not too many people have that number."

It was all in block capitals.

BEEN TALKING TO DADDY'S LITTLE GIRL HAVE YOU? OSCAR WON'T BE HAPPY. WATCH OUT FOR THE BRAT. YOURS THAT IS. BE A SHAME IF ANYTHING HAPPENED TO HIM. YOU KNOW, IF HE WENT MISSING. AND PAPA. NOW THERE'S A THOUGHT. PARKINSON'S, NASTY, THAT. PROBLEMS WALKING, THEY SAY.

How could they possibly know? she asked herself. She'd barely hung up from the call with Juliet.

Reading it again made her blood run cold.

CHAPTER 30 DAY 14

THE OLD MAN SURVEYED the platter of food in front of him and breathed deeply. Lovely. Saturday morning.

The place was just beginning to crowd with breakfasters. Young and old. Singles and couples. As ever, the elderly gent was turned out immaculately. A habit he'd instilled in his daughter. A brown-and-white checked shirt, trousers ironed to a knife crease and highly polished brown brogues with a casual sports jacket. And that, added to the distinguished short-cropped white hair against the ebony complexion, made for an imposing individual.

A wonderful aroma of freshly baked bread. Gail's bread. Delicious. Plus, that weekend feeling. Not that the day of the week mattered to him as he'd been retired for at least ten years. This was his occasional indulgence, overindulgence in fact, and he revelled in it. Two poached eggs on two slices of crosscut fried white bread. Bacon, chipolatas, tomatoes, mushrooms, baked beans, French fries and a steaming mug of tea.

It was all a far cry from the food he'd been brought up on back home where his mother would serve up, any one or a combination of cornmeal porridge, Johnny cake with salt mackerel and mint tea, callaloo with ripe plantain and hardo bread. All of it a lifetime ago. And all a good deal healthier than this morning's fare. Still, a good English fry-up. Hard to beat. He ate slowly, savouring each mouthful.

Occasionally he'd close his eyes and think of the baby. Against all the odds his daughter Tamsin had become a mother. A son, Matty. A grandson. His namesake. Pascale would have been so thrilled.

A muscled young man, shirt sleeves rolled up and a worn pair of builder's denim jeans, approached the table. "This one taken, mate?" He pointed to the seat opposite the old man.

"Nah, man. Y'all okay."

"Thanks, chum," he said, planting his equally stacked plate of food on the table.

"Hello, Mr Pierre." A member of staff, an eager young girl in the bakery's livery of white shirt and black jeans, smiled down at Matthew. "Been a coupla weeks since you was last here. All right are we then?"

"I'm fine, darlin'. Bit slower, but all fine."

"That's the ticket, love. Gimme a shout if you need anything else."

The old man smiled, nodded his thanks. It had taken him half an hour to walk the short stop from home to here. Parkinson's Disease was no respecter of class, gender or age. And Matthew Pierre's was gradually invading every aspect of his life. No matter how his daughter protested, he'd made it clear he'd use a stick to steady himself when he was forced to, and not a moment before.

The buzz of conversation gradually increased as more people arrived, seating themselves randomly around the place. Gail's in Queen's Park had an almost clublike atmosphere of friendliness. A place to come and pass the time of day with any of the variety of drinks, pastries and hot dishes on offer.

Two heavyset individuals came into the bakery. In their forties, with glossy black hair and dark suits and ties, they might have been twins. Staring around the place, frowning, apparently concerned, but by what? They seemed to be looking for something or perhaps someone.

After a few seconds one of them spotted Matthew and nudged the other. Then they both disappeared briefly before reappearing with mugs of coffee which they planted on a table nearby and sat themselves opposite one another, lapsing into animated conversation. Every now and then one or other of the two men would glance pointedly in Matthew's direction.

He'd seen them of course, had no idea who they were and, nodding amicably in their direction, notably received no acknowledging response.

"Friends of yours?" said the young man opposite Matthew, replacing his own mug of coffee on the table between the two of them, before starting on his own food, shovelling heaps of the steaming fare into his mouth as though he'd not eaten in a month.

"Ain't never seen them before," confessed Matthew. "But they lookin' friendly and polite to me."

"I wouldn't be so sure," whispered the other, swallowing, then leaned towards the old man so as not to be overheard. "They're up to something."

"They fine, man. Y'all need to have a little trust in folks."

"If you say so. They don't look too friendly to me. Still ..." He shrugged, returning his attention to his plate. "Whatever you say."

Finishing the last of his fry-up Matthew sat back feeling well satisfied. "Ain't nothing like an English breakfast," he murmured. A couple of other customers nearby who'd overheard smiled at Matthew with knowing looks.

"Too right." The young man smiled, chasing a piece of fried bread around the sauce on his plate. "Sets you up, d'unt it?"

"Matthew Pierre," said Matthew, pursuing the exchange and extending a palm.

"Ben Eastman ... Benny," he replied, taking Matthew's slender hand in his own rather more substantial fist.

"Been nice to talk, son. Mebbe I'll catch you again. But it's time for me to go now," said Matthew, edging himself out and away from the table before clambering laboriously to his feet. "Gonna take a while to get home."

"Got far to go?"

"Not far. But I'm moving bit slower than I used to," he explained, unfolding himself to his full six feet and leaning on the table a moment to steady himself.

"Need a hand, Matthew? It's no trouble. I could walk with you if you like, take your arm?" The old gent looked frail and vulnerable. A twig that might skitter away in a light breeze.

"I'm gonna be just fine now. Need to work these old bones'a mine. Doc says to keep up the exercise. You just enjoy your coffee. Good talking to you, son." He nodded at Ben, an avuncular hand on the young man's shoulder as he made his way to the door.

A moment later Ben watched as the two who'd been looking at Matthew got to their feet and followed the old man out of the restaurant. Something felt off.

Getting up, Ben, nodding to the young woman who'd been talking with Matthew when he arrived, moved quickly to the door, and went out. The older man had gone only a short distance and the two behind him had nearly caught up. Ben quickened his pace.

Matthew turned his head, stopped a moment, seeming to catch his balance, and spotting Ben, waved his hand.

The two between stopped immediately and looked in all directions until they saw Ben waving back. One scowled and the other nudged him to cross the street, where they turned a corner and went out of sight.

"See ya again, I hope," Ben called and headed across the street himself, deciding both to respect the older man's wishes and to keep him in view until he was safely home.

CHAPTER 31 DAY 15

IT WAS AN LGBTQ EVENING at the Tilbury club and, the crowd oblivious to or else deliberately ignoring recent events by choice, the floor was packed. The atmosphere was warm and friendly, with a smoke-laden aroma of hash, perfume, tobacco, and sweat floating around the place.

She'd dressed ambiguously, choosing straight black jeans, a high-neck, tight-sleeved, multicolour patchwork print tulle stretch bodysuit by Diesel, to which she'd added low-heel black boots. She'd blow waved the unruly curls almost straight, making a boyish side parting.

And with the object of being noticed she'd clearly achieved her aim, judging by the number of propositions she was receiving. In the so-called gay ear, the left, she wore a gold teardrop earring. To add to the mix, the male cologne 1 Million by Paco Rabanne. Let the punters form their own conclusions, she'd decided.

The music, occasional slow pieces like 'Girls like Girls' by Hayley Kiyoko, or the more up-tempo 'Tomboy' by Princess Nokia, was great to dance to. Then there were the older classics including Tom Robinson's 'Glad to be Gay', which had practically the whole place singing together. Fifteen hundred voices raised to the chorus of an iconic anthem. Otherwise, the club bounced to the familiar beat of house music.

She'd visited the other two clubs in the last couple of nights and found nothing that would assist. No clues. No leads. Zilch. Now she was at the Tilbury. The place it had all started. The same bunch of red-outfitted youngsters were behind the backlit bar, with the signature cumulus of white hair in charge. She nodded in his direction and, spotting her, he raised a hand in acknowledgement, then beckoned her over.

"Hi." She grinned.

"Hi, love. What can I get you? Like the threads. You're looking cool, babe." He was wiping a glass dry with a red and black dishcloth, while his number two DJ, the enormous and self-styled, hugely smiling Papa Doc, handled the sound.

The light show of lasers and strobes together with mixed images of people, places and the abstract playing on the walls and giant screens was handled by software which only needed occasional adjustment of interference by the DJ.

"I'm flattered," she said, hoisting herself onto a barstool. "Vodka?"

"Of course."

"Chilled?"

"Sure, what's your poison?"

"Got a Beluga Gold?" She sounded doubtful.

In reply, Dexie glanced back at the glass-fronted fridge. "In the freezer, sweetheart."

"Really? Bit expensive, isn't it?" she asked, surprised.

"Only for special customers."

"I'm impressed. Hester caters to a wide variety of clients."

"My idea, Tammy. I suggested Hester keep a small selection of the best of everything. You know, gin, single malts, vodka, of course, tequila; we've even got a decent champagne. She lets me run the bar here as I want, and also to help out with suggestions on organisation at the other two clubs."

"Okay, then. Mine's a double Beluga. Lemon, no ice."

While he fixed her drink Tammy looked around. "Good crowd tonight."

"Yeah. Been quiet on the street for a bit. No surprises there. Thank Christ it's been looking up. Here you go," he said, planting the tumbler of vodka in front of her.

She picked up the drink and took a long pull, feeling the delicious iciness on her tongue, letting it swirl sensuously around her mouth before swallowing.

"Dex," she said, "can you help me out here? We've got nothing at all to go on so far. Absolutely nothing. No DNA we can use. No murder weapon. No witnesses. Tell me, do you have any new attendees? I know it's a lot to ask with the numbers here, but you know, people you don't immediately recognise?"

"You get to know people, Tammy. All types. What they drink. How they dress and who they get off with. Which days they come. Even how they dance. I reckon I could ID at least two thirds, maybe more of the crowd. I've got a brilliant memory. So's Hester," he added, aware that Tammy had already picked up that fact.

"So, who do I talk to? Who're the newcomers? I've tried the other two places, dressed to be noticed, walked out late at night on my own, hoping to attract attention."

"Isn't that dangerous, Tammy. I mean, on your own?"

She shrugged in response, drank the rest of the vodka in one, but said nothing. Dexie, looking crestfallen, couldn't offer more assistance.

"Tell you what," he suggested, brightening a bit. "Take a look in the side bar. A couple of new faces there." He thought about it, then, "Big guy. Could be a builder? Cleft chin. Easy to spot. Big mouth. Got a lot to say for himself."

Tammy felt a frisson in the pit of her stomach recalling the blurred images she'd seen on the club's CCTV. Our man? she wondered. "Cleft chin, you say? I've not spotted him here up to now. Been hiding himself away perhaps. So not a member then?"

"No. If he were we'd have a name and address for you."

Dexie caught the eye of one of the bar staff, a stocky lad in his late teens, and, nodding at the used glasses behind the bar, made a washing motion with his hands which the boy immediately picked up. "He's usually in the smaller bar, so you'll have missed him if you've stuck to the main dance area."

"Okay. Might be promising. Anyone else?"

"Hmm." Dexie had picked up another glass and was drying it absent-mindedly as though deep in thought. "Maybe," he pondered. "An older guy. Fifties perhaps? Greying a bit. Horn-rimmed specs. Always wears a three-piece, three-button suit, whatever the weather. An oddball. Nurses a drink all evening. Lager. Never seen him talk to anyone. He just sits there the whole time staring around at everyone. He's no trouble. Looks too timid to say boo to a goose."

"Is he a member?" she asked.

"Nope. Again, you'll need to make your own approaches. See how you get on."

"And timid, you say? Hmm! They're sometimes the most dangerous. Still, thanks. Very observant. I think I'll treat myself to a quick blend with the crowd first. Can't resist it."

She needed no reminding she was here on a mission, but despite herself, acknowledged she'd not had the chance to chill out so much in a long time. No reason why she shouldn't mix business with a little cheer, she decided, joining in with a bouncing group of young people and throwing herself into a brief period of abandonment.

Then, within moments, thoughts of the text and her purpose in coming here brought her up short. People were beginning to stand around watching her dance, some complimentary remarks there, but one she particularly overheard: "Wasn't she here the other day asking questions?"

A voice in response: "Is that a she? Or a he? Bit of both?"

"Enough," she berated herself guiltily, exiting the dance area and making for the quieter bar where, as had been suggested, she might have a better chance of hearing and being heard.

Having worked her way through the crowd she found herself in an area of high, circular pedestal tables with fixed stools and a scattering of armchairs around low tables. Less crowded, but still fairly busy. She got to the bar, climbed onto a stool and ordered another vodka from a red-jacketed bar girl. This one at a more realistic price. Then she twisted around to survey the place. Here at least the hubbub was mainly chatter rather than the relentless beat of drums and base guitars, though the wide entrance only reduced the sound marginally.

She spotted him almost at once. Sitting in an easy chair where he had a wide view of the dancers was the middle-aged man in the three-button suit. He was heavyset and bespectacled, with greying hair, toad-like eyes and a pink complexion, showing a sheen of sweat on his upper lip and forehead. An innocuous-looking character. He might have been a teacher, or a professional man. Tammy observed him leaning forward, elbows on knees, chin in his palms, intently watching the crowd. In front of him on the low table was an apparently untouched beer. Despite the eclectic collection of clubbers, here was one individual who seemed entirely out of place.

The armchair opposite the man was free so Tammy, placing her vodka on the table, sat herself down without being invited, and attempted to catch the man's eye, enquiring, "May I join you?"

He showed no sign of having heard her, merely continuing to stare unblinking at the clubbers. Impossible to form any impression about the individual, who for all Dexie's belief in his apparent diffidence, seemed to Tammy to be determinedly searching about for something or someone. Having watched him for several moments Tammy decided to make a further attempt to break the ice and speak to him.

"Hello." She smiled. "I'm Tammy. I don't think I've seen you here before."

There was still no response, and Tammy spoke again, only louder this time. "It's really noisy in here, isn't it? This is supposed to be the quiet area." Still nothing.

Then, "Hello there," she tried once more, louder still. "Is there anybody home?"

Finally eliciting a response of sorts, the man inclined his face in her direction. His eyes, a watery grey, looked vacant behind the horn-rimmed glasses. Unseeing, unfocused. "What?" he muttered. "What do you want?"

"I was just saying…"

Turning away from Tammy to gaze back at the dance area, he said, half to himself, "I'm looking at the people. What are they? Men? Women? Freaks. All of them. Someone'll stop it. One day. Maybe I will."

"I'm Tammy," she ploughed on relentless and, if rather less certainly, extending a hand, which he didn't see or else deliberately ignored.

"The women," he said.

"Yes? The women?" she urged. What was it with the man? He seemed to be totally out of reach.

"Not real, are they. Just men pretending. It's a sin. Not legal. Can't be. Needs to be put an end to."

"Do you mean there should be a law against it, or something?" She was floundering, trying to keep up the threadbare dialogue.

Angling back to her, while concentrating intently at a spot over her shoulder, the man said, "What are you? You're a man, aren't you? A bloke? That voice. Too deep. No-one can sex change a voice. Why're you dressed as a woman?"

"Because I am a woman and I like the way I dress. Don't you?" It was a half-hearted enquiry to which no response was expected.

But she was entirely unprepared for his next comment, a remark that left Tammy feeling as though the place were closing in on her.

"I did it you know." He smiled. "Someone had to."

"What did you do?" she asked very quietly, searching the man's face for something, anything recognisably sane.

"I'm Edward," he said abruptly, looking her in the eye at last. "Edward Seward," he added, grinning hugely this time.

"Hello, Edward," she responded, taken aback. "I'm Tammy. Tammy Pierre."

"And what is it you're telling me you did?"

"I dealt with it. With them," he said earnestly. "They won't be any more trouble now. Promise. Cross my heart and hope to die. I followed them and dealt with them. Sorted them all."

"Were there many you dealt with, Edward?" she asked, testing the water. How to deal with an individual like this, short of continuing to talk in the hope of gleaning something useable. Anything that could be worked on.

The oppressiveness was like doors, exits, all slamming around her wherever she looked. She felt hemmed in, although she could simply get up and walk away at any time she chose.

Without warning Seward got to his feet. He was a short man and stocky; crammed into his three-piece suit, he reminded her a bit of John Manus. No wonder he looked hot in the club atmosphere. That, or whatever it was among the dancers that so fascinated him making him sweat.

He was standing over her now, and looking down at Tammy. Pointing a fat finger in her face, he said, "You. Just like the others, aren't you. Well, no more of that, mister. In due course. Just wait for it. We'll have you sorted too. Count on it."

With that, he stalked off, leaving Tammy more troubled than she'd have cared to admit.

CHAPTER 32 DAY 16

"TAMMY, THIS IS ABSOLUTE RECKLESSNESS. Even by your standards of lunacy.

"Belmarsh? The all-male prison?" Dov was pacing the living room of his North London flat, stepping between the mounds of books and sundry antique furniture and objets d'art, his working stock, that littered the floor.

Looking relaxed in a white T-shirt and denim jeans, matching Dov's own, Tammy was sprawled back in an easy chair.

"You don't have to do this, you know." He looked anguished, he sounded almost pleading, and her heart went out to him. But still.

"Oh, but I do, Dov," she insisted.

"Why do you have to? Where's the requirement? Who's demanding it?"

"No-one's demanding anything. It's just that I promised someone I would," she said simply.

"Really? Who?"

"Judge Jeffreys' mother, Beth."

"Tammy, if what happened to Jeffreys were to happen to you…" Flinging his arms outwards in a gesture of hopelessness, he left the comment hanging.

"In a prison?"

"Why not?"

"It won't."

"Don't be arrogant, Tammy," he said, turning from his continuous pacing and pointing at her accusingly.

"You're not invulnerable, you know. And, you're still recovering from the terrible beatings you've sustained in your last two outings."

"I know, Dov. And I also know you've only got my interests and safety in mind. But I'm not stupid, and really, I don't need reminding about the need for care and caution."

Changing the subject, Dov asked, "Anyway, what happened to your plan to tempt the killer, if it is just the one, by using yourself as bait?"

"That's still on hold. I've had other things to think about up to now."

Returning to his previous enquiry, he said, "And what are you hoping to gain by putting yourself at risk in Belmarsh?"

"Access to Dominic Pope."

"Haven't I come across that name?" said Dov thoughtfully, planting himself on a low Victorian nursing chair opposite Tammy. "Wasn't he the sex offender who raped and killed his victims?"

"That's right."

"All children, weren't they?"

"Those we know about."

Dov gazed distractedly out the window. "Hell!" he muttered, scratching the back of his head.

"Jeffreys gave him forty years without parole."

"But you're investigating adult killings, not children. What possible use can he be to you?"

"I've no idea. It's really just a fishing trip."

"For God's sake, Tammy. Do you have any idea what Belmarsh is like? It's the UK's top security prison, with a reputation for bullying and intimidation. I mean we're talking real violence here. Are you even aware? Did you know, in 2020 a man was found beaten to death. Horrific head injuries."

Leaning forward and clasping Dov's hands in her palms, Tammy said, "I do know, darling. Of course I do. I've made my own enquiries."

"And how are you going to keep up the pretence you're not a woman in a shared cell?"

"Forty percent of the cells are single occupancy. Bob Walker ..."

"Your Chief Superintendent."

"Not mine, Dov. But yes, Chief Superintendent ..."

"Don't tell me this was all his idea?"

"Quite the opposite. He tried to dissuade me."

"What? What are you talking about?"

"Simply that a Chief Superintendent can't be seen being a party to this sort of deception. If it were to go wrong what possible excuse or justification would he have for having put me in any sort of danger?"

"He'll get you in, though?"

"Yes. Perhaps, if I can't organise it myself. But his involvement stops there. I'll do what I can to see Pope. I'm told he's in the same top security facility that they'll be putting me in. When I'm ready I'll have to think of some way of getting myself out."

"You'll be on your own?"

"Entirely."

"I'll think of a way of getting you out."

"No, Dov. You will not. We're looking to get any information that might lead us to stop these killings. If you interrupt things before I'm ready to attempt an exit, think of the danger you may put me in if word gets out before I do. I've got to have a clear run to find out whatever I can."

"You've said yourself there may be more than one killer. What does that mean? Two? Three?"

"I really don't know," she sighed. "I'm playing this whole thing by ear."

"I suppose there's no chance you might ask to see him as a visitor during visiting hours?"

"What, you mean turn up for a chat and try to convince him I'm a reformed killer looking for information that might help the police with their enquiries. Dov, please. Be real."

There was a long pause, then Dov said, "Well if there really is nothing I can do …"

"Actually," she responded. "There is. Can you do me a favour and start nosing around all three club venues for me? Look for anything that might help. The girls that may have been touting for business there. The barman was concerned for the club. Frankly, from what I understand about their apparent ages, I'm more concerned for the girls. I doubt their presence has anything to do with the killings, but it's something worth looking into."

"Alright, Tammy," he said, sounding resigned. "Whatever you say."

CHAPTER 33 DAY 16

"THE BABY IS DUE to be born within days, Mrs Giordano." The imposing surroundings of the Savoy tea room. Under the magnificent atrium a white latticework gazebo housed a pianist playing soft music.

"A boy? It has to be a boy. You promised." The woman was looking at Mario Kerkut earnestly. Her accent was Italian, American. She and her husband were seated opposite the Kerkut brothers, with an afternoon tea spread of finger sandwiches and patisserie together with a teapot and crockery laid out on the low table.

Mario was at his soft-spoken best. "A boy, we've seen the scans," he lied. They'd not risked taking the girl to hospital for a proper check-up, despite the recent tragedy they'd been a party to. There'd be obvious problems with age, she was just fourteen, identity, and the absolute certainty the girl would talk to anyone she could to try to make an escape.

Jay, ignoring his brother's black looks, seemed bored, fidgeting constantly. Clearly impatient to get the deal done and be away.

The woman was in her mid to late forties, and likely too old to adopt. The two-piece Giorgio Armani suit in ochre complemented her olive complexion, and she was perfectly made up, her short dark hair beautifully blow waved. The watch, which she constantly ran her fingers over in a nervous gesture, was a gold Jaeger-LeCoultre, and had not gone unnoticed by Mario.

The husband wore a simple two-piece suit in navy blue. He might have been a brother of the Kerkuts, except he was older, probably early fifties, and greying slightly at the temples. He too wore a designer watch. Mario had already spotted the Vacheron Constantin. The man exuded wealth and success.

Mario considered the price he'd asked for the baby and started calculating his approach to doubling it without it seeming too blatant.

"Which hospital will the boy be born in," the husband asked of Mario. He sounded native Italian, as the surname suggested.

"A small private hospital," Mario replied reassuringly. "Where the service and the standard of medical care are the finest in the UK. You need not be concerned for the safety or well-being of your baby boy, Sir. Or of the mother, come to think of it." Brushing some imaginary crumbs from his lap Mario gave the couple his most convincing smile.

"We are both so excited. We've tried everything. Drugs, dates of ovulation." She suddenly looked embarrassed. Then went on, "IVF. We've spent a fortune. But now, at last, our own. And a boy. Sweetheart?" She glanced at her husband as though seeking agreement.

"A boy," he said, taking his wife's hands in his own. Then looking at Mario, he added, "It has been a long wait. But now, no more. Thanks to you, my friend."

Mario let the comment settle. Then said softly, "There is of course, the fee. We mustn't forget that, must we. In all the excitement. Sorry to sound mercenary. But we do owe the mother as well as ourselves, of course."

"I understand, I understand," responded Mr Giordano, reaching into an inside pocket for his wallet. "Fifty thousand pounds, you said, with half in advance. Am I correct?"

Looking somewhat nettled, Mario said, "I'm sorry, Mr Giordano, I thought I'd made it clear, no cheques…"

"You want cash?" said Mr Giordano, glancing nervously at his wife. "Yes, yes of course, I can arrange that, but I'll need a couple of days."

"No, Mr Giordano." Mario's voice was raised slightly, and he spoke in short staccato bursts. "You've forgotten? I thought I'd made it crystal-clear when we were first in touch. We want the transaction to be conducted wholly in cryptocurrency. I mean, I assumed you understood? No cash. No cheques."

"Oh! I'm sorry. We've been so taken up with the excitement of a baby, I quite forgot."

There was a silence lasting several moments, only broken by the gentle playing of the pianist within the surrounds of the pergola.

Then, trying not to look too annoyed, Mario went on, as though trying to coax a baby to walk, "I assume you do have cryptocurrency availability?"

"Yes, yes. Of course," Giordano replied hastily, turning guiltily away from his wife, who simply looked puzzled.

"So is there problem?"

"No, of course not. I just hadn't realised —"

"Well, no harm done," Mario interrupted, looking relieved.

"Will Bitcoin be acceptable?"

"No, it won't," said Mario sharply, irritated once more. "It's the last thing we want. Much too volatile."

Somewhat crestfallen, Giordano asked, "Well, tell me, which currency would be acceptable?"

"I was going to say, you surprise me, holding funds in Bitcoin. But then as a successful businessman and obvious risk taker I do see the logic."

"For fuck's sake," muttered Jay, barely under his breath. "How much longer is this going to take."

Mrs Giordano looked shocked, seemed about to cry. "This isn't how I thought it was going to be." Glancing at her husband, she asked, "Rafael, who are these people? I thought you said everything was going to be fine. I mean, what the hell is going on here? Do we have a baby or don't we? And why don't we try a legit adoption agency again, instead of these two?"

"Mrs Giordano," offered Mario, leaning forward confidentially and sounding as smooth as silk. "Please ignore my brother. He means no offence, do you, Jason?"

"Well, if you say so," responded Mrs Giordano. "But..."

Before she could go on, Mario added, "My brother suffers from hypertension, don't you, Jay?"

Without waiting for a reply, he went on, "It's Jay who has done all the work here selecting a baby for you, Mrs Giordano. He just wants the event to proceed as smoothly as possible, and for you both to be proud and happy parents of a beautiful baby boy."

"Well, if you say so," said the wife again, dubiously.

"Isn't that right, Jay? You want this lovely couple to be happy with what we've arranged for them. Hmm?"

"Yeah, yeah," murmured Jay. "A happy couple," he said, then asked, "so what about the money, then? When're we gonna be paid for the kid?"

Mario, turning back to the couple and restraining himself, asked, "About the money. May we proceed now?"

"I am happy to accommodate you, Mr Kerkut. Tell me which currency you require and I will make the transfer, as we sit here."

Then as an afterthought, he added, "Right now."

"Tether, please, Mr Giordano."

"Tether?"

"That's right," said Mario, trying not to sigh too obviously.

"You mean, US Dollar Tether? USDT?"

"At last, we're getting somewhere," muttered Jay.

"Precisely."

Seeming a lot happier, Mr Giordano took his mobile from an inside pocket and proceeded to get into his account. "I'll get the transfer from Bitcoin to Tether underway right now. It may take a while."

"I know how it works, Mr Giordano. I have been there before, you know."

"Of course," said Giordano, fiddling with his phone.

"When you've made the transfer, I'll give you the address of my Exodus account."

"What's that?"

"You don't know? You surprise me."

"I have reserves in Bitcoin, Mr Kerkut, but don't normally deal in it. I gamble with it only. It's a sort of pastime of mine. But otherwise, all my business affairs are open and above board. So I don't know what is Exodus. Perhaps you will tell me?"

"It's not complicated. It's simply a means of keeping and moving around these currencies I work in, entirely undetected. Too many cases of crooks hacking into Crypto accounts and helping themselves." He grinned conspiratorially.

"Very well," said Giordano, "I'm ready. If you will give me the Exodus address I will transfer the first twenty-five thousand as agreed. Then the second tranche, making up to the full sum of fifty thousand when you have delivered the child."

There was complete silence for several seconds. Nobody said a word.

Mario looked taken aback.

Then Jason spoke. "What's he talkin' about, Mario? We never said anything about two twenty-fives. We agreed 50K up front and 50K on delivery. That's 100K, mister."

Giordano shook his head as though to clear it of some imaginary mental blockage. "But…but…"

"No buts, mister," said Jason. "That's the price. Take it or leave it. We got plenty more customers out there looking for a kid."

"Raffy," said the wife, again looking close to tears, "I don't like the sound of this one bit. I mean, what is going on here? I think we should leave now before we get any further into this."

"Amore, we have come this far. These gentlemen are highly recommended. If we start again it could be months before another suitable child is found. We have had a minor misunderstanding here. Let us proceed. I'm sure all will be well."

"Sorry, I don't like it, Raffy. Not one bit." Mrs Giordano, close to tears, dabbed at her eyes with a lace handkerchief.

"Listen, lady," said Jason placatingly. "We don't mean to cause no offence, but we've got other people waiting. So, are you two going ahead, or is the deal off?"

"Call it off, Raffy," she pleaded with her husband, having recovered herself and now decided, putting the hanky away in her bag. "Please, honey. I'll wait. Another few months won't make any difference."

But Rafael, ignoring his wife, said to Mario, "Let me have your Exodus address and I'll do the first 50K now. Let's get on with this before I also change my mind."

"Good man," said Mario, getting to his feet, followed by the towering Jason. "We expect to be able to meet you in a week."

"Mr Kerkut?"

"Yes. Was there something else we haven't covered?"

"Erm, yes, there was. Is," Rafael said hesitantly. "Do I not get some sort of receipt? You know, 50K after all. It's a lot of money."

"Well no, Mr Giordano. It'd hardly be appropriate. I mean. A receipt? This is all supposed to be entirely discreet. Isn't it? Tell me if I'm wrong."

"No, no. I just wondered."

"Tell you what," said Mario, removing his watch and offering it over. "How would it be if I let you hold on to my gold Rolex. Sort of a returnable deposit. It's worth a lot more than you're paying for the baby."

Rafael, looking acutely embarrassed, said, "No really. It's all right. After all, we're both men of the world, aren't we. You hang on to the watch. I know I can trust you. My wife and I will see you in a week, unless the birth is delayed."

A moment later the two brothers had left, leaving in their wake a note of something unsavoury hanging in the air.

"A week," said Mrs Giordano, shaking her head doubtfully. "You really think you'll see them again? Personally, I doubt it. You've just handed over fifty thousand hard earned pounds, with no baby. Twice the asking price fiddled at the last second and no proof of anything."

"It will be fine, amore. We can afford it, and if the only way to get a baby is this way, then so be it. After all, he offered me his watch, didn't he?"

"Guessing you'd be too proud or too embarrassed to take it. Alright," she sighed. "Let's see how things turn out. I shan't get my hopes up too far, though. I couldn't stand another disappointment like the last few."

CHAPTER 34 DAY 17

HAVING SLEPT RESTLESSLY, she'd awoken nervous in the knowledge that this would be the first time she'd attended a meeting in such eminent company.

She'd deliberately dressed soberly, selecting a navy two-piece suit, with jacket lapels and straight, narrow trousers and a matching navy blouse, the outfit given a touch of colour by the addition of an Etsy scarf in lilac shantung. Pale lipstick, no mascara and low-heel footwear by Jimmy Choo. Armour in place, she should have been ready for anything, but actually felt anything but.

She took a taxi which would drop her right outside. No need to worry about looking harassed on arrival or risk being caught in the rain. In the event, it turned out sunny.

Approaching early to meet John Manus prior to going down to COBRA, she found him already in the reception area. He was wearing a dark suit that fitted him, for once. He looked less florid. Maybe he found challenging events like this calming, for he seemed supremely relaxed. "Been here before, Tammy?"

She thought guiltily about the two lines of cocaine she'd done this morning to give herself some Dutch courage. She'd ditched her stash when Matty came along, but had felt the need when under pressure to go back to her drug of choice. So she'd restocked. Had it worked? Probably not. It was after all only a temporary fix.

"First time, John."

"You'll be fine," he reassured her, assessing correctly that she was a tad apprehensive, out of her comfort zone.

Tammy raised her eyebrows in reply but said nothing, her pulse starting to rise in anticipation of what lay ahead this morning. Then they went downstairs to the Briefing Room together.

COBRA is based at the Cabinet Office at 70 Whitehall, adjacent to Downing Street. The building, comprising three historically linked properties as well as what's left of Henry VIII's 1530-built tennis courts, houses meetings when there are national emergencies to address, such as the threat of an imminent terrorist attack.

CTC or Counter Terrorism Command, also known as SO15, is a Specialist Operations unit within London's Met, combining intelligence ops and investigative functions. When required, it will work in conjunction with MI5, which latter engage in intel gathering and the identification of suspects.

MI5 don't carry guns. CTC do, and use them as needed, and without hesitation, but strictly in accordance with the protocol established in KRATOS, otherwise known as critical rules of engagement.

The meeting room includes a magnificent twenty-five-foot mahogany boardroom table. Giant TV screens cover the back wall showing live views of London between sessions.

People attending COBRA will be any or all of those who can and are needed to contribute, including the PM, Home Secretary, other government ministers, senior police officers, and the actual heads of CTC and MI5.

In attendance on this occasion were DCI John Manus and Detective Chief Superintendent Bob Walker representing the Met. Chairing the meeting was the Home Secretary, Michael Templeton, a stooped, intense-looking individual, together with his Permanent Under-Secretary, Edwin Fellows, an impossibly young man with improbable spikey black hair. Also participating was the head of CTC, the burly Nick Holden, a man who always displayed a wildly optimistic approach to life. Probably unique in his vocation. MI5, unable to attend at short notice, would be briefed later with minutes of the meeting.

CHAPTER 34 • DAY 17 • 215

This was to be the second COBRA since the recent train atrocity. The first had been adjourned without resolution, due to the all-too frequent clash between politics, led by the Home Secretary, and the need for operational independence, led by Bob Walker and backed by John Manus, Nick Holden and the London Met chief, Miranda Miller, the latter unable to be present this time.

Tammy was aware of the problems even before the start of the meeting, perceiving the atmosphere of opposition, or maybe out and out dislike, between the Home Secretary and Bob Walker.

Templeton opened the meeting with a brief resumé of the aims of the meeting, particularly in light of the recent terrorist attack on Northern Region Rail, which had resulted in the deaths of seven people, the members of two families sitting close to each other, and injuries to a further thirty.

Those present looked grave.

Discussion inevitably turned to recollection of the horrific bus and tube bombings on the 7th and 21st of July 2005. More than fifty were killed, hundreds injured.

What was perhaps most creditable in the light of those two atrocities, was the magnificent way the CTC and MI5, together with police forces around the country, had worked together and prevented more of the same. This entailed work on the operational side of things, as against the political, whose interventions were frequently problematic. Would today be a case in point?

Tammy was introduced as a private investigator with a police background known to Bob Walker, who had recommended her for a number of successful missions.

"Ms Pierre, young lady, we're really glad to have you here, but can you explain how you think you may be able to assist us in this inquiry?" asked the Home Secretary, focusing all his attention on her. The voice of privilege, she realised. That of a stratum of society known for its entitlement. To what, she wasn't sure. But she knew she was forming immediate reservations about the man.

The 'young lady' in particular rankled as patronising and actually, damn rude, but she kept her cool. She explained, "Bob Walker recently asked me to assist the Met in looking at several murders that had taken place in or close to some of the venues where clubs owned by one Hester Lamont are situated."

"Why you, particularly?"

"The club has specific LGBTQ nights. Bob felt that the nature of the clubs and the murders might prove problematic for the run-of-the-mill cop. The victims were all transsexuals."

"Really, Ms Pierre?" said the Home Secretary, looking decidedly perplexed.

"Can you perhaps enlighten us all, then? Are you supposed to be assisting in the search for a sexually orientated killer, or else a terrorist person or persons?"

"Both," she responded bluntly, reaching out for the jug to pour herself some of the mineral water.

"And whatever do you imagine a young person like you might be able to offer that our regular police and security services wouldn't have the capacity to cope with?" He looked smug, unconvinced by anything Tammy might have to offer, even at this early stage. "I mean, you're no longer with the force, are you? Hmm? Got none of the backup or resources we can provide."

Before responding she glanced around the room, but nobody offered anything further so, after taking her time drinking from her glass, she went on, "I've had a number of … ah, relationships, shall we say, that it was felt might stand me in better stead when it came to assessing the type of clientele, and the likelihood of my getting close to some of the patrons in seeking answers."

"So, to put it bluntly, Ms Pierre, you were brought in because you're a lesbian?"

"Just one moment, Michael," protested Nick Holden, head of CTC, sounding irritated. "For heaven's sake. I think we might cut our guest a bit more slack as one well versed and familiar with that sort of scene. Don't you?"

"The general idea, Nick. Thanks for that," added Bob Walker, also pouring himself some mineral water from the jug on the table.

"I appreciate that, Mr Holden," said Tammy quietly, noting the predicted undercurrent of animosity among those present.

"And pray tell, Ms Pierre," continued the Home Secretary, brushing a flop of hair from his forehead, "how can your investigation of homosexually orientated crimes have any bearing upon or relationship to the terrorist outrages we've been witnessing?"

"I understand from a colleague," responded Tammy, "that a boatload of illegal immigrants, mostly young women, who it is thought might have been brought in to use as prostitutes, were accompanied by four men of Middle Eastern appearance."

"And just who is this colleague?"

"I'm not at liberty to say, but I am told that the four men who accompanied the girls have been followed to some of London's mosques. In particular, the East London Mosque."

"This colleague of yours? Not by any chance a Mr Dovid Jordan, or some of his accomplices?"

Tammy remained mute.

"I see," said Templeton. "Man keeps popping up where he's not wanted."

"He's been useful to us on a number of occasions in situations where our presence would have been problematic," offered Nick Holden, sitting back and folding his arms.

"Israeli, isn't he?" said Templeton, looking as though the idea was thoroughly distasteful to him.

Then, turning to Tammy, he put to her, "Without wishing to offend, Ms Pierre, how well do you know this Jordan man? We've reason to believe he's involved with Mossad."

"He's a friend."

"That's all?"

"Correct."

"A lover, perhaps?"

"I can't see what that has to do with this meeting."

Templeton raised his eyebrows. "I understand. Perfectly," he added, as a purposeful afterthought.

"What do you understand, Home Secretary?"

"Are you a Jew?" put in Templeton's aide unexpectedly. Edwin Fellows looked slightly amused at the prospect. "I mean, you're bla ... I mean a person of colour."

She was finding it increasingly difficult restraining herself under this needless provocation, and replied, "So, persons of colour can't be Jewish?"

"That amulet you wear. Jewish lettering?"

"I'm a Jewess, Mr Fellows."

Then, close to her limit, she got slowly to her feet and took the initiative for the first time. "And you've really taken up more than enough of my time, sir. If you'll all please excuse me, I'm not sure I can be of any more use here."

As she was about to leave the room, she noted John Manus was flushed bright red with embarrassment. Bob Walker called out that he'd speak to her later.

The last comment she picked up was a furious rebuke from Nick Holden, saying it was time Templeton found himself a new aide, ideally an adult. But then something stopped Tammy as she was on the point of exiting the conference room.

They'd barely stopped bickering when they were interrupted by a shirt-sleeved young man who burst into the room unannounced. He looked frantic.

All eyes turned in his direction.

"What is it, Peter?" asked a worried-looking Home Secretary.

"News just in from forensics and the pathologist, sir."

The lad was out of breath. Seemed scared. He went on, "Some of the bodies have just been identified, sir. The train bomb?"

CHAPTER 35 DAY 16

UNDATED

So lonely. I just wanted to make friends, that's all. They didn't understand. So I got angry. Then I killed. And killed again.

They called me pinko shit and buggered the hell out of me. Like razor blades up my arse it was. I screamed. They laughed. Bled a lot. Ruined sheets. Mum thrashed me. For bleeding. Can you dig it? I was seven years old. Got handed around like so much garbage to be sampled by as many as there were in the place at any one time. Six? Seven? Eight? I lost count. Never-ending. My daily vision of hell.

Thing is, they were all white. So how come I get called pinko? Mum was black. Dad was white, long gone. I guess, anything to taunt me as I was different to her. She did nothing to stop it. Encouraged it. Earned from it. Made me fucking swallow. I gagged, nearly choked till I got used to it. Not that you ever can. That salt taste. Makes no difference now. Can't make a proper relationship.

I want friends. Proper friends, not just people to be pretend polite with. Really. So lonely. I've waited. And waited. This long. No more. Now I want revenge. I'll kill when I can.

Friendship or death. Their choice. Both maybe. Cut and slice. Cut and slice. Remove extraneous genitalia. Just the ticket. What the doctor ordered.

I'm okay really. Doing what comes naturally. Press talking about serial killings. I'm no psychopath. They hurt me, now I'll hurt them. Any of them. All of them.

Love it. Love it all.

* * * * *

DAY 16

THE TWO COUPLES WERE SITTING in a tearoom of the Savoy, as before, the pianist on the central gazebo playing soft dinner jazz.

There was a buzz of chatter and the clink of bone china as guests relaxed in the soft surroundings, away from the noisy shuffle of the Strand traffic outside. Staff unhurriedly moving back and forth served trays of tea and multi-layered cake stands filled with Savoy baked delicacies.

Mr Giordano was dressed as he had previously, in what looked like a Savile Row grey and black pinstripe, with silk shirt and dark tie. His wife, Mario Kerkut saw, was dressed in an Yves Saint Laurent dress in a dark turquoise, the colour again a magnificent contrast to her Mediterranean complexion.

What Mario had also noticed, and judging by the glance he got from his brother in acknowledgement that he too had seen, was the gold Patek Philippe Neptune watch on her wrist. Priced at around £23,000, the couple would have no difficulty telling the time, nor any difficulty paying for the baby. Patek Philippe this time and Jaeger-LeCoultre last time.

On this occasion the brothers were accompanied by a Silver Cross Balmoral pram, in black. The traditional big cycle wheels and concertina folding hood so familiar a sight on our streets in the past. With the price now at £2,700 the pram had become the epitome of established middle-class affluence.

Inside, securely wrapped in a blue Babygro with a blue knitted woollen cap and sleeping peacefully, care of a fingertip of gin sucked off Jay's finger in a nod to a long-dead nineteenth-century custom, was a beautiful, chubby-cheeked babe.

"Raffy," breathed Mrs Giordano, clasping her hands together excitedly. "He's beautiful. Beautiful. Beautiful. Oh, Raff, I can't wait to hold him." Looking into the pram she could see the baby's pink cheeks as he slept on, his gentle breathing like a summer breeze to her ears.

"Best wait for the moment," said Mario, trying not to look too alarmed. "If the little one cries ... we don't want him disturbing the other guests, do we?" he added, almost as an afterthought, drinking from his cup of tea.

"Of course. Of course," she responded enthusiastically, barely able to contain herself.

"What about our money," growled Jay, who was looking increasingly agitated. His tea sat on the small antique table, untouched and now stone cold.

"Raffy," his wife beamed, "pay the man. Then we can go with our son."

"Yes, yes, of course, amore. Right now." He sighed happily, suggesting an element of relief, as though he'd not actually been certain they'd ever see a baby or the return of his money if a baby were not forthcoming.

Reaching into the inside pocket of his jacket, he extracted his mobile phone and started tapping away. "Same Exodus address as before?" he asked.

"That's correct," replied Mario smoothly.

"Mr Kerkut?" Mrs Giordano ventured. "You have been so kind, we would deem it an honour if we may call the boy Mario? After you, of course."

"Mrs Giordano," responded Mario, smoothly taking the cup from his lips. "The honour would be all mine."

"What about me?" growled Jay. "What's wrong with my name, then?"

"Oh, yes, yes, Mr Jay. We'll call him Mario Jay. Mario Jay Giordano." She was too taken up with the baby, her excitement rendering her oblivious to Jay's increasing agitation.

"Come on, come on," Jay muttered. "When's our money coming?"

"Fifty thousand, right?" Mr Giordano smiled, referring to the agreed price.

"Whaddaya mean, fifty thou'? We said a third, that's fifty down and a hundred to complete."

"But! But! That's not what we said. Mr Mario? When we met here last week." He turned distractedly to the other brother, who'd clearly been caught unawares, but who had equally quickly recovered himself.

"Oh, I think we did, Mr Giordano. One hundred and fifty thousand pounds for a healthy newborn baby boy. That's what we agreed, and we're now delivering. Not strictly legal, these off the books adoptions, but fulfilling a need. Wouldn't you both agree?" He turned and smiled at Mrs Giordano, who looked bereft as she could see her dream swiftly evaporating before her eyes.

There was a stunned silence lasting what seemed like an age, but was in reality no more than a few seconds, the quiet finally broken by Mr Giordano.

"Mr Kerkut, please don't take me for an innocent fool. I'm a businessman, and a successful one, I deal in numbers all day. We both know what was agreed here, in these tea rooms just one week ago. You increased the price then, from the initially negotiated fifty thousand to one hundred, without my acquiescence. Now you're telling me it's one hundred and fifty thousand."

His voice was rising, and Mario glanced around the room as though alarmed they might be overheard at some of the tables nearby.

Gesturing they should all calm down, Mario said, "Look, if we made an error in the price, please accept my profound apologies." He held his palms together in earnest supplication.

"You must understand, it is not easy to fulfil a request like yours. But, I'm sorry to have to say, the closing price requires a further one hundred thousand pounds to complete. There is no risk to you, the honest buyer, but there is considerable risk to us. You must appreciate ..."

"We appreciate nothing, Mr Kerkut," said Giordano, angrily getting to his feet. "As far as we're concerned, the deal is off. You don't take me for a fool. Amore?"

He glanced down at his wife, who was still gazing adoringly at the baby, the little one now making tiny noises suggesting he might awaken at any moment.

"Come, amore. We're leaving. There'll be other deals out there."

"But, Raffy; he is so beautiful. And he's here now. We can afford it. We can be home with our son in under an hour. Think of it, Raffy. Our own boy. And he's here. Now. We can't just abandon him."

"Not the point. We're being done over. Taken for fools. And that I can't stand. We're leaving. Now!" he added emphatically.

"Please, Raffy," she begged, holding on to his forearm, now close to tears. "Please. If I never ask for anything else in my whole life. Let me have this one thing?"

Glancing down at his still seated wife, Giordano shook his head in a wonder of resignation and started tapping at his mobile again without a further word.

"Come on," rasped Jay, also getting to his feet at the same time as his brother. "Be quick, mister. You got the kid. What's taking you so fucking long?"

"Jay, Jay," said Mario, recovering the smooth demeanour. "Do forgive my twin, he tends to get a little overwrought when a human cargo is involved."

"It's done," said Giordano. "You've got your money. Now go, dammit. And leave us alone."

But there was no need for the brothers to be dismissed, for they were already leaving the couple and making for the exit, hunched over like a pair of Dickens's Fagins.

Resuming his seat, Giordano sat quietly for several moments, regaining his composure, his wife looking at him anxiously. Eventually he said, "Alright, amore," taking his wife's hands in his. "You have your baby. Your son."

"Our son, Raffy. Our own son."

"Of course," he replied, looking into the pram for the first time. "Our son. We will give him the best money can buy, amore. The best food, the best education, best clothes."

He stopped.

"No," he decided. "No. Not important. We will give him what matters most. We will give him the best of love. All our love."

"Oh, Raffy. Thank you. Thank you, my own love."

Giordano waited until he'd finished drinking his tea, sufficient time to regain his composure, then said, "Come. We'll leave the pram for the concierge to forward on to our home. He has the address."

In the foyer of the hotel Mrs Giordano leaned into the pram and tenderly extracted the child. "Mario, mi ..." She stopped abruptly.

But Rafael, having guessed at her sudden reticence, said, "Giovanni, mi amore, after your father."

"Giovanni," she repeated, hugging the child tight to her bosom.

The top-hatted doorman, with a nod of familiarity to Giordano, handed over the keys to his two-tone brown and ivory Bentley, parked in the hotel's undercover access road, incidentally, the only road in England where drivers take to the right.

The baby cot was already secured on the back seat, where Mrs Giordano climbed in, almost beside herself with joy. Unable to contain herself a moment longer from examining the tot, her son, the heir to her husband's considerable fortune, she pulled aside his nappies.

The guests in the lobby of the hotel, the doormen, the taxi drivers, random guests, all heard it. Something they would find hard to forget.

The world seemed to stand still, as though undecided what and where to go next. There was no sound of traffic. A plane overhead made no sound. People mouthed words that could not be heard like an old black-and-white silent film.

Then came the cry. A drawn-out, uncontained wail, an animal scream, a howl of the uncontainable rage of a woman in utter despair, a mother who'd been duped, denied, mocked, and destroyed.

A mother, no longer a mother.

CHAPTER 36 DAY 17

"YES, PETER," said the Home Secretary, looking and sounding worried. "What have you got for us? We're all listening."

For a moment the young man gazed around the room as though lost for words, then he whispered, "It's Norman Cutler, sir."

There was a collective gasp around the room as the news was taken in. The momentary silence was then broken.

"God, no!" said Templeton. Then focusing on the assembled company, he announced, "As I'm sure you are all well aware, Norman Cutler is, or was, Permanent Under-Secretary to the MoD."

A murmur of disjointed comment rattled around the conference table.

"Who else died?" asked Bob Walker. "Was his family with him?"

The Home Secretary glanced up; he had tears in his eyes. "Norman hadn't had a proper holiday in years. His wife finally persuaded him ..."

"The little girls too?" murmured John Manus. "Not the children. Please, not that."

Peter merely shrugged and said nothing further.

"Alright, Peter. Thank you," said Nick Holden, seemingly having taken over the chairing of the meeting, and for once, unsurprisingly, less than his usual ebullient self. "That'll be all."

Petty squabbles set aside, the discussion continued in earnest for some time, with areas of investigation and the ever-present need to find more personnel to assist.

Any CCTV footage that could be recovered from the train would be studied, together with anything from the embarking station that might indicate whether the family had unwittingly picked up a planted device in a bag, a case, or more than likely a rucksack.

Somewhere a switch would have had to have been made. All vague conjecture at this stage.

During a lull in the conversation, the Home Secretary looked in Tammy's direction and, catching her eye, said ruefully, "I must apologise, Ms Pierre. We're all overwrought here. I know."

He raised a hand before she could say anything. "It's not an excuse for our behaviour. A reason, perhaps, but not an excuse."

"Thank you, sir," she said quietly, resuming her seat. "No harm done."

Then, looking uncomfortable for the first time and nervously drumming his fingers on the table, Templeton's aide added, "Ms Pierre, please. Erm ... my comments were uncalled for and unprofessional. I apologise. Unreservedly. We're all a bit, well, you know ..."

"Thank you, Mr Fellows. Point taken," said Tammy.

She wondered just how sincere the "unreserved" apology was, but realised there was nothing to be gained by making any further issue of it. She'd lived with a lifetime of subtle and not so subtle abuse. One more insult would hardly make any difference.

Letting the atmosphere settle, Nick Holden then asked, "Ms Pierre, Bob tells me you've undertaken some pretty risky assignments. Obviously, no-one here wants you to put yourself in harm's way, but both Bob and John seem to think you may be able to help us in some way. What was it you had in mind, if you don't mind my asking?"

She thought about her response for a few moments, smoothed the lap of her skirt, then said, "At this stage, as we really know practically nothing, I was proposing to simply test the water by looking into one of the mosques believed to have been the destination of the four who came across."

"You'd go into the women's section, obviously."

"I think not, Nick. When I was in Syria, for the most part I was able to pass myself off as a man. I've the height, the voice, the presence. It'll be easier for me to nose around and to enlist the help of fellow men, as it were, rather than seek information from women, who in my experience, particularly within the confines of a mosque, will be far more circumspect about helping." She was addressing the whole room, looking from man to man to get some sort of reaction, and noted the doubtful expressions on several of the faces staring intently at her.

"The Islamic community," she went on, "is still very much a patriarchy. No women will want to be accused of stepping out of line. It's too risky where we may be dealing with possible terrorists."

Nick, leaning forward on his elbows and looking extremely concerned, said, "Tammy, if it were discovered you were female in a mosque, you could find yourself in real trouble. Worshippers wouldn't take kindly to what you have in mind."

"I'll take that chance, Nick. I can talk my way out of most situations and on the physical side, I really can take care of myself."

"Madness," sighed Templeton. "Sorry," he said, addressing Tammy. "But this is total madness. We really can't be seen to be a party to this sort of adventure, Ms Pierre. I advise against it, absolutely."

"I understand, Home Secretary," she said quietly. "In which case, I will simply take my chances."

"While undertaking to look into the Clubhouse murders at the same time?"

"Exactly. Somewhere there is a link to be found. It will be my job to find it."

CHAPTER 37 DAY 18

MIDDAY FRIDAY, and the East London Mosque was crowded with worshippers.

She'd considered calling ahead to request permission to visit. Mosques are friendly, welcoming places where people of different faiths may visit to observe or simply join in worshipping. But she wanted to observe incognito, so she'd dressed as a male, as she'd said she would, in an ankle-length dark thobe, her head covered with a tight-fitting kufi with her short hair tucked in.

Noted as a stranger as she entered, she was greeted warmly, and shown where to leave her sandals. Built some twenty years ago, the interior exuded restrained magnificence, with an elaborate, wide circular skylight, pillars down both sides of the wide praying area and ranks of places for prayer mats, like the backs of playing cards, marked in the marble flooring.

The delicate fragrances of bakhoor and oudh permeated the whole area.

Realising that a lot of the worshippers were familiar with each other, she deliberately avoided eye contact with anyone near her, not knowing how any conversation, once started, might continue.

While trying to look as unobtrusive as possible, she followed the imam leading the prayers and copied the actions of those closest to her, prostrating herself kneeling forward, her forehead touching the prayer mat at the same time as the others. But still, she felt uncomfortable, knowing she was playing false.

Then she saw the men. All four, unmistakably them, recognisable by their size, if nothing else, each bearded and with a long-tailed turban, standing to one side of the large praying area, arms folded, surveying the congregants as though they were sentries. Dov's people had managed some blurred photos, taken from a distance, but it was them. Little doubt of that.

Prayers lasted approximately thirty minutes, after which time people began dispersing. What now? she wondered. Leave? Having achieved nothing? In which case she might just as well have watched who entered and left the mosque from outside.

Then she caught the eye of a young man, similarly attired to herself, standing nearby gazing at the four burly individuals. Risking a conversation she whispered, "Any idea who they are?"

"They started coming here recently, but don't usually join in prayers. It's like they're on the lookout for someone or something." He stared at the men, puzzled, then turned back to Tammy and said, "I'm Deepak. Deepak Pandit," and extended his hand.

"Ahmed Choudhury," came Tammy's quick response, as she took the hand of the other.

"Hi, Ahmed. Hey! I haven't seen you here before either. Even with these numbers you get to know faces."

"I'm usually in West London," said Tammy, thinking fast. "I'm here in Stratford for a couple of weeks, so thought I'd pay a visit. Have to say, those four don't look too friendly."

All too aware her approach was unplanned and frankly, even in her own eyes, amateurish, she decided to wing it anyway. It wouldn't be the first time, and as long as you kept your head, anything might emerge. After all, how do you plan to make contact with strangers who may correctly suspect your motives and publicly call you out. The last thing she'd want if the four strangers were to overhear.

"I wonder what they're up to," mused the younger man.

"Recruiting?" offered Tammy.

"I hope not." He frowned. "We're a nice balanced community here. The last thing we want is ..."

He stopped suddenly as one of the four men approached them, a belligerent look on his face.

What next? Tammy wondered, unconsciously bracing herself for a fight, which common sense told her would never happen in these surroundings.

He was as tall as Tammy, taller even. Catching her eye as he stood in her space, he hissed at Deepak, "Who's he? Don't know him."

"His name, is ..."

But Tammy interrupted, a restraining arm on Deepak's forearm, saying, "It's alright, Deepak." Then turning to the man, Tammy extended a hand and said, "My name is Ahmed. Ahmed Choudhury."

Ignoring the offer of friendship, the man, looking her up and down in a distinctly suspicious way, said, "Ant ghayr marghub huna."

Turning to Deepak for assistance, Tammy replied, "I'm sorry, I don't speak much Arabic."

"Not wanted here," said the man, his lips drawn back like a Dobermann Pinscher to reveal blackened teeth.

It was impossible to gauge the individual, or what his next move might be. Equally difficult to know how to respond, other than to be polite. Although, she had to admit to herself, recalling Proverbs 15:1, this might not be one of those situations where a soft answer would "turneth away wrath."

Still, worth a try, she decided. "I'm visiting the area on business. I usually attend the West London Mosque."

He came up close to her now, and she could smell his breath, the sweet aroma of the stimulant khat, mixed with, astonishingly, that of alcohol. Forbidden in the Muslim faith, Tammy wondered what it said about the man.

His other three colleagues now approached, and Tammy noted Deepak beginning to look fearful. "Don't worry," she whispered. "It'll be fine."

"But ..." started Deepak.

All four men now surrounded Tammy and Deepak, the latter looking distinctly scared.

The first of the men who'd approached said, "Tusim ithe nahim cahude ho."

"He says you're not wanted here," translated Deepak.

"Yes," said Tammy. "I heard the first time."

Then, keeping a rein on her temper, which was threatening to boil over, and smiling at the four men, Tammy added, "I'd like to say it's been a pleasure, gentlemen. But you know how these things are."

Before any comment could be offered in response, Tammy made her way towards the exit, ushering Deepak protectively in front of her, while resisting the temptation to see if they were being followed.

Outside the mosque the street was still crowded with worshippers milling around, chatting before gradually dispersing.

A few drops of rain scattered the pavement, kicking up dust. Tammy felt a chill breeze around her neck, which echoed her mood. Traffic, as always in bad weather, had slowed to a crawl. There'd be little to report to Bob beyond recommending twenty-four-hour surveillance. CCTV coverage in the capital would prove invaluable.

"They're not of our community," said Deepak, wrapping his arms about himself.

"How do you mean?" Tammy asked.

"Our religion is very divided. I knew when I first set eyes on them. They pray differently to us."

Then the four exited the mosque together, apparently making for Tammy and Deepak, and not looking as though they were about to engage the pair in conversation.

"Quick," said Tammy, pressing a business card into Deepak's hand, and, seeing his surprised expression, added, "I'll explain when we have more time. We'll split up. Hurry now," she urged, pointing to a black cab going in the opposite direction just as the traffic started to move again.

Seeing the momentary indecision on the faces of the four, Tammy weaved between the slow-moving traffic and raced to the other side of the street, ducking into a small lock-up shop specialising in female Islamic wear. She dragged the kufi from her head, fluffing out her short curls, and in a moment of inspiration, grabbed a black hijab from a rack and gasped to the young assistant, "Quick. I'm being followed. Can I use your toilet?"

The girl, a lovely thing in a pale green hijab, looked bewildered, simply pointing to the back of the shop, where Tammy ran, dragging off the thobe as she went. Once in the loo, she hurriedly folded the garment and stuffed it behind the toilet bowl. Then she pulled on the hijab, after applying a little light lipstick and running a comb through her hair. The jeans and blouse she'd worn under the thobe were sufficiently nondescript to draw no undue attention.

"You'll do." She smiled, surveying herself in the tiny mirror, hoping she'd got it right. Otherwise, there'd be little if any room for manoeuvre. The consequences of miscalculation on her part didn't bear thinking about, she realised, recalling the warning expressed by the Home Secretary.

The four were in the shop when she emerged, circling the interior like feline predators. They all looked very much interchangeable in terms of height, dress and general appearance. Within the confines of the tiny area they all appeared much bigger than they had in the mosque. Clustering together like four large chess pieces, they muttered among themselves, glancing in her direction from time to time, as though seeing through the disguise.

The unaccustomed hijab scraped against Tammy's cheeks making her sweat and she wondered if it was noticeable to the men. One, with a nervous tic in his cheek, eyed her up and down suspiciously, more closely than the other three.

Without wishing to appear too much in a hurry Tammy looked around the shelves and hangers in the little shop, with as much interest as she could feign, aware the man with the tic was following her with his eyes, frowning suspiciously as though there was something he couldn't quite fathom. He edged up to her until he was practically touching her. She could smell the betel on his breath, see the red veering to black staining on his teeth she'd noted in the mosque. If things got difficult in the shop, she could handle two without difficulty. Three might be problematic. Four was out of the question.

So she moved smoothly and casually away from the man, continuing to handle garments and scarves on display, all the time getting closer to the door. The man with the tic continued to shadow her, and it was becoming increasingly clear she'd painted herself into a corner.

The girl behind the counter could sense the menace in the increasingly oppressive atmosphere, and looked frightened, started arranging and rearranging things on display. Other customers, aware of nothing untoward, came and left, with no-one requiring any attention from the assistant.

The last thing Tammy needed right now was to have her cover blown, even if the four, suspecting something of her, could have had no idea what it was she might be up to. With what they likely had in mind themselves as part of their sojourn in the UK, it wouldn't need the brain of a genius to form their own conclusions about anyone they decided was interested in them, nor how they'd be prepared to deal with any interference with their plans.

Deliberately ignoring the men Tammy sidled her way towards the door to the street, only to find her way barred by the one with the tic.

Moving nonchalantly, Tammy could now see there was no way out without addressing the individual. "Excuse me." She smiled, still avoiding the man's direct gaze.

CHAPTER 37 • DAY 18 • 239

Traffic hummed past the shop, a car horn sounded, a sudden gust blew a swathe of wet leaves across the pavement.

"I am knowing your voice," he said softly.

"Looking straight into his eyes, Tammy responded, "I don't think so, janaba." I don't think so, sir.

"I am hearing your voice, just now." He paused as though searching for the memory. Then he said, "In the mosque. I am hearing your voice in the mosque."

As his tone became higher-pitched and more agitated, his tic more pronounced, the other three men approached. "Who are you, and what are you wanting?" he said, pulling aside his loose jacket to reveal a knife with a curved blade in a scabbard at his waist.

"I think you are a man, pretending to be a woman," he went on, grasping the shoulder of her blouse, not realising the chance he was taking. "Maybe we will take you with us to find out? Perhaps remove some of your clothes now? They have changing room at the back."

The situation was fast getting out of hand, with the absolute need to calm things down. Have the men focus on something other than her. "Kuri, girl," called Tammy, almost conversationally, "dial 999 now. I am being attacked."

Then she started to ring the number on her own mobile.

"What is it you are doing, kuti?" he said, leaning towards Tammy.

"I'm also dialling for the police," she replied. "And don't call me kuti." She took a wild guess that the word was an insult directed at women. Except that he thought she was male.

In the growing confusion one of the men said, "Leave her, Muhammed. We have other work here. Let her go."

"We can have her stripped in a moment, Irfan. We take her now." The tic was becoming more pronounced, the hand gripping her shoulder ever tighter, the nails digging into her flesh like predator's teeth.

Tammy's pulse had slowed to half its normal rate as she prepared herself. Clear-headed and calm, she reached in her jeans back pocket for the mini Gerber 06 automatic knife with the 3.6-inch aluminium blade she always carried. She felt the handle of the weapon, its familiar and reassuring finger choil or moulds, nestling in her palm, but didn't withdraw it immediately. A touch of the release button would let the blade snap out, but then she'd be committed to a course she'd wanted to avoid at all costs.

The girl at the back of the shop was crying now, as Tammy's mobile was responded to.

"Emergency. Which service?"

Looking around at the four men Tammy said quietly, "Your call, gentlemen. What's it to be?"

The shop was inconveniently empty now, no-one to hide behind, the atmosphere oppressive. The men's sweat was overpowering, as she saw her position compromised and the absurd impression she would create in the eyes of those at the COBRA meeting.

Assuming, that is, that she'd ever get the chance to debate it with them. Three would be manageable, she'd already assessed, just. Four was one too many. A curved blade or blades against her toothpick. The savage wounds from her recent trip to New York and the still-troublesome scars would hamper any response she might pursue.

The man with the tic and two of the others were now pressed up hard against her. She heard, "Put your phone down, Kuti, or we will put it down for you."

She was out of options. The surveillance of the mosque, a failed mission. Busted flush.

The voice on Tammy's phone repeated, "Emergency. Which service?"

The shop assistant, terrified eyes open wide, ended her own call.

No-one spoke as the silence ballooned, cloying, unpredictable.

CHAPTER 37 • DAY 18 • 241

In the way a given situation out of control may plot its own path, irrespective of the intentions of those involved, this matter resolved itself as swiftly as it had menaced her.

One of the men announced, "We need to get on. This is a waste of our time. Come. Please, brothers. Let her go."

The man called Irfan pushed open the shop door, beckoning her, his eyes narrowed as he said, "We will see you again, Kuti."

"I've no doubt we will," answered Tammy, swiftly exiting the place.

CHAPTER 38 DAY 19

"TAMMY, CAN YOU COME NOW?" The voice was whispered, sounded frantic.

"He's here now."

"Who is?"

"The other man I told you about."

"The one with the cleft chin?"

"He's in the smaller bar."

"Is he talking to anyone?"

"No. He's just standing around. Big bloke. Can't miss him. Sizing up the place, maybe? I don't know. As if he's looking for his next ..."

"On my way. Try not to panic."

Early evening, and with traffic fairly light for once, despite the impending rush hour, Tammy made it from Bruton Street, where she'd been struggling to catch up with correspondence highlighted as urgent by Mrs Gilchrist, to Tilbury in about forty-five minutes.

The casual jeans and denim jacket she'd worn for the day were ideal for the club's informal atmosphere, and as she walked in the place was already humming with activity. Strobe lights flickered, and with the familiar aroma of hash, an almost community atmosphere greeted the visitor. Spotting the familiar white cloud of hair and red jacket behind the backlit bar, looking nervously to his left and right, she nodded to him, ordered a bitter lemon, and made for the smaller drinks area.

As he'd said, the man was easily spotted; around six feet tall, he was wearing khaki chinos, shiny black Doc Martens, and a leather bomber jacket with open-neck check shirt. He had one hand in a trouser pocket, the other holding a pint. Never easy to know how best to approach a stranger, particularly when you had to virtually shout to be heard above the noise. Still, plumping for the direct tactic, she said simply, "Hi."

"What?" came back the none too promising response.

His skin was pock-marked with a sort of teenage acne, and he had the look of a man for whom any excuse would do, for an argument or, better yet, a fight. But what struck Tammy most was the man's eyes. If it were possible to classify eyes as those of a killer, those blue-grey eyes were just that. Vacant, lifeless, absent.

"I just said hi," she repeated.

"Piss off," he muttered, turning away from her.

"No way to treat a lady, now is it." She smiled hopefully, realising she was getting precisely nowhere.

Turning to face her for the first time, he looked her up and down as though she were an exhibit on a second-hand market stall. "Lady? Lady? Who's a fucking lady. Not you, butch. That's for sure."

He sneered, then paused for a moment as though trying to formulate an idea, before adding, "You're a trans, ain't you? Bloke calling himself a lady. Don't make me laugh."

"Lots of trans people here on trans evenings, chum, of which this is one, but not me. I'm all woman."

Then before he could come back at her, she added, "Don't like trans people, do you?"

"Why, should I? Perverts, the lot of 'em."

"So why are you here? Doesn't make sense."

"Do a good pint here," he said, taking a long drag from his. "Got the day wrong, didn't I. Anyway, what's it to you?"

"Nothing," she sighed. "Just making conversation."

He moved as though he was about to walk away, and Tammy accepted she'd need to try an alternative tack if she was to keep him talking. "Didn't I see you here the night they found that girl dead in toilets?"

He looked as though he'd been punched in the gut. "What girl? No, I wasn't here that night. Anyway, it wasn't no girl. It was a bloke like you. Got what was coming to her. Him." He corrected himself.

"You seem to know all about it, don't you?"

"Read about it in the papers, I guess."

"Been some nasty killings here the last few weeks," she prodded, waiting for further reaction.

"Someone needs to deal with 'em," he said disinterestedly, taking a further long draught of his beer.

"Would that be someone like you, do you reckon?"

"You're asking a lot of questions, mister," he said, sounding like Edward Seward. "Could get you into a right load of trouble."

Sometimes a totally unrelated remark from left field could throw an individual and produce an entirely unexpected result.

"You're a good-looking bloke, you know," she tried. "My type."

He stood for several seconds looking at Tammy, perplexed, his heavy brows knit, the pint, or what was left of it, weighing heavily in his hand, uncertain what to say or do next, then he said, "Your type, am I?" He moved closer to her, till she could smell him, an unwashed body and sour breath. "Think I'm a poof, do you? A limp-wristed fudge packer?"

"Can I get you another drink?" she interrupted, smiling. "Yours needs replenishing."

"They've got tarts working this place," he muttered. "Pregnant some of them, they were. Disgusting."

"Were?" she heard.

"Dealt with now," he said under his breath. "Must be. Don't see 'em no more. More for someone to do, though."

She wasn't sure whom he thought he was addressing. And what the hell did he mean by, "More for someone to do, though?" What had been done so far? And by whom? Him? The music seemed to get louder and the atmosphere increasingly oppressive. She could barely focus her mind.

"I'll have you, mister," he whispered. Then, looking down at Tammy's crotch, "What've you got down there? Eh? A big cock? Or maybe you've had it all off? Hmm? Fucking trans. I'll have you. And them." He gestured around the place, before stalking off.

He might have been the man in the CCTV, but the images were too unclear to be certain.

She'd suggest John Manus approach the man for an informal interview. Get his take on it, if the man were prepared to be spoken to. A big if on the fabric of this encounter. Not enough evidence to arrest him.

On her suggestion, Manus had already had Seward in for a chat, which had produced nothing of value, beyond Manus's opinion of Seward's mental state.

Watching the man's back as he trailed off, she considered those hands of his. Pointing at people. Holding the pint jar as though it were no more than a thimble. Builder's hands. Big enough and strong enough to squeeze the life out of a wild animal. She thought of the women who might have succumbed to those fists, and possibly more, dismembered bodies of innocent youngsters, and felt a chill like an iced blanket wrap itself round her.

CHAPTER 39 DAY 20

"I'M GOING TO JAIL, JOHN."

Not sure whether she should be saying anything or not, she'd finally decided that she might increase her options while not compromising the discretion of her plans if just one more person knew. That is, in addition to Bob Walker and Dov. And, come to think of it, Beth Jeffreys.

Seated back, casually turned out in a pair of flared skinny jeans, a pink T-shirt and matching jacket, with navy blue, white-soled Gucci trainers, she looked as though prison was the last place on earth she'd be planning to explore. Watching John Manus shifting about uncomfortably, he'd nodded noncommittally, she wondered whether perhaps she'd have been better off saying nothing. He wasn't that easy to make out, being a man with old-fashioned notions of courtesy and reserve, together with a tendency to keep his opinions, the personal ones that is, to himself.

However, she noted right now that Manus appeared seriously concerned, as well he might. Regarding her quizzically, this time he shook his head almost imperceptibly. "What's the crime, Tammy? Already committed? Or merely planned?"

Appearing more florid than usual, his suit as tight as ever, John Manus ignored the steaming coffee on the occasional table by his side, and leaned forward on his elbows, hands dangling between his knees, his eyebrows raised as though deeply distressed, which he clearly was. "Do I really want to hear this?" he asked, echoing her own recent comment to Dexie regarding his planned surgery.

They were on the penthouse floor of the New Scotland Yard building which Tammy had arrived at some fifteen minutes earlier. Despite the early afternoon, outside was dim as twilight, clouds lay heavy in the sky, and rain pattered miserably against the windows.

Looking for all like a favoured uncle, Manus asked, "Jail? Tammy? Where did this plan come from? A book, by any chance? Something by Barbara Vine? I don't mean to sound sceptical, but …"

"John, this isn't a joke, you know."

Manus was perspiring slightly, ever more harried with concern. "I wasn't joking, Tammy. We can't afford to lose you."

"You won't," she insisted, nevertheless noting his discomfiture, and in truth, more worried about letting him down than anxious for her own safety.

"It'll never work, my dear. I don't mean to patronise you, but how did you come up with this scheme?"

"*Brubaker*."

"Brubaker?" he queried, looking thoroughly confused.

"*Brubaker*, John. The film. From some forty years ago. Starring Robert Redford and based on real events, it's the story of a man, Henry Brubaker, who, before taking up the post of governor of Wakefield State prison in Arkansas, aimed to clean up a corrupt and violent prison system by having himself secretly incarcerated in order to assess at first hand what was going on inside and what needed to be done about it."

"And does he succeed?" asked Manus. "Does he get out in one piece?"

"Just about."

"It doesn't sound too positive, Tammy."

"He put in a lot of reforms, sacked corrupt individuals, and finally got himself sacked."

"And you're hoping to, what? Follow his example? Reform the UK prison system?"

"Of course not, John. I'm going in incognito for the sole purpose of gaining information."

"And Brubaker? Sacked? All for what?"

"Two years after the sacking, John, two dozen prisoners brought a successful legal action against the prison, resulting in its closure. The new governor was not re-elected."

Manus shook his head, clearly still unconvinced. "I can see nothing is going to change your mind, Tammy."

Ignoring his concern, Tammy changed the subject and said, "I gather the press conference didn't go well?"

"In this sort of situation the press are like circling vultures."

"Don't I know it," she returned.

"They've already labelled these killings as the Clubhouse Executions. They're calling the killer the Tilbury Ripper."

"It'll be bad for Hester," said Tammy. "Horrifying for the victims. Yet when I'm in any of the three clubs, attendance is always up."

"The ghouls, the curious, the young risk takers. Just try to stop them from going."

"To be expected, I suppose."

"So, of course, nothing short of an arrest, or arrests, will appease them," added Manus.

"Nothing forthcoming from any of the families, partners, friends of the deceased?"

"We've drawn a blank so far," said Manus, pulling at an earlobe. "So, the killings appear to be almost random, yet not entirely, as they all seem to focus on apparent transsexuals."

"What about serial killers? Anything useful on the PNC?"

"Nothing that ties in with what we're faced with here." Manus shrugged. "A few years ago up north, we had a series of four unsolved killings. The only thing in common with the Clubhouse murders was the close proximity of the murders to each other, all in north Blackburn, with broken necks in the case of three victims, all male in fact, and a slit throat of one young woman. No suggestion of transsexualism. No clubs involved. No apparent motive. Unlikely any connection with these in the south."

They were interrupted by the appearance of Harry Ricks, as sartorially elegant as ever, the Rolex prominent. He'd not seen Tammy, who'd bypassed Ricks's floor on her way in, and spotting her with Manus found it hard to disguise his discomfiture and dislike. "Boss," he said. "You're needed downstairs."

"I'll be there shortly," Manus responded sharply.

"You're needed now, boss."

Looking thoroughly irritated, Manus snapped, "I said, shortly, Ricks."

Then, locking eyes with Tammy, Ricks pointed. "And what's she doing here?"

Beneath the flush, Tammy watched as Manus went slowly white, the colour draining from his face. "I think you should go back down, Ricks, before you jeopardise your career further than you have already."

Then, without further word he turned away from the chastened detective constable.

With neither offering any comment, an understanding passed between Tammy and Manus. She'd laughed when Manus had joked about their uneven heights. Now, she felt herself drawn towards this man whose tough exterior disguised his natural warmth.

Picking up her coffee, Tammy blew on the surface pensively before taking a tentative sip of the scalding liquid, then offered, "You know, trying to make sense of all these assorted killings is like trying to sort out the Hanger Lane Gyratory on a traffic-clogged day."

"Except we don't have anything like Alexander the Great's sword to cut through it," Manus added ruefully.

He was a man with modest origins; his grandmother had been one of the last of her generation to be employed in service: the cook, in charge of the kitchens in a thirty-two-bed stately residence in the home counties. Her notion of loyalty and service had been passed down to Manus's mother, a regular churchgoing woman like her mother, who'd worked in a tiny haberdashery until marrying Manus's father, a heavy smoker, who worked as the village postman in the same area, and whom she'd met at a church bazaar. An utterly devoted couple, Manus was their second child, their first, a girl, had died during birth, almost taking Manus's mother with her, a loss she'd found almost impossible to sustain. Manus's father had died ironically of pancreatic cancer, a second tragedy, then his mother suffered a fatal stroke a few short months later after the unbearable death of her man.

All this was more than half a century ago, but the values of honesty, loyalty and consistency were embedded in John Manus's psyche. In his time on the force, he'd dealt with marital and child abuse, fraud of every description, and people of every type and hue. He'd grown accustomed to the unusual, the unique, the eccentric. He was a great people manager, and his subordinates held him in the esteem he merited. Furthermore, Manus wasn't by any means new to murder investigation, having, in his career, witnessed the whole gamut of revenge situations, random killings, and sexually motivated homicides.

But now, in the present instance, the two things that were entirely unique in his career were the apparently motiveless murders of a number of harmless transsexuals, and, not least, Tammy. She impressed him with her commitment and ability, but, if he were honest, he found her unfathomable. He'd never come across another as idiosyncratic and unpredictable as she, and the notion that she would willingly have herself incarcerated in a prison like Belmarsh without even the governor being aware left him quite bemused. Still, he wasn't about to attempt to dissuade her from what he felt was an insane project.

"What do you know about transsexuals, Tammy?" Manus enquired. "It's all relatively new to me." He shrugged, almost helplessly. "What strange times we live in. I mean, whatever happened to men and women?"

"Not all that new, John. Go back to the nineteenth century. Doctor James Barrie, born Rosemary Bulkley, lived in an age when there were no female doctors. Not even female university students. So what did she do? She dressed as a man, and got away with it. Despite a high-pitched voice and short stature, she fooled them all, qualified as a doctor and went on to a successful career, carrying out the first successful caesarean operation in history.

Her sex was only discovered after her death, when, against her stipulations, her clothing was removed and her gender revealed. What was intriguing were the stretch marks discovered on her body, suggesting she'd born a child or children. So, a woman, fronting as male, with likely a secret life as a female. About as ahead of its time as might ever have been possible."

"Interesting," said Manus. "But then I have heard of April Ashley, the first widely publicised transsexual. She was very beautiful. I wonder whether she suffered much in the way of abuse?"

"It's getting easier for women," said Tammy. "When I was a youngster I knew I was ambitious but wasn't sure what the chances were of a woman making it in a man's world. Then, out of the blue, I heard a woman professional on TV say she'd always wanted to be an economist, but realised if she were to fulfil her life's ambition she would have to stop thinking intuitively, like a woman, and start to think logically, like a man. Well, she was wrong, because you see, we women gain over men in all walks, because we are able to think logically, but we also have intuition as long as we know how and when to apply it. It puts us far ahead of the game."

Manus grinned, finally drinking from his mug of now tepid coffee, and using a handkerchief to wipe away a line of froth from his top lip. "Okay, I think you've got it taped, Tammy. But what about this prison jaunt you're planning? You do realise what Belmarsh is like? If it were discovered you are a woman, it doesn't bear thinking about, particularly if they felt they were being observed. How're you going to share a cell and get away with it?"

"Bob Walker tells me there's a fair proportion of single cells and he'll contrive to get me in one. He'll have to."

"What about the showers, Tammy?"

"You've been in Belmarsh?"

"Of course."

"So you'll know that there are shower cubicles, and apparently most of the prisoners prefer to wear boxers rather than walk around naked."

"How will you get out when you want to? How will you get out if you need to? If no-one is to know? Including the governor? What if you're discovered? Have you considered any of that?"

Tammy steepled her hands, closed her eyes thoughtfully. "I'll have to play it by ear, John."

Manus sighed. Like one defeated. "A bit random, don't you think? This whole thing? I mean, as I keep saying, hopelessly risky."

"Maybe, but I want to speak with Dominic Pope."

"I wondered who it was you hoped to target. So, the killer who has castrated."

"Exactly. And worse. Children and likely adults too. It would draw too much attention to seek to talk to him during visiting hours. So I'm going to see if I can get close to him in prison."

Manus shook his head, but offered nothing further.

"I'll have a buzz cut," Tammy explained. "It'll show up a livid scar at the side of my head, the result of a recent knife attack, which should go some way towards enhancing my male credentials."

"I understand, that and your height, the baritone voice." Manus breathed. "I still think it's crazy. You should be aware, that slight French accent of yours might attract some unwanted attention too."

Manus had stopped talking and was looking curiously at Tammy. "Is everything alright, Tammy? You've suddenly gone very pale."

"You mean you can tell, John?"

She sounded amused, but felt anything but. For, while she refused to believe in them, she'd just been visited by the most appalling premonition. She could hear a thin voice calling out to her, a child's voice, echoing in her head, pleading yet unable to reach her, nor could she reach it for all that struggle on her part.

CHAPTER 40 DAY 20

THE THREE MEN SAT HUNCHED over Styrofoam cups of coffee in a Starbucks on Kingsway.

They looked like prosperous businessmen judging by the Savile row suits and silk ties. One of them, a man with floppy red hair, constantly shot his cuffs, allowing a gold Rolex to peep out as though quite unintentionally, letting it be seen.

The place was packed out, which served their purposes ideally. Their discussion wouldn't be overheard in what amounted to a hastily convened meeting in a poor choice of venue, located as it was not that far from Victoria Embankment and the Yard. They, that is, the Kerkut brothers and DC Harry Ricks.

"Why did we have to meet face to face?" asked Mario. "What's wrong with WhatsApp? Or Teams? Zoom? Anyone could spot us here."

"I don't do social media," grumbled Ricks. "And anyway, I like it better this way."

"If you say so," replied Mario doubtfully. "So what was so urgent it wouldn't wait for a better time and place."

"You're crazy, you know," muttered Ricks.

"Who you calling crazy, mister?" Jason Kerkut leaned forward menacingly, a finger pointing at Ricks's nose, but Ricks just grinned back at him.

"Leave it, Jay," admonished Mario, a restraining hand on his brother's forearm. "Let's hear what he has to say. Alright, Harry?" he asked. "What's the problem?"

"The problem is, you're wasting time and getting nowhere."

"Fuckin' wise guy," muttered Jay, snatching his arm away from his brother's grasp.

"Go on then, Harry," urged Mario. "We're listening."

"You brought the scrubbers in to lower the tone at the clubs, have people stay away, didn't you? Hopefully, buy out the Lamont woman cheap. Use the place for laundering. S'not working, boys."

Ricks fixed each of the Kerkuts with his attention. "Has it not occurred to you two, no-one's staying away. Not even with the killings."

"So, we make her an offer she can't refuse," said Mario.

"What? You mean, rough her up a bit?"

"Whatever it takes," said Mario.

"A bit crude for you, isn't it? Although, come of think of it ..." Ricks looked thoughtful. "When I remember the mess you left at the Dagenham squat for me to clear up. Two dead. How many more?"

"No more, Harry," answered Mario quietly. "That was a one-off and won't happen again."

"A one-off? A one-off?" Ricks leaned back, gazed up at the ceiling ruefully, shaking his head. "Don't make me laugh."

"So, what's on your mind?" asked Mario.

"I'll tell you what's on my mind," Ricks countered. "The Karen Richardson thing."

"Nothing to do with us, Harry," Mario said.

"A bloody joke, if you ask me. Amateurish!" Ricks retorted.

"Who're you calling amateur, mister?" growled Jason.

Ricks threw up his arms in frustration. "I might have known. Christ! Jason. Did she see you? Even get a glimpse? What were you thinking?"

"Alright, Harry, cool it. She's dead now. Jay made a mistake," said Mario, trying to soothe the situation.

CHAPTER 40 • DAY 20 • 257

"A mistake? Is that what you call it? Hell, man. How many other mistakes have there been like that one? Give me a number?"

"None, Harry," replied Mario, looking hopefully at his brother.

"I just hope you're bloody right," said Ricks, idly moving his coffee cup around the table. "Last thing we need right now is a homicidal maniac to deal with."

"Who're you calling a fuckin' homicidal maniac, mister." Jay was getting increasingly restless.

"Alright, Jay. Enough," said Mario. "Let's stick to what we came here to talk about. He's not talking about you."

"Aren't I?" murmured Ricks under his breath.

Then, sounding impatient he asked, "Look, can we get on with this?"

"So, once again, what do you suggest we do, Harry?" Mario turned all his attention now from his brother to Ricks. "We need the clubs. We've got the girls. We can traffic people into the UK. Those four Muslims we brought in paid a fortune. We might bring in more. What's to stop us?" Mario asked.

"Mario," asked Ricks, looking curious. "How did you find those four Muslims you brought over?"

"We didn't. It was suggested to us as a lucrative source of revenue."

"Go on."

"We were scoping out the clubs early on. Probably stood out as we weren't in the usual casualwear the others were sporting."

"And?" encouraged Ricks.

"We were approached. Tall skinny guy, a lot of chat to start off, checking up on us, I guess, but basically said, did we want to earn some money. Big money. Hedged around a bit more, then finally said he knew of Muslims who wanted to come over, but he didn't have the cash or means to bring them in. On a stab in the dark, he said he thought we might be able to do something. He was just working a hunch, that's all."

"But he chose the right people to ask."

"That's right. Said his name was Mikey. He wanted a kickback per unit, and said we could keep whatever else we could make. He'd keep the supply coming. That's how it started, and so far we've had the one trip. Four units, that's four blokes. Bunch of tarts too. Nearly went disastrously wrong. As you know. That's another story, another time. Won't make the same cock-up again."

"Wonder why he wants to bring in Muslims, as against any other groups," said Ricks.

"Working with terrorists? For terrorists? A terrorist himself? Who knows?" said Mario.

Ricks pulled at an earlobe. "Who was this guy? Tall you say?"

"And skinny. Looked half-starved," said Mario. "Probably was, if he was that desperate he needed to approach total strangers with his plans. It was his idea to bring in the girls as well. Enough of them willing to pay big bucks to get into the UK. He made the right guess again, didn't he? Gonna prove useful for us."

"Was he black? White? Oriental?"

"He was white."

"A white terrorist? Muslim? I don't think so. No way."

"Oh, I don't know though," came back Mario. "Muslims from Northern Cyprus, Turkey and so on, they're all white."

"If that's what you think," accepted Ricks. "I'm still a cop, you know, supposedly working on these Clubhouse killings, where you met this bloke. Although, victims are nothing but a load of trans trash. Killer's doing us all a favour if you ask me." Then he noticed Jason glaring at him and turned away, quickly shifting the subject around. "Any distinguishing features?"

"None I can recall." Mario thought about it for a moment. "There was one thing, maybe. It's probably nothing, but I thought I detected a slight northern accent. Maybe Midlands? That's all."

"So, if you traffic people in, Muslims, whatever, you've still got the problem of what to do with those tarts on your hands right now, haven't you."

"They'll earn for us. Even if we don't use them to lower standards at the clubs. The babies will bring in big money."

"Forget the babies. You need to be practical, Mario. For crying out loud. You of all people should know. The squat's a piss house. I wouldn't let my dog live there. Girls have to be fed and clothed. Need to be locked in and supervised all day and all night. Who's got the time? Anyone there right now? Or could the girls just break out?"

"We've got someone, Harry."

"Really? Who've you got?"

"A couple, in fact. One's an old scrubber called Tess. She used to be on the game till she got too old. She's twenty-eight now. Lost her looks. Tough as old boots. She's helped by another ex-hoe, Belinda. Thirty-eight. Looks about ninety. Also hard as nails. They keep the doors locked, girls mostly in their rooms. Unless they're out working. In which case Tess is still around to keep an eye on stuff."

"That's another thing, mate," added Ricks. "No proper sanitation in the squat, filthy bogs and baths. Girls must be starting to stink by now. Not good for trade."

"Harry," said Mario. "We're still buggering around. Why don't we cut to the chase. You're the man with all the bright ideas. So, we're listening. And we're waiting."

"Okay, so here's the deal. And you just need to keep it simple. Mario, you don't seem to know, you're sitting on a goldmine."

"Really? A goldmine?" He stared out the window at the passing traffic. A double-decker rumbled past, casting its shadow into the coffee bar which was getting ever more stifling with the lunchtime crowd. Squeezing past, an attractive young woman, tall with long black hair, possibly an office worker judging by her outfit, bumped into their table, slopping some of the coffee from her cup onto the floor. "Oops! Sorry, mate," she tittered.

"Fuck's sake," grunted Jason.

"Still, no 'arm done, eh?" She moved on, straightening her jacket with her free hand, still giggling.

Seamlessly turning his attention back to Ricks, Mario asked, "So what's this goldmine that I seem to have overlooked?"

"Yeah, wise guy," put in Jason. "What's this fuckin' goldmine?"

"I already said, forget babies, guys. Takes too long. And way too risky. Money's okay, I know. £100K per brat? Right? But that's nine months fucking about. Plus the risks if they cop it. As we've already experienced. And, by the way, just so's you know, if it happens again, I won't be there to clear up the bloody mess. Once was enough."

"For crying out loud, Harry. How much longer are you going to keep us waiting? All day?"

"Okay, okay." He held his hands up as though in surrender. "Offer the girls for sale."

"What?"

"Individually. Mainly to Middle Eastern buyers. They like them young. Younger the better. Under twenty-two years old you'll get £150K, no sweat. Under thirteen, you're talking £250K plus. They like virgins."

"What?" Mario sounded amazed.

"I'm telling you, sell what you've got. Your current stock. How many there, fifteen? Twenty? Clean 'em up. New clothes, make-up, hairdos. Do one or two at a time. Put them up in a smart hotel. Savoy. Dorchester. Hilton. That way, with promises of jobs, travel and big money, they won't be so inclined to run away or need so much supervision. You can get paid in any currency you like. Crypto if you prefer."

"How come we've never got involved in any of this before?" Mario asked.

"Burgeoning trade, my friend. In the supplying countries my contacts check out girls hoping to come to the UK to get jobs. Easy to pick out. I've got guys, "dickers," at the stations who look out for girls on their own, or mothers and daughters. Photo them in railway points of embarkation in Ukraine, Romania, Albania. WhatsApp the pics to guys, my guys, already waiting in UK railway stations who promise the girls jobs as soon as they spot them arriving. Couldn't be easier. Limitless stock of willing young tarts who don't know what they're gonna be in for."

"So whaddaya need us for, mister?" put in Jason.

"Like I said, I'm a cop, Jason. Going to stay that way. On the inside track, as it were. Smell what's going on while making loot selling hoes to rich Saudi Muslims. Working with you two we could clean up. I'll source, you'll sell. I've got all the contacts we'll need to get stock over here. You can concentrate on keeping the girls sweet once they arrive, that is until you can organise sales."

"Been busy, haven't you, Harry?" pondered Mario.

"Division of labour, my friend. Simple as that."

"Been doing this for long?"

"Long enough." Ricks smiled, deliberately fingering the gold watch. "One thing, though. We may have a problem."

"Go on," said Mario.

"There's more and more private security firms employing UK army veterans to intercept the pick-ups before the girls are whisked away. It needs to be dealt with."

"Don't worry, Harry," said Mario reassuringly. "When the girls see two smart guys like us coming towards them, it'll put their minds at rest. We'll park the limo where it can easily be seen. Their eyes'll be popping out. And, we'll deal with the vets if there's an issue."

"Good. One less difficulty," said Ricks.

"How do we split the take," asked Mario.

"Fifty-fifty," replied Ricks, smirking.

Mario smiled back at Ricks shaking his head. "I think not, Harry. There's two of us and one of you. Once you bring the girls in your job's done. We've got to groom them, keep them happy in five-star accommodation. Feed and clothe, only the best. Then negotiate with the Saudis. Up to now you've worked more or less alone. Doing what with the girls you've sourced? Selling them on the cheap into prostitution?"

"I s'pose," said Ricks, looking slightly abashed.

"Have you sold any for £150K? £200K?"

"Not so far," said Ricks.

"Thought not. That's why you've approached us, isn't it? You know we've got the better contacts; and we have, believe me. We'll split three ways. You'll do better than you ever dreamed possible, my friend. My deal. Take it or leave it."

Ricks paused for several seconds, looking irritated, but it was clear he wouldn't improve on the offer. Extending his hand across the table to Mario, he said, "Done."

"Okay, Harry," said Mario. "Now, one more potential problem. Well, two actually."

"Go on."

"The Muslims."

"Ah, yeah. Those four you brought in on the boat. Where are they now?" Ricks asked.

"No idea." He shrugged. "East London, among other places, we heard. But it was a great little earner. Even after paying the skinny guy, Mikey, his kickback."

"Maybe, but like I said we don't want complications. If those four are here to cause trouble."

He paused an instant, then continued, "Have jihads and Christ knows what else, we begin to attract the attention of the anti-terror people. MI5, CTC, SO15, you name it. There's already been that bomb on the Northern Region train. Took out a government man. No leads so far. No-one's claimed credit. Yet. All too risky. We don't need it. I don't need it. Forget the Muslims."

"Alright, Harry, point taken."

"What's problem number two?"

"The black bitch. Pierre. She's poking around. And by all accounts she's good. We've met her." He looked pointedly at Jason, who said nothing.

"Yeah, I've met her too," put in Ricks. "Arrogant fuck. Needs taking down, if you ask me. She was up at the Yard. Now working with Manus and the team. We could have a problem there. Bitten off a lot, she has, by all accounts. But then, she's also managed some meaty deals in the past. I heard she was sniffing about. We also heard about East London, like you, in particular the East London Mosque. That's one place, anyway, where the four have been spotted."

"Interesting. Oscar Mountford wants her…"

"Dead?" exclaimed Ricks.

"Maybe later. But for now, humiliated. Seems a waste of time to me. His choice. He's sore she put him where he is, and he wants revenge. Killing would be too easy, he reckons. Oscar's got some notion she should be put in the frame for murder."

"Do me a favour, Mario. How's that to be managed?"

"I don't know, but Jay and I seem to be somehow committed to it. Far as Oscar's concerned."

"Come on, Mario," said Jay, clumsily getting to his feet. "We're finished here. Let's go."

Outside the coffee bar, as they walked towards the Drury Lane car park, Jason said to his brother, "Ricks don't want us to bother with Muslims. Says we'll earn enough with the hoes. Whaddaya reckon, Mario?"

"I reckon we don't tell him. What he doesn't know won't hurt him. We'll do both, girls and Muslims. He organises the girls coming over. Been doing it for long enough, it seems to me. I'll handle the sales. We'll also deal with the jihadis. Mikey, our club contact. We'll clean up."

"Sounds okay to me, bro."

"Say, Jason, how old is the youngest we've got?"

"About fourteen, maybe fifteen. Why?"

"We'll spruce her up," offered Mario enthusiastically. "Put her in pigtails and a kiddy's dress, make her look like a twelve-year-old, hole her up at the Savoy, introduce her to a Saudi. I know one or two already. If they like the merchandise, they'll introduce us to more customers."

"Two hundred K, Mario? Per sale? Nice, bro. Fuckin' nice." Then Jason stopped for a moment. "He don't like social media? So what's wrong with the fuckin' phone?"

"Maybe, Jay. Take your point. Still, I think he was right; deal like this is better face to face. Worth taking the chance."

Moments after the Kerkuts had left, Ricks's phone bleeped and he saw it was his mother. "Yes?" he said curtly.

"Oh, Harry, love, could you perhaps help me out a bit?"

"Money, is it? Again?"

"Don't talk like that, darling. But you know how it is since your dad passed on."

"You mean died?"

"Harry, you're upsetting me now." She quickly sounded close to tears. "Never used to be like this when Daddy was around."

"How much?"

Swallowing back her sadness, his mother said, "That gardener you sent us, love. I mean after Daddy … Well, the garden was in such a mess. It used to be his pride and joy."

"What do you want?"

"He was so expensive."

"Done a good job, though. Yeah?"

"Not so wonderful. I s'pose he tidied up a bit. But, Harry, I've had to raid my savings. He wanted fifteen hundred pounds."

"Should have thought about that before, shouldn't you. I can't spare that kind of cash. Not made of money, you know."

"Oh, but, Harry, please …" She was crying now.

"Haven't got time for this," said Ricks, cutting the call.

A moment later he tapped out a new number and the call was answered almost immediately. "'Allo, 'arry. Awight?"

"She paid you, she told me."

"Just like you said, fifteen 'undred."

"Okay, Ben. You keep five hundred, I'll have the other grand. Old cow needs to mow her own fucking lawn in the future."

CHAPTER 41 DAY 21

UNSELFCONSCIOUSLY NAKED, the woman walked around the Hilton Hotel suite overlooking the greenery of a gloriously sunny Hyde Park.

In clear view from their window on the fifteenth floor was the eighteen-foot-high statue of Achilles, short sword at the ready in his right hand, round shield held aloft in his left. Commemorating Arthur Wellesley, the Duke of Wellington, the magnificent bronze made from thirty-three tons of cannon captured during the Duke's French campaigns, displayed a magnificent male nudity giving a diametric counterpoint to the woman's statuesque feminine physique.

Almost as tall as Tammy, she was ivory white with long black hair that tumbled to her shoulders.

"That was nice," said Tammy, lying on the huge bed, propped up on one elbow, similarly naked.

"Again?" suggested the woman, coming towards Tammy with a look that suggested she just couldn't wait.

"Coffee first, Aaliyah. I need time to get my breath back. I'm not as young as you."

"Maybe not, but you're no more than thirty? Thirty-two?"

"Thirty-eight," sighed Tammy, "and not getting any younger."

"Well, I'm thirty in two months, you know. Not so much younger than you."

Changing her position to sit up on the bed, her legs bent at the knee, arms wrapped around them, Tammy replied, "Wearing rather better, I'd say."

"You have a beautiful, beautiful body, Tammy. But those scars? Some old, some looking very new. Dov told me you've been in some difficult situations."

"You might say that," Tammy agreed.

"Does it worry you that they show up white against your dark skin?"

"Not really. The surgeons have all done good work. They'll fade to fine lines eventually." Then under her breath, and almost as an afterthought, added, "I hope."

"And I see you are showing tiny stretch marks? You have a child? Children? How did you manage to keep those marks so faint?"

"I've got a baby, few months old. Matty, after my father. And since you ask, I kept the stretch marks to a minimum by using industrial quantities of Bio-Oil. British manufacturing could have operated for a year on the oil I used."

"Ha!" Aaliyah laughed. "You are so funny, darling."

"So, tell me, how long have you been an agent with Mossad? Dov tells me nothing. For all I know he might be married to you."

"I wish," offered Aaliyah, sitting down on the bed next to Tammy and taking her hand in her own.

"Really," said Tammy, sitting up straighter. "I thought..."

"No, darling. I'm like you. Want it every which way."

The thought occurred, though she wasn't sure she wanted to know the answer. But it had to be asked. "So, did you and Dov? I mean, do you and Dov?"

"Once or twice. That's all."

"But..."

"But nothing, Tammy," she said, putting her hand affectionately on Tammy's shoulder. "He hasn't taken vows of celibacy. And promiscuity isn't your sole prerogative, you know."

"It's just that I thought..."

CHAPTER 41 • DAY 21 • 269

"I know what you thought, Tammy. What you're thinking. Hurts, doesn't it, when the boot's on the other foot."

Tammy remained silent.

"It's you he loves, Tammy. You must know that."

"I do. Of course I do. He's told me often enough. But I can't change, Aaliyah. I am what I am."

"Well, don't change, darling. Be what you are. Who you are. But let him be, too. You don't have him in chains, you know. And he's not your little dog, snapping at your heels. He's a gorgeous hunk of independent male."

Tammy nodded dolefully in agreement, then brightening asked, "The coffee?"

"I'll get it," Aaliyah offered, walking towards the coffee-making facilities. "How do you like it?"

"Oh, black please. No sugar."

Side by side once again on the bed, mugs of coffee in hand, Aaliyah said tentatively, "Tammy?"

She guessed what was coming, and had no idea how she was going to respond.

"Is it Dov's baby, darling? I assume it is?"

Glancing down at her coffee, Tammy then looked back at Aaliyah, focusing her gaze before considering her response. The pause was fractionally too long, and immediately perceived by the other.

"Oh my God, Tammy," exclaimed Aaliyah. "It's not Dov's? If it's not Dov's baby, then whose is it?"

"It's not that simple."

"It never is darling."

"It'd take too long to explain."

"You don't know, do you? You don't know whose baby it is, do you?"

"Please don't tell Dov, Aaliyah," she begged.

"I shan't tell him anything, Tammy. But you know how he worries about you."

"Aaliyah, did Dov ask you to see me because he wants to know if Matty is his baby?"

Replacing her mug on the bedside table, Aaliyah said, "Of course not. He wouldn't be so devious. He's a man, darling. So we both know men have no idea how to be artful. If he wants to know something, he'll ask. He must have already asked you by now since you mention it?"

"Okay." She shrugged. "It's come up. Let's leave it there, shall we?"

"Listen, Dov suggested I talk to you to tell you I'd seen Harry Ricks and the Kerkut brothers together in Starbucks."

"Recently?"

"A few days ago."

"How close did you get to them?"

"I was lucky, got a spot near enough to pick up some of what they were saying. I bumped into their table and spilled the coffee of one of them."

"So? What did you hear?"

"Fragments of conversation. They were very sotto voce. But I picked up enough to satisfy me that they're working together. You know we'd already followed the four big men who came over on the boat with the girls to an East London mosque. But this was something different. Names I couldn't catch, but no talk of East London."

"And?" asked Tammy.

"So; here's something you won't know, as yet."

"I'm listening."

"When the boat beached, we recorded the two Kerkut brothers as part of the welcoming committee."

"Why wasn't I told?" complained Tammy, flexing her arms from her sides in frustration.

"We weren't sure ourselves at the time. Dov was going to tell you but decided to let me give you my own first-hand account of the spotting of the three in the coffee house. Something else, Tammy."

"Well?"

"These guys don't mess around. The tillerman was overheard demanding more money for the trip on account of the dangers with the weather."

"What then?"

"They shot him down in cold blood. Local police have been left to work out what's happened. We've not interfered. We don't want anything to cloud the bigger picture, like the local plod getting involved at this stage."

"How do you know what they all look like, Aaliyah?"

"Really? Come on, Tammy. You know who I work for. We're well aware of the Clubhouse killings and a possible connection somewhere between whoever's involved with some of those and the recent train outrages."

"Ricks?"

"We're having him followed. Discreetly. He's been seen entering and leaving what looks like a slum in East London. There's been girls, women, seen coming and going. At first they were traced mainly to the Tilbury Clubhouse, but recently there's been less movement. We don't know what's going on. But girls, some very young-looking, have been seen exiting the place, dressed to the nines and being picked up in a smart limo. Dov said he thought they may be being sold to Middle Eastern buyers looking for underage sex partners."

"And? Are these the girls that were picked up on a beach in Folkestone?"

"Almost certainly."

"Poor kids. Probably risked the Channel crossing in the hope of something better in the UK."

Restlessly getting off the bed, Tammy began to prowl around the room like a caged tiger. "We need to do something fast. But …"

"But … You know we have no arrest powers in the UK."

Aaliyah followed Tammy around the room with her eyes. "I can only let you note the address we have, so you can check him out. And, Tammy, don't jump the gun. Hmm? You need to be sure of your ground before you give John Manus the nod to raid the place. I'll keep you in the loop, don't worry."

"Don't worry?" said Tammy. "I'm practically screaming to get something done." She paused a moment, then asked, "Will I see you again, Aaliyah?"

"Unlikely, darling. I'm back in Israel tomorrow."

"Pity. It would have been good. You're special, you know, Aaliyah."

"I know, darling. But then so are you."

CHAPTER 42 DAY 22

AT JOHN MANUS'S REQUEST Tammy had gone to Charing Cross nick where they were holding a man who fitted the description she'd given of the one seen at the Tilbury club displaying a deep cleft chin.

"He was making himself a nuisance with some of the clubbers and we got a call from Dexie, who was working the bar at the time. You know him, don't you?" asked Manus.

"That's right. He's helpful. Well, they all are. Every reason to be."

"We've pulled him in for an informal chat. He's in one of the interview rooms. Not under arrest, and very belligerent. Only reluctantly agreed to come in."

"Sounds like the man I met," said Tammy.

"But here's the thing," said Manus. "He's got a record going back years. Done time for rape. Carrying an offensive weapon. Affray. He's knifed one person. Slashed their throat. Used a kitchen knife. They survived. Amazingly. Messed-up job."

"Sounds familiar. We've had one of those already, haven't we?" suggested Tammy.

"A more sophisticated weapon this time."

"Perhaps he's learning," said Tammy sardonically. "Perfecting his craft."

"But we've got inconsistencies displayed in each modus suggesting he's unlikely to have been responsible for all of the killings."

"Let's see what he has to say for himself. Should be interesting."

"Would you like to sit in on the interview?"

"Absolutely, John."

Outside the interview room a CCTV screen showed a very angry-looking man, in jeans and sweatshirt, clean-shaven and with a short army-style haircut, restlessly pacing the little room.

Tammy looked. "Him," she said, nodding.

"His name is Patrick Laing."

Once inside the interview room, Tammy and Manus sat at one side of the table on utility plastic chairs, indicating that Laing sit opposite them. A young PC stood inside the interview room at the door.

"Thank you for agreeing to come in, Mr Laing."

Laing sat back in his chair, arms folded defensively across his chest. "I'm thirsty." He sounded belligerent. "I want something to drink. Tea or a coffee."

"This isn't a hotel, Mr Laing. We can manage a cup of water," Manus said, glancing at the young PC, who taking the hint left the room, returning a couple of minutes later with a cardboard cup he placed on the table between the three participants.

Laing gulped it all back, then smiled smugly at Manus and Tammy. "That's what I call service," he said.

Ignoring the taunt, Manus turned to the recording machine on his right and flipped a switch, then announced, "This is an informal interview, Mr Laing, albeit under caution. I am Detective Chief Inspector John Manus and sitting with me is private investigator Tamsin Pierre of Pierre Search and Security.

"I have to advise you that this interview is being recorded. You do not have to say anything. But it may harm your defence if you do not mention when questioned something you later rely on in court. Anything you do say may be given in evidence. Do you understand, Mr Laing?"

"Hmm!" muttered Laing, wiping his lips with the back of his hand. "I suppose."

"For the tape, will you please state your name."

"Patrick Laing," he murmured, barely above a whisper.

"Louder, please? If you would, for the tape."

"Patrick Laing," he said, his voice raised.

"As you have been told, you may seek or be provided with legal representation should you so desire."

"Waste of fucking time," said Laing.

"And you are not under arrest and therefore may leave this interview at any time you choose."

"Don't make me laugh," said Laing, rocking back in his chair.

Ignoring him, Manus went on, "You were asked to come in and assist with our enquiries following complaints from several of the clubbers frequenting the Tilbury venue, that is one of the three centres known as The Clubhouse, and also from the barman, Decimus Debrun, known as Dexie, that you were harassing them."

"What kind of name is that?" he added, running his fingers distractedly through his hair. "A midnight runner, is he? Fucking black poofter."

Sighing, Manus went on, "The Tilbury club, and incidentally the other two venues as well, retains extensive computer records of the dates attendees frequent the clubs, Mr Laing. And it seems that on each occasion a murder has taken place, in or close to the Tilbury venue, you were in attendance."

"Just a minute, boss. What's this got to do with me? You said I was here to answer questions about harassing clubbers? Now we're talking about murder? I think I'll leave now," he said, scraping his chair back and getting to his feet.

Then he stopped short, like a horse suddenly reined in, and stared at Tammy.

"It's you, innit? Tried chattin' me up at the Tilbury. Didn't know whether you was a poofter or a bird."

"You have an extensive record, Mr Laing; you've committed some pretty savage crimes. Why don't you sit down for the moment." Manus indicated the chair which Laing reluctantly sat in again. "This won't take long."

"I done my time," he said sullenly.

"Why do you go to that club, Mr Laing," asked Tammy.

"Beer's good. I live in the area," he said, folding his arms ever tighter over his chest. "No crime to drink there, is it?"

"There must be other pubs with decent beer near you, aren't there?"

"I just picked the wrong nights. Skanks, tarts, queers, trannies. You name it. Something needs to be done. Something is being done. About time too."

"By you, Mr Laing?" asked Tammy. "Are you the one doing something about it right now?"

He shrugged, but didn't answer.

"I think you go there to scope the place out, Mr Laing. Isn't that what you go there for? After all, there's enough indication which nights are LGBTQ. You're not forced to go in."

Again, Laing didn't respond, so Tammy helped him. "No reply? I'll take that as a yes, then."

"Take whatever you want. I broke no-one's neck and didn't cut no-one's bits off."

"You seem to know all about the killings?"

"All on the news. Fucking good reading." And then in an echo of Edward Seward's comments, added, "Someone's got summink right, ain't they."

Opening a blue cardboard file on the table in front of him, Manus extracted some printed sheets, and scanning them said to the man, "Tell me, Mr Laing, where were you on the nights of …" before proceeding to read out all the dates the various murders had taken place.

Laing stared at Manus and Tammy, both amused and perplexed. "Where was I? Where was I," he asked with incredulity. "Where was you, you tosser. How the fuck should I ..."

But holding his hand up, interrupting Laing's fluid flow, Manus said, "I can tell you where you were on at least four of the occasions in question, Mr Laing."

"Oh yeah? Go on then. I'm all ears." He'd folded his arms across his chest again, and leaning back in the plastic chair, which threatened to buckle under his weight, said, "You're a joke, mister. Got nuffink on me, mate.

"Anyway," he said, scraping back his chair once more, "if you ain't arrestin' me, I'm pissin' off."

As Manus and Tammy exited the interview room, Tammy caught the eye of the young PC and pointed to the cup Laing had left behind. "Keep that," she whispered. "The DNA might prove useful."

The PC nodded with a smile and went over to retrieve the article.

Back in the canteen over hot coffees, Manus, who'd noted the exchange, said, "You know, we're supposed to get permission before testing for DNA."

"I know, John. Just curious. Let's see what it throws up, if anything. After all, our killers haven't asked permission to kill."

"Fair enough, Tammy. Can't hurt to check."

Then Tammy said, "He was right of course. We've got nothing on him at all."

"He might have killed Julie Crosbie, you know, broken her neck. Did you see those hands? Then Liz Armstrong. Could be Laing again. Pity about the blurred CCTV images. And Karen Richardson, the almost failed job? I'll get someone to go back in the records to see if there's any similarity between the two killings that might tie Laing to the Richardson murder."

"But less likely the other two, Anna Proby and Rolande Jeffreys. That sort of surgery doesn't seem to be his modus."

"Dead end," said Manus, shaking his head, before adding, "pardon the pun."

"Somewhere," said Tammy, "there's a link between the clubs and the Kerkut brothers. They've brought in a boatload of girls, possibly working the clubs, and at the same time ferried in four potential terrorists."

"You went to one of the mosques, didn't you? Any use?"

"Dubious," she sighed.

"Dressed as a man, I understand?"

"Correct, John. As a man."

Manus sounded pensive. "And now you're planning a repeat performance at Belmarsh."

"We've discussed this already, John."

"I know. I know," he said, holding his hands up in surrender. "You certainly like putting yourself in harm's way, Tammy."

Ignoring the comment, Tammy went on, "The four characters that my friend Dov reported had been followed when they arrived were all there at the mosque in East London when I attended on spec. They've noted and are aware of me, and aware of the gender question I posed, so I can't be seen by them again. I reported to Nick at CTC and he said he's had them under surveillance from the time Dov alerted CTC and MI5 of their presence." She shrugged. "You're probably in the loop here anyway?"

"I am. They all keep me up to date." Manus nodded.

"So that's it. For the moment," she added, drinking coffee from the Styrofoam cup.

"So, as we know, you're involved in two apparently unrelated sets of crimes," suggested Manus. "The Clubhouse killings and the possible terrorist threat?"

Manus's face went unexpectedly red, and his brow shimmered perspiration as he put a hand to his chest, heaving for breath. "Tablets," he muttered, patting down his jacket pockets before finding what he wanted and putting a tablet under his tongue.

"What is it, John?" She felt frantic. Stupidly helpless. "Blood pressure? Heart?"

"I'm fine, Tammy. Really, I'm fine."

"At least let me get you a glass of water," said Tammy, rising to her feet.

"No not necessary. Oh, well, okay. No need to fuss, though."

She was back in a moment and Manus drank gratefully from the tumbler. "Let's move on, then."

He was still perspiring heavily, but the crisis seemed to be over. For the moment, at least. Tammy gazed at him intently, noting him barely perceptibly shake his head, and didn't press him further. Whatever drove the dear man, she would neither fathom nor try to dissuade. "Well, if you're sure," she said doubtfully, before reluctantly continuing.

"As you heard at the COBRA meeting, I was asked if I could handle both investigations at the same time. The reason I said yes was because somewhere I think they're likely tied in together. The four illegal Muslims involved with the girls on the same boat, introduced to the clubs. Not sure yet where the murders fit in with all this, but maybe Pope can come up with some ideas. Is Laing our killer? Or is he one of them? If he is, it doesn't help us with the Muslim link, but then he could be a lone killer. Either way, if we can get to one solution it may well lead to the other. Call it women's intuition." She smiled.

"It's helluva lot to have on your plate at once."

"It is," she agreed, realising the huge affection she was developing for the man and his obvious concern for her safety. "But then I've got CTC, MI5, SO15 and the whole of the Met behind me, haven't I?"

"True enough." Manus smiled. Then he asked, "Are you really still intent on going to jail, Tammy?"

"Yes, very much so. I know it's risky, John." She held up her hands as Manus had a few moments ago. "But I think the man Dominic Pope, a convicted and unique killer, might know something I can use. Whatever it is I may be able to glean from him. Prison tends to have a calming effect on some miscreants."

"Some, maybe. Not all."

He stared off at nothing in particular, then said as though an afterthought, "But Pope? Really?"

"I just don't know. But these are unusual crimes, involving specifically transsexuals; and any avenue, however unconventional, is worth chasing."

"If you say so," Manus responded dubiously.

"Then again, looking at the terrorist element. We know of several extremists inside who might hopefully have begun to mellow."

"I wish I had your optimism, Tammy. How about all those who've become radicalised instead?"

"I am aware," she answered, feeling the first seedling of doubt in her own mind. "It's a chance I'll have to take. Needs must when the devil drives."

"God, I hope not," Manus said, catching her glance. "I say again, I wish you luck, Tammy. Can't say I have your faith in what you're going to do. For what it's worth, it's been a while since there were any incidents in or near any of the clubs."

She reached to put a restraining hand on Manus's wrist, counselling earnestly, "Best not to tempt providence, John."

CHAPTER 43 DAY 23

DAISY MEEKINS WAS JUST TURNED SIXTEEN, the age of consent, when she visited a Clubhouse venue for the first time. The apple of her father's eye, he'd not turned a hair when she'd guiltily confessed to preferring women to men.

"It is what it is, love," he'd said with a smile. "And you are what you are. And that's my beautiful daughter."

"Really?" she'd asked, having expected a very different answer from her retired army officer parent. Alexander Meekins, who lived with his wife and daughter in prestigious Rainham, Essex, one of the most desirable of the Medway towns, had been brought up in a traditional British home. Public school followed by a career in the army, and later, unexpectedly from his own point of view, a successful life as a property developer.

His daughter had been born almost three months prematurely, after her mother, Sarah Meekins, started contractions early when she'd fallen while running for shelter from a storm. She weighed just three pounds when she was born. Their local GP, aware of the difficulties her mother had had conceiving at forty-four, had said, "I want to make sure we keep this baby."

But they needn't have fretted, for Daisy was a feisty tot and gradually caught up, until she could face the others in her class at school on their terms. Still small, she was just five feet one, she had the strength and constitution of an ox.

It led her into gymnastics, where her physique and agility made her a competitor of almost Olympic standard. But the Olympics were not what she was aiming for, despite her PE teacher's constant pressure. Daisy wanted to be a nurse and carer, ideally of elderly people. Her own mother was now sixty years of age and with health issues emerging during the pregnancy had aged prematurely.

Like her husband, Sarah Meekins was not fazed in any way by their daughter's confession. As a teenager she'd known herself what it was for the all-enveloping pash for another girl that could emerge from nowhere.

"Call me when you're ready, and I'll pick you up," Alexander offered. Easily tired, the couple tended to turn in early and Daisy, aware of that and her father being eight years older than his wife, felt she was quite capable of seeing her own way home.

She was of the generation that seldom had much time for the news. Nonetheless, there'd been enough local talk of the killings, principally in the Tilbury area, and of the fact that there seemed to be a blessed lull. She'd initially decided to go up West to a Soho club she'd heard of, and not told her parents about her last-minute change of mind. A schoolfriend she was meeting had suggested the Clubhouse in Tilbury, close to the docks, as being sufficiently decadent in their young minds, to obviate the need for the longer journey into London. Alexander, had he known, would have forbidden it.

And it had been worth it. She and her friend had danced together, cuddled and eventually kissed. It was uninhibited heaven, and they planned to travel home together. Except that events don't always pan out the way you expect and they'd become separated in the throng during the course of the evening, unable to connect by mobile due to the poor signal. Still, Daisy knew she'd be safe as groups of clubbers tended to leave together.

Before leaving home, she'd said, "Bye, Pops. Love you."

"You too, elfin," his nickname for her, "take care."

"Always, Dad." She grinned happily.

And in the end, it would work out fine with Daisy aiming to catch the last train home from Tilbury, a twenty-minute fast connection to Rainham. Pops would never know.

Except once again things hadn't quite worked out as she'd planned.

Her mother, already weary, had taken to her bed early. If only she had more energy these days. But her age and the pregnancy had taken their toll. She'd see her treasure in the morning. God's gift. And so unexpected when it had happened, at last.

*****

Just seen a little buttercup. A pixie. Those legs. To die for. To die with. Even because of...?

Skirt's much too short. She'll catch her death. As it were. Wonder what she's hiding under it. Is she a she? Or is she not? Hee, hee, hee.

I'm suited and booted. Always look smart. Gives the girls confidence when we meet.

But why do they insist on walking alone? In the dark? Don't they know how dangerous it is? There's people out there. Some of the girls leaving the club ...

She needs to be told. Accompanied. I'll see to it. My good deed for the day. Friends with benefits. Not lonely anymore.

Love it. Love it all.

CHAPTER 44 DAY 24

THE UNTRACEABLE TEXT said simply:

WATCH YOUR BACK TRANS BITCH.
YOUR TURN NEXT.

She was hardly surprised, indeed had expected something of the sort would find its way to her at some stage. Thought it might have come sooner.

Yet still, the message when she read it left her profoundly disturbed. It hadn't been the first threatening message she'd received, thinking about those cryptic missives she'd been sent warning her off in recent cases, and it wouldn't be the last. But somehow the personal threat here seemed more acute.

Resolving to put it out of her mind, at least for now, particularly in view of the latest development, she addressed the team. She'd immediately picked up the sense of dejection in the room. An uncomfortable shuffling of feet, eyes focusing on anything and nothing. Not altogether surprising considering the lack of progress thus far and the brutality of the murders.

"As you will all be aware there has been another killing." Facing the group, Tammy was as sombre as everyone else. Most of them were seated at their workstations on the fifth floor, New Scotland Yard on the Victoria Embankment. "Discovered in the early hours, we're waiting for pathology to give us an approximate time of death. My guess would be around midnight when numbers at Clubhouse tend to thin out."

A handful preferred to remain standing, among them DC Harry Ricks, who openly sneered at her whenever he caught her attention. She was perfectly in touch with what he was trying to do and wasn't in the least fazed. There was something about the man, his open hostility. It was unlikely with his attitude he'd ever make commissioner. So far he hadn't made it past detective constable, having failed his exams more than once, she'd heard. Yet, the Rolex? The expensive suits?

"Our victim lived in Rainham, Essex. Just a short walk for her from the club to Tilbury railway station," she continued. "About ten minutes, or half a mile in fact, so presumably she felt safe to be on her own. Security cameras, even with the supplementary ones fitted, operate outside the premises but hardly film much further than the entrance, as you know. So, no help there."

"Tammy?" This from a young, pale-faced constable from the back of the room.

"Yes, Lenny." She'd made a point of committing as many of their names to memory as possible. It was flattering to be remembered, and at the same time it helped to produce cooperation from a team, wherever based, and thence results.

"Is the gov coming in this morning?"

"On his way, Len. Been held up but should be here shortly."

Tammy surveyed the room before continuing, then noticed one of the WDCs, in a navy-blue hijab, with a raised hand. "Yes, Farida?"

"Is the modus the same in this murder as in the previous?"

"I'm afraid so. One significant difference which I'll deal with in a moment." Tammy strode back and forth, like a university lecturer, gripping the lapels of her denim jacket as she talked in order to see and be seen by as many of those present as possible.

Before she could add anything, Ricks smirked. "I hear this Daisy was going through the process of hormonal reassignment before arranging surgery."

"Really. That's news to me, DC Ricks," Tammy sighed. "And where did you glean that pearl of information, may I ask? The body was only discovered hours ago."

Ignoring Tammy's enquiry, Ricks went on, "Let me guess, the killer did it for him. Helped him reassign."

There was a murmur of astonishment among the detectives.

"DC Ricks, you're already out of date. Pathology has confirmed in their opinion, and on an initial cursory examination, Daisy was a biological woman. We've heard nothing at this end to suggest otherwise."

Becoming hardened to crimes of this nature through experience was one thing, a macabre sense of humour such as Ricks displayed was anything but funny.

Pointedly disregarding the DC's last comment, Tammy made to continue, but was interrupted again by Ricks, who was standing with his legs spread, arms folded belligerently across his chest. "Don't you think with the way you look you could be up in the firing line yourself some time? Doesn't it bother you?"

Not to be put off, Tammy said, "Thank you for your concern, DC Ricks. I'm touched. Now, don't you think we might move on? We're not here to discuss my prospects."

It was his following remark that left her ice cold.

"After all, who knows? It could be your turn next."

Your turn next? That contact this morning? Whatever Ricks was up to Tammy didn't have him pegged as a murderer. Still, the text could easily be a touch of mischief, designed to unsettle her, which it had. A grinning Ricks was clearly enjoying himself, having detected her discomfiture. Something she hoped the rest hadn't logged on to.

Before she could respond, John Manus walked in, in his overtight suit, looking as florid as usual. "Morning, Tammy. Morning, everyone." There were no apologies for his tardiness, nor any expected. "Tammy been filling you in, has she?" There were murmurs of assent.

"Particularly horrific murder, body badly hacked about, emphasis on the sex organs again. Likely penetration with a knife. We're awaiting further from pathology. God help us. The significant difference, Farida, was the fight that Daisy put up, unlike the others so far. I'll dwell on that in a moment."

Ricks made no comment.

"Anything else, gov?" a keen young DC at the front addressed Manus.

"Tammy?" Manus turned to her. "I know you went down there particularly early."

"Yes. I checked out the space outside the police tapes, beyond SOCO's immediate area of interest, and found one thing." Holding up a plastic evidence bag, she announced, "This button. Spotted it in the gutter. There's generally a lot of detritus near any of the clubs in the early hours, but anything and everything that might have helped us had been washed away leaving the kerbs clear. All except this heavy gold and silver military button."

Then Manus intervened, holding up a second evidence bag. "One more thing, Tammy. Forensics found this tiny strip of cloth grasped in Daisy's palm."

"Have they tested it for DNA yet, John?"

"Scheduled," he replied. "And marked urgent."

"You think the button and the bit of cloth could have come off the clothing of our killer," asked Farida.

"It's a real possibility. During a struggle any one of our victims might have grabbed the button, albeit not deliberately, pulling it free of a jacket or coat, whatever the killer was wearing. So it might not have involved Daisy. The cloth is the more useful clue at this stage. Remember, all the killings were carried out within a hundred-yard radius of each other."

"Is that it, then?" said Ricks, whose fatuous interruptions were starting to annoy Tammy.

"Be quiet, Ricks," admonished Manus. "Unless you've got something useful to add.

"Daisy Meekins put up a tremendous fight. Poor, poor kid," said Tammy, seeking to hide her own distress, indicating the big screen and display boards where pictures of all the murder victims together made for a gruesome chamber of horrors.

She touched the screen, pointed to Daisy. "Look at the marks on her arms, her face and upper chest. It's as though her attacker might first have tried to strangle her with some sort of tie; see the bruises on her neck? Marks of a ligature? SOCO found some cloth fibres to support this theory, which forensics will go over.

"When that didn't work the killer resorted as in previous killings to the knife. A straight blade again this time. Left-handed killer. A signature repeated. Can't imagine why they tried strangulation when the only other like it was the one who actually killed inside the club. It singles out this case. Was our killer the same man? Or was he merely emulating the first in the hope of confusing us? Who knows?

"We're scratching around here, I know," she went on. "I think you'll need to go through all the victims' phone records. Look for patterns, look for numbers that might indicate any contacts in common."

Farida said, "We have done that already, Tammy."

"I know it's a long slog," Tammy conceded. "But still ..."

"Do it again, Farida," interrupted Manus, pulling at his too-tight shirt collar. "Lenny can help you."

"Yes, gov."

"Thank you, Tammy," Manus said. "If you leave the button on the evidence table for the team to view. For the rest of you, get over to the clubs again, talk to people. Think, have you missed anything, however trivial."

Tammy put in, "I'll get over to forensics to see if they've picked up anything further. Incidentally, when you people go down to the Tilbury club to question staff and so on, take a look at the lockers, get staff to agree, of course. See if you can find any article of clothing with a button missing."

"Are you saying it could be a member of staff at Tilbury," Lenny asked.

"Nope," Tammy responded. "Unlikely. After all, you don't spit on your own doorstep, to put it gently." There was a ripple of eased tension.

"But we leave no stone, et cetera."

"So," said Manus, "I'm not going to spend more time trying to find a motive. We've all spent time considering hate, revenge, thrill or sexual intention, and come up with nothing remotely plausible."

Tammy watched as the mood in the room fluctuated from intrigue to horror, back to the sense of hopelessness with which she'd been greeted on entering the place.

"As before, I want you to talk to Daisy's next of kin. That is the parents. Once they've been told," said Manus, "I dread to think what their reaction will be. They've already reported their daughter missing."

He paused a moment, then continued, "Bill, can you organise FLO? They'll need all the support they can get. I think she was probably the youngest of our victims. Then, look to school friends. Other than the Clubhouse, where else did she hang out? If anywhere. You all know the routine. Repeat it, over and over, if necessary, with all the others, too."

"I'd also suggest talking to Hester, the Clubhouse owner," offered Tammy. "She's there most of the time. The barman, DJ, is also worth chatting to."

"Thanks, Tammy," said Manus. "Also, let's have another look at the PNC. The National Computer's come up with nothing so far resembling what we've got, but still,

CHAPTER 44 • DAY 24 • 291

Farida? Will you check this out? I must re-emphasise, no stone unturned."

"Yes, gov," she answered, looking pleased she'd been entrusted with something important and specific.

"You know, John, we might have another chat with both Seward and Laing. Laing in particular could fit the bill. Made it clear he doesn't like trans people or gays."

"Got quite belligerent when we questioned him," said Manus.

"Mind you," added Tammy. "A lot of what Laing said was echoed in Seward's attitude."

"Worth another go, Tammy. I'll have DI Bill Jenner talk to them, see if he can bring out anything new. He's been working late, among other things, mugging up on these cases. Unique, he says, in his experience. I'll have him liaise with you."

"Okay, thanks. I think that's it for the moment. A lot of work ahead of us," said Tammy.

"Not got very far, have you, miss?" Ricks gloated.

Ignoring the further interjection, Tammy added, "We've highlighted that there could be any number of killers involved. So for now, we'll keep an open mind on that front."

"Pick a card," gloated Ricks.

"I've said, that's enough, Ricks. If you've got nothing useful to add I suggest you keep quiet. Maybe attempt to do your job," snapped Manus.

Ricks shrugged, but said no more.

Manus added, "Thanks for the input, Tammy."

"No problem," she responded. "Your call now, John. You've got my take on the matter. I'll see what I can add as we go along. Heaven help us, let's hope we stop this before there are any more."

"All right, team," said Manus, addressing the room. "Let's get to it."

Tammy's mobile bleeped and she saw it was a text from the Home Office pathologist, Raymond Hawley, whom she'd first met while investigating the case of the missing wife of politician Oscar Mountford now presently in prison for multiple murders.

It simply read,

> Can you come in now, urgently? I've got something I think you ought to see.

CHAPTER 45 DAY 24

"BODY'S BURNED BEYOND RECOGNITION. All we've got, as you can see, is the skeletal remains and some lumpen traces of charred flesh."

The white-coated pathologist Raymond Hawley, middle-aged and on the short side, a somewhat harassed-looking gentleman, spoke with a slight American burr.

Inside the room was glaringly lit by banks of overhead fluorescent lights. The floor was covered in a slip-resistant, hygienic, and totally impermeable composition. The walls were white-tiled. Laid out in parallel were half a dozen stainless-steel slabs on supporting cylindrical bases, all bearing bodies discreetly covered, with the exception of the one presently being viewed. Along a side wall was a series of stainless-steel sinks and taps. And over each slab was an all-seeing, all-recording eye.

There was a strong smell of chemicals, not necessarily identifiable, but enough to assail the nostrils, and Tammy found herself half consciously wrinkling her nose.

Accompanying Tammy to examine the corpse, besuited Detective Inspector Bill Jenner, mentioned by John Manus, and now brought in to assist on the case. A tall individual, greying at the temples and in his fifties, he leaned over the remnants of a human being on the slab. Bill had thoughtfully been seconded to Tammy by Manus, who was otherwise tied up, with the object of giving her someone to bounce ideas and observations off. Bill was very much on a par with John Manus in terms of experience, the two having worked together on innumerable cases over the years.

"Can you tell whether it's male or female?" he asked the pathologist.

"Oh, male," came the emphatic response. "From skeletal remains we can identify cause of death, ancestry, and therefore race, age, height, and of course gender."

Tammy raised an enquiring eyebrow, absently straightening her denim jacket.

"Really? Can you be that sure?" queried the DI, pre-empting Tammy's intended question.

"Absolutely. Let me show you what I mean. First off, look at the comparatively narrow hips. A fairly sure initial sign we're looking at a male. Then, the subpubic angle is greater in females in order to facilitate childbirth." The pathologist pointed out the angle in the pelvis he was referring to. "That's male," he added, looking the DI in the eye as though anticipating a response, before going on.

"Furthermore, the robust nature of the skull is another signal we're looking at a man. Then again, males invariably have brow ridges, while females do not. The male chin is squarer, the forehead likely to slant back more than that of the female. The female skull is generally more rounded. Need I say more?" asked Hawley, resolutely clasping his fingers together in front of him.

"Sounds very much beyond dispute," said the DI.

Without making any response, the pathologist walked around the body as though deep in thought.

"You know, we also did some DNA testing on what we could find clinging to the skeleton uncorrupted by the fire. Not much, I can tell you. But we removed some of the teeth and found areas of the lower jaw within which one of the teeth had been embedded. We extracted some bone, enough to gain some of the DNA I referred to, and again, this was definitely male."

Sighing, he carried on, "The femur, largest bone in the body, gives another likely indication of gender, being generally shorter in the female. In this case the individual will have been at least six feet tall. Further, the acetabulum, the socket that secures the head of the femur, is larger in males.

Also, look at the throat. See? The laryngeal prominence is greater in the male."

"I think I understand." The DI nodded.

"I could still give you much more. Does that satisfy you so far?"

"Not entirely." The DI stroked his chin and, looking thoroughly perplexed, gazed at the skeletal remains from different angles as though a varied view might provide more answers.

"But really, Detective Inspector, what more could you possible hope for or expect at this stage?"

"You see," Jenner explained, "the fire that this skeleton was located in was that of a women's shelter. We've a list of all those that were there at the time the place went up, and I can tell you now, there were only females. No males' names given to us at all."

"Are you the SIO on this case?"

The DI stood away from the slab, stretched his back and sighed. "No. That's my colleague, DCI Manus. John Manus. I'll be reporting this visit to him later on."

"Am I to expect further fatalities from this fire?" asked Hawley.

"No," said the DI. "All the others got out, or were already out safely. This was the only individual that died. We're questioning those not too shocked to see if we can get an ID. Someone should be able to help. We need to know who he is, or was, and what he was doing in a women's shelter."

The pathologist moved back to stand next to Tammy and shoved his hands into the pockets of his white coat. "It might interest you to know, Detective Inspector, that despite the severity of the fire, and the state of the corpse, a partially melted name bracelet in nine carat gold was found on the wrist of the corpse. It's on the exhibit table over there."

He pointed to where he meant, and Tammy, following his eyes, went and picked up the bracelet before studying the largely erased name.

"C dot Udlow?" she wondered. "Or Budlow? Rudlow? I give up." She shrugged. "It's a lead of sorts, I suppose."

Hawley nodded, then put in, "There were still shreds of clothing adhering to the skeleton when it was found." He indicated a few fibres to illustrate the point.

"Nothing distinctive there," said Tammy. "Apart, perhaps, from that bit of clothing you've drawn our attention to. What would you call that colour, anyway? Violet, amethyst?"

"Take your pick." The DI looked down at the bones arrayed on the slab, and muttered, "Poor bloke."

"Poor bloke? Actually, I don't think so. At least I'm not sure." The pathologist caught the DI's attention again.

"How's that? You don't think so? Whyever not?"

"Because the clothes found on the body, what was left of them, were women's clothes, Detective Inspector. Look over there."

He pointed to a stainless-steel table where further fragments had been laid together like a macabre jigsaw puzzle. No doubt about it, they were all looking at a dress.

"What's that?" asked Tammy.

"You heard me," explained the pathologist. "I said women's clothes. What we're looking at here is, I'm betting, an example of either a transsexual or else a cross-dressing individual."

"So, a male dressing as a female?" put in the DI, sounding perplexed.

"Could be, but until we've done further DNA tests we won't know if this person had had female hormone therapy," said Hawley, pushing his hands back in the pockets of his white coat.

"Don't get it," said the DI.

"What don't you get, Bill?" said Tammy, getting further involved.

"None of it. A man can't just decide he's a woman by putting on women's clothing."

"I think you're wrong, Bill. You see, irrespective of the pathology you are what you self-identify as."

"Really? So if I call myself a woman, I'm a woman?"

"Yes. But only if you really believe it to be so. That is if you think, act and feel like you imagine a woman does."

"I'd agree," said the pathologist.

"So you see, Bill, if this is not a cross-dresser, this is likely a woman. At least in her own mind. Not sure we can argue with that. Do you understand?"

Jenner shrugged, and just looked blank.

"Let me go on, then," offered Tammy. "Look at me frankly, Bill. I've a man's physique, I'm nearly six one, have a male outlook that relies more on logic than intuition, female reproductive organs, high levels of testosterone giving rise to male muscle definition and a deep voice. But I am a woman. And I mean, all woman. And yes, I do enjoy relationships with both men and women."

"Okay. I think I see where you're coming from," Jenner responded, still sounding doubtful. "But what about children. Do you have …? I mean, can you have …?"

"I'll say, I can have." Tammy grinned. "I am the besotted mother of little Matty. My baby boy. As I said, I am a woman. Need I add anything?"

"Right, I think I've got it," said Jenner, smiling at last. "That's something about being in the police."

"What's that," said Tammy.

"You never stop learning."

"One more thing you should be aware of," said the pathologist, interrupting the other two.

Tammy and the DI turned to him with interest.

"We're listening," said Tammy.

"This woman wasn't burned to death."

"What?" exclaimed the DI. "What do you mean, wasn't burned to death. How else did she die, if not in the fire?"

"Not immediately clear perhaps from the damaged bones we have." He indicated the area below the skull. "But this person suffered a broken neck," said Hawley. "The hyoid bone is fractured, a common cause of asphyxiation."

"Murder, then?" asked Tammy.

"We've more," explained Hawley, in the impersonal attitude of a university lecturer.

"See?" He pointed one long finger to the spinal column in the area of the neck before continuing. "There are seven cervical vertebrae. Look, numbers C6, C7 situated below the skull occur closest to the shoulders. Observe closely numbers C4 and C5 and you will note the transverse cut?"

"Now you point it out," said Jenner, "it's pretty clear."

Tammy nodded her understanding as well.

"What we have here," continued Hawley, "is cause of death being a slash occasioned by a straight-edged knife, with power enough to cut through neck muscle and nerve tissue penetrating as far as the spinal vertebrae. Any deeper and the head would have been severed. Incidentally, this was almost certainly a left-handed killer."

"Good grief," murmured Tammy.

"This individual was dead before the fire ever started," the pathologist went on. "So you were correct, Ms Pierre, this is a clear case of murder. And if you want my opinion," he added, "whilst it has much in common with the other street killings, what separates this one is the sheer ferocity of the attack."

He regarded his visitors. "I would add, it's likely the killer was known to the victim."

"Why do you say that, Mr Hawley?" Tammy asked.

"Because there are no signs on the skeletal fingers of any attempt to deflect a knife. Normally, there'd be cuts to the metacarpal bones and phalanges, where the flesh had been penetrated during an attempt to repel an attack, hold back a knife."

"I see," said Tammy.

"In my professional opinion," Hawley continued, "this bears all the hallmarks of a revenge killing."

CHAPTER 46 DAY 25

"TAMMY?"

"What's the problem. You sound alarmed. Talk to me."

It had been a sunny start to the day, brightness beaming into the small modern office complex. She'd finally got around to sitting at her desk for long enough to start catching up with texts, emails and telephone voicemails. Mrs Gilchrist had looked in from time to time with apparently mixed feelings about the chaos on Tammy's work surface, together with a satisfied acknowledgement that the mountainous backlog was finally being addressed.

"We've got a man standing outside the club. My main one in Tilbury, that is. I've seen him outside a few times, but it never gelled that he was suspicious. I think he may have been inside once or twice as well. Can't be certain. More obvious when he's on his own. Easy to miss when there's a large crowd. But, you see, I've recently seen him outside Dagenham and also Dartford.

"He was here last night when I looked out at around midnight, saw him following one of the kids. At least, that's what it looked like. I was going to run after him to see if she was alright. But to be honest, Tammy, I was a bit scared. Chickened out. I'm sorry. He's a big fellah."

"Why didn't you call me, then?"

"I don't know. It was late, and, and ..."

"Okay, calm down."

Unable to resist the itch, she helped herself to a panatella, the first in some time, ignoring Mrs Gilchrist's disapproving glare as she brought in more papers for Tammy's signature. You're not supposed to inhale cigars, but somebody forgot to tell Tammy, who gulped a lungful contentedly, feeling her head swim.

"Go on, then," she prompted, tapping the glowing tip into the large glass Art Deco dolphin ashtray.

"I could see them at the end of the road, he was getting closer, like he was going to say something to her. Then just as he reached out to touch her shoulder, a car came past, and he pulled back, started walking in the opposite direction."

"You say he's there now?"

"That's right."

"I'll be there in twenty," said Tammy, dragging her jacket from the back of her chair and rushing from the office to the astonishment of her PA, who eschewed the desire to question her boss.

In the short time since leaving the office it had clouded over heavily, angry skies making the atmosphere gloomy and threatening. Pulling up near the club, Tammy spotted the man immediately. In a black T-shirt and chinos, clean-shaven, with hair down to his shoulders, he was taller and burlier than Patrick Laing, whom she'd questioned fruitlessly.

She watched him for a while as he wandered up and down the quiet street, appearing aimless, occasionally peering in at the club as though contemplating whether to go in. Her eyes narrowed. There was something odd about the guy, nothing she could put her finger on. Just a vague notion that something here wasn't right.

Favouring the direct approach, albeit a cautious one, Tammy addressed the man, introducing herself.

"What!?" he said, leaning back as though he'd been hit, and gazing down his nose at her quizzically.

"I said hi, I'm Tammy. I haven't seen you around this area before."

The man frowned back at her but said nothing, merely bunching his shoulders and stuffing his hands in his pockets.

"Would you like to come into the club? They do a nice set lunch at the bar. Steak and chips? Fish and chips?"

"I watch the girls," he said, so softly she could barely hear him. "When they come out in the night."

"Do you now?" said Tammy. "You like that, do you?"

"They're like porcelain."

"How's that, sir?"

Talking to himself he offered, "Beautiful and fragile."

She tried to make eye contact with the individual, but without success. "You like porcelain, do you?"

"It needs constant polishing and protecting." He sounded concerned at the prospect of any piece being damaged.

"Is that what you do, then? Polish and protect it. Do you have any porcelain of your own?"

"I follow them sometimes. Make sure they're safe. They don't like it when I try to talk to them. They run away, some of them, all of them. I don't mean to frighten them. My little porcelain flowers," he whispered.

"You haven't told me your name," Tammy urged.

The man leaned across Tammy menacingly; he smelled of lavender. "Name? Whose name? What do you want to know my name for?"

"Just being sociable." She shrugged, smiling in what she hoped was an encouraging manner. "I told you I'm Tammy. What's your name?"

After several seconds he replied, "Hector."

"Well then, Hector. Do you have a second name?"

Another long pause, then, "Binns. I'm Hector Binns," he muttered.

"Do you think any of the girls get scared when you try to talk to them, Hector?"

"Some of them are boys. Men." He gave it some thought, then added cryptically, "I know. I've seen."

"What have you seen, Hector? Tell me?" she urged, aware she was making little progress.

He looked as though he was having difficulty marshalling his thoughts. "People coming out of the toilets. The wrong ones. I see these things."

"Do you now? Something wrong there, Hector? Something you don't approve of?"

"It doesn't seem right."

"Tell me, then."

Making eye contact with Tammy for the first time, Hector said, "I'm a gentle man unless people make me angry."

"What do you do then? Hmm? If they make you angry?"

"My mum always said she wanted a girl. But she got me instead."

"Does that upset you?"

"I try to talk to them when they leave the club. When they're on their own."

"I think I understand, Hector," she said solicitously, before adding, "and tell me why, then?"

"Why? I'll tell you why. To find out how they do it."

"Do what, Hector?"

"Get to be a girl. So I can make Mum happy. But they always run away. The girls. At least I think they do. Porcelain breaks so easily. I've seen at least one or maybe two, broken. Shattered. Lying in the gutter."

"Did you break them, Hector? Did they annoy you when they couldn't help with your questions?"

"I don't know," he murmured. "I saw someone else with the girls. I don't think it was me."

CHAPTER 47 DAY 26

"IT'S A BAD LINE, OSCAR. Say again?" Mario Kerkut was disturbed from sleep when the call came through at 2.00 am, and not best pleased being woken at that hour.

"I said, Ricks has picked up some mumblings on the grapevine."

"What sort of mumblings?" Mario turned over, shoving aside the naked young blond, who murmured her irritation.

"It seems our meddlesome private investigator may be planning to have herself incarcerated in one of His Majesty's securer residences."

"What the hell for? Is she mad? And anyway where, Holloway?"

"Apparently not. She's a bit more ambitious than that."

"So, which one does she have in mind? No, don't tell me, Wakefield?"

"You may not be too far from the truth."

"Come on, Oscar! Wakefield?" Mario sounded incredulous. "That's a men's facility, for crying out loud. What's she planning to do there, be the resident tart? Do their tea and cakes? A bit of cooking and mending?"

"Ricks tells me she's been roped in by the Yard to see if she can help with these East London murders they're scratching around with."

"How's going to a men's lock-up going to help?"

"Ricks thinks she may want to talk to anyone who knows anything about multiple murders. Maybe find an actual serial killer and see if they've a handle on who or what might be going on here. Just any info, links, hints she can pick up. Whatever."

"What's wrong with asking a prisoner during visiting?"

"Nothing. Only no-one is going to confide in their past as a killer to a stranger across a visitor's table. If you want insight, confessions, hints as to someone's involvement, you need complicity. Trust. Confidence."

"What? From a convicted serial killer? That's a long shot, isn't it? Who's she hoping to team up with, Jack the Ripper's great grandson?"

"Who knows? Press are already labelling the killings work of the Tilbury Ripper."

"I don't look at the news."

"I'm making an educated guess she'll have to go in disguised as a male. Bloody lunacy, if you ask me. No other way she'd gain admittance. Except as a visitor, which we've discounted. So it looks as though she's going to try to fool them."

"Really? What about the medical? The shower block?"

"Some of the prisons have a percentage of single-cell occupancy. Inmates, like in this dump, Mario, don't walk around in the nude. We go to the individual shower stalls in our shorts, in some cases T-shirts. There's no more slopping out. It's ancient. Cells have their own bogs these days."

"Mmm!" mused Mario. "I suppose, she is around six one, flat chest. Broad shoulders. She might just get away with it … But for how long? A few hours? And what's she going to do about the audience when she has a shit or piss. She'll be on full view. If she's discovered, they'll crucify her. Places are full of bloody psychopaths."

"Thing is, if Ricks can find out where she is he can get word inside and we can have her dealt with."

"That'll save me and Jason the trouble."

"You haven't exactly been active on that front, Mario. She's still walking the streets and in one piece. Not what I had planned."

"She's hard to pin down. Doesn't stick to any routine we could track."

"If you want a job to be done ..." Oscar's voice rose.

"Okay, Oscar. Cool it."

"Don't tell me to cool it, you total cretin. When I get out of here ..."

"How're you going to get out, Oscar," Mario interrupted. "They'll never let you go. You know that, come on, man. You're inside for good."

"I don't think so, Mario."

"I'm listening." Mario grunted as his companion shifted on the bed. "Chrissake, woman."

"My lawyers are working on appeals against all the convictions."

"You've got, what? Four murder convictions against you? Including your own son? Your PA? That security man? Then there's the pilot who killed your boy. How can you possibly overturn them all? You'll get no press or public sympathy. You're rated as a monster."

"All circumstantial evidence, Mario. Not one iota of real proof. Everything based on unreliable testimony from one, a convicted criminal and two, a lawyer lying through his teeth, thinking he'd get a reduced sentence by turning King's evidence. Which the latter, incidentally, didn't work out. He will be inside for the rest his life. Otherwise, if he ever came out and I'd gained my freedom, I'd make him wish he'd stayed inside. I'd have the fucker shredded."

"Okay, Oscar, I wish you luck." Mario sounded genuinely alarmed, no doubt thinking of his own future if things went seriously awry.

"Tell you something else, Mario."

"Yeah?"

"That train bomb that killed the Under-Secretary to the Defence Secretary?"

"You?"

"Use your imagination, Mario. If you have any. They think it was an Islamist cell. Terrible people, the Muslim community. Amazing what you can organise from jail with a little connivance from the warders. And, of course, Harry Ricks. Complicated man, our Mr Ricks. Difficult childhood, I believe." He spoke through a hiccupping fit of laughter.

"A lot of people died, Oscar."

"Sheep, my man. Just sheep. Watch out for more where that came from."

Then Mario's voice changed as he addressed his bed companion, "Whaddaya mean you're trying to sleep? I pay you enough, don't I? You don't like it, you piss off, Daria. You get preferential treatment here, 'cos I choose to give it. Look after the bitches, Okay? That's your job. Keep them quiet, sure. But don't push your luck. There's plenty more where you came from, missy. Got a house full of you scrubbers, haven't I."

"Alright, lover boy," she nuzzled his cheek, wanting to vomit but keeping up the pretence.

"It's not luck I want," said Oscar, resuming the dialogue, "but a competent defence lawyer. Then maybe I'll get out of this shithole and deal with things myself, rather than relying on incompetent people like you, Mario."

"Hey look, Oscar …" But Mario was talking to a hollow void.

CHAPTER 48 DAY 27

SHE'D JUST FINISHED her usual breakfast of four quarters of a wholemeal slice, each individually spread with Marmite, peanut butter, Danish blue and honey, and eaten, as always, in that order. And all washed down with a huge mug of strong black coffee. She was set up for the day.

Risky was lapping milk from his own designated bowl, Maria was brewing more coffee, and Matty was in his highchair glugging contentedly from a bottle held unsteadily aloft in tiny chubby hands. Remembering how close she'd come to losing him, she found herself welling up. Then annoyed with herself for admitting her own weakness, she banished the thought.

"Is everything alright, madame," Maria asked, concerned.

"I'm fine, Maria, just fine. It's just ..." she started, before letting it go.

Maria didn't look convinced, but said nothing, though momentarily there was a palpable tension in the room.

Tammy knew that Maria planned on taking Matty to visit his grandfather, as had become a once or twice weekly routine. She joined them for at least part of the time whenever she could fit it into her work schedule, preferring to include walking or riding to or from together.

Worries about threats like those from the Kerkut brothers were kept at bay, but always present. She'd been relieved when Dov had also found time to accompany Maria and Matty a few times recently.

She enjoyed what was becoming family time, certainly, but knew that in her line of work they were wise precautions, as well. And her frequent phone calls to Matthew likewise brought her comfort on both fronts.

The atmosphere now looked like changing as Tammy picked up a call from frantic parents who'd been given her contact details by Hester Lamont. Their son, whom they'd recently understood frequented somewhere called Clubhouse in the Tilbury area of East London, was missing. Hadn't been seen for several days.

At age eight, Alex Hedges had been bigger than the other lads at his prep school, while at eighteen he'd gained the considerable accolade of a rugby blue at Oxford. He'd been tipped to play for England. Inevitably he would join the family business based both in the UK and US, comprising a number of five-star hotels, once he'd graduated with a business studies degree. He was now twenty-one, and in his final year at university. The Hedges family were nothing if not wealthy and were desperate to find their son. True to their class and background, they'd not wanted to make a fuss. Had logged their concern with the police and then spoken to Hester.

What the family didn't know was that Alex had a problem. A problem he'd never dreamed of talking about. Because Alex, for all his size, strength and masculinity, dreamed of one day transitioning to a woman. Despite that, Alex was sexually attracted to women. Did that mean if he transitioned, he would be technically gay? Lesbian? The young man was bewildered by his own preferences but found a measure of community at Clubhouse.

The couple lived with a staff of five, comprising butler, chef, chauffeur, cleaning lady-come-maid, and security guard, in a vast four-storey detached red-brick mansion in the Avenue Road near Regent's Park, North West London.

The home was an eclectic gallery of art, including impressionists, pre- and post-Renaissance works together with a selection of Pre-Raphaelites. The place was littered with marble: statues on plinths, columns, and an extravagant fireplace.

Against this impressive backdrop the couple seemed almost modest by comparison. Outshone by the grandeur of the place, as it were. Michael Hedges, probably in his sixties, the white hair doing little to dispel the appearance of age, was a little man with jug ears and a Mr Punch nose. He wore navy silk trousers, a navy shirt, gold-edged slippers and a finely embroidered smoking jacket. His appearance and jerky manner might have been those of a marionette. But were more likely nerves with what the couple feared they might be confronting. Newspapers and magazines such as The Times and The Economist lay scattered by the Queen Anne armchair, one of a pair, from which he'd just risen to greet Tammy. Clearly a man committed to, if not obsessed by, his business, she'd heard him murmur under his breath as he approached her, "Hmm! Stock's up by two points."

Geraldine, his wife, towering over her husband and considerably younger, was a strawberry bottle-blond. She wore an unpretentious grey dress, low heels, minimal make-up and a simple gold necklace with heart-shaped pendant.

Aware of the address she was going to meet the couple, Tammy had dressed to impress without going too far. An Yves Saint Laurent trouser suit in deep blue with a blue V-neck blouse, a Charmeuse silk scarf in coral providing a contrast. Her own pendant with its Hebrew inscription nestled comfortably between her breasts.

She was seated in one of two burgundy leather Chesterfields opposite the couple, the Porsche parked on their extensive drive. They'd provided the usual mid-morning fare of coffee and biscuits, brought in by their young Filipino maid, cup and plate placed on an antique occasional table by Tammy's side.

"Tell me about your son," Tammy asked, directing the question to whichever of the two chose to respond.

"He's a good lad." Michael, sipping from a lead crystal tumbler of whisky, spoke first, the voice showing signs of quavering with age, or possibly fear. "Never could understand why he'd want to go to that damn silly club."

Geraldine fiddled with her cup of tea, irresolution coming off her in waves. "He had problems, you see. He was confused, but we never found out why. Just that for all his academic ability and sports skills, there was something wrong. He is a very private person, would never be open about anything." She'd replaced her cup on her side table, and looking at it, left it to go cold. "Then there was this peculiar club Michael just mentioned. LG ... something or other? Some very strange people frequent it we'd heard."

"Made our own enquiries about this so-called discotheque, don'tcha know," added Michael. "Blowed if I could understand what he'd see in the place. Son of mine." He shook his head, bewildered, drank the last of his scotch and climbed wearily to his feet before making for the drinks cabinet. "Sure I can't tempt you, Ms Pierre?"

"No, I'm fine, thank you, Mr Hedges."

"Michael, please. Michael. No need to be formal." He poured himself a generous refill and shuffled slowly back to his seat like one carrying the weight of the world on his shoulders. "Don't know your own kids these days, what?"

There was no way Tammy could reach out to comfort the old man. All she could do was watch helplessly, as he tried to retain some semblance of dignity.

"Darling, I'm sure if there's anything to be done Miss Pierre will do all in her power to find Alex. I'm sure this will all be resolved. A silly mistake." Geraldine smiled as she spoke, but Tammy could see the tears threatening to give away her attempt to be stoic.

Seeking to move on, Tammy asked gently, "Do you know if he made any friends there? The club, that is?"

"No," said Geraldine. "On the playing fields he was at home. A team player. Elsewhere he was a bit of a loner. No friends that we knew of."

"Girlfriends?"

"As a matter of fact, he did. So he said," replied Geraldine. "I saw him with one, by chance, outside Kings Cross station, clinging on his arm. A real raven-haired beauty. No idea where they were going. I didn't ask, even when I did have the chance." She glanced down at her untouched tea. Then smiled up at Tammy hopelessly. "I never asked," she repeated, as though to emphasise the point. "It seemed wrong to intrude. He'd tell me if he wanted to."

"Of course," sympathised Tammy. "Was there, or is there anything at all in Alex's life you feel I should know? Anything that might help me get a make on what moved him? No matter how small or trivial?"

Geraldine looked enquiringly at her husband, who nodded his agreement, before clearing her throat like one about to deliver a speech. She hesitated, as though she might be betraying a confidence. "Miss Pierre, there was one thing."

Tammy leaned forward as though it might help her hear or understand better what Geraldine was about to confide.

Then sounding bolder, almost confrontational, Geraldine said, "My son has a criminal record."

"I'm listening," encouraged Tammy, trying not to appear too shocked at the revelation.

"I think he may occasionally have cross-dressed. I never caught him doing it, but I noticed he sometimes had what looked like traces of lipstick. Traces only that is, that he had been wearing and assumed ... No, wondered ... Well, the club. You know. Was he ...?"

"You said he had a criminal record?" asked Tammy, wanting to get back to the point.

"From the scraps of information I picked up after the event, and later, during the trial. An incident occurred." She stopped for a moment, assessing Tammy as one she could trust to take her seriously. "I believe he was ridiculed by someone in a pub when one day he'd failed to remove all evidence of the cosmetic. The man laughed at that and the fancy waistcoat Alex treasured. Called him names. I won't go into that."

"I do understand," said Tammy, quite sure she knew what sort of names Geraldine meant.

"No-one wants to be laughed at or humiliated in public," Geraldine continued.

Then Michael added, "Boy was gentle to the point of timidity, despite his size and strength. But, you see, he had a temper. My lad. Almost uncontrollable when he was really angry."

"He lost his temper with the one who mocked him?" Tammy enquired.

Geraldine said, "You might put it that way. The pub was crowded. Dozens of witnesses. Alex lost it completely. Broke the man's nose and jaw too, in three places. Lucky not to lose the sight in one eye, the man. They had to practically drag Alex off. Police arrived and arrested him, charged him, and the court sentenced him to three months. He was sent to Belmarsh. Judge was furious. Wasn't interested in any defence of provocation."

"Belmarsh?" said Tammy, wide-eyed. "Supposed to be a terrible place, they say." Her pulse was racing as she started exploring possibilities.

Then Michael put in, "Said he'd be out in six weeks if he behaved."

"Maybe less," said Tammy. "In some cases. But not a nice place to be."

"I'm a wealthy man, Miss Pierre. I made it my business to approach the governor and a number of the warders. See the boy was treated well. Expensive business, altogether, but I got the lad out in less than a month."

"What about the university?" Tammy asked. "Was he sent down?"

"Threatened. But I dealt with that too. You see, Miss Pierre, money talks. And I've a lot of it to spare."

"You've both been really helpful," said Tammy, getting to her feet, not wanting to press the obviously weary couple further. "And I've taken up more of your time than I intended. I'll do all I can to locate your son. You must understand though, no promises."

"Miss Pierre?" Geraldine ventured.

"I wish you'd both call me Tammy."

"Of course. Of course," said Geraldine. "Tammy, you've been so kind. But up to now we've not asked you what your professional fees will be."

"Don't worry, I'm retained by the club owner."

"Nonsense," said Michael, drinking from his refilled tumbler. "You tell me your rate and I'll pay you double."

"Please," said Tammy, raising one hand. "Not necessary." Then from the back of her mind an enquiry wormed its way. "Tell me about the fancy waistcoat you mentioned. Anything in particular you remember about it? Style? Tailor made? Fashion? Colour?"

"Only the colour," the couple said, in unison.

"What was that? The colour, I mean?" asked Tammy, not certain what she was hoping for at that moment.

"The colour?" said Geraldine. "It was his favourite. Amethyst."

"Violet? Amethyst?" Alex Hedges? It all fitted. Cross dressing. Favourite colour. The DNA would be the clincher. Then, heaven help, the business of telling Michael and Geraldine. They'd be devastated.

CHAPTER 49 DAY 28

"TAMMY," SAID MANUS, at his ever too-tight collar, the irony of a policeman collaring himself not entirely overlooked by Tammy. "What are you going to do about the toilet arrangements in Belmarsh. Have you given it any thought at all? Cells are open and loos aren't private, you know. You can be seen by every cell within sight during the day."

They were walking through Regent's Park, alongside the boating lake. It was a sunny day with a stiff breeze blowing leaves around their feet as they paced. Mothers with prams, kids with footballs, dogs chasing each other around, and incongruously, a small number of besuited businesspeople interweaving the melee. A picture of nirvana in the centre of London. A latter-day Bruegel.

She'd been testy with Maria that morning, called her out for leaving a minor ruffle in the counterpane on her bed. The paperwork in her Mayfair office might be an unholy mess, but the home in Queen's Park, her sanctuary, had to be perfection. She made no apology for her obsession with the clean and the tidy. The place was a show flat of modern elegance.

"I'm sorry, Madame, but while you were in the shower, Risky and Matty ..." She'd looked utterly crestfallen.

"Don't worry, Maria," she softened, pulling on a pair of stretch leather Karen Millen jeans. "It's only me. Ignore it. A bit edgy today. Really, no big deal." She'd given up exhorting Maria to call her Tammy.

But now, lighting up her third panatella of the morning, against her avowed self-imposed temperance, inhaling deeply and hoping for a tobacco hit, which in her present state failed to materialise, she'd have been loath to admit it, but she was nervous. She'd overindulged before leaving home that morning with a couple of lines, the high all too quickly followed by the come down. Now she was attempting to rationalise her fears of discovery by reminding herself, perhaps convincing herself, of the absolute need for this mission to succeed. If she couldn't carry it off the men inside would be merciless. Physical attack even attempted rape she could cope with. What occupied her thoughts and fears were the other possibilities. A thrown cocktail of boiling water laced with sugar made a sticky paste guaranteed to disfigure. As bad, or worse, was the prospect of catching what in prison slang was known as 'a buck fifty'. A cut needing to be closed by around a hundred and fifty stitches. She shuddered at the prospect of destroyed looks. Would Dov still want her? Would she ever find another lover? Male or female? If Manus noticed her discomfiture, he remained silent.

"Frank Sinatra used to shower seven times a day," said Tammy, coming in from left field. Then explained, "I'll sit down on the loo once, when I need to, first thing, when it's not too light, and shower maybe two or three times a day where I can use the shower block loos. They'll see me as eccentric. Again, no-one will see what goes on at night when the lights are dimmed a bit, and the wicket gate locked, so I'll be clear there."

"You make it all sound so easy. If you're found out ... Tammy, not to put too fine a point on it, what if you need to pee during the day and can't use the shower block?"

"Thought of that. I've got a pee funnel."

Manus kicked a pebble disconsolately. "As if there wasn't already enough risk, Tammy. The place is laced with psychopaths. Pope, who you want to talk to, slaughtered a whole family. I wouldn't give tuppence for your chances if ..."

"I'll be able to pee standing up," she said, as though Manus hadn't spoken. "With my back to everyone."

"What about clothing checks? All prisoners are subject to these on entry to any prison."

"Bob will have somehow circumvented that."

"Impossible." Manus shoved his hands in his pockets, frustrated.

"Ask him."

"How will you get this funnel thing in undetected?"

"You don't want to know, John."

"You're right. I won't ask any more questions. I can see I'm getting nowhere." Then a thought occurred to him. "Tammy, with all this talk of what you'll do once inside, the one thing we've not discussed, is how the dickens are you going to get into the place?"

"It's a work in progress, John. No decisions yet."

"But you're planning to go in imminently. All convicted criminals are transported by SERCO in a clearly marked SERCO vehicle, from the Old Bailey to prison. You can't expect them to deliver you, and you can hardly walk up to Belmarsh's gates and ask to be admitted."

"Working on it." She looked away from Manus, sounded obstinate.

Manus gazed out at the boats cruising the lake, wondered whether he might have chosen a less complicated way of life. Then realised, nothing would change his love of the job and the commitment to those for whom he felt responsible. "Okay, Tammy," he conceded. "Entirely against my better judgement, and strictly off the record, I may have a suggestion."

"Go on."

"Occasionally, albeit rarely, if there isn't a SERCO vehicle available, we've transported convicted defendants to jail by taxi. A larger SUV, like those supplied by Addison Lee, might have the presence to carry it off. Dead of night," he added, sounding doubtful. "Maybe, I don't know for sure. Rumour's already afoot inside, believe it or not, that you murdered five members of a rival cocaine gang. We'll let that stand, although there may be the question of why you're not in the High Security Unit."

A couple of rowers cruised past, a young couple without a care, the sun kissing the backs of their necks. "Can't deal with everything now. Just got to suck it and see." She shrugged.

"One thing you won't be able to avoid is the need to be accompanied in your cab by the regulation pair of warders and at least one uniform, required to sign you in. They'll need to be the real thing, not three random guys from the local theatre club."

"I'll give it some thought, John," she said. Then in a moment of inspiration, she remembered the comments made by Michael Hedges. People were bribable. But could the same two warders be found as had looked out for Alex Hedges? What about a uniform to accompany them? She wouldn't hold her breath. Michael would help, of course. He had to. Anything to locate his son.

"Give it some thought? You'll need to do better than that. Anyway, Tammy, that's all I can do for you. Ball's now in your court." He sounded closed off.

Turning to face Manus, a hand on his shoulder, Tammy smiled, if somewhat wanly. "John, I am truly touched by your concern. But I have to do this."

"One last thing, Tammy."

"Yup?"

"I've done some nosing around and found one of Pope's acolytes inside Belmarsh is a Jamaican, Lloyd Kendall. I got hold of his girlfriend, an occasional prostitute, Debbie Calder, who's been nicked a few times. We suggested she get word to her boyfriend when next he calls, hopefully imminently, that you're a killer, on your way in. He might find it of interest, perhaps he'll want to introduce his patron to you."

"That's appreciated, John." As she turned away from the DCI, her early morning nerves morphed into realisation of the enormity of what she was undertaking. Too late to turn back. Not that she would have countenanced a change of heart.

Failure was unthinkable.

But that didn't mean it couldn't happen.

CHAPTER 50 DAY 29

WORD WAS OUT that the prison was awaiting a new inmate. A fresh bright star. One Thomas, Tommy Peters. In for a long stretch. He'd wiped out a rival gang of cocaine dealers, John Manus had already briefed Tammy.

Small articles had appeared in the press to support the story. No more information was available at this stage. It had been a mission to keep a story like that to a minimum. But, five men dead. All head shots, brains scattered in rooms laden with blood and gelatinous grey gore.

The inmates of Belmarsh were expectant. A hoped-for amusing diversion from their otherwise stupefyingly mundane daily routine.

The stench was the first thing she noticed on entering the place, a casserole of shit and piss such as might assail the throat and nostrils within the confines of the water-filled pit of the hippo house at any zoo. That and the hollow, echoing noise of animal howling, arguing, fighting accompanied by the smashing of cutlery and tin cups against the bars of cells into which prisoners, many of them dangerously unpredictable, were generally incarcerated for up to twenty-three hours a day.

It was the noise of a twenty-first-century bedlam. A madhouse of wild beasts who'd killed, in many cases, to get in, would kill to get out if they could. Over sixty gangs within the prison walls pursued rivalries initiated on London's streets. Blood on the floor, beatings, broken limbs and boiling water laced with sugar producing the glutinous mix Tammy had feared might be her fate, thrown over victims as part of the everyday family atmosphere.

What Tammy didn't already know about the prison's regime she'd shortly be finding out. To her own cost. But still, she felt the risks were worth the reward if she could secure the leads she wanted.

* * * * *

The cells measure just ten feet by seven and are heated to an inhuman 40 degrees Celsius, despite ongoing complaints from prisoners and human rights groups. Rumour has it that prison staff want to ensure prisoners don't get too comfortable. Little chance of that, it seems.

Belmarsh is a Category A Prison holding prisoners from all over the United Kingdom. Distributed across four residential units, 40 percent are single-occupancy cells, necessary if Tammy was to promote the fiction of her gender. While 60 percent are multi-occupancy, designed for two but frequently holding three inmates with resultant intimidation, abuse and humiliation among those unfortunate enough to be forced into those cramped conditions.

Worth noting, inmates at Belmarsh are offered access to education, workshops, and two gyms, sadly benefits not taken up by many.

A listener scheme for prisoners at risk from suicide or self-harm is in operation at the facility. In recent times it has proved to be spectacularly unsuccessful, with dozens of suicides or unexplained deaths being recorded each year.

A support group for foreign national prisoners, many of them Muslim, operates in the prison providing advice on immigration law. It was to this group that Tammy hoped to make some sort of contact, to sound out what if anything they might know about the recent past or else planned terrorist attacks, if, that is, they could be persuaded to confide in Tammy.

There is in addition, the HSU, or High Security Unit, for the most dangerous or most vulnerable, from which no prisoner has ever escaped. She'd hoped she'd be placed in the same block as the man she was targeting, not necessarily the HSU. All a bit chancy.

In the event, she would find there was no need to search for Pope. He was already planning to have her incarcerated in the same block as he. Of course, the whole venture would be regarded as the polar opposite, if there was such a thing, of a slam dunk if she missed him.

No chance of that.

With all it has on offer, one might be forgiven for thinking that time spent in Belmarsh compared favourably with a Center Parcs holiday camp. Nothing could be further from the truth. In November 2009, an inspection report from the Chief Inspector of Prisons criticised the 'extremely high' amount of force used to control inmates at the prison. The report also stated that an unusually high number of prisoners had reported being intimidated or victimised by staff at Belmarsh. That is, if they didn't already have the overtures of other prisoners to deal with.

Among the prison's more notable luminaries are, or have been, Stephen Port, the 'Grindr Killer', a multiple rapist and murderer of four men. Delroy Grant, the 'Night Stalker', a serial rapist and burglar with likely over a hundred offences. And Abu Hamza al-Masri, the one-eyed, one-handed imam at Finsbury Park Mosque, sentenced to seven years for inciting violence and now, having been found guilty of terrorist-related offences in the United States following his extradition, incarcerated for life without the possibility of parole.

Joining this eclectic celebrity line up: one Dominic Pope. The man serving a forty-year sentence with no chance of parole before thirty years had been served, effectively a whole of life tariff. He killed young women, as many as eight, though he refused to be drawn on numbers, mainly through strangulation, sometimes during intercourse, like serial killer John Christie.

He was sentenced by Judge Roland Jeffreys, the latter having been subjected to a tirade of hysterical threats and abuse when Pope had been taken down after the trial. Jeffreys' mother had expressed her fears for her son's safety when she and Tammy had met. Fears that had already been borne out by Jeffreys' horrific slaughter. A revenge effected by Pope from behind his prison bars? All options were on the table.

In the prison's High Security Unit, a prison within a prison surrounded by twenty-foot walls, with ninety-six cameras and three layers of wire mesh ceilings, Pope had enjoyed the unique distinction of being the most feared within the company of the most feared in the time he'd spent there.

Now resident in the main body of the prison, still no-one argued with him, except on pain of his raging reprisals. All new inmates at Belmarsh were subjected to Pope's unique welcome and hospitality. They never forgot it. In some cases they bore the scars for the rest of their lives.

* * * * *

Dominic Pope lay back on the bed of a three-man cell he had to himself. The larger than regulation bed supported an ivory-coloured duvet, and there were fresh flowers on the bedside table. A thirty-six-inch screen adorned one wall, and a small Mitsubishi air conditioning unit kept the otherwise unbearable forty-degree temperature marginally at bay. An eclectic collection of books was lined up on a shelf opposite the TV.

To the casual observer, Dickens, Trollope, Tolstoy, de Maupassant, and at the other end of the intellectual spectrum, crime thrillers by the likes of Belinda Bauer, Barbara Vine and Harlan Coben. Intriguingly, next to the vase of flowers on his bedside table, sat an autobiography of Albert Pierrepoint, Britain's last hangman. An individual who, of all people, eventually disavowed capital punishment, calling it nothing more than a primitive desire for revenge. Clearly, there was no accounting for some people's tastes. The toilet under the window had an added modesty board, care of Pope's friends among the warders, who happily attended his every need.

Two men stood in the cell, with legs wide and arms folded. Neither looked the type you'd want to bump into on a dark night. In a black T-shirt and jeans, Lloyd Kendall, a black Schwarzenegger with an uncertain temper, stood around six three and was doing a ten-year stretch for GBH. His companion, Alf Chapelle, wearing a floppy grey tracksuit, and carrying as much weight as a super tanker, several inches taller than Kendall, had murdered his wife and her lover when he'd found them in flagrante. Chapelle sported, if that was the best way of describing it, a facial tattoo of a black scorpion, its head and body over his nose and forehead, legs like pincers grasping his cheeks down to his collar. People inside never argued with him. He still had fifteen years ahead of him before any chance of parole. The three men ruled their wing on the third floor or landing known, for some reason, as 'the two's'.

"What's your news, gentlemen?" Pope was in navy trousers, ironed to a fine crease, and a white shirt in shantung with a paisley silk tie. In civilian life he'd been a banker and foreign exchange dealer, and knew it added to his cachet behind bars to be thus dressed, that plus the casual Eton accent. Not that he needed anything more to supplement an already fearsome reputation.

"New guy comin' in any day, boss. Man's a shotta. Real badman," said Kendall, looking down at Pope.

Dominic Pope moistened his lips and prepared to engage with the newcomer, Thomas, Tommy Peters. A badman, eh? Some gentle tuition might be required here. But would Tommy be prepared to engage with him?

CHAPTER 51 DAY 30

"There's ten dead."

"How?"

"Does it matter how? It's what you wanted, isn't it?"

"Don't you talk down to me, you snotty piece of working-class shit. You get paid well for what you do."

"Doesn't mean I approve of it, Oscar."

"God's sake, man, don't start getting moral on me now. And it's Mr Mountford to you, sonny. What I need to know is, did it look right? What was captured on the train's CCTV?"

"What we arranged. Asian kid with a school satchel takes it off his back. Leaves it in the gangway. Looks up at the camera and grins. Then walks away, just as you planned."

"And the bomb?"

"Went off half a minute later."

"Good. Good. Should produce the backlash wanted against our friends in the bearded community. Incidentally, what was in the kid's satchel?"

"Search me. School books I'd imagine."

"Half a minute, you say. Cutting it fine, wasn't it?"

"Not my problem…Mr Mountford."

"Pipe bomb, was it?"

"What else?"

"Mm! Like last time," said Mountford half to himself, sounding pleased with what he'd heard so far.

The caller didn't respond.

"Out of interest, who did you get to plant the device?"

"The supplies for making the bomb, I got to Muhammed Dhelavi, father of Rakish, the boy who was spotted planting the satchel on the train. He was the one, Dhelavi, who went to France to bring back the other three Muslims, when the boat they were in nearly went down. Man's got a distinguishing nervous tic in his cheek."

"And where did you get the supplies from? No, don't tell me. So, who actually planted the thing?"

"Jason volunteered. He left it in a Buroni briefcase planted in the luggage area close to where the kid was spotted."

"Jason Kerkut?" His voice raised.

"Right."

"Man's a homicidal maniac. A Buroni briefcase, you say? That's a Maxwell-Scott luxury item. If any of it survived the bomb it'll almost certainly have Jason's DNA on it. And anyway, he didn't need to do it himself."

"No accounting for taste, is there."

"But the first bomb, on the Northern Region, the one that killed Cutler, was planted in a carryall, which the family then took onto the train themselves. So there would have been no risk to anyone transporting it but the family."

"Jason again, I believe. Mario was furious with him."

"Alright, Harry, you've done your bit. I shan't need to call on you again. You can slink back under the stone you crawled from."

"Thank you, Mr Mountford. Praise from you, indeed…"

* * * * *

"Another damned terrorist outrage. What the hell is this woman of yours doing about it, Bob?" The Home Secretary was practically apoplectic.

"She's working undercover at the moment." Even as he said it, Bob Walker acknowledged seriously, perhaps for the first time, the risk to himself personally, quite apart from the danger Tammy was putting herself in if anything went dramatically wrong. An injured civilian woman taken from a men's facility to hospital. Unthinkable. Unconscionable. Bob Walker's career would be over. A trickle of perspiration ran down his back.

"Another madcap scheme?" Templeton held his arms open in exasperation. "Undercover where? Doing what? From all I've been hearing about her ..."

"Probably risking her life for this investigation, Mike." The DCS nervously doodled on the notepad in front of him. Impossible to get through to the Home Sec when he was in this sort of mood.

"Well, who asked her to? Come to think of it, what the hell are we doing about it?" raged Templeton.

Cabinet Office Briefing Room A. The strong aroma of percolated coffee and an undercurrent of sweat in the mainly shirt-sleeved attendants. A hastily convened meeting of COBRA. A critical emergency, for which press and public would be demanding immediate answers. The question: Could answers be supplied? The atmosphere, among some in attendance, edging towards panic suggested not.

Present, as before, Home Secretary Michael Templeton, who'd made the opening comment, pale-faced and drawn, running his fingers distractedly through his hair.

To his left, his Permanent Under-Secretary, Edwin Fellows, tie askew, who looked blank. Then the usually unflappable DCS Bob Walker, conversing quietly with a more florid than usual John Manus.

On the opposite side of the conference table, the Head of CTC, Nick Holden, shirt rolled up to the elbows, collar undone, shifting impatiently in his chair as though any movement on his part might be sufficient to produce some sort of useful result.

Joining the others this time, on Nick's right, Miranda Miller, fiftyish, broad-beamed Met chief, immaculate in uniform, neatly cut chestnut-coloured hair, quietly observing the others at the table, notepad and pen at the ready.

Also in attendance, having been apprised of the content of the previous meeting, seated next to Miranda Miller was David Sinclair, head of MI5, who also acted as a floater between that agency and MI6. Small, balding and softly spoken, with an impossibly high IQ and inconspicuous to the point of invisibility, David was generally reckoned to be the best MI5 had ever had in charge. A former eighty-a-day man, David sat with a cigarette smouldering in an ashtray by his right hand, a ribbon of smoke winding lazily towards the ceiling. Occasionally he would take up the king size between his index and middle fingers to tap ash into the glass bowl, unable to entirely relinquish the habit. But he never drew on it. No-one commented or complained.

"Mike," said Bob, "everyone here is doing their bit. We've given Tammy a broad brief. She's been investigating the East London killings, and at the same time scoping the mosque where it's believed some of the illegals have planted themselves."

"Well, if it's too much for her, take her off the job, man." Templeton was having difficulty controlling his temper.

"We simply have nothing to go on," put in Bob. "CCTV of the carriage where the blast took place, shows a young Asian boy deliberately dropping his school satchel while smirking up at the camera. The bag was later found damaged, but with nothing more than partially burned books in it. So it couldn't have been his plant, although we accept the contempt displayed.

"Our people have identified the bomb as having been left with other luggage on a rack in a Buroni briefcase. We only got a glimpse of a possible suspect, a heavyset man in his thirties or forties wearing a city suit. The last person you'd expect to see in the role of terrorist bomber."

"Alright," said Templeton, belligerently banging the heel of his fist on the table in time with his comments that followed, "I intend to go round this table, now, and get input from everyone here. What are you doing? What progress do you believe you've made? None, as far as I can see. And what do you propose next? Personally, Bob, I suggest we take this Pierre woman off the job. The taxpayer has better things to do than finance an expensive PI who's producing nothing. Undercover, you say? Pah!"

"The taxpayer isn't paying her anything, Mike."

"Well then, who's funding her? She can't be doing all this for nothing."

"Hester Lamont, owner of the Clubhouse clubs, who first employed her is paying her."

"And that's it?" said Templeton. "She could be risking her life for a PI's retainer. What is she, man? Barmy?"

"No, Home Secretary. She's not barmy. She's a professional. She's committed and she intends to see this through, as I've seen on every job she's been involved in."

Templeton shrugged, mildly rebuked, and countered, "She's still given us sweet nothing."

"Hang on, though! She's only been involved a few days," protested Bob. "We've hardly given her a fair chance."

"And what about those dead on the train, DCS Walker? Do you think they got a fair chance?"

"For God's sake," put in Nick. "We're behaving like a bloody rabble."

"I have every confidence in Tammy Pierre, Home Secretary. She's an experienced PI and one who's prepared to take risks, if need be, to back up her theories," offered John Manus.

"What theories, John. Let's have the benefit of your inside knowledge of the woman. Theories, you say? What theories?" he repeated.

"Gentlemen, please," Miranda Miller tried to cut in.

"We've got teams working the mosques investigating all known or potential troublemakers," continued Nick. "I have crews hammering on doors, engaging in stop and search. We're still examining the CCTV images to see if there's anything at all that might have been missed."

"It's not enough then is it. You need to do more," argued Templeton.

"There is no more, Mike. You know the protocol...," said Nick.

"I don't give a damn for protocol. I want fucking results, people."

The meeting was threatening to decline into chaos. David Sinclair, leaving the smouldering butt in the ashtray while stirring his coffee, milky and stone cold, the way he preferred it, glanced around the room. Live images of London showed on the large screens down one wall, giving a false impression of a safe city.

He spoke so softly everyone had to cease arguing to hear him.

"We need to give the Pierre woman time and space. By all the accounts I've received she is somewhat unconventional. Takes chances some might say are unnecessary. But." And here he stopped for a moment. "She gets results. And her boyfriend, Dov Jordan, is an asset. He's an occasional operative with Mossad. We've worked with that team, albeit discreetly, for years. We don't broadcast it, even within security. They also get results.

"Bob," said David. "Do you have any idea at all what this undercover operation of Ms Pierre's is?"

Trying to sound calm, though he knew Sinclair was too fly to be fooled, he replied, "No idea, David. On this she left us all out of the loop."

"I see. Thanks, Bob. Finally, one more thing no-one has brought up." David paused again, for effect. Then said, "Oscar Mountford."

People looked up, perplexed.

"Oscar Mountford?" muttered Templeton. "What's he got to do with all this? He's not a terrorist. He doesn't arrange to have bombs delivered."

"A known extremist of the right," explained David. "An agent provocateur, to our knowledge. Convicted of organising several murders, including his own son. These two bomb explosions don't have the mark of planned, or even random terrorist outrages. They're too subtle. Not a Middle Easterner in sight, apart from the boy, planted no doubt to confuse. Which it has. All designed to divert us from what might otherwise have seemed the obvious. I'll wager they're the work of Mountford, working from behind bars."

"Can you be certain, David?" Miranda Miller asked.

Turning to face her, David said, "No, of course not. But my gut tells me there's a link between the Clubhouse issues, the illegal sex workers there, Mountford, and the bombings. I smell it, that's all. He'll be looking to discredit the Muslim community, stir up unrest wherever he can. He's the one we need to be looking at. The street killings are a separate matter so far. But as many as three murderers? I'm aware we've nothing there to go on. At the moment," he added. "Won't be easy to find."

Sinclair stirred his cold drink, watching the liquid swirl under his spoon, before going on, "Then there's that other question, the Kerkut brothers. The elephants in the room. Let's not forget them. Friends of Mountford, we know. Apparently, Mossad have tied them in with the imported illegals. Almost certainly brought them over. Another likely association there?"

Addressing the whole room, while tapping his Montblanc pen on his notepad, Sinclair sighed. "Oh, what a tangled web we weave ..."

"When first we practise to deceive," murmured Miranda.

Nodding his acknowledgement, while reserving his final comments for Bob and Manus, David pressed, "Keep Ms Pierre on the books, gentlemen. I believe she'll produce the results we want. All in good time."

He drank his coffee, finishing it with great satisfaction before retrieving the remains of his smoke. "Try to stop her from doing anything too rash. Hm?"

Bob Walker raised one eyebrow but made no further comment.

CHAPTER 52 DAY 31

HANDCUFFED AND FLANKED by the two crooked warders Michael Hedges had successfully sought out and coerced, both burly and sullen, Tammy had a rare opportunity to see things from the point of view of a convicted felon.

Bribery hardly came into the picture with what Michael had on them. Still, he'd decided a nominal contribution to the prison's benevolent fund would keep them happy. Add one taxi driver, up front next to a uniform, who looked tense but said little.

They'd put a magnetic flashing blue light on the roof of the cab to add hoped-for veracity as they drove away from Charing Cross nick where she'd been ostensibly transferred, for no known reason, after the sentencing.

They had to manage without a siren. No problem on London's darkened roads. Traffic was sparse. The night clear. The moon bright.

And now they were roaring through London's streets on their way to Tammy's date with, who knew whom or what? Maria and her papa had been told she was away for a few days. Not to worry. Dov didn't need to be told any more than he already knew. Manus had done what could be done to assist. Bob Walker was understandably keeping a low profile. There was a collective holding of breath.

The game, if it could be regarded as such, was very much underway. She'd be okay, she believed and prayed, once she was incarcerated. But right now, she was shivering with fear, her clasped hands resting on her knees, all her worst worries crowding in. What if …? What if …?

She carried minimal personal belongings to be held by the prison once she was inside. Wallet with three twenty-pound notes. False ID in the form of a single credit card, without an actual account, so hopefully no question of it being too closely examined. House keys for a non-existent address outside London. Burner phone, ready for use, but with no numbers that could be followed up, and which she wouldn't be allowed to use anyway. Only the prison phone permitted, and then only for outgoing calls once the required credits had been accrued. A small kitbag allowed by the authorities, with changes of T-shirts, boxer shorts, denim jeans and tops, a couple of tracksuits. And as a last-minute addition, a few Western/cowboy-style men's checked shirts picked up in Gap. That was about it.

She'd had her skull shaved, allowing the still livid scar at the side of her head, compliments of a man called Bear who'd attacked her during an earlier investigation, to be prominent as part of her credentials as a hard man. Her nails had been filed down and stripped of all vestiges of varnish, and she'd removed the gold amulet with its Hebrew inscription.

Finally, in an act of personal savagery, she'd shaved off her eyebrows. The look, emulating that of killer Bernie Rose in the film Drive, was its own statement. Maria had seen it all. Looked on horrified but said nothing. About some things, she was quickly learning, she knew better than to enquire.

It had all happened too fast to be taken in, but signed in she was and now, at 3.00 am and lodged in the first night centre with what was known as a new inmate's first night pack, comprising a toilet roll, comb, shampoo, body wash and gel, she was sitting on her bunk wondering what she should do about sleep. As with all new prisoners she'd been lodged in house block 3. Shortly, probably in the morning, she would be allocated a cell.

For now, whether because of the hour or else overtures made on her behalf, she'd managed to avoid the strip search, which in some cases in the past had required a new prisoner to squat over a mirror. Ostensibly now banned, it took no account of warders' present interpretation of the rules. Such a test would have seen Tammy's crusade at a premature end. The humiliation that would follow would have made her a laughing stock. Whatever she thought the risks her venture might have involved before admission, were now made starkly worse with the reality she now faced.

The prison regime would see Tammy committed to an induction programme designed to give all new prisoners information on how to make routine requests and complaints, followed by a second part to the programme which would allow use of facilities such as the gym. Much of this was subject to unscheduled delays.

Lights came on at 8.00 am, so she would use the toilet before that, behind a closed door. And after? She'd have to wait and see. An awful lot of speculation here. It was getting worse. Like a rollercoaster careering out of control. She'd managed to smuggle in the funnel, and there were always the shower block loos. Anything for some light relief, in a manner of speaking.

Dreading the morning, she spent the night, what there was left of it, thrashing about restlessly on the lumpy bed, eventually falling into a fitful sleep, only to startle awake panicked she'd overslept. When she checked the hour, she saw it was 7.50 am. She had just enough time to ready herself before lights came on and cell doors were opened up.

Even so she was unprepared for the moment when it happened. The noise that continued throughout the night, the banging and screaming from cell to cell, or cage to cage as some of the inmates put it, went unabated when the doors were unlocked. If anything, the resemblance to a Victorian asylum became even more acute.

She would soon find a Middle Eastern bazaar of drug dealing, Spice being the narcotic of choice, particularly among some of the younger prisoners, unable to cope with the bullying and harassment, who simply preferred to zone out. No-one had told her she'd be allowed just one shower a day, late afternoon, before lights out. Forget the loos in the shower block. As well she had the funnel.

Breakfast, which was Continental, comprised a modest couple of slices of bread with a mini pot of jam, a packet of cereal, sachets of tea and coffee, some milk and a flask of hot water. Normally collected by the prisoners, hers had been thoughtfully left inside her cell. There wouldn't be much further thoughtfulness along these lines. Nothing like her usual nutritious fare.

She felt a long, long way from home, and more than just a bit lonely.

She'd just swallowed her last bit of bread when one of the two earlier escorts appeared at her cell door. Barney? Barney. She hadn't taken much note of the two men's names. For the first time she noticed his neck. It was so wide it appeared as though it was part of his shaven head.

"You're outta here, sonny," said Barney, indicating the direction with his thumb. "Get your stuff together and foller me."

"Where are we going?" she enquired, trying not to sound too obviously unsure of herself, and remembering to keep the pitch of her voice as low as possible.

"House block 1. Lifers like you. You're gonna love it. Got a welcoming party. Just for you."

"What about induction…? Aren't I supposed to…?"

"You'll find out all about induction where you're going, mate. No worries. 'Ave you done your will, yet? Hah!" He guffawed. "Too late now, son, if you ain't."

It was at this stage that her nerves began to calm down. Up to this moment she'd had to contend with the unknown. Now she was entering the realm of the known. People, she knew, she could always deal with.

She had no idea how wrong she could be.

CHAPTER 53 DAY 32

JOHN MANUS, AT TAMMY'S BEHEST, had decided to publish pictures of the young Asian boy seen smirking at the surveillance camera on the train seconds before the second outrage which had killed, at the time, ten, and now, with further deaths, the present toll was fourteen. Had anyone witnessed the youngster behaving strangely at the time? Did anyone recognise him?

No-one immediately came forward and there was no denying another blank had been drawn.

The press, at first supportive, quickly became infuriated at the continued lack of progress. How could there possibly be any witnesses, they wanted to know, when all those closest to the bomb had died, or else were too shocked to offer anything?

But Manus had done the right thing. And quite unknowingly he'd struck gold. Seated opposite him in one of the Yard's hospitality suites, and wearing traditional Muslim garb, was a lad called Deepak Pandit.

Deepak explained to Manus what had happened outside the East London Mosque. He'd retained Tammy's card, puzzled at her appearance and the accusations of those who'd sought to attack her, claiming she was a woman. Then, he'd seen the press pictures of the boy on the train and begun to put two and two ...

Mrs Gilchrist had directed the boy to John Manus who was delighted, in fact excited, to meet up with him.

"I'm so glad you've come in, Deepak." The lad had been offered a drink and asked for an orange juice, which sat on the low table in front of him. "So, I'm listening. What more have you got for me? A name? An address?" He thought about that last one, then said, "Well, maybe not an address. But anything at all we can use?"

"I know his name," said Deepak.

"You do?" said Manus, astonished.

"Yes, sir. From the published pictures. It's Rakish Dhelavi, and his father, whose name I do not know, is one of the men who accosted Tammy." Deepak had to turn over the name Tammy in the back of his mind, having previously accepted it was Ahmed.

"Heavens!" said Manus. "To risk the life of a boy so young? How could anyone?" Shaking his head, he sat back and folded his arms. "What is he, ten, twelve. What sort of mind …?"

"Not so young, Mr Manus."

"Really? What am I, a couple of years out?"

"Mr Manus, Rakish is small for his age, but he is in fact eighteen."

"Eighteen?" Manus sounded incredulous. "Even so. The dangers involved. Didn't he care? He might have been killed. We're talking barely half a minute here between him exiting the area and the bomb going off."

"His family are committed to jihad in the UK, Mr Manus. They'll do whatever they think necessary." He toyed with his glass of orange for a moment, then putting it to his lips took a long and satisfying draught before replacing it on the table.

"Is there anything we can do to identify his people? I'm not willing to see Tammy put herself on the line by returning to the mosque." He sighed, and said softly, "As if she wasn't already in enough of harm's way."

"Miss Tammy would recognise at least one of them, even though she won't know his name."

"She would?" Manus's interest perked up. "Which one, then?"

"Rakish's father," said Deepak. "He has a nervous tic when he gets angry or upset. It's very noticeable."

"Do we know anything else about him?" Manus asked.

"The talk in the mosque is that he helped locate and then bring in from France the three he's been seen with. I actually heard one of them say it had been a terrible crossing because of rough seas. The boat nearly sank."

"I wonder who organised and financed the crossing?"

"It may not be relevant, but ..."

"Go on, young man. Then I'll decide if it's something we can use."

"Does the name Kerkut mean anything to you?"

"Does it?" Manus leaned forward, elbows on his knees, his attention sharpened.

"I overheard a conversation in the mosque with Rakish's father, he said there were two brothers of that name waiting for the boat on the shore when it arrived. He said he knew them."

"A lead, at last?" Manus was clearly relieved. "I wonder who else was involved? I can't see the Kerkuts risking a penny of their own hard stolen cash on a venture likely to be as tricky as this. Anything more, Deepak?"

"I secretly listened in and they talked about someone with the name Oliver? Or perhaps it was Oberon? Ogden? I can't be sure."

"Oscar?" Manus prompted.

"Oscar," the boy breathed. "Oscar Manford."

"Mountford, Deepak. Oscar Mountford."

"You know him, Mr Manus?"

"I should say I do. He's serving a life sentence for murder. It would be like him to finance something like this."

The day had started overcast, but now, as if on cue, a beam of sunshine lightened the room and atmosphere. One of life's welcome if inexplicable coincidences. Manus adjusted his tie, found himself beginning to smile slightly. A breakthrough? Of sorts, perhaps. Too soon to get over-optimistic. But any port in a storm? Straw in the wind? A start? Whatever.

Deepak regarded Manus intensely. "Rakish is not a nice person, Mr Manus."

"I can see we have a problem here, Deepak. Rakish's performance on the train is hardly an endorsement for the improvement of socio-political relationships." Manus helped himself to a biscuit from the tray, thoughtfully left by a member of his team, and poured himself a hot coffee from the cafetière into the waiting mug.

Deepak then delivered the second welcome coincidence of the morning. The morning was proving more fruitful than Manus had dared hope. "Rakish and his father both have criminal records, Mr Manus."

Manus considered the possibilities for several moments, then said, "That is the most significant piece of information we've had so far into these two terrorist explosions."

"I'm delighted to have been of assistance, Mr Manus. Is that all?"

"Well, Deepak, we still have the problem of fixing a firm ID on these two. We'll need more than an eyewitness account of the boy's identity. That may take some time, however certain you are of his ID."

"How may I help, sir? Perhaps by trying to get information through the mosque?"

"It's tempting, son, but could be dangerous if word got to either of these two that you were asking questions."

Deepak finished off the juice, then turning to Manus said, "Tell me what you want me to do, sir, and I will happily oblige."

"That's very kind of you, Deepak." Manus blew on the surface of his coffee and took a sip, then he said, "You know, there are all sorts of definitions of what police work entails." Deepak smiled politely. "But for me," said Manus, "police work is all about investigation and inspiration in roughly equal parts. Throw a bit of luck into the mix, like our present conversation, and you have a recipe for progress."

"How very clever." Deepak smiled.

"Not really. I think you'd find most of the officers in the force would agree with that definition."

"And do you have any inspiration, Mr Manus?"

Manus gave Deepak's enquiry several moments of deliberation, then, sounding genuinely optimistic for the first time in their chat, said, "Do you know what? I believe I have. Foolish of me not to have seen the possibility earlier. The boy, Rakish, left his satchel behind when he escaped from the train. It was damaged, but survived the explosion. We have it in custody. If, as you say, he has a criminal record, we'll have his and his father's DNA. We'll be able to ID them properly through the bag, without spending hours looking through photographs trying to find a match."

DI Bill Jenner came in at that moment, and said, "A quick word, gov?"

"Go ahead, Bill," invited Manus.

"We've got a raft of DNA results in. They make interesting reading."

"I'm listening."

"Can I speak in front of the lad?"

"In general terms, Bill. Don't mention any names."

"All the killings, those outside the clubs, barring numbers one, three and four, show a common DNA. Whether found on clothes or bodies. Or both, come to think of it."

"Yesss!" said Manus, punching a fist into his palm. "Now tell me you've got a match with the satchel."

"Well, yes and no."

"Why yes and no?"

"Because we've IDed the boy as Rakish Dhelavi, who, when we checked him out, has a criminal record."

"We're already ahead of you on that front. You'll be able to find the father's ID now as well."

"Got that too."

"Good man. And it is?"

"It's Muhammed Dhelavi."

"Well done, Bill."

"One thing though, gov."

"Go on, then. Spoil the party."

"None of the samples of DNA found on any of the victims matches that of either of the Dhelavis."

* * * * *

Feeling restless. Need another hit. That last one was good. Better than mainlining. The parting of the flesh, you might say. Like the opening of the Red Sea to let me and Moses through.

Bit of a challenge there. I liked that. Almost came in my pants. Worth the effort, though. Silly bitch put up a fight. Not a good idea when you're dealing with the Phantom Slasher. Tilbury Ripper, did I hear someone say? Don't insult me.

Thing is, they're all leaving the club in twos and threes, or by taxi.

I'm crying now. It all comes back at odd moments when I least expect it. Remembering the only one I truly loved. Let me down. The fucker. Nearly took that one's head off.

They won't be unfaithful to anyone else. Can't, can they? Not now. Hee, hee.

Love it. Love it all really.

CHAPTER 54 DAY 32

"IN 'ERE, MATE. 'Urry up. Looks like 'e'se waiting for yuh," said the first man.

"Need to show the cunt who runs things in here," responded the second. "We'll have him eating outta the palms of our hands. That is if he can still chew when we're done."

"Heard he's a cocky fucker," added the third man.

"Won't be for much longer, eh!" said the first, laughing raucously.

The cell was dark and gloomy, whether because of a lack of natural light, or because of her mood, she wouldn't have been able to say.

Seated on her bunk, her chin in her palms, she heard movement outside her cell, shuffled footsteps, whispered comments, something being dragged along the landing, unaware it was she who was being discussed. Only conscious of her sense of solitude and that of being hemmed in within the shrinking bounds of her tiny cell, the hairs on her forearms and back of her neck crawled and stood to attention. Something brewing. A kettle drum hammered in her chest, till she forced two slow, deep breaths. Calm now. Ready.

Everything then happened very quickly. Too quickly to permit any mental or physical preparation. Even for an advanced exponent, like she, of Krav Maga.

Three oversized males appeared at her cell door, the first of these hauling what looked like a stained ancient grey mattress. The other two followed on behind as the door only allowed for a single file admittance.

Utterly bemused, and before she could move to defend herself, she was swiftly dragged to her feet by the second and third warder, slammed up against the wall and battered senseless by their night sticks.

She knew she must not scream and risk giving the game away. Though it was almost impossible, at times, her jaw hinged wide in a silent shriek. She longed for unconsciousness, but until that release, was aware of every hammer blow. Every jolt. Every shock to her protesting body. Explosions in her head. Bombs going off. Screams, shouts and tin cups rattled against cell bars by inmates who knew full well what was going on, all adding to the confusion.

The warders knew exactly where they were aiming, going for the common peroneal nerve in the mid-thigh, the back of it, which was visible, rather than the preferred front. The batons were swung in a fast-snapping strike action, to include the biceps, not the unreachable triceps, and randomly across her back, some dangerously close to her neck. The aim was to cause transitory neuropraxia (not a term the warders would have been aware of), causing spasmodic muscle pain, even paralysis which might last for days or, in some cases, weeks. They knew just when to stop the assault; after all, they didn't want him dead, not yet. Later maybe. Right now, there'd be too many questions to answer. He'd only just arrived.

Slipping in and out of consciousness, for how long she wasn't clear, from time to time she caught the sound of muffled conversation. "Shall we wake 'im up, boss? Seems a pity. Looks so peaceful."

She dreamed? Or perhaps she didn't dream of an interested face hovering over her; maybe that of a ghoul, studying her with curiosity. The countenance was a Halloween mask. Stark white with at its centre a black head and thorax over the nose and forehead from which emerged jagged tentacles spreading across the cheeks as far as the neck. A tarantula, clinging to a compliant aspect? A scene from Alien? Only this wasn't a fiction.

The three men stood over Tammy's senseless body, those she believed she'd fantasised. Not the warders. A small man, around seventy, maybe more, with a narrow intelligent face, dark brown eyes, immaculately turned out in finely pressed trousers and a double-cuff white shirt, and incongruously, considering the location, a dark silk tie. Dominic Pope was accompanied by Alf Chapelle, the man with the facial tattoo, a vacant if brutal face, and Lloyd Kendall, Caribbean, handsome, an enquiring look, both in jeans and T-shirts.

The clipped accent of an educated individual came back. "Not yet, Alfred. By all accounts our friend is handy with a gun. Unfortunately, he wasn't allowed one in his cell. Tends to leave one at something of a disadvantage."

"Not so 'andy wivout, is'e," Alf laughed. "Look at 'im now. Couldn't tuck up 'is nan in bed, could'e. Hah!"

"Killed a lot of people, Alf. Our new guest, Mr Tommy Peters. A man to be reckoned with, I'd say. As soon as he's able to grace us with the pleasure of his conscious company, always assuming, that is, he does wake up, we will engage him in conversation. Then it will be for us to receive him into this little community, in our own inimitable fashion."

"Right. We'll give 'im a welcome 'e'll remember."

"You mean in addition to that he's just been subjected to?" Pope smiled, satisfied.

Turning to the other man, Pope enquired, "What do we reckon, Lloyd? Any thoughts to add to our mental perambulations?"

"Nice one, that, boss. Nah. Don't know what the blud's about yet. Tell you one ting…?"

"What's that, Lloyd?"

"Like you said, Dom, dude cut down five, man. All shot in the head. Mus' be dealing caine in a big way. Leas' that's the word on the street."

"Whose word, Lloyd?"

"Me garlfren' Grace. Me have call her las' night."

"Mm! I see." Then looking her over again, like a prize pig for auction, Pope observed, "Nasty scar that at the side of our friend's head. Been in a fight, perhaps?"

"No worries, boss," offered Alf. "When he wakes up, we'll give 'im another on the other side of 'is 'ead. 'E'll 'ave a matchin' pair then."

"Impressive, Alfred. A sense of humour? You reveal hidden depths. Or do I mean shallows?" he pondered.

It was dark when Tammy finally regained consciousness, still on the floor where she'd been intentionally left. Doors were locked for the night. The place felt oppressive. And all too apparent, the stink of men, of bodily functions and noise which had continued unabated every time she'd been remotely aware of her surroundings.

A meal of shepherd's pie left in her cell was stone cold. Carefully checking out her condition, arms, legs and neck, she reckoned there were no broken bones, though she was aware of what must have been horrifying bruising. She hurt everywhere, muscles, bones, and worst thing, all the recent scars she'd sustained. She was cradled in pain. In agony. Crying would have permitted some release, though it couldn't be chanced.

But now she had an idea of what she was up against, she started to prepare for the following day. First off, she ate all of the shepherd's pie, disgusting though it was. She saved the chocolate bar left behind for the morning. She would almost certainly need the energy.

Then, despite a desperate, drug-like weariness, she began the arduous task of getting herself back into the sort of condition to effect a credible defence against any further unprovoked attacks by the kindly prison staff. There wouldn't be a repeat of the overtures of the welcoming committee. In due course they would understand. She'd see to that, whatever it took.

She spent two hours loosening up, fighting through the pain, concentrating on press ups, squats, shoulder loosening, shadow boxing until, running with sweat, she finally allowed herself to fall into an exhausted sleep. As she drifted off she realised she'd not had a shower since before being admitted. She felt tacky and uncomfortable.

Probably the least of her problems.

CHAPTER 55 DAY 33

THEY'D TAKEN A DNA SAMPLE when he was just sixteen and been convicted of violent affray. Rakish Dhelavi had been easily traceable this time as his address, that on record, had remained unchanged, the same as that of his parents.

Manus had attended the boy's home in Walthamstow, an Edwardian terraced house in a nondescript street, with his DI Bill Jenner, and he'd reluctantly agreed to be interviewed under caution at Charing Cross nick. Manus had also tried to get in touch with the father, who hadn't been home. He would have been furious had he known his son was about to be questioned and would almost certainly have refused to allow it. Manus felt that the father's attitude while being interviewed under caution, in the wholly unlikely event he'd ever agree to it, might have been instructive. There'd always be another day, he consoled himself.

But the mother, Meera, a dignified middle-aged lady with lines of tiredness at the corners of her eyes, looked at her son, concerned, and asked, "What have you been up to now, abni?"

"Nutting, Ommi. I swear." Manus couldn't get over the fact that, close up, the boy looked even younger than he had on the CCTV images. He might have passed for ten years old. A kid in white trainers and a blue tracksuit with a hoodie.

His mother glared at him, pulling her blue patterned sari tighter about her waist, unconvinced. "We don't want any trouble, sir. If the boy has been ..."

"I assure you, Ms Dhelavi, this is a purely routine enquiry. The lad is not compelled to accompany us."

"Oh no?" Mrs Dhelavi was absolutely clear. "If you need to question my son you take him now. I want to know what he has been doing. My husband has been away for a few days, but he's back now and he will hear of this."

The interview at Charing Cross was a dismal affair. A gloomy room with a chipped blue laminate-topped table and two plastic chairs on either side. Rakish had refused the offer of legal assistance, and so after the usual introductions, the recording machine was turned on and his questioning commenced. Nick Holden of CTC had been informed and hurried over from his office; he was watching proceedings outside the interview room from a monitor.

Manus, dispensing with a possible easy opening, launched straight in, "What do you know of the recent bomb outrage on the Southern Region train, Rakish?"

"What? Bomb?" he replied, shocked. Then recovering himself he said, "No comment."

"We have you clearly on CCTV, Rakish," probed Manus.

"No comment." He slouched back in his chair, provoking the two men with his own brand of affected disdain.

"The DNA found on your satchel, your DNA I might add, puts you clearly on that train just before the explosion."

"No comment." He closed his eyes.

"We don't need eyewitness evidence, you know. What we have here is irrefutable."

"No comment."

And so it proceeded. In response to questions about the boy's presence on the train, and what he knew of his father's involvement in the explosion, they got a repeated, 'No comment,' from the young man. He was more experienced at this sort of thing than might have been anticipated, judging by his apparent naivety.

It was time for a change of tack, one Manus introduced with a winning smile at the lad. "You might have been killed yourself, you know. Dangerous situation for you to have been in."

"No comment." The young man was starting to get restive. Kept shifting about on the plastic chair. Then after a few moments considering his situation, he said, "You tell me I don't need to answer any questions. That I can remain silent. That I can leave whenever I want ... So," he continued defiantly, getting to his feet, "now I am going."

"Of course, Rakish. As I said, whenever you want. Let me escort you out. Incidentally, do you think your father has seen these CCTV images?"

"How would I know?" he said, folding his arms across his chest.

"They've been on the TV news, on social media. All over the place."

"What do I care?" Now moving his hands to his pockets.

"Do you think your father would have worried if you had been killed in the explosion?"

"That would never happen," retorted Rakish.

"Really? The time between you grinning at the CCTV like a belly-filled Cheshire Cat and the bomb detonating was less than half a minute. And where was your father when all this was happening? Not on the train, that's for sure, young man."

For the first time, Rakish looked a bit troubled, his forehead creased.

"The near miss you experienced, young man, suggests your father cared more about planting the idea that you caused the explosion than about your safety."

"No comment." Rakish agitatedly wrung his hands together, but the questioning was beginning to have an effect.

So far, DI Jenner had added nothing to the session, thinking that to do so might dilute the impact his colleague was having. Manus, on the other hand, decided now was the time to drive home his advantage.

"Have you heard of someone called Oscar Mountford?"

"Who? Who's that?" Rakish hadn't moved to leave the room, merely staring at Manus as though waiting to hear he'd won some sort of prize.

"He was an MP. Involved in a number of murders he organised. He's inside serving forty years, and he never touched a soul. Merely got others to do his dirty work for him." Manus had got up and faced Rakish.

"So what's that got to do with me?"

"I'd have thought that was obvious, wouldn't you?"

"You mean, what you already said, you think my father was setting me up?"

"Rather looks that way; don't you think?"

"I didn't plant any bombs, and you can't prove I did," he announced aggressively.

"Correct. You did nothing. It was your father who organised the planting of the bomb. What you don't seem to have factored in is the possibility that you could go to jail, simply for being an accessory. Are you ready for that?"

"My father would not allow that."

"Forty years, Rakish. You could go in for forty years if you're found guilty in this way, even if only as an accomplice."

Rakish replied, "I don't believe it."

"You'd better believe it, young man. Your father has murdered dozens, and purely at random. How many Muslims do you think he's killed among that lot? If Oscar killed his own son, do you not think there's even a slim possibility your father could sacrifice you in the same way? Make you the fall guy if it suited him? Do you want to be that? So far, you've done nothing, although on circumstantial evidence we could put you away for a long time. Think about it, Rakish. Have you been doing the dirty work of others?"

Rakish looked sullen but said nothing, only evidencing a sense of confusion as he turned things over in his mind.

"You're no longer a child, Rakish," said Manus, relentlessly seeking to press home his advantage. "You're eighteen and have reached your majority. There's every chance you'd take the rap."

"No!" the boy unexpectedly screamed, the sound echoing around the walls of the cramped interview room.

The dynamics among the three had shifted perceptibly with Manus continuing to force the boy into revealing more.

"Well, tell us what you do know. We can help you, Rakish. You don't need to be doing this on your own."

"I don't know anything. I want Ommi here, or else my Abba."

"Of course, you do, Rakish. And we'll start to arrange that right now." Turning off the tape and addressing Bill Jenner, Manus said, "We'll halt the interview here, Bill, while you contact the mother, and if he's available, the father. We'll need their mobile numbers, Rakish," said Manus, shoving a notepad and pencil to the boy.

Manus caught Bill Jenner's eye with a look that said, Don't hurry too much. Jenner understood, picked up the scrap of paper, and nodded accordingly.

When Jenner had left the room, Manus turned to the boy who'd resumed his seat, and said, "Look, son, we're off the record right now, so just between ourselves, that first train bomb, the one that killed the government minister and his family, among others, was that you?"

"What? What are you saying?" Rakish's face had gone the colour of rancid cheese.

"Simple enough, isn't it. I want to know, did you plant that first bomb? You can talk quite freely. No witnesses, no recording. Just you and me. Explain what happened and I'll do all in my power to see you're treated fairly. But we will need your absolute cooperation. Do you follow?"

Rakish sat unmoving, unspeaking. The implications of all Manus had just said beginning to sink in. He put his elbows on the table, his head in his hands and started crying.

"It wasn't me. It wasn't me," he wailed. "It was Abba. Not me."

"Your father, Rakish? All by himself?"

"Yes." He turned this way and that. "No." He was becoming disorientated, glancing this way and that, clearly not understanding where he was or what to say next.

Then sounding desperate, dragging his fingers through his hair, he added, "Abba told Ommi he was going to meet a man called Ricks. A friend of someone called Osbert?"

Making the same mistake as Deepak had over the name. "Could that have been Oscar, lad? I've already talked about him to you," Manus prompted.

The boy closed his eyes to concentrate, then nodded. "It was Oscar, not Osbert. That was the name. I don't think he meant to say that in front of me. He looked annoyed when he said it. Ommi asked who he was, and what of this man called Oscar, but Abba wouldn't say. He only mentioned him the one time, Ricks that is, but I saw them both walking together when Abba met him that same day. I'd followed him. He didn't see me."

Rakish paused as though he'd just been struck by a thought. "I listened in as far as I could. They were too far away and I didn't want to get too close to be discovered."

"What did you hear, son?" Manus held his breath, hoping the boy wouldn't change his mind about what he'd been about to reveal.

"Nothing. Nothing at all," said Rakish. He waited several seconds, and finally, as if an afterthought, said, "Only, I heard the man Ricks say something like, 'Leave it to me, Muhammed. I can supply all you'll need.'"

Progress, thought Manus. But with Ricks's record of reliability, could one be sure he would, or could, supply the necessary equipment to make a bomb? Assuming it was a bomb that was being discussed. He wouldn't question Ricks just yet. Leave a man enough rope ...

Rakish went on, "Then again I saw them another time through the window of the local Starbucks, with their heads together, having a coffee."

"Anyone else, son?" asked Manus. "Anything else, no matter how insignificant it may seem to you."

They were interrupted by the return of Bill Jenner, who merely shook his head when he caught Manus's eye.

"No joy, Bill?"

"Nothing."

"Do you mind if we continue the interview, Rakish?" Manus was adopting a more formal approach. "You're not obliged to stay, as has already been made clear to you. But you've not been charged with anything, and it might help you at a later date if you've cooperated now at this early stage."

The boy looked beaten, his head sunk between his shoulders, but still he said, "Okay. I'll say what I can."

"Good lad," said Manus in attempt to reassure the boy as far as he could.

"Can we get you a drink? Tea? Coffee? Water?"

He shrugged. "Water please?"

"Okay, John, I'll get it," said the DI, leaving again.

"I'm listening, lad." Manus had his hands on the table, fingers interlocked in a casual pose on the tabletop.

"I never wanted to be involved in any of this, but from the time I was thirteen all I remember my Abba talking about was jihad and death to the infidel."

"Go on," urged Manus.

Rakish tried unsuccessfully to catch Manus's eye, looking for some sympathy perhaps, before adding, "I didn't plant any bombs. I swear it. Please believe me."

"Where did your father get the bomb-making materials?" Manus persisted.

"I don't know. But he made the bombs himself in the garden shed. When I saw what he was doing I became very frightened."

"Did your mother know what he was up to?"

"No. If she had she would have stopped him. Ommi is a very strong woman. I think Abba is a bit scared of her."

"Son, who carried the bombs onto the trains?"

"I don't know. Really, I don't. Perhaps this man, Ricks?"

"Do you not realise how close to death you came?"

"Abba said, 'We'll make the police look stupid. They'll never trace us.' He said to drop my satchel as though it had a bomb in it, then walk away. Smile at the camera. You know, taunt the police."

"Weren't you frightened by all this?"

"When the explosion came I was knocked off my feet. I was shocked when it went off as early as it did. I'm now thinking Abba didn't care whether I was hurt or not."

At that Rakish started weeping again, his head in his hands. "I do not have a father."

In the same moment, DI Jenner returned with the tumbler of water which he placed in front of the boy who sounded positively humble. "Thank you, sir." He drank the water down in one.

"All right, lad," said Manus, aware of what he'd made the lad face up to. "You've done very well. If it's any help we're not charging you today, and if your account holds up I'd say we won't have a case against you."

They were well nigh at the end of the session and decided to let the boy go. It was unlikely they'd learn any more from him. He looked exhausted and contrite.

Once Rakish had been shown out by Bill Jenner, Nick Holden came in to join the two for the post-mortem. Easing his considerable bulk onto the plastic chair recently occupied by Rakish, he said, "Well done, John. Got a result there."

"I'm wondering what's in it for Ricks?" said Manus. "He's putting his career, his reputation, his freedom on the line."

"Money?" suggested Bill Jenner. "Have you seen the Rolex? The Savile Row suits?"

"That and bitter personal prejudice. He doesn't like any of the ethnics. He's an old-fashioned hate-filled bigot," was Manus's take on Ricks.

"Will you take him off the case, John?" asked Bill.

"You'll want to keep an eye on him, won't you?" offered Nick. "I'd say keep him where you can keep a constant bead on the man."

"Of course. Last thing we want is Ricks going to ground. We'll leave him alone and see if we can catch him out." Manus got to his feet and stretched his legs.

"This is a tiny operation," said Nick. "We're not looking at a major terrorist cell. Ricks's name, Rakish mentioned, smacks of his close involvement, that means the Kerkuts are likely to be there too, and by association that makes me think of Oscar, whom the boy has said he heard them talking about. It's got his signature. Small, tight-knit, under his control, with everything far removed from him. Designed to discredit the Muslim community which is what I'd expect of Mountford with his extremist views. If anyone's a terrorist, gentlemen, he is."

"I wonder if the person planting the bomb on the Southern Region train was, by any chance, Jason Kerkut?" mused Manus. "Seen to have been left in a briefcase by a smartly dressed man. If so, why him and not Rakish's father? Probably knew he'd be picked up by CCTV. Dhelavi Senior, that is. But then Kerkut, if it was him, would have had the same problem. Knowing Jason, he probably volunteered. Wanted a bit of fun. Man's a genuine, solid gold psychopath."

"Will you be bringing in MI5?" asked Jenner.

"Not at this stage. And certainly not if I can avoid it. I've seen more than enough of the round table bickering in COBRA meetings. And," he emphasised, "enough of 5 and 6 getting at each other's throats. You'll understand what I'm getting at, won't you, Nick."

"All too well," Nick agreed.

"For now," Manus went on, "we'll keep matters between ourselves and, if I feel we must, the Home Secretary."

"Agreed. John, before we split up; I've been meaning to enquire, where's your enterprising Ms Pierre these days?"

he said, effecting to leave, and casting an eye over the dismal interior of the interview room.

"Nick. Don't even ask. It was her contact from the mosque, young Deepak Pandit, who started this ball rolling. At first she wasn't even sure whether the mosque outing had been a waste of time."

"Looks like it's brought up the most significant lead so far," said Nick. "Give her my best, and let her know I'll be convening a COBRA meeting to let them know too."

Manus, his head down in contemplation, said quietly, "Of course. And I'll get back to you, Nick, if she survives what she has in mind."

CHAPTER 56 DAY 33

8:00 AM

LIGHTS CAME ON and cell doors were opened up. She made sure she'd used the facilities in good time. She could hear prisoners eating the breakfast they'd collected the night before.

But no-one had told her about that. There'd been the cold shepherd's pie during the night, but she'd missed out on breakfast, having been barely conscious most of the day and into the early evening. Her stomach pinched and growled, and she ate the chocolate bar, slowly to gain maximum benefit of the brief sugar shot.

A stocky young female warder looked in. An innocent somewhat pasty-faced woman. She was wearing the regulation short sleeve white shirt with navy blue epaulettes and tie, and matching navy trousers. "You okay, love? Had any sleep? You was late in, wasn't you, night before. You were out all day yesterday. Like a light. I heard what happened. You didn't look too good, darling. Some of them screws is real bastards."

She stopped talking for a moment and squinted at Tammy. "What's happened to your eyebrows, love? No, don't tell me. None of my business. Gawd, you're a odd one. Had any breakfast? Don't look like it. I'll see what I can do for you, mate. Tommy, isn't it? Peters?"

"That's right," Tammy answered quietly, hearing the incessant chat like bat wings flapping in her brain.

"Nasty scar that, on your head. Blimey! Been in a fight sometime, have you, darling?" she said with concern.

"Something like that," said Tammy, wondering where this was all going.

"I'm Sarah, love." Then she asked, "You German or Itie? Got a funny way of talking."

"French," said Tammy. "At least, part French."

Sarah didn't look as though she'd heard, instead looking over her shoulder and said, "Listen, it can be a bit tough on New Booties."

"What?"

"Them as haven't done time before." She had a hand on her hip, surveying Tammy with interest. "Like you, I heard."

"I'll keep that in mind."

"Look, I know what happened when you got here. Word gets around this place."

"Not quite the warm welcome I was expecting, Sarah," she sighed.

Putting her finger to her lips, Sarah said, "Sorry, love, but the talk is, they haven't finished with you yet."

Getting to her feet, Tammy put a hand on Sarah's shoulder. "I really appreciate you giving me the heads up on this."

So that was it. They weren't finished with her yet. She wondered whether she'd get a chance to talk to Pope at all before she became hospitalised. Or whether this whole venture was going to prove a vainglorious folly on her part.

"Good luck, darling," said Sarah before moving on. She paused for just a moment, her head on one side, surveying Tammy as though she'd missed something. "Know what? Grow some hair, darling, and you'd be quite fanciable. Still, I'll get you some breakfast in a mo'."

She lay back on the bed propped up against a pillow, breathing deeply to steady her nerves. She'd already decided how she would handle things if there was an attempted repeat performance.

The dawn chorus of shouting, screaming and metal banging up against prison bars gradually diminished. The sound drained away like water from a bath, as though the prison were awaiting an event. From her bed she could see no sign of movement outside her cell. No warders doing the rounds. No prisoners being taken out for morning exercise in the prison yard. The silence grew, was unsettling. A moment to ponder her imminent fate.

Her thoughts strayed to baby Matty, chubby fingers and toes, giggling; her papa, always ready with considered advice; recollections of her feisty mama. Dov had begged her not to do this. Would she see any of them again? She was feeling trapped. Increasingly so.

Footsteps approached. Three sets by the sound of it, echoing along the landing in her direction, dragging something. The mattress, obviously. The third-floor landing. The two's. She wouldn't wait and they wouldn't catch her unawares this time. But then they would realise that anyway. Climbing off the bed, she stood facing the cell door, with legs spread and arms folded, defiantly, check shirt open at the collar, revealing the T-shirt underneath. Inconsequentially she realised that Sarah hadn't yet brought her the promised breakfast.

The cell door would only admit the warders one at a time, it gave her a slight advantage. If she were able to capitalise on it. A moot point. Unlikely, if she was realistic.

She could practically hear the thudding of her heart in her ears, at her temples, in her chest. Life is unpredictable, but we make the most of our opportunities and cope with whatever cards we're dealt, however unpalatable, as best we can.

The first one presented himself on the threshold of her dwelling. He was tall, taller than she, and with short sleeves his arms resembled the hams in her local butcher's. He had the look of one intent on a task. One not easily to be diverted. Here was a problem. It didn't require a psychology degree to recognise the shimmering glow of hatred.

Behind him, another warder, as big as the first, and grinning inanely, dragging the mattress.

A third man making up the rear wasn't smiling.

Neither was number one, who greeted her politely, "Mornin', nigger. 'Ave a good night's sleep, did yah? Fancy another kip, do yah? See what we can do for yah, then."

"Good morning, gentlemen. How may I help you?" The fear evaporated, replaced with a cool assessment of her situation. As usual in these threatening situations, her pulse had slowed to just thirty beats per minute. Tammy gave her most charming smile. Inevitably their size gave her pause, if more than one managed to crowd into her cell the odds would clearly stack up further in their favour. But only one came in at that moment.

"D'yo hear that, fellahs. I fink we got a frog 'ere. 'Ow abaht that? A wog frog." Then turning his attention to Tammy, he said, "Enough of this shit, sonny jim," and advanced into the cell with a raised fist aimed at Tammy's head.

The boxer's mantra, much like that of the Krav Maga exponent, is never lose your temper. That way you lose control and then you lose the battle.

Tammy didn't lose her temper, not now, not ever, though she was piqued and not about to surrender to a beating like the last one she'd succumbed to.

Moving her head easily to one side to avoid the blow, she caught the man's wrist and upper arm, seeing him grin at her in the second before she brought the elbow down across her raised knee, snapping it like a twig.

The scream could be heard across all three landings and started alarm bells ringing.

The stretcher brought for the injured warder was superfluous. It was quicker and simpler to help him walk away, but not before he'd explained what his comrades would be visiting upon Tammy in the coming days.

She couldn't resist responding, "Of course. If you give me a bit of notice, I'll have tea and cakes ready for all of you."

The other warders looked askance at Tammy. An older one among them asked, "What the hell has been going on

CHAPTER 56 • DAY 33 • 363

here? You're for Seg, young man. Just arrived and already causing trouble." Then turning to a younger colleague he said, "Cuff him, Wilf. Then take him down."

But before that could happen, a short, impeccably turned-out gentleman, accompanied by two heavyset companions, intervened, addressing the older warder, "It's alright, Bert. Frank here slipped and fell against the railing. Nothing to worry about. No need for cuffs or Segregation Unit. The boy's fine."

"Alright, Dom. If you say so," the other responded doubtfully. "We'll leave it for now. But I'm telling you, I don't like the look of it. Not one bit."

A moment later, Sarah arrived, grinning hugely. "See you been busy, love. Seems like I nearly forgot something."

"Really? What was that, Sarah?"

"Breakfast, darling. Looks like you could do with some."

All very well and kind, thought Tammy.

But what's up next?

CHAPTER 57 DAY 34

"HI, JOHN."

"Bob. Is everything alright? You sound concerned."

"As well I might be. We might both be."

"I know, I know. Have you heard anything yet?"

John Manus was seated at his desk on the fifth floor of New Scotland Yard. The surface was covered in neat piles of paper, each with a different colour Post-it note indicating the case in question. The bright sunlight that beamed into the offices did nothing to reflect John's mood which was one of almost uncontainable concern. He noted that despite his usually calm demeanour, Bob's voice betrayed an equally grave anxiety.

"Not a word. I was hoping you might have."

Manus picked up a ballpoint and doodled aimlessly on the pad in front of him. "Did she tell you how long she was planning on staying inside? That is, always assuming she can get out when she wants."

"The whole thing is so hush hush, not even the governor of Belmarsh knows. She is entirely on her own. Nothing I could say would dissuade her from what she had in mind."

"Same here. If she's found out …" He didn't add anything, although he couldn't help recalling the smirk on Harry Ricks's countenance each time he'd faced him in the last couple of days.

Bob asked, "How long has it been? Do we even know?"

"Three nights, four, max, by my reckoning. We spoke about three days ago and she was clearly planning on going in then, or maybe the day after." Manus glanced down at the doodle and saw he'd sketched a window with prison bars.

"Christ," he murmured, screwing up the paper and throwing it impatiently across the room where it missed the wastepaper basket.

"Interesting times, John."

"Given the choice I think I'd rather be bored."

"You and me both. Keep in touch," said Bob, before signing off.

"Of course," he replied, adding, "she's amazing, I know. But still, God save us from mavericks."

John Manus had barely ended the call when his mobile buzzed again. The number meant nothing to him. "Manus," he answered.

"Mr John Manus?"

"That's right." Manus noted the throaty accent and guessed he was speaking to an Israeli.

"I'm Dov Jordan, a long-time friend of Tammy's. You and I have not had much in the way of contact, beyond that is what Tammy has relayed to me, but I assume we both know what's happening?"

"That's right."

"Are you happy about it?"

"Absolutely not."

"I tried to dissuade her."

"So did I."

"I think my people ..."

"Would that be Mossad, by any chance?"

"Let's just say, my people for now."

"Your choice."

"As I was saying, I think my people can locate her, that is the cell block in Belmarsh, without too much difficulty. What worries me is that if we interfere in any way, we might be putting her in more danger."

"Things can happen very fast behind those walls," said Manus. "Tempers are on a hair trigger. Inmates are invariably on the lookout for a fight. A wrong glance, a wrong comment."

"I've some disturbing stories about the warders too."

"Being locked up with numbers of psychopaths, bully boys, gangs, drug dealers and the like, it's small wonder it gets to some of our lads."

"Alright, John. May I call you John?"

"Of course. And you're Dov?"

"That's right. And, John, I don't think I've ever felt so damned helpless."

"We all do."

"If there's anything we can do…"

"I shan't forget. Sure, we'll talk soon."

* * * * *

"Bring me up to date, Mario. What the hell is going on? Has she been located yet? Or not?"

"Ricks thinks she's in Belmarsh. He's got the contacts. Said they'd had a new inmate coupla nights ago. Tall skinny black bloke, shaved head, big scar at the side.

"They called 'him' Tommy Peters."

"That's her then, isn't it? Tammy Pierre. Bit obvious, wouldn't you say?"

"Maybe. But then she's not expecting to be found out, so Tommy? Tammy? Avoids slip ups."

"Well, looks like she just slipped up, doesn't it? Do we know which cell block?"

"Ricks is working on it. Oscar, do you still just want her humiliated? Or more. She's trouble, as long as she's around. We could have her finished off. No problem. Make it look like an accident."

Mountford turned the idea over and over before saying, "Okay. The embarrassment was my ego trip. I wanted to make her squirm because of what she'd done to me. When you find out where she is, arrange an accident.

"Can't be too soon. Don't call me till it's done."

CHAPTER 58 DAY 34

SHE ATE QUICKLY, unaware of the cereal having any taste. The bread and jam were a poor parody of her usual nutritious morning fare at home but would have to do.

Not having the slightest notion what next to expect she lay back on the bed and closed her eyes, controlling her breathing and gradually unwinding. She ached everywhere, what she'd been able to view at the backs of her legs showed a physical terrain of aubergine and purple bruising, but as soon as the opportunity presented itself she would again go through her loosening up regime. Right now, she would avoid any distractions and simply wait.

From inside her cage she could hear the clamour of dispute, pick up the occasional sound or glimpse of prisoners doing trades in the brief interludes allowed between lockdowns. Judging by the aroma that floated into her vicinity, the stench of rotting fish, a scent she would find clung to clothing, both hers and that of other inmates, she guessed there was a lot of Toochie, that is, Spice being traded.

Around mid-morning she heard the footsteps. Two sets of padded paces, soft soles like those of trainers. A third pair clicking against the metal landing much like a pair of brogues.

They're coming for me, she thought, getting gingerly to her feet to greet her visitors. As before, she stood with legs planted apart, arms folded, and took a deep breath. Her pulse slowed again. It calmed the nerves and oxygenated the brain. An aid to clear thinking, she'd found, long ago.

Men and women have distinctive ways of walking, sitting, talking. If she was to be a man, she'd need to sound like a man. She had the deep voice and the appearance. The manner of speech was something she'd need to think about.

Women embellish, are generally more garrulous, more expansive. Men tend to abbreviate, grunt, murmur, keep responses short. She seemed to have got away with things up to now. There'd been no opportunity to engage in anything approaching a real conversation. Still, she couldn't be too brief, too inarticulate. She was, after all, educated. The acid test would depend upon her contact with the man who'd be making his way to see her. Dominic Pope.

The first thing she saw looking around her open door was a vision from a horror film. She'd not hallucinated while semi-conscious. The face looked as though octopus tentacles had spread across the cheeks and forehead. The nose and centre of the forehead were black. When it smiled, the teeth, those that remained, were black stumps. What really struck home was the eyes. Tiny, black, unblinking. Alf Chapelle, in a baggy tracksuit, Dominic Pope's man. Dominic was as immaculate as she'd been led to believe in a suit and tie; behind him another of Pope's parish: handsome black man, Lloyd Kendall, all in denim.

Chapelle spoke first, a gravelly voice as though he needed to clear his throat. "Washall we do wiv 'im, Mr Pope? The usual? I can cut 'im if you like."

The knife, presumably taken from the cell block's kitchen, was about seven inches long, held casually in Chapelle's right fist, point down in a stabbing attitude.

Looking Chapelle in the eye, Tammy said softly, "Morning, mister. How's it to be, my friend? Tea and toast? Or something stronger. Right out of coconut milk, so, sorry, no piña coladas today."

"What the fuck's 'e on abaht, boss?" said Chapelle, advancing a step into the cell, the knife leaning that much closer to Tammy, the man straining an invisible leash, just looking for any excuse to launch an attack.

"Well, why don't we wait and see what the young man has in mind, Alfred," said Pope, looking interestedly at Tammy. "Your call, Mr Peters. Alfred here seems to be seeking a little input from you."

Tammy hadn't moved a muscle, continuing to stare out Chapelle. It was now time to engage the man in conversation, see what he could contribute to a friendly dialogue. She could practically smell the man's endocrine glands in operation, presenting a charge of adrenalin that the individual himself would find well-nigh impossible to contain once he'd been let loose by Pope. No wonder new inmates left this jail with souvenirs of their induction by the character his two accomplices addressed as boss.

Transferring her attention to the knife, Tammy said, "Well now, Alfred. What are we going to do? I mean, ask yourself, 'Do I feel lucky?' Well do you, sir?" She'd amended the original quote to favour the man with the satirical rather than the crass. He might well be a punk, but there was no need for unnecessary provocation.

"It seems, Alfred, we have something of a movie buff in our midst." Pope smiled. "Consider the familiar Clint Eastwood quote as the redoubtable *Dirty Harry*. Then observe our colleague's ghoulish shaven eyebrows, care of killer Bernie Rose in the film *Drive*, if I'm not mistaken? What does that leave us with?" asked Pope, easing his way around Chapelle into the cell.

"I don't know, Mr Pope. What does that leave you with?" Tammy asked.

Turning to Chapelle, Pope asked, "Well, Alfred, I think we know the answer to Mr Peters' enquiry. You were never the luckiest of individuals, that is until you met me, and so I suggest you and Lloyd leave me to discuss matters in private with our new guest here."

"Okay, boss," said Chapelle with a shrug. "Whatever you say."

"You be okay on your own, Dom?" Kendall sounded unconvinced.

"Thanks for your concern, Lloyd. I'm sure I'll be fine."

Seeking a better view of Tammy, Lloyd briefly edged around Pope, caught her eye, noted her interest, then deciding the sociable approach was the better of the options available, raised his clenched fist and said, "Bruv?"

Tammy responded by brushing knuckles with Lloyd, presuming that indicated some measure of man-on-man acceptance achieved by her. Kendall stopped for a moment, regarding Tammy with interest, then as though he'd made a decision said, "Y'all watch yourself in dis place. Take care, man, hmm? Don't want to get duppy. Some fiend cut you."

The two men drifted away uncertainly, while Pope, smiling, asked, "Mind if I take a pew?"

"Help yourself," said Tammy, with some sense of relief at a possible crisis averted.

Then she asked, "Duppy? Fiend?"

"Seems you've hit it off with Lloyd. He's warning you to be careful of fiends, or drug addicts."

"And duppy? Sounds like something I heard Bob Marley singing about."

"To be precise," said Pope, "duppy is urban slang with a Jamaican root for becoming a ghost or spirit. In short, getting yourself killed. How come you don't know that? You're black. Where were you brought up?"

"I'm middle class, my friend. Do I sound like Lloyd?"

"I suppose not. In fact, word on the street is no-one knows much about you at all, Mr Peters. Does that surprise you?" Pope concentrated on straightening the crease in his trousers.

"I don't know, should it?" said Tammy, sitting back on the bed with her arms around drawn-up knees.

"Rumour has it, five members of a drug dealing gang dispatched? Only rumour, mind. But convicted where? The Old Bailey? The warders haven't been any help. As in the dark as the rest of us. I should have thought that with that accolade on your CV it would surely indicate you've had plenty of previous encounters with others of the same ilk, dealt with in the same way?"

"A few." Tammy shrugged.

"Care to enlighten me?" Pope asked.

"I think not," Tammy said. Then changing tack she said, "While you're here, Dom, okay to call you Dom?"

"Of course," he replied, shifting around to get more comfortable on the cell's one rickety chair.

"Could you use a tea?"

Pope, to give him due credit, kept his surprise at this unexpected offer of hospitality well hidden. "Why not," he enthused, reaching into his trouser pocket to pull out a Dunhill briar pipe of the type favoured by Sherlock Holmes and a small pouch of tobacco, from which he extracted a quantity of the crushed leaves, packed them into the bowl of the pipe and tamped it all down with the tip of his thumb. A flame from a flip-top lighter followed, and Tammy watched fascinated while Pope started puffing away contentedly. The cell was soon filled with a fug of sweet-smelling tobacco.

"I thought smoking was forbidden. Health grounds? How do you manage to get away with it?" she asked.

"Friends in high places," he replied.

While Tammy busied herself with filling and boiling a kettle of water, setting out mugs and milk and sugar on the tiny table, Pope took his interrogation of Tammy a subtle step further. "When I said no-one knows much about you, Tommy, I'm led to believe that includes our esteemed governor, Brian Cudlipp. Now how can that be possible?"

"Search me," said Tammy.

"Given the choice, I'd prefer not," he said, looking up and down at her drab tracksuit.

Easing up for the first time since her incarceration, Tammy, testing the water, said, "I think we understand each other, Dom. We're what you might call, en rapport. Hmm?"

"Of course," he said, then observed, "that accent. French, I presume?"

Back on the bed, blowing on the surface of the steaming mug, she responded, "Part French."

"I referred to your interest in film, Tommy. Another comes to mind."

"Oh, yeah?"

"Don't tell me you don't know what I'm talking about. I'll repeat, no-one knows who you are, why you're here, how you got here, including the governor."

"A total mystery," she suggested unhelpfully.

"Come on, Tommy." Placing his mug on the table, his hands either side of it, Pope, the pipe clenched between his teeth, said, "We both know I'm referring to Robert Redford's role in *Brubaker*. It's exactly the same scenario."

He stared at her, fascinated, then, "Just what in heaven's name are you up to? Research for a film? A book? Are you really a convicted felon? God help you in this place if you're not and it gets found out."

Tammy, looking blank, finished more of her tea without comment.

CHAPTER 59 DAY 35

"WELL, HAVE YOU FOUND HER yet? Is the bitch still alive?" Mountford's temper was on the rise, his voice beginning to crack with the strain of it all.

"We think she's in Belmarsh, but we can't be certain." Ricks's voice wobbled with anxiety.

"What the fuck do you mean, you can't be certain, you total wanker. Do I need to break out of here and kill the tart myself?"

"No, Oscar, of course not."

"Oscar? Oscar? Whaddaya mean Oscar? It's Mr Mountford to you, you total tosser."

"She's only been missing three nights and we're doing all we can to locate her, but the prison service is in lockdown. If they know where she is they're not saying."

"What about your boss, Manus? Has he died too?"

"No, sir. But I've dropped hints which he has ignored."

"Well drop a few more, you fucking moron. And what about your wonderful contacts in Belmarsh? Where are they right now? Retired to the South of France?"

"We still don't know for sure it is Belmarsh, Mr Mountford, and if I push the boat out now and it's another prison she's in I don't want to use up my credit. Also, my two main Belmarsh contacts are on leave."

"On leave? On leave?" Mountford was screaming now.

"Well get them back from leave. Or maybe hand back the Rolex I lent you by mistake."

"I'll do what I can, Mr Mountford. I promise I will."

"God save us all. Wherever the hell did I find you?"

His voice dropped to a whisper. "Now hear this, my man, either you get your finger out and see to our black friend or I'll have a chat with the Kerkuts about terminating your career. Permanently. If you get my drift."

CHAPTER 60 DAY 36

POPE HELD OUT A WARNING to Tammy.

"Cudlipp's making enquiries, you know. He's a man who operates on a short fuse. No-one crosses him more than once. Whatever you're up to, he'll let play out, no matter the consequences for you. Which could be dire. And he could confine you to Seg. Genuine felon or not. Bare room. No bed, no blankets. No water. No toilet. No fun. Believe me. After that, and depending on developments, you can expect a summons to his presence."

"I'm not worried about segregation. If anything, I'll welcome it." She held her breath, waiting for the next remark, and wasn't disappointed.

"Brave talk, Mr Peters. Or maybe, just foolish. So," Pope ventured. "We've both been guilty of a similar crime."

"Not exactly," corrected Tammy. "Yours was personal. Mine was strictly business."

"Business?" Pope protested. "Is that what you call it? And how do you know about me?"

"Google, Dom. Before I was admitted I made a search of the place and our companions. Course, you came up."

"Fair enough."

"Quite a reputation you've got."

"It's a damned millstone around my neck."

"Well, now there's a confession if ever I heard one. 'Nother cup?"

"Why not," said Pope, stretching his arms behind his head to ease his aching back.

"Tell me, Dom. If you don't mind me asking, are you from an Italian background?"

"Why do you ask?" He looked at Tammy quizzically.
"Oh, I know. The skin colour. Swarthy, they tell me. I tan easily. Or did when I was free."

"So, Italian?"

"No. Cypriot. Northern Cyprus to be precise. Similar complexion. My people originally came to this country somewhere around 1950. Made a life here. David was born in 1979." He seemed reluctant to enlarge, other than to say, "He's forty-four now."

Interesting coincidence, she thought. The Kerkuts are from a Cypriot background too. They and Pope would have made for interesting bedfellows. Though Dom killed for his own twisted reasons, not as means to an end like the Kerkuts, who are principally interested in money.

Boiling another kettle, Tammy probed as gently as she could. "Why a millstone, Dom?"

"Why? I'll tell you why. Because I've a reputation to maintain in here."

"So I've heard. It's quite something to have," she said, placing the second mug in front of him before resuming her place on the bed.

"I was a young thug, you know. Any excuse to get into a fight. I'm not tall like my crew, but my God, I could handle myself in those days. Unstoppable, if you ask me."

"And now?" she asked, interested.

"And now I'm saddled with it. I used to revel in violence. What you'd call a borderline psychopath."

"Did you say borderline?" Tammy asked, astonished. "With your reputation, I'd have said full blown."

"A matter of semantics, Tommy. Okay, I killed a lot of people, adults, children. I hid a lot of victims the authorities never knew about. They were just listed as missing persons. I made sure I operated in different parts of the country so nothing would link one killing to another, and nothing would be tied to me. But as I say, most were never found. I dug their graves deep. I'm in here for forty years, for what they do know about. If I told them the rest they'd keep me in for a hundred years. At least, metaphorically. Either way I'll die in this place," he sighed.

"A lot of people, eh?" She was sitting on the side of the bed, her feet resting on the floor of the cell, leaning back propped against the mattress.

"Whatever was available. And, as I said, got away with nearly all of it. Until here happened, of course."

"Sounds like a shopping list."

"It was very much. Trouble is, I loved it, the crunch of bones breaking under my grip. Flesh opening at the introduction of my knife. It gave me a sense of peace. Even a sense of purpose. Impossible to explain, I'm afraid." He gave a half smile at the recollection.

"Is that what you needed?" She tried to catch his eye, but he consistently looked away from her. But she persisted. "Was a normal life so off your radar?"

"No!" He waited a moment, thought about his response. "Well, yes. I suppose. As I think I've made abundantly clear, I loved the thrill of the kill. And again, your life is hardly normal either."

Ignoring the comment, she went on to press Pope. "And now?"

"I'm weary of it."

"Really? You're kidding me."

"It happens."

"Once a killer…"

"Not that simple, Tommy." He spread his hands, palms up. "Maybe it's just the hormones drying up. Who knows?"

"So, what made it happen in the first place? Bad homelife? School? Someone kicked the shit out of you?"

"All perfect, at least in the beginning, no complaints whatsoever; at least on the face of it." That sounded promising, even ominous, but she didn't interrupt his flow.

"Parents idolised me," he continued. "I was school captain. Blues at rugby and cricket. First class honours in law, would you believe? The London School of Economics, no less. I was everybody's blue-eyed boy."

She still wasn't making headway, interesting though it all was. Then, picking up on something she felt might lead somewhere, she asked, "So, is borderline psychopathy hereditary?" She finished her mug, and leaning forward, placed it next to his on the table, in a mute act of unity.

He gazed up at the ceiling, looking for inspiration? "I sincerely hope not. Certainly not where my parents were concerned, anyway."

"I'm interested," urged Tammy as casually as she could, intuition telling her he still had further to travel. "Go on."

"An incident occurred after I'd graduated that was to turn my life around."

Tammy smiled encouragingly, letting the remark hang for the moment. "Okay. Keep going," she said eventually.

"My parents' marriage began to show signs of stress. They bickered more and more. Sometimes it was trivial things. Other times it was to do with their lifestyle, which Mother felt should have been far better, in her opinion, than it was. She was always the dominant personality between them. Even looked the part. Taller than he. Prominent nose. Square jaw. Slight moustache on her upper lip. In comparison he appeared almost effeminate."

"Couldn't your father do something about the lifestyle? Improve it? Whatever?" She shifted her position on the bed trying to get comfortable but not wanting to distract him from his flow.

"Not really. They were both accountants, not business people, so while the earnings provided a good standard of living, it wasn't spectacular, and certainly not enough for the lifestyle she craved."

"Tough," Tammy observed.

"Worse than that, she became more and more disgruntled. She took to demeaning him in public, highlighting every shortcoming she could find. It went on for months without end. Father always kept his temper. Stiff upper lip and so on. He never got angry. He wasn't that sort of person. But she provoked and provoked, until one day he said quietly, 'If you don't stop, Martha, I shall kill you.'"

"Okay. Anyone would ..." She paused for thought, then, "Jesus, I bloody would."

"Exactly."

"So, did he keep his temper?"

"She was laughing at him. Mocking him. Calling him names. Letting him know she thought he was inadequate, in every sense of the word. Particularly, and this was the clincher, in bed. She hinted she'd had affairs, dozens of them, under his nose and without his knowledge and that the worst of her lovers was a better performer than he."

"And still he kept cool? I'd have gone mental by now."

"I was raging, wishing he'd do something, thinking that if he didn't, I'd bloody step in myself, but Dad smiled on. Said nothing. The consummate pacificist. He was brilliant. Walked calmly up to Mum as she ridiculed him, and, putting his hands on her shoulders in a gesture of friendship and reconciliation, broke her neck."

"Christ."

"He did it in so skilled a way I couldn't believe he'd never done anything like it before."

"You say, skilled? And, never before?"

"What I mean to say is, she died quickly, of course, but at the same time with a brief hiatus. Just long enough for her to realise what he'd done to her. If you'd seen the look on her face. Eyes wide. Mouth open. It was wonderful to witness. Because of the way she'd treated Dad I'd grown to despise her, and in that time, all women too. Particularly those who resembled her in some way. I started to dream of doing what Dad had done. God, he went up in my estimation."

"So, you started killing?"

"I told you I was an inherent thug. It was easy to make the transition to out and out killer. So now I went at it with purpose. Killing that is. Not immediately, though. I needed to test the water. Falsifying my identity, I organised a couple of dates, countryside walks, woodland exploration. Examining the flora and fauna. I was a natural-born assassin. Each time I killed I was Dad killing Mother. It was all I could do to restrain myself from letting out war cries at the critical moment. Then I got to enjoy killing for its own sake, whatever and whomever I could find. Like you, Tommy, I'm a movie buff. Watched the film *Natural Born Killers* at least twenty times. More. The joy spread."

"Well, to repeat, Dom, for you it was personal, least at the start, before you got to obsess. For me, it was business all the way, man. Only buzz I got was a job well done. A patch taken over. Increased income. Power. An aphrodisiac, like a side benefit. But then you don't need me to tell you that."

There was a lull in the conversation. Movement on their landing. People walking around. Voices, some raised, some muffled.

Tammy studied his face, still trying to figure out the man. Finally, she asked, "Tell me, mate, did you never have anything out there for any one human being at all?"

Dom was uncertain whether or not to go on. He showed every sign he was wrestling with a personal quandary. His brow furrowed, he scraped his fingers through tousled hair, fidgeted with the mug on the table. Then, having finally decided to disclose, he said, "I have a son." He spoke quietly as though afraid someone might be listening.

She recognised the confidence granted, and said nothing, hoping he might reveal more.

"David. Pope. Now, Eckstein. Not surprisingly he changed his name."

"Do you ever get to see him?"

"God no. He won't have anything to do with me. Daddy's a serial killer."

"He has a point, wouldn't you say?"

"Whatever I am, or appear to be, to you and the outside world, he's still my boy. Nothing will ever stop me from loving him. He's the only one I do. Or ever did."

"Human after all, man. Hmm? Or maybe I mean, after a fashion. Did you play any part in raising him?"

"All of it. The silly cow I was married to wasn't interested in kids and buggered off by the time he was seven or eight. She'd have gone as soon as he was born, given the chance, but she needed my financial support till she found something else. No idea how she managed later. You see, I was away a lot, and the boy tried to tell me something, each time I got back. I never knew what. But he was often distressed, the little lad. I was always too busy to listen. Years later it occurred to me from what he hinted at she may have abused him, or else, had him abused. Never saw her again. Thank God. Christ knows what I saw in her in the first place." He pondered the issue, then said, "She kept a tidy home. She was convenient for a time. Things that count, after all."

"How'd you rear the boy?"

"I tried to make him happy, secure. You know. I had no time to kill, as it were, so I actually did something useful, apart from the FX trading, for once."

"That it?" she pushed, to get further behind the wall protecting his past. "Anything else you want to talk about?"

"I couldn't contain my hatred of women. And whilst I wasn't out on the hunt, I'm afraid I wittingly or otherwise sowed the seeds of hate during the whole of his young life."

"And did he take your attitude on board? What did you think? He was going to copy Daddy?"

"No." Pope smiled to himself. "A big lad. Tall and exceptionally strong, he was gentle as they come." An echo there of Michael Hedges' description of his own son. "More relevant though, he liked girls. Just as well. It wouldn't have done to breed another killer like me."

"And now? How does he earn his keep?"

"He's a serial entrepreneur, lives in Blackburn, drives a luxury car I've been told. I'm proud of him. Can you believe that?"

"Look, you've given me a lotta time, Dom," she said, shifting her position in an indication she wanted to be alone. "It's been a blast."

Looking at Tammy full on, he replied, "It's probably the first time I've had a chance to confide in anyone in years. Possibly ever. Incidentally, there was one other thing I failed to mention."

"I'm listening."

"Where do we go with this?" he said quietly. Then, having decided to go on, "One night, when I was about seven years old, Mother came into my bedroom after I'd been put down for the night."

Tammy made no comment and he went on. "I thought she was going to kiss me goodnight and tuck me as usual."

Tammy enquired, "She had something else in mind?"

"That's right."

"Let me guess," said Tammy.

"It wasn't nice."

"Just the one time?"

"That's right. I did what I could to forget it. Otherwise, a happy upbringing, I suppose, but this grey shadow always lurked in the corner of my vision. After Dad did what he did the recollection came back to me with a vengeance, and certainly further coloured my perception of women."

"And your dad?"

"A kindly individual. Couldn't believe what he'd done. Pleaded diminished responsibility and still got ten years. Died a broken man three years in. The bitch had effectively killed him. I got angrier and angrier by the minute."

"I see where you're coming from."

"I loved Dad, but saw him as essentially weak, apart from the one aberration. One thing you haven't asked, don't you want to know why I killed that family of five?"

"Tell me," she responded, a shiver of anticipation running down her spine.

Pope stood up and stretched his legs, wandered around the confined space. "I told you earlier, in civvy street I was a foreign exchange dealer in a fringe bank. I got an intro to a wealthy family who I dealt with mostly through the telephone or emails. They bought and sold foreign currencies in huge quantities. I felt it would be good policy to meet up. When I suggested it, the wife insisted she entertain me at their mansion in Holland Park. What I came across shocked me. The husband was a brilliant self-made businessman, but amiable like my father, to the point of effeminacy. The mother was as close to a carbon copy of my mother as you'd find, even down to the incipient moustache.

"But what really appalled me was their three sons, aged fifteen to eighteen. I'd only eaten there a handful of times, when this liberal, farsighted family decided to happily confide in me that the two eldest of their sons were thinking of having transsexual surgery. It was all I could do to contain my rage. They were men, for God's sake. Not bloody women. I became obsessed with the whole thing. Couldn't eat, couldn't sleep for the knowledge, spreading in my head like a cancer. The next time they entertained me I took an eight-inch blade and slaughtered them all, unable to resist the temptation to castrate, well emasculate, the two eldest. It was cathartic. But there was no covering my tracks this time. I ended up in here. You can see why my son disowned me."

"That's one helluva history, Dom. Obvious question; did what you'd experienced leave you gay?"

"Nope. But unable to form any sort of normal loving relationships with women, which, after my stupid bitch of a wife left, I couldn't anyway, so I used prostitutes."

Turning over all she'd been told, she suggested, "I'm guessing you've covered it all now?"

"Pretty much, I reckon. Thanks for listening, Tommy." He nodded with finality. She'd got as much as she would from him.

"Any time," she said.

"Incidentally, Tommy, what're you going to do with all this superfluous information I've given you?" Aware the revelations might impact his reputation and power within the prison community.

"Good point, Dom," she responded, considering the options. "Probably chew it over with you from time to time if they leave me in this cell block. We'll both have enough time to talk, won't we. Years, in fact. Maybe I'll tell you my life story too."

Pope yawned, stretched, made to go, relieved at Tammy's assurances. "I look forward to the privilege, Tommy."

Some activity was happening outside her cell, but at that moment she was unsighted. It wouldn't be for long.

Instead, she debated. A lot of work to do here. More information than she'd expected to glean. The son, Eckstein, would need to be followed up. Impossible to know where that would go; but it was a lead of sorts. Actually, more a line of enquiry. If she were honest with herself, the hope that talking to a serial killer would lead her to the East London murderer, was speculative at best. Still, a man who despises women with a chilling down on potential or perceived transsexuals? If she were in Belmarsh long enough she'd tap Pope for any other contacts he might have had with the same inclinations as his. He did admit he'd castrated the boys.

Feeling a tad disappointed, she was left with the sole option of mixing in with the Islamic crowd, if she was able in whatever time she had left in the prison.

She was about to find out what she'd been unaware of a moment or two ago. The sound of heavy footsteps echoed along the landing. Menacing. The cell block became quiet as an empty church. No disputes, no deals, no banging of tin cutlery against the bars.

"Hear that?" asked Pope, cupping an ear.

"You mean the silence," she said.

"I'd better make myself scarce."

"Oh!"

"They're coming for you, Tommy. Best of luck, young man. You're sure as hell gonna need it."

"I'll be ready."

Pope shook his head in disbelief. "I'll say one thing for you, you sound like the real thing, son. If you're not, you've got me fooled. But I say again, how can a felon ostensibly guilty of five murders, at least you say, get in here with people so much in the dark about you?"

"They won't be for all time," she said cryptically. "Truth will out."

CHAPTER 61 DAY 37

THE FOOTSTEPS GOT CLOSER, clattering along the landing. Three maybe four sets of them. Their paces heavy and deliberate like something feral.

But not out hunting for food, these were predators solely seeking a kill. She was being tracked, their prey, and she was already cornered. No hiding place. Nowhere to run. The silence grew more oppressive.

A cloud moved across the sun, obscuring it, throwing the cell into comparative darkness.

A bead of perspiration ran down the centre of her back. Two more between her breasts till her stomach felt wet, her tracksuit sticky.

She took the same stance as before to meet them. A twist of fear, then the hair stood up on her arms, her bones felt icy, and a serpent of uncertainty slithered around the base of her gut. She breathed in, pulse slowing, calming herself.

Inconsequentially, she realised she'd not had a shower since arriving at the prison. Was that sweat or simply fear she could smell on her own body.

She indulged herself with a momentary thought of baby Matthew. He'd be all but orphaned, unless Dov were to accept the findings of any DNA test he might organise and take the lad on, whatever the results.

They were at her cell door. Four men in T-shirts and tracksuit bottoms, all over six feet, with beer bellies, the front two, shaven-headed. All of them with extensive tattoos on their arms.

The fear evaporated, to be replaced by anger, immediately overtaken by a rational assessment of her situation. Which was bleak.

Their mutterings had been heard ahead of the men. "Skinny bloke, I've heard. Shouldn't be no trouble. Ah baht we break bofe 'is arms, an' maybe 'is legs an' all? Hah!"

The first man presenting himself at her open door, his eyes bloodshot, insane, spoke softly. She preferred shouting because that signalled a loss of control. This man was entirely in charge of himself and the situation. "You hurt one of my mates, mister. Now we're gonna make you pay, nigger. Gonna teach you respect for white people."

His breath, stinking of sour milk and alcohol, made her nose wrinkle in disgust, the back of her throat sting as though she'd ingested what he expelled. It suited her that he didn't rush into the cell but shuffled in slowly. It gave her time to think, albeit with bare seconds in hand.

Krav Maga had been her saviour before. But she'd not always faced four assailants at the same time. Thankfully, with there being no other choice, they approached in single file. She noted there was no mattress this time, but the men all carried batons, as was to be expected. Applied directly to her flesh she realised there'd be a lot of blood. Specifically, hers.

After that, things happened in slow motion.

The man at the front stepped into her space, with a baton raised above his head. She swiftly shot an arm up and grasped him by the wrist, seeing him grin, then the grin quickly fading as she twisted his arm around and up his back in a half-nelson. "'Ave to do better'n that, nigger," the man said, struggling against her lock.

"How's this then, sir?" she said, pushing the arm further up his back.

He wasn't about to give in, so Tammy pushed harder and harder still, the man now grunting in pain. "Fuck you, pretty boy."

"Do you think so, sweetie?" She panted with the effort. "Fancy a kiss?"

"You mutherfucker. Get 'im, Sean," he called to the man immediately behind him. "Before 'e ..."

But Sean was impeded by the sound of a hideous crack and a scream, then the man's falling body as Tammy broke the arm at the shoulder. He lay, struggling in agony, the arm at a crazy angle.

Almost indistinguishable from the first man, Sean blundered into the cell swinging his baton to the left and right like a maniac. One blow hit her on the shoulder, another, despite her swaying to avoid it, glanced off her skull, leaving her dizzy for a moment. Acting as fast as her depleted reflexes would allow, she stuck her index and middle fingers into the man's eyes. It was like prodding hard-boiled eggs. She watched as he scrabbled frantically at his face, noting blood trickling from one eye. She'd dealt with him as hard as she'd intended.

The third man now attempted to clamber over the first two but found his way in to her cell restricted. Nonetheless, ignoring their moans and fallen bodies he made it close enough to attack her.

Some noise was now making itself heard in the cell block, building up as prisoners awoke to the fact that the destruction of one of their number still hadn't taken place. Metal utensils banged relentlessly against cell bars and men hooted encouragement.

He'd moved quickly during Tammy's moment of distraction, man number three. She felt the impact of the baton on her other shoulder, her hip, her neck, the latter splitting the skin causing profuse bleeding, and impeding her breathing. Explosions of pain with each; she felt herself fading and realised she was in big trouble. Like the first man, he made the mistake of raising the baton above shoulder height and she immediately grabbed the opportunity to latch on to his forearm with one hand, his elbow with the other while bringing down the arm across her raised knee.

The sound of a sharp snap and the man's bellowing as the broken radius and ulna pierced the flesh in two jagged white points like iceberg tips, were acknowledged throughout the cell block with a further response of cheers and yells.

The fourth man, looking at the carnage, simply shrugged, made his decision, and ambled away.

Tammy, ignoring the pile of bodies in her cell, sat down heavily on the edge of her bed, her head in her hands, breathing deeply, trying to recover herself. Her tracksuit top was wet with blood at the shoulder, she was spent and felt close to oblivion, dark shadows closing in at the edges of her sight.

Unaware of other warders dragging the bodies out of her cell, their groans barely registering, she glanced up to see Lloyd Kendall standing over her. "Taken a hammering, bro. Need to get that seen to," he suggested, looking at her neck. "Dom's damned impressed."

"Delighted to hear it, Lloyd. I'll be okay if I just sit awhile and unwind."

"Your call, my man," said Lloyd, looking at her, concerned. "Still think you should go to medical, get yourself patched up."

"I agree with Lloyd here." Pope had just arrived back on the scene. "No need to be a hero, young man. You've made your point."

But Pope got no further when a slim young warder with acne looked in and said, "Governor wants to see you, mate. Are you for it? Says if they brought back flogging he'd buy his own cat o' nine. Anyway, after you seen 'im, you're going to Seg. Be nice and comfy there."

CHAPTER 62 DAY 37

THE GOVERNOR'S OFFICE was a spacious room with a light wood desk planted in the centre, bare of any embellishments or personal items, an all-white décor and a wall of filing cabinets lined up like sentries on guard. Situated behind the governor was a large wall-mounted screen.

A man in his fifties, Brian Cudlipp sat behind his desk in a freshly laundered, blue open-neck shirt, his sleeves rolled up to reveal forearms as hairy as a silverback gorilla. Tammy stood before him like a recalcitrant school child, struggling to keep her exhausted self from failing her, and said nothing, waiting, fascinated to see what the governor would say, noting he appeared the epitome of elegance. So she was surprised when he spoke.

"Who the hell are you and what the fuck are you doing in my nick, sonny? And just look at the state of you."

The old scars, throbbing, the ugly bruise to her head and the wound that had brought forth blood when she was struck on the neck. She was hurting everywhere. Blades of pain cut into her all over. Blood soaked through her tracksuit top which she'd not had an opportunity to change. She was weary, hadn't anticipated the savagery of the events of the last two days. The last thing she needed right now was a fight with the raging man she was facing.

She'd planned to have more time. Inside, that is. Both to talk to Pope, draw him out some more, and then to see what information she could garner from the Islamic prison community. The latter, probably a long shot, she accepted. The number of so-called terrorists within that group, whatever crimes had brought them into Belmarsh, would be minimal, if any.

So, now her time in here was up. She hoped. Cudlipp was a quite unknown quantity. The moment had come to confess. But with his discretion, he could easily plant her in Seg for a few days. A horrific prospect.

She took a deep breath. "My name is Tammy Pierre and I am a private investigator looking into the East London killings by the so-called Tilbury Ripper."

"You're what?" His mouth hung open for several moments in disbelief.

Tammy stood in silence before the man, noting he was so angry beads of sweat laced his brow, a vein stood out on his temple.

"Answer me, for crying out loud," he said, standing and banging a bunched fist on the desk so hard that it made her jump.

"I'm a PI, Mr Cudlipp, investigating multiple murders around the Tilbury area."

"And who the hell asked you to meddle in what is strictly a police matter?" Spittle was forming at the corners of his mouth.

"Where do you come in to all this? And a woman, you say? This your idea of a joke. 'Cos if it is, no-one's laughing in here, sonny. Do I even mean, sonny?"

"I was retained by the owner of the clubs, Ms Hester Lamont, to look into a murder that had taken place on one of her sets of premises when she felt the police were somewhat at a loss due to the nature of her clubs and clientele."

"You mean a mix of gay and transsexual people." There was a trace of contempt in his voice. "I've read all about it. We all have."

"Not only," she explained. "There were a few nights a week when the concentration was LGBTQQ, but the rest of the week was for all comers, straight, gay, trans and so on."

"And you like dressing up as man, judging by what I'm seeing here."

"Not particularly. In fact, it's only when the occasion demands it."

"And just what did you imagine you'd find in my nick? The killer, for God's sake?"

"I wanted to speak with a multiple murderer, you've got at least one here, to see if I could pick up any leads or hints as to what makes that sort of individual tick. Maybe it would help and maybe not. But it was worth a punt."

Cudlipp, who'd sat back down, swung his director's chair to the left and right in a gesture of impatience.

"You've been talking with Dominic Pope, our resident celebrity. God knows how many killings to his credit. He's boasted about them often enough."

"Do you mind if I sit down, Mr Cudlipp?"

Ignoring the request, Cudlipp asked, "How the devil did you get in here? There's been snippets of useless news in some of the press, national, local, none of it substantiated by anyone on my team. How the killing of five members of a drug trafficking gang fails to be widely reported, or even verified, gaining only minimal coverage is way beyond me."

"Do you mind if I sit down, Mr Cudlipp." With the threat of Seg hanging over her, she decided not to push her luck claiming the initiative by sitting down anyway.

"Obviously you've had help getting in here. I learned almost as soon as you were admitted of your presence, but decided to see where it and you were going."

"It's a long story, sir."

"Try me. I've got all day, and all night too, if need be."

He got up from his desk and went over to a low filing cabinet upon which a cafetière rested, poured himself a mug of coffee then resumed his seat. Tammy's mouth watered at the smell, but she wouldn't give Cudlipp the satisfaction of turning down any request for a drink herself. "Who do you know in the force, Ms Pierre?"

"I know several officers, sir."

"Who, for example? John Manus is working on the Tilbury killings, I do know. Good man. Well respected. You've worked with him?"

"I have," she said, shifting from one foot to another.

"And did he sanction this merry jaunt of yours?"

"Of course not." She folded her arms, fatigue seeping further into her bones. Much more of this and she'd keel over.

"Who else? Who else do you know?"

If she didn't tell him he'd probably find out anyway, so she offered, "Detective Chief Superintendent Bob Walker."

"You know Bob, do you? And does he know about this escapade of yours? I cannot believe he'd have anything to do with it."

"Neither Bob nor John has any inkling of what I'm up to. I merely told John I'd be away for a couple of days, but didn't elaborate. And nothing of any sort was mentioned to Bob."

Taking his time over his coffee, Cudlipp asked, "And how have you come to know DCS Walker, whom you refer to in such familiar terms?"

"He was my boss when I was a DI."

"You're an ex-copper?" He looked astonished.

"That's right." She switched to the other leg. She'd allow him one more question, then she'd sit, whatever the man said, or did.

For the first time he looked interested. "And have you made any progress while you've been in here? Has Pope been of any use?"

Enough of this nonsense, she decided and with enormous relief, sat down firmly on the padded seat in front of Cudlipp's desk.

"I didn't say you could sit down, Ms Pierre," he shouted, pointing at her accusingly.

CHAPTER 62 • DAY 37 • 395

"And I didn't say you could keep me standing indefinitely, Mr Cudlipp."

To her surprise he made no issue of it, merely reiterating his enquiry. "Has Pope been any help?"

"It's too soon to tell." She wasn't about to mention any of Pope's confidences. "I've a couple of lines to follow up."

"Now about my men." He paused again, open-mouthed as Tammy got back up, walked over to the cabinet, and poured herself a mug of coffee, before returning to her seat. "Cheeky blighter," he said.

"What about your men, Brian?"

Raising his eyebrows in surprise at the sound of Tammy's familiarity, he said, "You've put several in hospital."

"Unfortunate. Maybe they should have thought about that before attacking me in my cage. I won't enlarge."

"Where did you learn to fight like you did?" She noted Cudlipp's tone had mellowed considerably since her arrival in his office.

"My boyfriend coached me in Krav Maga."

"I know, the Israeli system. Clearly very effective. Maybe I should have my staff learn it, if only to protect themselves from the likes of you," he said, a faint smile playing about the corners of his mouth.

Then leaning back in his swivel chair, steepling his fingers, Cudlipp commented, "You know, I could have your PI licence revoked."

"Try it."

"What!"

"I said, try it," she repeated. "And if you do I'll make sure the press get details of the attacks that took place, when four big men under your supervision weren't able to subdue a relatively helpless woman investigating multiple murders in an attempt to safeguard the public."

"Really?"

"Truly."

"And who do you think will stand as witness to all this, if we decide to cover it up?"

"Lloyd Kendall, for one. We clicked. And I'll wager, Dominic Pope."

"Pope? He's a bloody multiple murderer," Cudlipp protested.

"Too right, Brian." She paused for a moment to sip from the coffee mug, feeling the scalding liquid slip gloriously down her throat. "Just think, the press will love it. The public will soak it up."

"Bloody women," muttered Cudlipp.

"What was that?"

"Nothing, nothing," he responded.

"So where next, governor?"

"Where indeed?" he asked, very much at a loss. Then, as though struggling, he sighed, "Very well. I'll have a warder bring your things here from your cell. You can clean up in my en-suite."

He indicated a door to his left. "Take a shower and change. I'll have one of the medics bring some plaster for that neck. Do you want it stitched?"

"Not necessary," she said, astonished at the man's sudden change of tack, but not about to question it.

"Then I'll have you driven home in an unmarked car."

"One thing," she added. "Can you ask one of your female warders if they have an eyebrow pencil I might borrow? I can't turn up at home without eyebrows, looking like, like, *The Creature from the Black Lagoon.*

"Oh," she thought again, "and maybe some lipstick? Any colour will do."

She was in the shower for a full half hour, at first horrified at the sight of herself in the wall mirror. Haggard and drawn. A bloodied, smooth-skulled spectre.

The borrowed make-up made her look and feel a bit more like a human being. As for the prison stink clinging to her, she searched around Brian's toiletries and found aftershave and cologne, the latter she applied liberally. With her neck wound dressed and plastered by the obliging female warder, and a change of tracksuit, she emerged both fresher and refreshed.

Back in Cudlipp's office the governor introduced her to Sergeant Comings, a good-looking young man in uniform, who would drive her home.

"For what you've put yourself through, I hope your time here doesn't prove to have been completely wasted," said Cudlipp, both looking and sounding doubtful.

"Time will tell," Tammy replied. "Can't say I'll be sorry to leave this place."

Cudlipp's eyebrows were raised.

"You might do me one favour, Brian."

"I hesitate to ask. Go on."

"Give me an intro to Pope's son."

"David Eckstein?"

"The same. He's in Blackburn."

"I know where he is. What do you want with him?"

"I'll let you know when I find out myself, Brian."

"I'll see what I can do for you. When did you have in mind for a visit?"

"Tomorrow."

"Tomorrow? God, you don't waste time, do you."

"Thanks, Brian. You're a star," she said, getting ready to go.

Just as she was leaving the governor extended a hand. "I'll say one thing for you, Ms Pierre."

"Oh, please, Tammy," she replied, taking his bear-like hand in her own.

"Tammy. Okay, Tammy," he agreed reluctantly.

"And what was it you were about to say?"

"I was about to say, you've sure got balls."

"Acclamation indeed, Brian." She grinned. "Albeit not entirely accurate, though."

CHAPTER 63 DAY 38

"WELL? WHAT'S HAPPENED?" Mountford was testy, his voice rising in frustration.

"I need to hear something positive, man. Ease the monotony of this place. Food's like pigswill. The stink of unwashed bodies. The stench of this all-pervasive Spice drug. Toochie, they call it. I'd kill for a decent claret.

"I get no respect in here. You'd think they'd recognise a politician when they see one. Understand class when it's presented to them on a plate. When they hear one of us speak." He turned over in his mind what he wanted to say, then admitted, "Well, ex-politician. Instead, they talk to me as though I were no better than the peasant class they represent. Inarticulate buffoons. You wait when I get out of here…"

"Oscar, you've been sentenced to forty years…"

"Don't argue with me, Mario. Breeding will out. Always. My appeal will be lodged shortly."

"I hope you won't be disappointed."

"Don't preach to me, you idiot. Tell me the bitch is dead. That's all I want to hear. Has the whore been killed yet? If not, why not?"

"No, Oscar. Not yet."

"Not yet? Not yet?" Mountford's voice had reached screaming pitch. "What the fuck is going on?"

"Ricks got word to his contacts in Belmarsh and they gave her a welcoming warm up …"

"What does that mean? Dinner at Claridge's care of Gordon Ramsay?"

"She was beaten in her cell."

Mario was floundering. "I don't think Ricks made it quite clear she was wanted dead."

"And now?"

"I spelled it out for him. Exactly what you wanted."

"In words of half syllables, I trust."

"He got four warders to go to her cell, with clear instructions."

"So? Why isn't she dead yet?"

"I don't think they were expecting her to be able to defend herself in the way she ..."

"God give me strength. So where is she now?"

"She's out, Oscar."

"Out? After what just four days? I thought she'd be there for a week, at least. Assuming she survived that long. Give us time to deal with her."

"The governor organised a lift home for her."

"This is better than a Michael McIntyre comedy show," he bellowed. "Did he hire a Rolls-Royce for her as well?"

There was a rising commotion in the background, voices complaining that Oscar was causing a disturbance.

Then the call was cut.

CHAPTER 64 DAY 38

SHE'D SLEPT THE NIGHT with Matty in her arms, unafraid of the possibility of overlaying.

It was a rarity, and his warmth and softness were irresistible. Little hands grasping her fingers, toes up against her chest. His contented breathing a reminder that above everything else this was what it was all about.

Risky, pleased to see her home, had pressed her flanks against Tammy's legs, leaving the food that had been put out for her by Maria, miaowing until her mistress fed her personally.

Maria had cried when Tammy first arrived home. "Oh, Madame Pierre! What has happened? What have you done?"

"Actually, Maria, I haven't done anything," she said, intending to elaborate, when her mobile interrupted them. "Tammy Pierre," she announced somewhat distracted, before spotting who it was.

"Tammy! I heard you were out," said Manus. "I also heard you had a hard time in there. Cudlipp gave me the full SP. Seems he was impressed. But tell me, did you achieve anything? Was it worth the risks involved?"

"A few bruises, John. And did I achieve anything? The sixty-four-thousand-dollar question. Frankly, if I were to do a cost benefit analysis, I'd have to say the results would be no better than debatable."

"I understand you got to see Pope?"

"The reason for the visit. And if there was anything gained, it was info about his son who is based in Blackburn. And maybe, less relevantly, some insight into the man, Pope, himself."

"I'm listening."

Tammy described all that had been discussed with Pope, and how off-beam one's general perception or, at any rate, her own of what a made up a serial killer was. This was an educated, articulate man, running his wing of the prison, more or less because it was expected if he was to retain the respect and control of the prisoners.

"The son was so appalled at his father's record, that rather than risk any possibility of his being linked to him, however remote, he'd changed his name to Eckstein. David Eckstein."

"And what did you learn about this man Eckstein?"

"Apparently he is a wealthy entrepreneur, well known and liked, in the Blackburn area."

"Family man?"

"Pope didn't say."

She paused as Maria pressed a mug of hot coffee into her hand. "Thanks," she whispered. "Just what I needed. You're an angel."

"Look, Tammy, I can see you're busy, let's catch up later." He paused for a moment, then asked, "What's on your schedule for today?"

"Well, I'm about to call Bob and bring him up to date, then I'm driving to Blackburn to see our friend Eckstein."

"But you've only just got out, Tammy." Manus was incredulous. "Surely you could give yourself a day or two at the very least, to recover?"

"The victims haven't had that chance, John. And anyway, I'll enjoy the drive. It'll clear some of those leaden jail cobwebs I've gathered."

"Drive? It'll take you three and a half hours, at least. I don't know where you get the energy."

"Train takes about half an hour longer, possibly more."

"Longer than by car?"

"The way I drive." She smiled to herself.

"Well, try not to get stopped for speeding."

"I'll be careful. Not to worry. I'll only do the ton between the cameras."

"You're utterly incorrigible, Tammy. Okay, then," he sighed, resigned. "If you think it'll lead somewhere."

"I know I'm scratching around, but what else do we have? Incidentally, the DNA tests? Staff at the clubs?"

"There was some reluctance at first, but they've all now agreed to be tested."

Realising the beatings she'd been subjected to in Belmarsh would render her appearance her least likely asset, she'd applied an eyebrow pencil, base make-up to cover the facial bruises, a discreet coral lipstick, and gold hoop earrings. She'd opted for a knee-length beige tweed Chanel skirt and matching jacket, with a rayon challis blouse in chestnut brown. Jimmy Choo low heels, and she was ready to go. Appraising herself in the full-length wardrobe mirror before leaving home, she murmured, "You'll do."

Maria was carrying Matty into breakfast, having first passed Tammy her coffee. But now appraising her employer, she stopped dead, and gasped, "Oh, madame, you look so beautiful today. When only yesterday ..."

"Thank you, Maria." She smiled, giving her proffered son a parting kiss and a cuddle, and then after a pause, another kiss and a cuddle. "Maman will see you a bientôt, angel face." Then turning to Maria, she said, "I'm back later."

An hour later, Tammy was on her way. The tank full, the Lexus SUV, her standby, parked in the Kilburn mews lock-up. It was a glorious day, and she luxuriated in the leather smell of the marsala-brown and cream upholstery, easing her foot down on the accelerator and experiencing the familiar rush at the vehicle's surge in speed. She'd called ahead and Eckstein, having been contacted by Cudlipp who'd given him a resumé of her exploits in Belmarsh, had made the time to see her.

* * * * *

Eckstein Industries occupied two floors of a luxury office block on the outskirts of Blackburn. She'd been given access to the building's underground parking, littered, she noticed, with luxury cars, and was now in the lift on the way to see David Eckstein himself.

The man, in his mid-forties, was the quintessential opposite of his father, being very tall and ultra slim, with blond Aryan good looks and the most startling blue eyes Tammy had ever encountered. Oscar would approve, she mused quietly. Come to think of it, so would she. This was an attractive man, and one who bore his good looks with apparent reserve. He favoured a dark two-piece with an expensive-looking silk tie, unlike the current penchant for open-neck shirts in business.

Getting to his feet, as she was shown into his office, he announced in a gentle baritone, "Tammy Pierre, of course."

His handshake was firm, but not designed to intimidate, and his smile broad, revealing perfect, even white teeth. She also noticed he had a small strawberry mark on the back of one hand, just below the cuff. Some said that a birthmark of that sort was a sign of good luck. Others maintained it had a God-given spiritual connotation.

"Do take a seat. What can I offer you? Tea? Coffee? Something stronger?"

The office was the epitome of simple, uncluttered modernity, with a wide picture window looking out onto one of Blackburn's many beautiful parks. Noting Tammy's interest in the view, Eckstein remarked, "It's very restful, isn't it. When I'm stressed, or under intense pressure, I simply swivel my chair around and gaze out of the window for a few minutes. It's positively therapeutic."

Answering his question, Tammy said, "Coffee would be fine, David. Black please, no sugar. And yes, the view is spectacular."

He walked to the glass-fronted drinks cabinet over on one wall, and poured Tammy and himself black coffees from the steaming coffee jug into bone china cups and, placing hers on a small side table at her side, resumed his seat behind the stunning Taiko wood executive desk. The place and the individual shimmered wealth.

"I see you admiring the photographs," he said, as she glanced appraisingly around the room.

"They're magnificent, David. Africa, I presume?"

"That's right."

"A professional photographer?"

"Not exactly." He smiled. "I took them. All. Different parts of the continent, but mainly Sierra Leone, where I spent some time years ago on business."

"Towns, villages, tribes, wildlife. I get the feeling you must have really loved the place."

"I did," he said. "Absolutely loved it."

She decided to keep things conversational, unless pushed, to see where they'd lead.

"If I'm not being presumptuous, David, you head up a raft of big companies, what was the Africa connection? You speak of it in the past tense, but obviously made a huge success of your time there."

"Too right, Tammy. I made a packet out there. Helped set me up here. Import, export, vast warehouse in Blackburn, IT services, commercial property, you name it."

"Impressive," she noted, crossing her legs and smoothing her lap.

"I was a young man." He drank from his cup, clearly savouring the taste. "A risk taker. Buccaneer. Fancied myself as a latter-day Indiana Jones. A sort of soldier of fortune. Except that Jones was one of the good guys."

"And you weren't?" she asked, intrigued.

"Hardly. I was at the start of my career, and thought I was invincible. Untouchable. So, I went in for the industry that Sierra Leone is noted for."

"Diamonds?"

"That's right. But I went in for the illicit market. Diamond smuggling. We moved stock into Liberia where there's a highly lucrative market."

"Wasn't that very dangerous, David?" Tammy focused on her host, looking for any sort of indication of what made him tick. But not expecting much. And not getting anything. A man who'd chanced and successfully achieved what he had was not likely to give away much of himself.

"Sure, it was hazardous."

"I wonder. How hazardous?"

"Very," he explained, pulling up the double cuff on his shirt to reveal an ugly purple scar across his forearm. "That hazardous."

"Wow!" she responded. "How did you get that?"

"I was shot at several times. That one didn't miss."

"You make it sound almost routine."

"Never routine. But when you're involved, as I was, with diamond running, you're up against government forces, who're easily dealt with if you know where and what sort of bribes to offer. But then there is also the criminal fraternity, who come from all over the world to see what they can make, and ex-members of the once notorious RUF."

"RUF?" Tammy enquired.

"Yes, the Revolutionary United Front. They're financed through control of the country's diamond resources. They were responsible for the deaths of some fifty thousand civilians, and the displacement of two million more."

"My God. So much of that continent has suffered decades of unrest. Civilians inevitably bearing the brunt."

"That's right. The RUF was active from around 1991 until their activities were brought to an end by the United Nations in 2002. There's a rump left over. There always will be. One of those things when some militants refuse to admit defeat."

"And these are people you had to contend with while out in Africa?"

"More than contend with, Tammy. I made them into business partners and when things didn't go the way they wanted, they made me into an enemy."

"Hence the scar?"

"Hence the scar. At least the one you can see. I'm actually covered in them. I've been knifed, shot at, tortured, imprisoned. You name it."

"Horrifying," Tammy observed.

"Actually, no."

"No?"

"The money was a big compensation, of course. The danger was the draw. Nothing like the rush when you play the odds and win. During my time out there, two of my partners were killed. Mowed down, in each case, by a hail of machine-gun fire. In that theatre of activity you need to be aware of whom to play with and whom not to upset. They were unlucky. Or maybe, just careless."

Tammy shook her head. "Careless? I can't imagine going through what you seem to have welcomed."

"Oh, I don't know, Tammy. From what Brian Cudlipp tells me you took an enormous risk when you entered Belmarsh as a male."

"But I wasn't doing it for the money. And the only rush I got was when I left the place in one piece."

"Fair enough. Still." He paused. "That's me covered. Let's turn to you. I gather you wanted to see me about Dominic Pope."

"Your father," she said, aware of the dismissive tone.

"Biologically, I suppose. But that's all. As soon as I could I changed it to Eckstein."

Tammy puzzled over that. "What made you choose Eckstein, then?"

"Oh, lots of things. Pope is an extreme right winger, anti-coloured." He nodded at Tammy. "I'm surprised he gave you the time of day.

"Antisemitic," he went on. "I've noted the amulet you wear with its Hebrew inscription."

Nonplussed, she felt herself flush. "You really are observant, David."

"I am," he agreed. "So I chose a name which is German in origin, he doesn't like Germans, with Jewish Ashkenazi links. Perhaps somewhat juvenile behaviour, I know. But it fulfilled a need in me. I know full well why he's in jail. And hope to God they keep him there for good."

"Before he was convicted of the mass killings, before you knew what he was capable of, what was your relationship with him?" Tammy asked.

"I'd say, peculiar. My mother had never been a presence, and I had had the impression that Pope wanted to be a responsible father. She left when I was about seven. There'd been some abuse. Not nice. Not nice at all," he confessed. "I don't like to think of it."

"Unpleasant," offered Tammy.

Eckstein demurred from further comment on the subject, and Tammy discreetly left it alone.

"But Pope kept on and on about the treachery of women, how they couldn't be trusted. I assumed that was because Mother had vanished, and he was resentful."

"Was Pope tactile? Did he ever hug or kiss you?"

At this Eckstein laughed. "No way. Love wasn't in Pope's lexicon of acceptable behaviour."

"May I ask, are you married, David?"

"It never happened," said Eckstein, idly scribbling in ballpoint on the blotter on his desk. "Pope had done his damnedest to ensure I never made a permanent relationship with a woman."

"Never?"

"No," he said, adding, "but African women are the gentlest in the world. They're the only ones that gave me unconditional love. I'd have stayed out there permanently, but I was being chased in too many parts of the continent. You see, I'd upset a lot of the wrong sort of people."

"That it, David?"

"Pretty much. You know, Tammy, you'll think this eccentric, but I'd have been happy to be an African myself. I go back there as often as I can. Got a holiday booked shortly. Love it there."

"Really? If only to aggravate your father, perhaps? The desire to be African, I mean."

"Sure. That and because I felt at one with all of them. Except the gangsters, of course." He grinned, studying Tammy. A concentrated stare running up and down her, assessing what he saw, before asking, "While we're talking about me and the risks I've taken, how about you?"

"Me?" she asked, surprised. "What do you want to know about me?"

"That scar, for one thing," he replied, pointing to the ugly wound on Tammy's head.

"Oh, that," she responded, self-consciously touching the injury with her fingertips. "Hazard of the profession."

"Bit like me."

Tammy smiled back, diffident, at a loss. "Perhaps."

Covering her embarrassment, she moved on. "David, you've been very helpful. Before I go, is there anything else, however remote, you think might be worthy of note?"

"Not really." He thought for a moment, caught Tammy's eye, then said, "Pope had a real down on gays, you know. I came home once with an expensive Hermès silk scarf. Pope took one look at it and ripped it to shreds, beat the hell out of me, saying he wasn't having a son of his buying women's clothes."

"Very revealing."

"Oh, and I nearly forgot." David replaced the pen on his blotter.

"I should have been wise to Pope's peculiar behaviour. He not infrequently came home with mud on his boots and on more than one occasion with blood on his hands and clothes. I was too young, or maybe too naïve to question it."

Getting up to leave, Tammy thanked David once more, before he asked her, "Has this been of any use to you, do you think, Tammy?"

"Too soon to say. It's all grist to the mill, though. From Pope I learned that each time he killed it was like he was killing your mother. I wonder if we'll find any similar link to the Clubhouse murders. Nothing's emerged so far."

CHAPTER 65 DAY 38

THE WEATHER HELD for the drive back, which Tammy took at a more sedate pace, glorying in the English countryside, and again her freedom from the threats and oppressiveness of Belmarsh.

What a strange set of complexes and contradictions was David. She'd not in her lifetime met a successful man who was not both charismatic and attractive, and David was no exception to that rule. She couldn't help wondering whether he found her attractive. She knew she looked good this day, even with the itching shaven skull she'd longed to scratch several times during her interview.

What to make of a man who had dreams of being another nationality. Another race even.

Manus would want to know what had been achieved and she'd have to admit it couldn't be set out or quantified, any more than the Belmarsh sojourn. For all that, she knew the meetings with father and son had had some value. Had given her some insight, albeit tenuous, into the workings of the mind of one serial killer and the son brought up in the shadow of the same.

But would that be of any help in the current situation? Would it open any doors or avenues of enquiry? Gut feeling, she thought. Woman's intuition. Time would tell, but she had calculated that the risks would prove to be worth the eventual reward.

The M40 ahead was comparatively empty, similarly behind. An experienced driver, as a matter of course she checked her rear-view mirror from time to time, spotting a low-slung red vehicle keeping a constant distance from her. As an experiment she slowed down considerably and witnessed the other car slow down. When she accelerated it maintained pace with her.

She'd give him a run for his money and see what transpired. Approaching the Wendlebury junction she put her foot down, burning rubber, leaving a pall of black smoke in her wake, easily pushing the Porsche to over a hundred miles per hour. It took the red vehicle's driver by surprise, and though it similarly increased pace, they weren't fast enough to catch her and she lost them as she swerved off the M40 and into the Wendlebury system.

Driving twice around the interchange to be certain she'd lost the other driver, she eventually picked up the M40 once more, heading south.

It was as she eased her motor back up to around ninety miles per hour that she spotted the red car in the central lane ahead. She was close enough to make out the lines of a Ferrari. She knew her vehicles. She'd researched the options widely before plumping for the Panamera. This was an 812 Superfast she was trailing. Significantly faster than her own but with a marginally slower acceleration.

She'd not been spotted, so she swiftly pushed the Porsche into the overtaking lane until she was level with the Ferrari. Unable to make out the driver, possibly male, she was suddenly spotted by the other who swerved at her as though trying to shake her off, the two vehicles briefly touching.

Bugger, she thought. He'll have scratched my new car. Damn fool childish games she didn't have time for, she slowed down, trailing the red car, who presumably having spotted the next exit slip, accelerated, leaving the motorway. His turn to shake her.

Let him go, she thought. Life's too short.

Her mobile bleeped and she saw it was Manus. "Hi, John, what's news?"

"A lot of nothing, Tammy."

Manus couldn't hide his exasperation. "We've now spoken to all next of kin, friends, neighbours, employers. We've taken apart their social media, every one of the victims. Facebook, Instagram, WhatsApp, Twitter, even the commercial LinkedIn, emails, you name it. We've checked phone logs and not located a single potential suspect."

"It's as we thought, John. They're all random killings. Spur of the moment sort of thing. So, we've still got our three main, or three only, suspects to concentrate on."

"My money's on Patrick Laing. PC Collins told me you'd indicated he should keep a hold of the cup Laing had been drinking from when we interviewed him. Well done. DNA result isn't in yet, but when it is we'll invite Laing formally to submit to a test and draw the obvious conclusions if he refuses."

"How're the team bearing up right now?"

"Pretty depressed, to tell the truth. It's all so frustratingly vague. Nothing tangible we can hook on to."

"I can imagine. How about the press?"

"Bad. We had a briefing yesterday. A lot of somewhat angry journalists. Bob Walker is starting to get uneasy as well. He's facing pressure on all sides. I could hardly tell him to be patient."

"I know. I chatted with him when I left Eckstein's place. He wasn't happy."

CHAPTER 66 DAY 39

SHE FELT SOMETHING FALL ON HER CHEST, and anticipating another heavy pummelling, she started with alarm before realising what it was.

Turning over in bed and reaching out to cuddle Risky to her chest, she murmured, "Little monster. Can't you let de mama sleep just once in a while? Petite horreur! What time is it, anyway?"

She glanced at the mobile on her bedside table. "Crikey!" she exclaimed, then called out, "Maria?"

Poking her head around the door as though she'd been waiting there in anticipation of Tammy's call, she replied, "Yes, madame, I am here."

It had caught up with her, the events of the last few days. She hurt all over, whether from the beatings she'd received in Belmarsh or just general exhaustion, she couldn't say, probably both. But she remembered telling Maria not to wake her. She had finally acknowledged the need for a long sleep. But this? "Maria, it's three in the afternoon. Where've you been? I know I said not to wake me, but it's been nearly twenty hours."

"Yes, madame. And if I may say, you look rested."

"I wish I could say I felt it."

Pausing for a moment, she added, "Coffee please. And for heaven's sake, Maria, stop calling me madame. It's Tammy. Tammy," she repeated. "Okay?"

"Yes, madame."

"I give up," she murmured, throwing up her hands in exasperation.

Climbing out of bed, in a rather more modest than usual ankle-length negligee, she deposited a mewing Risky on the warm patch where she'd been sleeping, watched her curl up contentedly, then, grinning hugely, asked, "And how is my son and heir."

"Matty is lovely. He is so beautiful."

"Can't wait," said Tammy, striding into the kitchen where Matty was seated in his highchair, waving a pink plastic spoon around like the little dictator he was fast becoming, depositing its contents of baby food on the floor, his Babygro, and his face.

"Ma!" He smiled happily. The cherubim on the Sistine Chapel ceiling couldn't compare.

Hoisting the little Napoleon into her arms, the smell of fresh talc overtaking that of chewed food, Tammy nuzzled Matty's cheeks, neck and chest to the sound of his uproarious giggles. "Mon petit monstre," she said, handing the baby to Maria who nuzzled him some more before depositing him back into his highchair.

"He will break many hearts, I believe, madame."

"You think so, Maria?"

"I am already in love with him."

"You and me both," said Tammy, reaching for her mobile on the kitchen counter and removing mute. Almost immediately it rang out, telling her she had six missed messages. All from Bill Jenner advising her there'd been developments and would she call him asap.

* * * * *

Back at the Yard on the fifth floor, and a few smiles of acknowledgement from a worried-looking team, Farida and Lenny, with whom she'd spoken already, both nodded in her direction. Bill greeted her warmly, indicating they go over to check out what he had for her on the large screen. "Take a look at this, Tammy," he enthused.

He pressed the remote and brought up a video of a heaving crowd of dancers on the floor of a club Tammy immediately recognised as the Clubhouse. The long bar, staff in red jackets, Dexie's cumulous white crown, the side bar off the main area. The light show, strobes, and all. Video screens with a variety of weird and wonderful colourful images of people, places, and the unidentifiable. All unmistakeable. As was the atmosphere, even detectable over a video, of good-natured bonhomie.

"So, Bill, what am I looking for?" she asked, slipping a hand into the pocket of her denim jacket. Her scalp was itching but, feeling self-conscious enough about her dramatic change in appearance, she resisted the temptation to scratch it. She'd not failed to notice the surprised expressions on the faces of some of those around them.

"Let me know when you spot something," said Jenner intently.

As Tammy peered closely at the screen nothing immediately caught her attention from among the hundreds in the dance area, then, "Christ!" she whispered. "It's him, isn't it, Bill. Not all that clear a picture, but still, unmistakeable."

"Patrick Laing."

"The man who only goes to the Clubhouse because he likes the beer." Tammy stood back, folding her arms. "Can you make out the girl he's with? It looks like a girl from the back view."

"We've seen him with several others, as though maybe he's deciding who his next target is going to be. For us to have picked him out with the number we have here, he must have danced with literally dozens of them. As you say, the man who likes beer. We've a lot more video, but I won't run through it all right now, it'll take too long. But here's the thing."

Bill Jenner turned away from the screen to face Tammy head on, drawing out his comment for maximum impact. "We've found his DNA on the necks or shoulders of at least three of the victims."

"Wow! Have. You. Now," breathed Tammy, separating each word. "That's brilliant, Bill. A breakthrough, at last." She frowned, a moment of thought. "Bill, the DNA was taken from a cup he'd drunk from when we last interviewed him here. Without his permission it's not useable."

"I know," replied Jenner.

"And also, how reliable?"

"When we bring him in, Tammy, he'll be only too willing to give us a proper sample if he wants to prove his innocence, which, of course, he won't be able to. He won't know about the filched sample."

"What if he denies you the right to a sample?"

"He won't," said Jenner, restlessly moving about. "But if he does it'll just nail him further."

"Maybe."

Jenner pointed at the screen. "If you look, you'll see how he touches the girls' necks and shoulders when they dance."

"Yup. Tell me, do you have anything on video of him leaving with any of the dead girls? That'd be something of a clincher."

"No," said Jenner, smiling. "But we have something else."

"Okay," said Tammy, longing to scratch her head.

Cancelling the video, Jenner brought up a picture of one of the murdered girls' faces, Daisy Meekins, the most recent. "We've enlarged this," he said, "and cleaned it up as far as we can to give a clearer image. What do you see?" he asked.

"She has an imprint of something like the sole of a trainer across one cheek. Hell's teeth. Not content with murdering her, the killer's trodden on her face too."

"Exactly."

"Have you located the make of trainer?"

"Farida did."

"She's a clever girl. Go on, tell me then."

"It's a Cloud 5 Waterproof. Not cheap. Farida's been putting her pennies aside to buy a pair in rose fossil. Nice colour. Our man is wearing the glacier white. I'll show you in a moment."

"You've done well, Bill. Looks like we have our man. When will you make an arrest?"

"Tomorrow morning."

"Do you know where he lives, then? Can't see he'd have volunteered it at the last meeting."

"We had him discreetly followed. He's in Tilbury, not far from the club. Then we checked the electoral register, and to be further certain looked at the national census database."

"If that doesn't cover it ... Of course, his number plate would also be registered at DVLA." She nodded. Then added, "Nice address. I s'pose you know Tilbury is the most dangerous small town in Essex, and among the twenty most dangerous of all Essex's towns and cities."

"How on earth do you know that, Tammy?"

"Believe me, Bill, I am a mine of useless information. Goes with the trade, I reckon."

"Well," said Jenner, smiling. "It fits the man, doesn't it. He might have hand-picked the spot to live."

"Search warrant?"

"Applied for. We'll pick up Laing first, then as soon as we can we'll turn his place over."

"Mind if I accompany you on the arrest?"

"Sure. As long as you keep well out of the way."

"Of course. Then if it's alright with you I'll sit in on the interview."

"Be my guest."

CHAPTER 67 DAY 40

THEY'D MET FOR A DRINK and a summing up of where they were so far at Tammy's local. There was the murmur of conversation among the customers and the clink of glasses being filled or washed.

John Manus and Bill Jenner were seated at a round oak table opposite Tammy in the Black Swan on Salusbury Road. She was still in the denim two-piece she'd worn earlier in the day. Looking as weary as she felt, she'd delayed a shower and change to meet up with the two senior detectives for a post-mortem before turning in for the night.

The men were both on pints. Tammy had eschewed her customary vodka in favour of a large Monkey 47 gin, which she nursed and sipped neat for a while before adding the tonic that had been sitting next to it. She felt herself unwind a bit, ahead of focusing on the matter in hand.

"Dealt with," she said, both men looking perplexed.

"How's that?" asked Jenner.

"As I see it, we've two men in the frame. Edward Seward and Patrick Laing. They've both used that phrase in connection with the murders. As though the dealing referred to had been carried out by them or, at least, one of them."

"Not much to go on though, is it, Tammy?" said Manus, idly tapping his fingernails on the side of his glass. "I mean, it's a pretty common turn of phrase."

"I suppose," she sighed. "It was just a feeling I had. Call it women's intuition." She reflected she'd used the term before to John.

"Not to be discounted," agreed Jenner. "I've seen a killer brought to book based on the intuition of a senior female cop. But right now, the refined DNA results are what we're waiting for."

"You mean a match, if Laing can be persuaded," said Tammy, tipping back her tumbler of gin, drinking half the contents in one.

"Due any time now. I put a rocket under forensics," said Manus.

Toying with her glass, Tammy said, "The DNA on the cardboard cup Laing left in the interview room may not be permissible in court, but as for persuasion, Laing can't refuse us if he's under arrest. He's not just being brought in for a chat under caution, like the last time."

"Exactly." Manus nodded.

"Okay. What about Seward?" said Tammy. "Apart from some macabre remarks we've nothing on him."

"Not yet," put in Jenner. "We'll review Seward when we know where we are with Laing."

"Which will be tomorrow," said Tammy.

"Exactly," said Manus.

"What about this other character, Binns? Hector Binns?" Tammy asked.

"He's on the back burner as well for now. From what you say, Tammy, he seems too inoffensive to be our man."

"Sorry, fellas. I need some shuteye," said Tammy, stretching and loosening her stiff neck, rocking her head from side to side.

"Before we go, though, a quick run through," she suggested. "Yes? I know we've done this already, guys, but it can't hurt to review once more, especially as we've more victims since we last spoke."

"So. Julie Crosbie," she opened. "Part trans, and Liz Armstrong fully transitioned, both sustained a broken neck at the hands of the killer or killers. The only ones to die in this way.

"Next. The burned body in the women's refuge was a man, not a woman. We don't know what he was doing there. Cause of death? Still to be determined. Possibly strangled. Though Hawley pointed out the clear evidence of a knife wound. We'll need to look further."

Glancing at her drink, Tammy picked up the glass, looking pensive, and drank the rest in a single draught.

"Karen Richardson," she continued, "we know was a botched job, slit throat, which didn't leave her dead immediately, and pathology tells us it was a knife with a curved edge that killed her. So, different to the others it seems. Unless," she mused, "our killer used more than one knife.

"Of the remainder, Anna Proby, Teresa Finch, the judge, Jeffreys, and now Daisy Meekins, all died with a killing from behind, carried out with a single slash of a straight-edged knife. In Daisy's case, after a titanic fight in a street close to the club. She may have tried to run and been caught from behind. There'd be little likelihood of the killer sustaining blood on their person, unless perhaps on a sleeve if they moved away too slowly."

"Just how many killers are we looking at?" asked Jenner, scratching his head. "Three? Four?"

"Exactly," Tammy replied, shaking her head. "Trouble is, this is one Gordian knot we can't simply cut through. It'll need to be untangled, heaven help."

"We'll see what the search turns up when we go to Laing's home, whether or not he's in," said Jenner.

"Are you sure he will be in?" Tammy asked.

"No, to be honest. But he seems to sit around most of the morning before bestirring himself, from what's been observed so far," Manus said.

Knocking back the last of his pint, Jenner said, "Looks like he's always at home, or else at the club. We shouldn't have too much difficulty locating him."

"And so far, apart from that button picked up from the gutter near where Daisy Meekins was found, and a tiny strip of cloth, possibly the lining of a jacket, found in her hand, we've nothing else to go on," admitted Manus. "All very bleak, I'm afraid."

"There's something been nagging at me," said Tammy. "You know, several of the girls killed were spotted on CCTV dancing with Laing outside the small bar off the main area. He liked the beer, we know. Each of those girls, maybe, had just been for a drink as well before being spotted by Laing and then approached by him for a dance."

"And then a killing," offered Jenner.

"If we've got further DNA results by tomorrow we could have a clearer idea of whom amongst the victims Laing might have been in close contact with."

"Agreed," said Manus.

"Plus there's the mark of a trainer on the face of Daisy Meekins. Identified as a Cloud 5 Waterproof," offered Tammy, before adding again, "and that button and the scrap of cloth. Not much, but with three items to think about, murderers have been convicted on less."

"Fair comment," said Manus. "We'll take it up tomorrow. We've got Laing being brought in. That should make interesting viewing."

"Gotta go now," said Tammy, stifling the desire to wince, being gripped by a needle-sharp attack of endometriosis, as she got to her feet. "I need to cuddle something soft and warm before I turn in."

Beaming, Manus said, "How is the little lad, Tammy?"

"Heaven sent, John." She smiled through the pain, feeling her heart skip for an instant as she thought of her baby. "Catch you tomorrow.

"Incidentally, where will you take Laing?" she enquired on her way out.

"Charing Cross. Aim for midday," said Manus.

Outside the pub, Tammy closed her eyes and breathed in deep for just a moment. Bed called. Then she felt a tap on the shoulder, the distinctive smell of lavender, and a voice enquired, "Is it you?"

CHAPTER 67 • DAY 40 • 425

"What?" she said, startled, confronted by a burly-looking character with greasy hair down to his shoulders.

"You're the one called Tammy." She was aware of his height for the first time, something that added to his menace. He was wearing baggy trousers and, she noticed, a military-style donkey jacket, with distinctive gold and silver buttons on the front, one of which, she saw, was missing.

"Mr Binns, I do believe," said Tammy, unsuccessfully trying to make eye contact.

"You remember," he noted, looking her up and down as though she were an exhibit in an auction.

"Nice coat, Mr Bin ... Hector," she said, adopting the more intimate approach. "May I ask where you bought it?"

"You may," he sneered, leaning threateningly towards her. "But then that's for you to ask and me to know." Not so inoffensive after all.

"But since you asked nicely, Tammy," he added rudely, "I got it in a sale at the Army and Navy in Tilbury."

"Is this man bothering you, ma'am?" The gentleman smiling at Tammy was holding the leash of a very large dog.

"Hello," she exclaimed happily. "Tom Volkan, isn't it. From Hyde Park."

"You remember, then."

"Of course. Why would I not." She bent down and let the dog nuzzle her palm.

Tom was about to address Binns, whose brows were beetling in annoyance, when Tammy said, "It's okay, Tom. I'm used to dealing with big dogs and little men." Then, turning to Binns, and somewhat less sociably, she said, "The jacket, sir? I see you've a button missing."

Reaching into a pocket, Binns took hold of something, then leaning forward, his palm open, displayed the missing button. "I caught it in a door in the club. Satisfied?"

"Which door, Mr Binns?"

"God's sake. None of your business, lady," he hissed. "And we're not done here. See you soon," he muttered and stalked off.

It was then that Tammy noticed something which changed her whole perception of the case, for as Binns retreated, she spotted the distinctive trainers with the crenellated soles he was wearing. They were Cloud 5 Waterproofs.

CHAPTER 68 DAY 41

SHE COULD HEAR THE SCREAMING from the moment she walked into Charing Cross police station.

"What the hell's going on?" she asked the desk sergeant, an amused young man she'd come across on a previous visit. "Nicholls, isn't it?"

"Yes, ma'am," the sergeant replied, delighted to have been remembered.

"Someone being tortured, are they?"

"You'd think so, wouldn't you. Ms Pierre, yes?" he asked tentatively.

"Well done, sergeant." She smiled, impressed. "So what's all the commotion? Let me guess, they've got Patrick Laing in one of the interview rooms?"

"Right, Miss," said Nicholls, unthinkingly reverting to the traditional form of address, then looking embarrassed. "I mean … I mean …"

"Don't worry, sergeant. It doesn't matter. Miss, Ms. Whatever. Courtesy is all about attitude, sergeant. Not title."

"Thank you, ma'am," he said, mightily relieved.

"Not ma'am, sergeant. Tammy. Tammy will do just fine. So, now, okay if I go through? I am expected." She glanced at her watch. "It's 11.45 am. I thought the arrest was scheduled for noon?"

"It was," said Nicholls. "But you know … Best-laid plans."

"Too true." Tammy nodded. "And now, if I may?"

"Of course, of course. I'll escort you."

"Don't worry, young man. I know the way."

She tapped on the door of the interview room several times, but presumably couldn't be heard due to the racket within. So opening the door she stepped in gingerly to find John Manus and Bill Jenner seated in grey plastic chairs on one side of a grey Formica-topped table, both clearly perplexed and exhausted.

On the opposite side of the table was seated an intense-looking individual; a neatly besuited young woman of about thirty-five, in a pageboy hairstyle, wearing a white ruffle-necked blouse, Tammy presumed was a legal adviser. Laing paced the room on his side, restless as a caged rat, intermittently protesting, shouting his innocence and screaming with frustration at what he was being unfairly subjected to and what he was promising to do about it.

"Results are in," mouthed Jenner, ignoring Laing and catching Tammy's attention, before inclining his head towards the suspect in a clear and obvious statement.

"For the tape," John Manus said as Tammy approached the spare chair, "Ms Tammy Pierre, private investigator, has entered the room."

Three people in the confined space glanced at Tammy, the fourth, Patrick Laing, with spittle drooling from his mouth, screamed, "Get that fucking bitch outta here."

Then, before anyone could move and to the horror of those present, he ran round the table, brandishing a fist the size of a cannon ball, swinging it at Tammy's head. Easily parrying the blow, she sidestepped it and the man, punching the heel of her bootie against his thigh.

He went down with a crump, still protesting volubly, "Did you see that? She fucking attacked me. Fucking police brutality."

"Now, Mr Laing," said Tammy, standing over the man, hands in her jacket pockets. "In the first place, I'm not police. Secondly, be reasonable. Why don't we all sit down and let this interview proceed like adults. See if we can sort something out."

Getting shakily to his feet, Laing protested, "Sort summink out? Are kidding me? I'm under arrest. I'm accused of murder, for Chrissake. On what grounds? Eh? On what grounds?"

His advisor, shocked at her client's continuing outburst, and speaking in a cut-glass accent, said, "Mr Laing, you've elected to have a legal representative provided for you, and if I am to be of any assistance you really must sit down and offer some measure of cooperation."

"I'll sit down when I'm ready," said Laing sullenly, continuing to pace the room. Then indicating Tammy, he said to those present, "You saw what she just done to me."

"Mr Laing," said Manus, "if you don't sit down, we can't be sure the tape will pick up all you have to say."

"So?"

"So," put in Bill Jenner, "if you wish to protest your innocence it'll help your case if we can hear and record what comments you have to make in your own defence."

Scraping the chair back from the table, Laing planted himself in it and said reluctantly, "I'm listenin'."

Speaking up first, John Manus advised Laing that they had, that morning, received further results of DNA tests carried out on the murder victims and intended to compare them with samples to be taken from any suspects. Laing was not to know that thus far he was the only suspect to have been asked to test for DNA.

He'd agreed on sufferance and a lot of noisy protest, at the urging of his legal advisor, who'd earlier introduced herself as one Penelope Naismith.

Tammy, sitting back on one of the plastic chairs, crossed her legs, brushed her skirt flat with the back of her hand, and studied Laing with interest, wondering what his reaction would be to the revelations soon to be imparted. Not necessarily enough to indict at this stage, of course. At least not yet. But they'd pursue it further.

"I'll keep this simple, Mr Laing," opened Manus. "We have you on CCTV dancing with a number of individuals later identified as the victims of murder."

"So what!" Laing interrupted, placing his elbows on the table. "That makes me a murderer, does it?"

"If you'll let me finish, Mr Laing," said, Manus patiently.

"I'm all ears, mate. Can't wait."

"We have you identified dancing on four different occasions," Manus repeated, "with four persons all of whom we have found a common DNA on their necks and or shoulders, as yet unidentified. We believe that that same DNA will be found on some or all of the other victims. Forensic testing is continuing as we speak."

"So? Dancin' ain't no crime, mister."

"In each case the individual in question was later found murdered. Later, that is on the same evening as you were recorded having contact with them."

"Tough!"

Ignoring the remark, Manus went on, "We have reason to believe that the unidentified DNA will prove to be yours, Mr Laing."

"Oh yeah? Why's that, then?"

"We're not at liberty to say at this stage," said Manus, thinking of the surreptitiously obtained sample from the cardboard cup Laing had recently drunk from.

Intervening, Ms Naismith offered, "Detective, there are what, over a thousand people in any of the clubs at one time? Maybe, twice that number? How have you managed to find CCTV of my client amongst so many attendees? Were you seeking to single him out? And how many hours of recordings have you had to sift through to come up with these gems of evidence? A remarkable coincidence, don't you think?"

Jenner intervened, "These so-called gems of evidence make a powerful case against your client, Ms Naismith."

Gaining Manus's attention, Ms Naismith, tapping her pen impatiently on her notepad, said, "You've no reason to hold my client, detective. He's been arrested on the basis of groundless speculation."

"I disagree, Ms Naismith."

"You don't have a scrap of real evidence, detective. The link you've highlighted between my client and several victims of murder outside the club is tenuous at best, victimisation, to my mind, at worst."

"It's not really, ma'am, when you realise that Mr Laing claims to like the beer at the clubs, attending the Tilbury club in particular, the site of all the killings, and chooses to drink in the small bar off the main dancing area. A bar apparently frequented by at least four of the victims, whom he's engaged in conversation, later dancing with them, before ... Need I go on? I think that narrows things down somewhat, wouldn't you say?"

"I remain unconvinced, Detective Manus."

"Be that as it may, Ms Naismith, but I continue persuaded that Patrick Laing is the person we're seeking and accordingly he remains in custody until we have the further DNA results to hand."

"You've got just twenty-four hours, detective."

"This is a multiple murder investigation, ma'am. We'll apply to keep your client here for thirty-six hours. And if need be, on further application, ninety-six."

"Can I go now?" Laing asked his legal representative.

"I'm afraid not, Mr Laing. You've heard what DCI Manus has had to say on the matter."

"Before returning to your cell," Manus added, "you will leave all your clothing with an officer to be tested for DNA."

Getting up from his chair Laing pointed an accusing finger at Tammy. "It's her, isn't it. Fucking trans bitch. Think I don't know a bloke when I see one. When I get out of here, I'll have you, mister."

"Mr Laing," interceded a clearly nettled Ms Naismith. "Please don't make your situation any worse than it is at the moment. Let's not add threatening behaviour to this catalogue of nonsense we're having to listen to."

Laing, making his fist into the semblance of a gun, pointed it at Tammy, saying mysteriously, "Who knows?"

It was as he exited the interview room that Tammy spotted the trainers he was wearing but chose to make no immediate reference to them.

Cloud 5 Waterproofs.

CHAPTER 69 DAY 42

SEATED OPPOSITE EACH OTHER in Caffè Nero on Kingsway, John Manus pushed the laptop across the table and said, "Take a look at some of these images from the club, Tammy. Do you recognise anyone here?"

"Should I?" she asked, breaking her heated croissant into pieces before buttering the morsels and popping them into her mouth one at a time.

"I got Farida to take her time looking through hours of recording, specifically for the man you mentioned, Binns. A military-style donkey jacket, you said. There you go."

Peering into the screen, Tammy spotted Binns almost immediately, talking with Daisy Meekins, outside the smaller bar at the club. He had a hand casually placed on her shoulder. But what caught the attention was the military-style jacket Tammy had seen Binns wearing the other night. It had all its buttons intact.

"It's dated the evening Daisy was killed," said Manus.

"Well, well. Either we've no credible suspects, or we're gifted with two at the same time. When I bumped into him the other day, the jacket was minus a button. But it must have come off the same day, or evening because he had it in his pocket. So we've still got Laing to question again once we've his DNA in, but certainly now's the time to bring in Binns for questioning too.

"Also, we've another clue. Or quandary, depending on your point of view."

"Go on," prompted Manus.

"Our present suspects both wear those Cloud 5 Waterproof trainers."

"Okay. Now to digress for a moment, you did excellent work on the Muslim connection."

"I wouldn't call it excellent, John. More, a bit of luck finding Deepak Pandit, and his spotting Rakish in the news."

"Don't downplay yourself, Tammy."

She raised her eyebrows but made no comment.

"You can probably guess what comes next?"

"Of course," said Tammy, attending to her second croissant and depositing pieces smothered with melting butter into her mouth. Then, "You'll be looking to have a quiet chat with Muhammed Dhelavi. If you can find him."

"That's right. He'll have gone to ground, almost certainly when he hears what his wife and son have to tell him."

"Binns?"

"I was just going to say, Bill Jenner, accompanied by Farida, found him at the Tilbury club. He'll be interviewing Binns later today. He actually seemed willing to help? The man's a mystery." Manus shrugged.

"Meanwhile?"

"Meanwhile, can you come along for another interview with Laing this afternoon? We should have some more DNA results in."

"Sure," said Tammy. "What time?"

"3.00 pm?"

"I'll be there."

* * * * *

Manus and Jenner sat at the same spot in the interview room as previously while Tammy observed from behind.

Laing and his legal advisor sat on the opposite side of the table.

The man appeared to have calmed down, at least for the time being. He sat quietly with his hands in his lap.

CHAPTER 69 • DAY 42 • 435

Ms Naismith attended to her notes and files.

Opening, Manus said, "Mr Laing, for the purpose of this interview please remember you are still under caution." He then, as before, started the machine recording.

"Whatever," muttered Laing, gazing about with feigned disinterest.

Manus extracted a raft of sheets of paper from a buff folder, and addressed Laing. "It won't surprise you to learn, Mr Laing, that your DNA has been found on the persons of the following." He paused to ensure he had Laing's full attention. Then he continued, reading from the list on the table in front of him.

"Anna Proby, a fully transitioned female. Teresa Finch, a part-transitioned female. The judge, Jeffreys, fully transitioned and lastly, Daisy Meekins, who was a biological female with no history of attempted or planned transition. She is perhaps the odd one out. We're not sure what makes her a victim as she doesn't seem to conform to any of our potential killer or killers' protocol. We've learned what we can from families and friends of each deceased, all of whom, be advised, are totally and utterly devasted."

Laing sat stony-faced and unmoving, his hands still in his lap.

The atmosphere in the room had become taut, as though something unpredicted was about to happen. Tammy's palms were sweating slightly, and she self-consciously brushed them against the sides of her skirt.

"I can now reveal," continued Manus, "what I think we've all been fully expecting, that the results of the DNA testing exhibit your traces on every one of the four victims referred to. We've also detected Daisy Meekins's blood on the sleeve of your donkey jacket. I'd say our case is cut and dried, wouldn't you, young man? Why not keep this interview short by agreeing to a guilty plea? It will save so much time and aggravation."

Still Laing made no comment.

Then Tammy had an idea; picking up an evidence bag from the table, she extracted the heavy gold and silver button she'd found in the gutter and asked, "Recognise this, Mr Laing?"

Laing squinted at the object, then shrugged. "Same as them on me coat. What you people 're lookin' at right now."

"That's right, Mr Laing. Our forensics team. It seems you weren't aware you had a button missing. We believe Daisy Meekins tore it off your jacket when you struggled with her."

"Crap!" said Laing. "Your forensics team must 'ave their 'eads up their arses. I give 'em a jacket with all the buttons on. Christ, I'da known if one was missing. It were new, the coat. Got it in a sale at the Army and Navy in Tilbury. Loads there like it. Goin' like 'ot cakes, they was. Lots like it in the cloakroom at the club. Dead cheap and looked flash. I bet half the kids in the club walked off with the wrong ones. Who'd notice? They was all the same." He leaned forward, his elbows on the table. "And there weren't no struggle 'cos I ain't killed no-one."

There followed a prolonged silence during which time nobody moved. But from where she sat, Tammy, to her astonishment, and apparently unnoticed by Manus or Jenner, perceived the sheen of a tear trickle down Laing's cheek. Ms Naismith had seen it and was about to make a comment when, thinking better of it, she demurred.

Undeterred by the suspect's silence, Manus went on, "Well, Mr Laing, do you have nothing more to say for yourself?"

Laing made no comment, merely remained sitting like a statue staring at nothing.

"Very well, Mr Laing, then let me put this to you," Manus sighed. "The four people I've referred to were all subject to having their throats cut by a very sharp blade. Your blade, Mr Laing, of course. Where have you secreted it? It will be needed as evidence."

At last Laing bestirred himself, and with tears now flowing unchecked down his face, what followed left the three sitting opposite him dumfounded.

"She were alright, that Daisy," said Laing. "She were a right darlin'. Course she weren't no fuckin' bloke. Said she'd go out wiv me. Then she disappeared, din't she." By now Laing was sobbing, his face in his hands.

No-one said a word, merely waiting and wondering where this was all going.

Finally, Laing continued, "I went out to look for her. Gone up the street. Then I seen her. Lying there, blood coming out of her neck. She 'ad the mark of a trainer on her face. Some fucker trod on her. Not enough to kill her. I can tell you it was a Cloud 5 Waterproof. Everyone's gottem these days. Including me. I'd know that tread pattern anywhere."

"Anything else, Mr Laing," Manus enquired.

"I bent down to look at her, touched under her chin, looking for a pulse." Laing continued sobbing.

"She was sweet. Really nice. Said she'd go out wiv me," he repeated. "Why'd she 'ave to bugger off like that? Someone else musta seen her before I got there, an' dialled for an ambulance, 'cos I 'eard sirens, so I made meself scarce."

"Detective," interrupted Ms Naismith. "I think my client needs a break."

"Very well, Ms Naismith. We'll adjourn. Reconvene tomorrow."

CHAPTER 70 DAY 42

"WHAT DO YOU THINK, TAMMY? Is he our man? Laing? And are we any closer than before to the train bomber, or bombers?"

"Jury's out, John. You saw his performance. Looked genuine enough, didn't it? We'll talk with him again, probably tomorrow."

They were seated opposite one another in a coffee bar close to the Charing Cross nick. Manus looked tired and flushed. As well he might, floundering around with the twin nightmares facing them. But, as Tammy realised, the man was way too obstinate to be at home resting. And with his matchless career record, he would pursue this to the bitter end, whatever the consequences to his health. Reputation took precedence over everything else for John Manus. Though his wife, Pidge, would hardly be expected to agree.

The place wasn't overcrowded, beyond a smattering of smartly turned-out office workers grabbing a coffee before making for their trains, some taking their drinks with them in Styrofoam cups.

Gazing out of the café window at the passing rush hour traffic, and concentrating her thoughts, Tammy said, "I got a call earlier today from one of the staff at Tilbury saying a man with a Middle Eastern appearance had been nosing around the club looking for something or someone.

"He didn't ask for anyone by name, merely gave an outline detail. Easy enough to identify who he was looking for with his description of all that hair. Dexie was out at the time, but when he got back, he didn't have a clue who the man was or why he might want to talk to him. The only identifying feature she could give was that the man had a nervous tic."

"Our man with the tic. Mr Dhelavi, of course. Well that looks like another dead end," said Manus morosely.

"Not necessarily," said Tammy, sipping from her mug of coffee, before turning back to Manus. "Putting the shreds of info we've been picking up together, and based on no more than my gut feeling, Oscar, with his far right agenda, knows the Kerkuts. We believe Jason may have planted the bomb on the Southern Region train, not Rakish, who was just the fall guy."

"All of this smells like Oscar's attempts to blacken the Muslim community," continued Manus. "But the two males, Dhelavi and his son Rakish, don't constitute a community. Even if the other males brought over with Dhelavi were involved, and we've no evidence to suggest they were, we still don't have an extensive affiliation."

"As well we've kept the investigation to your small team, John."

"Agreed. You know, Tammy, after you'd left that first COBRA meeting, I got mutterings from Templeton about bringing in the cavalry. Others there shouted him down. Particularly Nick Holden of the CTC. Can you imagine the effects that would have had on community relations? We'd have uniforms multiplying like rabbits and whole fleets of detectives. Disaster. Thankfully, Miranda Miller, our Met chief, was in agreement with the approach we've jointly adopted. Our Home Secretary, apart from his own questionable prejudices, doesn't have a clue how to run this sort of operation."

"We've managed so far to keep this to a relatively discreet operation, despite the publicity and high profile of one of the bomb victims," said Tammy, absently placing and replacing the condiments on the table.

"That's right," said Manus. "And as you would expect, Nick and David Sinclair have conducted a low-key investigation. But frankly, with all the resources of the two agencies combined, we've probably made more progress, however minor, than they. And furthermore, the press haven't suggested any link between the bombs and the street killings," he offered.

"So far. Let's not hold our breath." She paused, looked down at Manus's coffee. "I'm going for a refill. Can I get you one?"

"Hmm? Oh, yes please. Same as before."

"Only, hot this time?" she suggested.

The humour was lost on Manus, who was increasingly slouched over with exhaustion.

Tammy smiled encouragingly and returned a few moments later with refills.

"Forensics are still looking at the evidence of the first bomb on Northern Region," said Manus. "Nothing definite," he added, gingerly picking up the cup of steaming black liquid and sipping from it. "But they've hinted it could be a pipe bomb like the one already IDed on the more recent Southern Region."

"Same modus, then," offered Tammy. "Mr Dhelavi's thumb print?"

"Looks that way, doesn't it," agreed Manus.

"What about the three big men who came over with Dhelavi on the boat with the girls?" Manus wondered, half to himself.

"Nothing so far from me. You, John?"

"Nothing this end either."

"They'll show their hands eventually."

"No doubt. In which case, to date all we've got is Oscar, with the three Middle Easterners, Dhelavi and no-one else."

"So," mused Tammy, "if we are making some progress on that front, however thin, we still have the ongoing mystery of the Clubhouse killings, and the remote possibility of a connection between that and the so-called Middle Eastern man with the tic. Our Mr Dhelavi."

"He did ask to see Dexie," put in Manus.

"Hardly a connection."

"And as I said, he didn't ask for him by name, so presumably doesn't know him."

"I think it's time to bring in Dhelavi, don't you think?" suggested Tammy, digressing. "A little chat maybe? Under caution, of course."

"We've got nothing definite on him, other than what we've learned from Rakish. Persuasive, I suppose, but still speculative. No hard evidence to hand. But yes, let's see if we can get hold of the man. We don't even know where to start looking. Judging by the wife's anger at her son's perceived behaviour, she might just give us some pointers as to where he might be."

"Best bet, he'll be found at the East London Mosque. Send in a team to make the arrest. There's bound to be opposition from the other three colleagues if they're all there at the same time."

"Of course, but then, we don't know for sure that the other three even know Dhelavi beyond, that is, their common boat trip."

"Hang on, though. They've all been seen talking together by me and Deepak at the East London Mosque."

"True," said Manus.

"But still, go in mob-handed. One time we need to be prepared."

"Absolutely."

"And Binns? How did Jenner get on?"

Studying his fast-cooling coffee, Manus said, "Bill reckons he's eccentric to the point of being totally unbalanced."

"Surprise me," said Tammy, pushing her empty mug away.

"One thing, though." Manus concentrated, before adding, "Binns did admit to having the coat with the military buttons."

"He could hardly deny it," said Tammy. "I bumped into him wearing a jacket that fitted that description, and he's seen on CCTV in the club."

CHAPTER 70 • DAY 42 • 443

"True. But he claims the coat was stolen later the same night he was recorded wearing it."

"He must have gone back to the club after I spoke with him. We could check on CCTV to see if he re-entered the premises."

"Good idea," said Manus.

"I think I'll institute another search of people, lockers and anything else I can think of at the Tilbury club. Seems to be our centre of activity. Who knows, maybe Binns forgot where he put the coat."

"Too much to hope we'll find it there."

"It springs eternal, John."

CHAPTER 71 DAY 43

THE SOUND OF A SCREAM occurred at the precise moment the flat of the man's hand connected with the girl's face, throwing her sideways.

Blood burst from her split lip, and the man could be heard shouting, "Shut the fuck up before I start to get really out of it, bitch." Then a second slap was heard, the scream this time, louder than before.

"What he does to her, Daria? Why he won't leave Elena alone?" said a young girl with curly blond hair, one of a dozen left in the filthy apartment of the twenty who had originally been ferried across the Channel.

Moments later, a clearly furious Ricks emerged from the other room, his shirt open at the collar and dishevelled, trousers askew.

"Don't know when they're well off," he muttered, gathering his jacket from the back of a chair, hurriedly straightening his appearance and storming off.

Seated in a corner of the room, one of their minders, Belinda, looked up as a sobbing Elena stumbled out following Ricks's departure.

After the advice tendered to sell the girls to Arab oil billionaires, their numbers had gradually diminished as the Kerkuts, with the help of Harry Ricks, made sure they were kept fed and clean, before being sold on.

Those who looked older than early to mid-teens, whatever the effects a choice of clothing and make-up could produce, were kept as baby-making machines. While the problem of nine months supervision was onerous, nonetheless the sale price of newborn babies more than compensated for the time and effort involved.

Presently, four of those left were showing various stages of pregnancy, care of the eager ministrations of one police constable, Harry Ricks. They were all slumped disconsolately on worn sofas and armchairs dotted about the room. Elena now joined them, flopping into the one unoccupied armchair. "If he make me pregnant, I kill him."

"You ain't killin' no-one, darlin'," said Belinda, hoisting her bulk feebly out of a chair surrounded by screwed-up sweet papers, redundant cigarette packs and overflowing ashtrays, and surveying the barely live fire. "Least not while I'm 'ere to keep an eye on you."

Daria surveyed their looks of hopeless resignation, realising she was powerless to help. The fire guttered on in the rusting hearth, but it gave little if any warmth, despite Belinda's half-hearted efforts to rouse a flame with an old iron poker.

It was then that the germ of an idea worked its way into Daria's consciousness. She'd all but given up hope her boyfriend would be able to help them all. If he could get to the UK. If he could find the flat. If he could do anything on his own. If he chose the right police station and was believed. Too many imponderables.

But if he couldn't, then she would. Whatever the consequences. Her heart fluttered like bat's wings in her chest.

CHAPTER 72 DAY 44

It's been too long. Days, and I'm yearning for company. Little Indian girl I saw at the club. Heard someone call her Farida.

I'll wait for her, see her again. Itching for love. She must be. Saw it in her eyes.

My kind of love. The type that comes and goes with a knife. Straight blade that'll cut through flesh and bone, opening it wide like a bloodied yawn.

Mustn't get careless, though. Shouldn't have trodden on that last one's face. Cow! They'll recognise the pattern of my sole. Still, loads like it. That shoe. They'll never know it's me. Hee, hee.

Farida. Farida.

I'll be the swan if you'll be my Leda.

* * * * *

THE WERE ALL GATHERED around the big screen on the fifth floor of the Yard. Farida had the remote in one hand. With the other she touched the screen from time to time negotiating the images she wanted to bring up.

John Manus and Tammy stood closer to the screen than the others who merely crowded around, shifting where necessary to get a better view. There was a general air of expectation in the place.

Furthermore, on the CCTV recording the atmosphere of friendliness in the club could practically be felt. People danced. People chatted. Over by the main bar, Dexie was in animated conversation with a tall blond girl who'd hoisted herself onto a bar stool despite the struggle she must have faced in her tight black mini skirt. The place was a community and without the horrors that had been occurring it would, by her reckoning, be a place Tammy would happily frequent in other circumstances.

"I've been through dozens of hours of CCTV time," said Farida. "Looking for? I don't know what. Anything I suppose that might help. Something out of the ordinary."

"Teacher's pet," muttered Ricks, incurring irritated looks from several of those nearest him.

Ignoring the remark, Manus said, "So what have you got for us, Farida?"

"Only this," she replied. "Look."

"The man with a tic," said Tammy, peering closely at the screen and picking him out from among the crowds of clubbers. Then addressing the team, she explained, "We've identified this man as one Muhammed Dhelavi." Then went on to outline what had been found out to date, and from whom the information had been gleaned.

"His son!" exclaimed a voice near the front.

"Right, it's Rakish," said Tammy. "Very much dragged out of him. And hot off the press. So you're about as up to date as we are, at this stage."

By now, overcome by weariness, her various wounds and scars tormenting her, Tammy fought to concentrate. No time to be losing the plot, but the huge burden of what she'd undertaken was taking its toll.

"Tammy," said Manus, frowning at her. "Are you okay? Looking a bit peaky."

"I'm fine," she said, breathing deeply and forcing herself to brighten up.

"Shouldn't have taken on a man's job if you can't handle the pressure," sneered Ricks, who abruptly shut up when he saw the look on Manus's face.

"Here," Farida pointed, as though there'd been no interruption to her narrative, "and here," she added, changing the view to show filming at different dates. "And here, here and here."

"The man with the tic again, Mr Dhelavi," said Manus. "He doesn't move about much, does he."

"Always by the wide entrance to the club," said Farida. "That made him easier to spot on CCTV. Easier than when I was actually in the crowd myself."

"You what?" exclaimed a horrified Manus.

"I thought I'd stand a better chance of spotting someone. Anyone, if I went down to the Tilbury club to look around. I only went when I was off duty."

"Alone?" Manus was raising his voice now.

"Yes, gov. We seemed to be making so little progress, and ..."

"Farida!" Manus exploded, his face reddening. "You've acted totally irresponsibly. Without notifying anyone here in case of emergency? How often did you ...? No. Don't answer that. I'm not sure I want to know."

"I'm sorry." Farida's voice was small and uncertain. "I just thought ..."

"Okay," said Tammy, flattened palms spread, gently pressing the air down, calming the situation. "I think Farida gets the picture, John. She's taken a silly risk, possibly putting herself in harm's way. Though, no more so than the hundreds of others there. Unless, that is, she left the club when it closed and travelled home alone?"

Farida shook her head.

"Fine," Tammy acknowledged. "Then why don't we move on. So, Farida, what do we derive from all this?"

"Two things," she replied, peeping to the left and right, like a child caught filching biscuits from the tin. "First, every time he's found on CCTV there's been a murder later on. Same evening, or night, if you will. Look how he stands around taking it all in as though he's deciding who to target next."

"Alright, well done, Farida," murmured Manus, relenting. "First-class police work. But still. No more of the same. I absolutely forbid it."

"Yes, gov."

But Tammy could see the spark of combat in Farida's eyes. Nothing Manus said or could say would put off the young PC. She recognised her younger self in Farida. Except, Farida had none of the height, combat skills or strength at Tammy's disposal to defend herself in any physical confrontation.

"So, we have another suspect," Manus continued, pushing his hands into his jacket pockets. "But is he the bomber with his contacts brought over in the boat? Increasingly likely. Does he know Oscar Mountford? The Kerkuts? Or is he a trans killer? In which case, we're looking at a loner. Maybe he's both? Either way, we've not enough to haul him in, yet, other than for an informal chat, as Tammy and I have agreed. Of course, he might have been at the club on other occasions when there were no murders."

"We could try tailing him from the club," offered Tammy. "Though that may tell us where he goes, but not what he does and with whom. Come to think of it, any tail at night is going to stick out like a sore thumb."

"That's right." Farida studied the backs of her nails. "And if he uses public transport, we'd likely lose him. If he drives, whilst we can pick him up on ANPR, he won't be our killer. Our individual with the knife won't want to chance his number plate being recorded."

"And, while I think of it," Tammy put in. "Hester has installed added CCTV on the entrance to all three clubs, sufficiently conspicuous to deter any would-be killers from trying anything close to the club premises. Those there already were inadequate, having too little sweep. She's told me Dexie'd been on at her for ages, but she seemed to have been on the edge of collapse for a time."

"Anything else for us?" asked Bill Jenner, who'd arrived a few moments ago to join the others.

There was little movement in the room, absorbed as they all were by what they'd seen and heard. Tammy had shaken off her weariness, become alive with adrenalin at sight of what Farida had turned up, and been up to.

"Yes," said Farida triumphantly. "You'll see the man keeps away from people. Doesn't appear to have any physical contact with any of the clubbers. Easier perhaps where he's standing as he's not in the centre of the throng. One other thing that doesn't fit."

"Go on, Farida," prompted Tammy.

"Well, if he was seen at the club, ostensibly asking after Dexie, why from all the occasions we have him on CCTV don't we see him approaching the bar?"

"Maybe he did, or had," suggested Tammy. "Just not picked up in the recordings we have."

"It's possible," agreed Farida.

"Excellent," said Manus, allowing himself to smile for the first time. "And what conclusions do you draw from that, Farida?"

"None," she replied.

"None?" asked Manus, disappointed.

"Just watch, as he exits the club."

The man with the tic shrugged as though satisfied he'd seen what he needed to, and turned to go. Then it happened. Someone bumped into him, apparently unintentionally, and Dhelavi lurched, putting one hand against the metal frame of the wide exit to support himself. It was a momentary thing, and he frowned in annoyance before hurrying out.

"When was this," Tammy asked.

"Same day Daisy Meekins was murdered," said Farida.

There was a collective murmur around the room. A shuffling of feet. An improving mood. It was the first time the hitherto demoralised team had had the opportunity to indulge in a moment of genuine optimism.

"Go on, Farida," prompted Manus. "You say it. We'll all hear it."

"DNA," Farida practically whispered. Then she took the image and blew it up as far as possible. On the frame was a thumb print. Smudged, perhaps. But almost certainly a clear source of DNA.

"I'll get forensics down there right away," offered Jenner.

"I already have," said Farida.

CHAPTER 73 DAY 44

IT WAS LATE when Tammy got home, ready to crash, exhausted, wiped out. She needed a large vodka, bison grass, neat. A long day, but some progress at last.

Then she heard adult voices from inside the apartment.

"What the...?" she exclaimed, taken aback as she strode into her home. "Dov? What are you doing here?"

"Delighted to see you too, Tammy."

"That's not what I meant."

He was seated in an armchair, in his usual denim jeans and jacket, with Matty on his lap looking up at Dov and chuckling happily.

"I've come to see my son. You seem to have forgotten this young man has a father. When were you considering getting in touch again, Tammy? I've hardly set eyes on the boy. At this rate I wouldn't have been seeing him again until he was due to be bar-mitzvahed."

"I know, Dov. I am sorry, sorry, sorry," she said, shaking her head remorsefully. "I've been so taken up with this business, I've not had time to think. Please don't be angry with me, darling. I couldn't bear it if you were. I know it's my fault."

"I'm not angry with you," said Dov, beaming down at Matty as the baby took hold of one of his fingers, grasping it in his own chubby paw.

The beam on Dov's face was one of almost unbearable love. Tammy felt herself welling up and had to fight to prevent the tears that threatened.

But it wasn't anger Tammy could read on his face, as he glanced back, it was disappointment. With her. What more revelations might now be expected? God, no! She held her breath as she waited for Dov to reintroduce the subject of the child's paternity. Please, not now, anything but that. Too weary to start a post-mortem. But he was too distracted by the baby to bring the subject up.

"I like the hair, Tammy."

"Please, Dov," she said, self-consciously touching the side of her cropped head. "Sarcasm doesn't suit you."

"Then, tell me. What did your little jaunt in Belmarsh achieve? Apart from putting your life at serious risk?"

"Don't pressure me, Dov. I'm tired," she said, slipping off her jacket and flopping into an armchair.

"Very well, Tammy, I won't push it. But really, was it worth it? Did you make contact with the man, Dominic Pope? Was he any use? Man's a serial killer. A card-carrying psychopath. Could you rely on anything he may have told you? I heard you put up quite a performance in there. Three on one? Impressed the governor."

"Which order would you like me to answer your questions, Dov?"

"Any order you like, Tammy. I'm just trying to get my head around why you'd go to the lengths you have for apparently so little return; you've volunteered nothing. So I'm presuming you got nothing, otherwise, knowing you as I do, if you'd learned anything useful, you'd have been singing it from the hilltops."

"Dov, let's pause for a moment," she digressed. "I want a drink. You?"

"Coffee's fine for me."

Climbing wearily to her feet, Tammy called to Maria, who was in the kitchen preparing a meal for everyone. "Darling, will you do Dov a coffee, you know the way he likes it, black and strong."

"Yes, madame," she called back.

"Madame?" asked Dov, rocking the baby and grinning despite himself.

"Don't ask," said Tammy. "She makes me feel like royalty."

CHAPTER 73 • DAY 44 • 455

"No, Tammy. That's how you make everyone feel about you."

"Moving on," said Tammy tolerantly. "Your enquiries. There's been no great revelations from any source. Just morsels. All of which, I believe, will begin to add up to something." Flopping back into her armchair, large vodka in hand, she knocked back half of the glass.

Maria, wiping one hand on her flowered apron, came in quietly with Dov's coffee and deposited it on the side table next to him with a shy smile in response to Dov's nod.

"Morsels?" Dov, blowing on the surface of the steaming mug, took up the exchange again. "Is that it? All those risks. And with a baby, too. Don't you think you've been a tad self-indulgent?"

Tammy stared at Dov for several moments without saying a word, then, "I met with Pope's son in Blackburn."

"Well, that's something new. Why haven't you told me this before?"

"I'm telling you now, Dov."

"Okay," Dov sighed, bending over Matty to nuzzle his tummy to the baby's squeals of delight. "So, tell me, what's Pope junior got to say for himself. What's he like, this guy with a psycho for a father? Does he resemble Pope senior in any way at all?"

"In no way, Dov. He is the polar opposite of his father. Aryan features, blue-eyed, tall and blond. A chequered history making a mint in Africa. Albeit probably by dubious means. Diamond running, it seems. As for psycho, David was so horrified by his father's crimes, he changed his name to Eckstein."

"I get the picture, Tammy. But what did you learn, for heaven's sake?"

"That Dominic Pope has a charming son, who's distanced himself from his father as far as he can."

"Bloody wasted journey, if you ask me," said Dov, disgruntled.

"We'll see."

"Will we?" asked Dov dubiously.

Changing the subject, none too subtly, Tammy posed, "What about Aaliyah? You suggested she contact me."

"More morsels?"

"More morsels. Don't knock it, Dov. They all add up. By the way, where is she?"

"She liked you, you know. But she's back in Israel on a new assignment. Tammy, sorry to belabour the point, but it seems to me, you're running hard and standing still."

"We'll get there. Eventually."

"While we're on the subject, what's COBRA been up to? I'd have thought they'd be round your throat demanding answers," said Dov, picking up the baby and kissing his bare tummy.

"John's been keeping them at bay. And yes, I know," she said, interrupting a threatened interjection from Dov. "They won't wait for ever."

"And you've got precious little for them. Right?"

"No more than you know, Dov."

"How long do you think it'll be before they take you off the job?"

She shrugged. "The Home Sec isn't fighting my corner. The only one there who seems to be backing me up, apart from John Manus and Bob Walker, is the head of CTC, Nick Holden."

"We know him, of course. Mossad has a lot of respect for the man."

Climbing to his feet, Dov handed the little one to Tammy. "Take special care of my son, Tammy."

CHAPTER 74 DAY 45

LOOKING A TAD LESS FLORID than usual, but still fidgeting with his too-tight collar, John Manus faced Tammy across the table at their usual coffee house, Caffè Nero, a mere spit from where the Kerkuts had met only recently on Kingsway.

"Got some news for you, Tammy."

She was nursing the Styrofoam mug in her palms, and inhaling the smell of good coffee.

"Things looking up, John?"

"Maybe." Manus blew on the surface of his coffee, then sipped from the mug. "Too soon to get excited, Tammy. But wait," lifting a hand in emphasis, "Bill organised a second search of the three club premises."

"With all the killings, but three, based near to but essentially outside the Tilbury club," said Tammy, "finding anything relevant inside any of the premises was always going to be a long shot."

"True. But nothing ventured. So I let Bill go ahead. I've asked him to join us, by the way."

"And? You found something?"

"There was nothing in either Dagenham or Dartford," he delayed.

"Not surprising, really," said Tammy. "But, let me guess, you found something in the Tilbury club, the main centre of trouble."

"Just might be," he breathed.

Leaning forward, excited, expectant, Tammy said, "I'm all ears, John."

"Bill and a team from uniform went through everything. A thorough search. And I mean absolutely everything. Cupboards in the kitchens. Bar areas, loft spaces. In front, behind, and on top of whatever invited it. They also went around the club buildings, in the street, backyard areas, among the wheely bins. You name it. If they'd looked before, they looked again."

Tammy sipped from her mug, but resisted the temptation to hurry Manus. In his own way and in his own time, she'd learned to let him follow his own line.

Letting her mind wander for a moment, she touched the pendant around her neck, the one with the protective Hebrew lettering, thought about her own vulnerabilities, particularly where her father and son were concerned. The threat made when she'd first come across the Kerkuts.

As though echoing her own thoughts, a police car with siren blasting roared past the window of the café. She shuddered involuntarily.

"Everything alright, Tammy. You look as though you've just been spooked."

"Nothing, John. Just ..."

She paused, gazed out of the window at passing pedestrians. "It'll seem foolish, I know, but it was a feeling that someone had just walked over my grave."

"Unlike you to be so down, Tammy."

"I know. I know." She shook her head to rid herself of her doubts. "It's just the breadth of what we're up against. Killings somehow linked with acts of terrorism, albeit tenuously. We've got some positive leads, of course, but not enough to make arrests. God forbid there should be another outrage on the trains. And while we're about it, what about COBRA?"

"The Home Secretary made some more noises about taking you off the case, as you'll be aware. I nipped that in the bud as soon as it was brought up."

"You won't keep him at bay indefinitely, John. On top of all that, are there pending threats to be levied against me? I ask myself. My son? My father? And by whom? We all know, though, don't we. The Kerkuts. Ricks." She shook her head again. "Sorry, John, I shouldn't ..."

"No, please, Tammy. I could move Ricks, but you already said to leave him where he is so we can keep an eye on him. It is best that way. If he's as involved as we suspect he may be, we'll wait till he buries himself."

"I was thinking, why not put a tracker on his car? You told me he frequently disappears for hours at a time. Where does he go? What does he get up to? Does he know the Kerkuts? Could the Rolex, the expensive suits et cetera be linked to any activities involving the brothers?"

She waited a beat, then as though another notion had just presented itself, she asked, "John, out of interest, what sort of motor does he drive? A pool car?"

Scratching the back of his head, Manus said, "As a matter of fact he chooses to drive his own car. A navy blue BMW M4 Coupé, which by all accounts he bought new."

Staring straight into Manus's eyes, Tammy said, "Christ, John. We're talking around a hundred K. Where the hell does he get the money to afford a car like that, and on a DC's pay?"

"You're right, of course. I'd thought of putting a tracker on his vehicle but had held back. Couldn't get my head around the idea that he was anything more than a flash exhibitionist. Seemed almost like a betrayal by me. Didn't want to admit to myself one of our team could be a bad 'un. Time to face what might be unpalatable facts."

"You'll organise it, John?"

"Take it as read. Now," he said, getting to his feet. "Another coffee?"

"You haven't told me what Bill found, John. I can hardly wait. But, okay," she agreed. "Coffee first."

This time there was a queue, and it took a while to be served. It was while she was idly gazing out the window that she saw something that made her sit up rigidly to attention. On the other side of Kingsway, between the chain links of moving traffic, a glimpse of the Kerkut brothers talking with, unmistakably, one Mr Harry Ricks. For a moment she debated whether to chase after them but demurred. It was sufficient just to see them together.

Relating what she'd seen to a worried-looking John Manus, he agreed that the tracker was probably an overdue item to bring in.

"So, tell me now, what did you find?" she asked eagerly.

"It was in one of the lockers. They'd all been checked during the first search, but it was always worth taking another look." Manus paused for a moment as a couple making for one of the window tables brushed past them.

"And? You found something."

Manus smiled guardedly. "We found the jacket with the button missing. The other buttons on that jacket matched the one you found in the gutter close to the last murder scene. But. The missing button wasn't on the outside of the jacket, it was the spare appended to the inner lining."

"So when a scrap of material was found in Daisy's hand, she must have pulled the button off in the struggle, tearing part of the lining with it."

"Exactly."

"Obvious question, John. Whose locker was it?"

"One of the bar people. Tim Fletcher. Sadly, that's where the lead runs out." After the brief excitement of the find, Manus's disappointment was almost palpable.

"Why's that? What's the problem?"

"Simple. Tim is a size 44-inch chest. He's short, around five seven and broad. This has no label inside to indicate who the maker might be. But it's a size 40 and made for a six-foot-tall individual."

"Is this the same sort of jacket being sold in the sale at the Army and Navy store in Tilbury?"

"Apparently. Like Patrick Laing's. Except his doesn't have a button missing."

"Same as Hector Binns's, although his was missing a button. At least it looked that way, till he took the missing item from a pocket. Said he'd caught it on a door or something."

"So, we're still all at sea."

Drinking from her now cooling coffee, Tammy suggested, "Not too difficult to see what's happened here, is it?"

"Someone's tried to lead us astray, but they picked the wrong locker."

"So not someone from the staff, then. They'd have an idea whose locker was whose. Presumably. Tell me, John, are the lockers secure?"

"Apparently not. They are simply metal cupboards without a key. People are told not to leave anything valuable in them."

"That means anyone from among the club crowd could have planted the jacket."

"Needle in a haystack," said Manus.

"What do you think then, John, from what we have so far? Binns? What about him?"

"My money is still on Laing, Tammy."

"A convincing performance from the gentleman under interrogation, but not enough to charge him with."

"Both he and Laing are tall enough to fit the bill for that size jacket," said Manus.

"Of course, we've assumed all along that we're looking for someone somehow connected with the club. It could be a total stranger. One we've not even begun to think of. Our killer could have got to the lockers and planted the jacket simply to confuse. The lockers are close to the cloakroom. It would have been easy."

"But then Binns being the arrogant bugger he is, post the Daisy killing, realising he'd lost a button, might just have merely gone back to the Army and Navy to get a spare. Proudly shown when he was questioned."

"While I think of it, any progress on the DNA?"

"Results came in this morning. Laing, whom we've let go, had traces of his DNA on Daisy's neck, in line with what he told us about checking her pulse. Ditto the blood on the sleeve of his jacket."

"And Binns?" Tammy asked.

"Same thing as we saw on the CCTV. His DNA on the shoulder of her clothing."

"What about the strip of cloth found in Daisy's palm?"

"Nothing, apart from her own, which you'd expect," said Manus, the earlier optimism having evaporated.

"No further," she sighed. "Bloody nightmare."

Just at that moment they were joined by a rushed-looking Bill Jenner. "Sorry I'm late," he apologised. "Have I missed much?"

"I've brought Tammy up to date, Bill. The button, the strip of cloth. We're debating, Laing or Binns?"

"What about Seward?" posed Bill.

"The long-shot outsider. Possibly coming up on the rails," said Tammy, looking grim. "Do we have his DNA?" she asked.

"No," Bill responded. "But we've several versions of DNA on the clothing of various girls killed."

"Dance partners during the evening?" offered Manus.

"And possibly our killer's," said Tammy.

Getting to his feet ready to leave, Manus said, "See what you can do about getting Seward's DNA, Bill. Any way you can. I suspect we're going to find he's our unknown quantity."

CHAPTER 75 DAY 46

"ARE YOU OUT of your tiny fucking mind, Ricks?"

"Wait a minute, Oscar."

"No, you wait a minute, you moron. How many times have I told you to steer clear of the East London doss where the tarts are?" Mountford's voice was strained with barely supressed rage.

"Someone needs to keep an eye on the place."

"Bullshit. Leave it to the Kerkuts. Those two fuckers never get their hands dirty. Someone else always carries the can."

"Oscar, I've had to replace the two scrubbers who were keeping an eye on the place. They've both pissed off."

"And the Kerkuts couldn't have done that?"

He waited for several moments, uninterrupted by Ricks, then as though in revelation, said, "Wait a minute, Ricks. What are they paying you?"

"What do you mean, Oscar?"

"Don't play dumb with me, sonny. What are the Kerkuts paying you for your assistance?"

"Bugger all, Oscar. You said you wanted me to keep an eye on them, so …"

"You must think I was born yesterday, Ricks. Tell me, what do you drive now? A Roller?"

"A BMW."

"Still wearing the Rolex?"

"Yes, but …"

"Words fail me, son. But if I find you're up my backside I'll have you taken care of. Don't think I can't."

"I'd never do you down, Oscar. You know that."

"Crap. I wouldn't trust you as far as I could throw my own grandmother. And she's been six feet under for twenty years."

"Please, Oscar …"

"How often do you go to East London, anyway?"

"Only when I have to."

"Did it ever occur to you, you might have been followed there. The Pierre bitch shouldn't be underestimated."

"I've not been followed."

"How can you be sure? Do you ever check your car for a tracking device?"

Mountford couldn't see Ricks's face. If he could, he'd not have failed to see it had gone chalk white.

"When I r-remember," he stammered.

CHAPTER 76 DAY 47

THERE WAS THE PIERCING SOUND of hysterical screaming from inside the crumbling house, movement and running feet, as armed police, using a battering ram, smashed their way through the front door.

38 Naseby Street, East London. Parked by the kerb, next to a black paddy wagon, a magnificent BMW M4 Coupé. John Manus and Bill Jenner led the way in, followed by Tammy Pierre.

Ricks must have seen or heard what was on the point of happening, because as they entered the place he was about to run up the stairs and presumably attempt an escape.

Tammy spoke first. "Why, Mr Ricks. Please don't go. We were hoping you'd entertain us to a tea or a coffee."

An overweight, middle-aged woman seated in a worn and fading armchair in a far corner of the room struggled to her feet. Her dyed blond hair was black at the roots. She wore a flowered dress with an uneven hem. Wrinkled stockings hugged ankles above her otherwise slippered feet. A smudge of red lipstick overlapped thin lips that openly sneered at the visitors.

The place was a scene of pandemonium with girls running around like headless chickens. A couple of ancient ladderback chairs got knocked over. Teas and soft drinks on the couple of kitchen tables in the room got spilled.

One person, in jeans and a T-shirt, more together than the rest, approached Tammy. "Thank God," she said. "I am Daria. My boyfriend, Cristian, arrived from Bucharest yesterday. That devil." She pointed to a cringing Ricks, who'd now changed his mind about trying to make a break for it. "That devil, Ricks," she went on, "was here when he arrived and beat him so badly I thought he might die. He is upstairs lying down. He was refused an ambulance by him," she spat in contempt.

"It's all rubbish," Ricks whined, presenting less than his usually sartorial appearance, his blue suit badly crinkled and his shirt open at the neck without a tie. "He attacked me first."

At the realisation it was the police that had entered the property and that everyone was safe, the place began to calm down, with girls beginning to cluster around, eager to find out what was going to happen next. Then they all started talking at once. One or two were crying with relief.

Tammy, turning to Manus, said, "John? Your play."

"Of course," he replied, before addressing a white-faced, shaking Ricks and reading him his rights.

"It's not what it seems," whimpered Ricks, wringing his hands. "Boss?" he pleaded to Manus.

"And what does it seem, Harry?" Tammy asked, barely keeping her rage under control. "You came to the wrong house? You're not supposed to be here?"

"Alright, Tammy," Manus said placatingly. "I'll take it from here."

"Bill, we'll need an ambulance, from what this young lady says." He glanced at Daria. "And an FLO to deal with the girls and start the process of rehousing, and if they wish, getting them home again."

"In hand," replied Jenner.

"We'll also need statements from all of them, asap."

"They'll be only too willing, I'll bet," said Tammy.

"It was the Kerkuts," said Ricks. "Never me. And look," he exclaimed, pointing at the window. "That's them now. That's their car going past, and they're both in it. I can see."

"Somehow, Harry, I don't think they will be stopping," said Tammy.

"Sorry, Tammy. I misjudged that badly."

"How, John? Don't beat yourself up about things."

Manus shook his head in irritation. "Should have used the damn tracker sooner."

CHAPTER 77 DAY 48

THEY'D MADE SMALL TALK, as one does before getting down to the serious business in hand.

"Smart car outside," said Bob. "Lamborghini? Ferrari? Maserati? I can never tell. All beautiful."

"Must have arrived after I got here," said Tammy. "What colour was it, Bob?"

"Bright red," he replied.

"Hmm," said Tammy. "Sounds like the car that chased me when I drove south from Blackburn the other day."

"Someone hereabouts is earning a lot of money." Bob sounded wistful, or perhaps simply impressed.

"Some of the club members are pretty well-to-do," Tammy said quietly, trying in vain to disguise her tiredness.

He could sense the weariness in her voice. "Tammy, you need a break."

"I'm fine." She shrugged, absently fidgeting with a BIC ballpoint, making aimless circles on a blank page of Hester's heavy leather-bound notepad. "Never better." Not even she believed that fiction.

She was seated in Hester Lamont's office at the Tilbury club, chatting to a worried-looking Bob Walker, her elbows resting on the desktop. A file of her notes together with a second folder of printed documents, photocopies and news cuttings sat alongside to it. Next to them a half-empty jug of plain tap water with a couple of tumblers. Despite the refreshment taken, her mouth felt foul and sticky.

"We've made good progress. You've made good progress," he corrected himself. "I mean, fantastic progress. Without you …"

"Thanks, Bob. But really, without John and Bill ... You know. They're across at the pathologist's this morning, seeing if there's anything more he can throw light on. I doubt it, though. He's given us all he's got. I told John you and I would be here and able to manage perfectly well."

She'd left the office door open as staff had trooped in and out, assisting with her enquiries. But she'd barely taken in Bob's comments. She was worn-out but refused to admit it to herself. The prospect terrified her. She was in control. She was always in control. Except that the iron resolve to always overcome the odds, whatever they were, was slipping from her grasp. She could feel it. Her palms were sweaty and a trickle of perspiration ran down her chest between her breasts.

Matty had been fretful, keeping her awake at night. Dov, now spending more time at her place, and seeing the state she was in, had found his offer of help welcome, but politely refused.

Maria had wanted to step in; after all, she'd asked, wasn't that why she was there? But no, Tammy wasn't about to let anyone but herself be Matty's mother. There were enough occasions when she had needed and would continue to need Maria's help, Dov's too. Though not as long as she was actually with her son.

But the long days, the short nights, the pummelling she'd taken, all sustained on coffee and adrenalin, had long ago begun to take their toll. Trouble was, the adrenalin, upon which Tammy had always relied, was fast evaporating.

She and Sherlock Holmes had that much in common. Running out of energy, the great detective had come close to a nervous breakdown prior to the case of The Devil's Foot. Recuperating on doctor's orders in Cornwall's Mount Bay, he'd been revived by the need to investigate the unexplained deaths of three siblings in the village.

Imminently she'd be running on empty, if she wasn't already, and she could no longer ignore it. Unlikely there'd be anything emerging at this stage of the proceedings to revive her flagging energy in the way that Holmes's situation had resolved.

Interrupting her thoughts, Bob, gazing thoughtfully ceilingward, said, "You've been present at all the interviews John and Bill have had with Ricks. You, more than just about anyone, have had a hand in securing all the information we need to arrest and ultimately convict Dhelavi, and Oscar Mountford for his part in the planning and or financing of either one or both of the bomb outrages. I've observed everything, together with Nick Holden, onscreen outside the interview room or in recordings later when I couldn't be present."

"Hours of questioning," she murmured, instantly regretting the dull tone of her voice. She was letting herself down in front of this man whom she respected beyond all others in the police force. She needed something to give her the burst of energy that would help put this thing to bed, once and for all.

The coffees delivered by one of the staff were sitting on the desk, untouched and cold. Hester, equally exhausted, had taken herself off for a brief break in town while Tammy and Bob debated their progress.

"We've got the results we hoped for and more." Bob sounded confident, crossed his legs and planted his hands in his lap.

"I know," she said, forcing herself to appear brighter. "We've got DNA from Ricks and Dhelavi on bomb-making equipment for the second one on Southern Region. Very careless. Especially from our DC Ricks. But only Dhelavi's DNA on the earlier one on Northern Region. I wonder who his materials supplier was? Probably Ricks, though we don't have his DNA to connect him. Maybe he was more careful on that occasion."

"That's still a mystery. We'll keep the file open, of course," said Bob.

"Anything else?" Tammy asked.

"Well, we've still no idea who the besuited individual was who apparently planted the second bomb. No DNA traces on that distinctive Buroni briefcase."

"Looks like a Kerkut signature to me," suggested Tammy. "Jason was carrying just such a briefcase when they accosted me at our first meeting outside my apartment."

"Could be possible. Also, come to think of it," added Bob, "we've no CCTV to indicate when and by whom the first bomb was planted in the wife of the minister's holdall."

"Someone must have moved pretty subtly to have escaped notice," she said, sitting back and straightening the lapels of her jacket.

"Evidently," agreed Bob. "Also, I'm led to believe that Ricks will be turning King's evidence anyway. He's intimated he'll be shopping the Kerkuts. Though, to be honest, we've nothing on them save the apparent meeting where they were spotted in Kingsway talking to Ricks."

"So, we've got two out of three sorted, so far," said Tammy. "The bombers and the freeing of the girls from that dump. We're left with finding the killer or killers of the girls."

"I don't know whether you're aware, but Ricks admitted informally, and outside of the interview room, that the original plan was to house all the girls in a five-star hotel presenting them to rich Middle Eastern buyers."

"Never happened. Hmm? Probably didn't want to lay out the cash. Wealthy tightwads."

"Another thing," mused Bob. "I wonder why they brought the girls in on a ramshackle boat across a dangerous Channel, when, according to Ricks, he had the contacts to alert his people in London's mainline stations of potential stock. As he put it."

"Getting harder to pick up girls away from the prying eyes of security people at the stations. Still, it'd have been better than nearly losing the lot of them at sea."

"Back to the present, then," said Tammy. "And these bloody killings. We've got titbits, tasters, bits of bait, haven't we. But nothing we can specifically pin on anyone."

"The Home Sec is still grinding his teeth," said Bob. "Despite Nick Holden fighting your corner. The Met Commissioner, Miranda Miller, is also very much on board. She's got a lot of time for you, Tammy."

"Is Templeton still making noises about having me removed from the investigation?"

"The killings are a police matter, not strictly within the immediate purview of the Home Secretary. Basically, he oversees law enforcement and matters of national security and immigration in England and Wales. That's his remit. Still, the man is a bigot, clearly doesn't like you, and he carries a lot of weight. We need to come up with something urgently before he makes an announcement about your departure."

"How urgent is urgent, Bob?"

Shaking his head, Bob said, "Any time. Could be today? Hmm! Maybe not. My money's on tomorrow."

She could feel her temperature rising. "Bloody hell! No credit at all for what's been achieved so far?"

"'Fraid not, Tammy."

She sat staring out of the office door for several moments, watching cleaners going about their business with buckets and mops, staff refilling shelves behind the two bars, deliveries of food and drink being trundled in on heavy-duty wheeled platform trucks. A peaceful scene undisturbed by the recent horrific events.

"Okay," she emphatically. "No point in moping. We've a job to do."

Bob smiled. "Of course."

"A quick run through, then we'll talk to the last of the staff we've not yet interviewed."

"You shoot first, Tammy."

"Right, then. First off. Two girls with broken necks. Could be the same, or two different killers. They'll need to stay on the back burner as we've nothing beyond blurred CCTV images to go on. Julie Crosbie and Liz Armstrong.

"Then the botched killing of Karen Richardson. A curved blade, but again, nothing more to go on. Note, a right-handed killer.

"Then three of the last four, that's Anna Proby, Teresa Finch and Judge Jeffreys, all transsexuals, whether surgically addressed or not, and all killed by a straight blade, by an apparently left-handed murderer."

"The odd one out here is Daisy Meekins," suggested Bob. "Our number four. A left-handed killer, yes, but she wasn't a transsexual. Remember Laing's performance? If he was her killer, and we've DNA evidence on his sleeve, and the boot print on the girl's face, then did he do the others too?"

"The other mystery is the skeleton in the women's refuge," said Tammy.

"Broken neck. And what appears to be a savagely cut throat," said Bob.

"And hey," remarked Tammy. "A left-handed killer again."

At that moment, Bob's mobile rang. He put it to his ear and Tammy heard him say, "Thanks, John. I'm with her now. No, that's okay, I'll let her know."

Putting the phone back in his jacket pocket, Bob addressed Tammy, looking grave. "News just in from the pathologist, John tells me, is that the skeletal remains found in the women's refuge are those of Alex Hedges, son of Michael and Geraldine Hedges, but nothing had been said until there was certainty."

"How certain, Bob?"

Bob ran his fingers through his hair, studied Tammy. "One hundred percent," he admitted. "No doubts at all."

"God, how awful. Michael wanted to pay me double my usual fee to find Alex, but I refused." She lit a cigar, her umpteenth that morning, and drew deeply on it, waving smoke from her eyes, sensing the lift it gave her.

"I assume they've not been immediately notified?"

"No, not yet, Tammy. We weren't sure whether you would want to break the news to them yourself?"

She indicated not, with a flap of her hands.

"Probably better if someone at family liaison does the job, then I'll meet them afterwards. I can hardly believe it. They adored him."

Out of the blue, Bob said, "Edward Seward is left-handed, you know."

"It's a pointer," agreed Tammy. "But if that's all we've got on him, we'll need a helluva lot more."

"The other evidence we've collected?" asked Bob.

"Nothing. The donkey jacket was a useless blind and led nowhere. The button certainly came off it with the bit of cloth, but that proves nothing. It was planted in the wrong locker to confuse, but by whom?" She shook her head in frustration, the scar at the side of her skull beginning to throb painfully.

"You know we found no DNA on the bit of lining found in Daisy's hand, beyond her own."

Bob's mobile rang again, and, nodding to her before putting it to his ear, the strain on his face evident, Tammy heard him say, "Yes, Home Secretary. Of course, I'll get in touch with Ms Pierre as soon as I can and notify her."

She felt her hairline burn and a trickle of sweat run down her forehead, which she prayed would not be noticed by Bob. But what she really felt was dismay. This was what failure was all about. He didn't need to say anything. But then, of course, he did.

Turning to Tammy, looking pale and beaten, he said, "I am so sorry, Tammy. But as of now, you're off the case."

CHAPTER 78 DAY 48

"OKAY," SHE ADMITTED, her arms outstretched in resignation. "If that's the way we go, so be it. But let's at least finish off the last of our interviews here before we cash in."

For the first time since she'd been retained on the case she felt utterly miserable. Like a chastised school child. The successes achieved so far outweighed by the enormity of the failure to catch the main culprit. The man labelled by the press as The Tilbury Ripper.

Had it been worth the time and risk? Would she do the same thing again under similar circumstances? The answer, of course, was yes. Professionals don't walk away just because someone else has doubts about their ability to deliver. What not everyone seemed to appreciate was that she, Tammy Pierre, had no doubts whatsoever about her talents. Her problem, right now, was to re-establish her sense of self-worth, while trying to convince people like the Home Secretary of her value to this investigation.

"I'll say one thing for you, Tammy." Bob smiled sadly. "You've got what it takes."

"Cudlipp told me I have balls," she said.

"Hmm! I doubt I could have put it better," said Bob, with a wry smile.

"Still, no time for jokes."

"Who's left on your list, Tammy? We've been here for hours. Is there anyone left to interview?"

Casting her eye down the list on her mobile, she said, "Only Dexie."

"Has he been any help?"

"Done the best he can, I suppose," replied Tammy, surveying the ashtray full of smoked panatella stubs.

"Which isn't much, beyond a bit of moral support for the staff, who are fond of him; and me, when I needed a bit of a boost. He's a timid man, been badly frightened by what's been going on. But like the others here, couldn't afford to stop working, so, among others, persuaded Hester to keep the clubs open."

"Probably in hindsight, not a good idea," said Bob.

"Let's get him in," she said, while reaching for yet another panatella, despite her solemn vow stop, or at least to cut back. Her tongue was beginning to feel like an extension of a cigar.

"I'll go," said Bob. "I saw him behind the bar."

Before Bob could get to his feet his mobile rang again. "Yes, Home Secretary. Of course, Home Secretary. As I believe I intimated earlier, as soon as I locate her. I realise it's urgent."

"Christ!" she muttered, her temper flaring. "I won't try to guess. It's pretty obvious. He just can't wait, can he? We'll finish up here, then I'll withdraw."

"Not the way I wanted it to end, Tammy," said Bob, exiting the room to fetch Dexie.

A few moments later Bob returned with a worried-looking, red-jacketed Dexie, stunning as ever, with her signature cloud of white hair and exotic white lips against an ebony complexion, who on entering the office looked down at the two cups of untouched coffee, and said, "Let me get fresh ones for you."

Tammy asked herself again, why would such a beautiful creature wish to transition from what she was to something, anything else. She considered Dexie to be female, to all appearances, though using a form of address indicating the DJ's desire to be treated as male. "We're fine, thanks, Dexie," said Tammy, riffling through her file of notes. "We're almost done here. Little left for us now."

"Any closer to a solution?"

"It's borderline hopeless," said Tammy. "We've got nothing to hang onto anyone. No clues, no leads."

He looked downcast. "A dead end, then? All that blood, sweat and tears, and for what?"

Blood? she pondered. Disturbingly apt. "All we've got," she said, "is one or maybe two unidentifiable killers on CCTV. The shape of weapons used, and the fact that our main person is likely to be left-handed."

She gave the matter a bit more thought. Then before she could add anything further, Bob offered, "There was the identified boot print on Daisy Meekins's face."

"Ah, yes," said Tammy. "The print was from a Cloud 5 Waterproof."

"Not much to go on, is it. At least ten, maybe twelve percent of the population is left-handed. I'm left-handed," Dexie said, holding up his hand. "Homer Simpson, wife Marge and son Bart are all occasionally left-handed. Plus, several of us in the club wear Cloud 5s. Where do we go from here, then?"

"It's all frustratingly bleak," Tammy admitted. "What's really worrying is whether our killer is sated, or whether there's going to be more of the same."

Dexie welled up, tears threatening to roll down his cheeks. "I'll have to get another job," he whispered. "The stress is getting to me. It's more than I can stand."

"But you identify as male, Dexie."

"I do," he replied, clasping his palms together in anguish between his thighs. "But what if the killer knows I'm going through the change? If it's someone from the club ...? They'll know I was once female."

"I see your point," said Tammy. "I wish I could make more encouraging noises. Look, we're not giving up yet. Hopefully," she added, trying not to think about Bob's instruction from the Home Secretary.

"Try to stay strong. And, of course, please don't be concerned about letting people down. No-one will blame you if you decide to leave."

"Do you need me for anything more?" Dexie asked bleakly. "Can I go now?"

"Sure. And, Dexie, really, thanks for all your input," said Tammy.

"Not much, I know," said Dexie.

"But it's all been very much appreciated," added Bob.

As Dexie got to his feet, he asked, "Did you make any headway in Belmarsh, Tammy?"

"What?" she said, perplexed. "I don't recall ... Did I tell you about Belmarsh?"

"I must have heard it from somewhere." Dexie shrugged. "Word gets around, you know."

Bob leaned forward, better to hear. Frowned in concentration.

"But, Dexie, no-one knew," said Tammy, exasperated. "How could they? It was all entirely hushed up."

Dexie shook his head in bewilderment. "Someone called Tommy Peters? You?" He pointed at Tammy. "A bloke? Or someone acting like one."

"I don't believe what I'm hearing, Dexie. Not one individual outside a tiny handful, was in the loop about what was planned."

As though he'd not heard her, Dexie said animatedly, "You need to talk to someone called David Eckstein. He's Dominic Pope's son. Changed his name to avoid being identified as Pope's. Rich businessman now in Blackburn. Pope was a serial killer, you know."

"I know, Dexie. But how do you know about all this?"

Ignoring her bemusement, Dexie continued, "His son will be able to point you in the right direction. Tell you what you need to look for."

"I still don't see ..." She glanced over at Bob, who made a noncommittal gesture, his outstretched hands palms up.

They both noticed a subtle change in the demeanour of Dexie. Something you couldn't put your finger on. He started rocking backwards and forwards in the seat he'd resumed, hugging himself like a person freezing. And they both listened as the man stared blankly ahead.

CHAPTER 78 • DAY 48 • 479

"They called me shit and buggered the hell out of me. Bled a lot ... Mum thrashed me. For bleeding. Can you dig it? ... seven years old. Got handed around ... so much garbage to be sampled by as many as were in the place at any one time. Seven? Eight? ... lost count ... daily vision of hell."

Tammy closed the leather-bound notebook, resting her folded hands on the cover, and gazed at Dexie aghast.

"What is it you're saying, Dexie? What is this vision of hell?"

"She did nothing to stop it. Encouraged it. Made me fucking swallow. ... nearly choked till I got used to it. Not that you ever can. That salt taste. Dad was never there. Always at work. Tried to tell him, but it was all deaf ears. Even after she left. Only once, he stopped to listen. Then called me queer. Beat the hell outta me. Black and blue. Couldn't sit or lie down for a week. Can't make a proper relationship."

"Dexie. Please," Tammy entreated. But the realisation was filtering through the veins and capillaries of her body. Icy hands ran down her spine making her shiver.

"Chrissie Ludlow. I loved her. The only one, ever. Let me down badly. Bought her a name bracelet. Gold, it was. Bitch. Refused sex. Tell you why? A bloke, pretending to be a girly girl. She ran from me, but I found her. In a women's shelter. Waited till the others were out, hands on her neck, not strong enough, so cut her throat, then torched the place."

Bob just sat unmoving, head down in an attitude of defeat; his face had gone grey.

"So lonely. I've waited. And waited. This long. No more ... revenge ... kill when I can. Remove ... genitalia. Trans shit."

His voice rising in agitation. *"What the doctor ordered. ... okay really. Doing what comes naturally. I'm no psychopath. They hurt me, now I'll hurt them. Any of them. All of them. Love it. Love it all."*

Shaking his head as though to clear it, Dexie grinned at Tammy and Bob. "Hey, guys. Why so glum?" Then, starting to get to his feet once more, he offered, "Look, your coffees are stone cold. Let me get you fresh ones."

"We're okay thanks, Dexie," said Tammy, waving him back into his seat.

"I'm fine," whispered a badly shaken Bob.

Then Tammy, calming herself, clearing her mind, sitting back in Hester's swivel chair and steepling her fingers, asked, "Tell me, Dexie ..."

"Yes, love." He smiled. "How can I help?"

"Did you kill Anna Proby, Teresa Finch, Judge Jeffreys, Daisy Meekins and the individual found burned in the women's shelter?"

"What! Are you mad? Come on, Tammy." He smiled winningly. "This is me; Decimus, Dexie. Your friend. How can you ask such a crazy question? And to me, of all people, lovey?"

"Dexie! Just give me a straight answer, please. Did you kill those girls? Yes or no?"

"Of course not. For God's sake. Can't you see, they were all killed by David Eckstein."

"Really, Dexie? How do you know?"

"It's his signature, isn't it," said Dexie. *"He likes to kill. It's his thing. Gets his rocks off that way. Cut and slice. Cut and slice. Lovely, lovely. Trans shit. All of them. Now dealt with. Then, home and tranquillity. Gin and tonic. Coronation street. East Enders. Peace. My coat, stolen from a clubber, in Tim's locker. Untraceable DNA. Hee hee. Gave you something to think about, didn't it. That threatening email you got, lady? It's his thing. Eckstein. Didn't you know? Cops are fucking useless.*

CHAPTER 78 • DAY 48 • 481

You're useless. Tommy Peters. Should'a wrapped this up ages ago. Call yourself a PI?

"As for you," he addressed Bob Walker. "Total wanker. Better off as the local vicar, mate. No DNA, mugs. See?" He held up his covered hands. "Allergic eczema? A joke. No-one asked me to take them off for a looksee. Leather gloves, yes? Morons, both of you. No trace of me on the girls." Then pointing to his eyes, he said, "Did you never notice? Brown eyes. Eckstein's are blue. Contacts, people. You two ...?" He shook his head in disbelief. "Like dealing with infants.

"I watched the women's shelter. Knew where Chrissie'd gone. She'd not escape me. The man bitch. I scoped the clubs too. Called myself Mikey. Spoke to the kids at Tilbury. Idiots. Even they didn't recognise me as a white man."

She experienced a moment of blinding clarity, chased by unreasoning exultation. They had him. The Tilbury Ripper. Sitting there. Right now. In front of her and Bob Walker, whom she saw determinedly reaching for his handcuffs. Then, dismay at the understanding of what the man had done.

And confusion as to the references to Eckstein. Brown eyes? Blue eyes? Her head swam. What was that about?

"I feel ill. Gonna be sick." In an instant Dexie'd jumped to his feet, and grabbed the heavy leather-bound notebook, swinging it around, hitting Tammy on the side of the head and likewise Bob Walker's, before whooping and dashing from the room.

AFTERWORD

"Decapitated, Tammy. Do you hear me? For God's sake. What do we do?"

"We call for an ambulance and for support from the nearest nick," she responded, unfazed by the Detective

Chief Superintendent's show of apparent and quite uncharacteristic panic, her adrenalin still pumping.

"Yes, yes. Of course. I'm sorry, Tammy," Bob said, attempting to compose himself. "But this thing has left me terribly shaken."

"I understand," she said solicitously, having never seen Bob Walker in such a state of discomfiture. Now coming up beside him, she peered first at the man with the staring eyes, perceiving the tic in his cheek.

"This one's alive, anyway," she announced dispassionately. "Our friend Mr Dhelavi, I do believe," she added, before making for the other flank of the car to examine the supposedly decapitated man.

A black face with a cloud of white hair that had become dislodged during the crash, revealing a skein of white skin at the top of the forehead. "Look, Bob," she said.

"What!" he replied, still agitated.

"We've found our killer," she announced.

Standing next to her, he asked, "How do you know?" Then realising what he was staring at, exclaimed, "This man is white! And he's alive. Thank God."

"This man is Dexie," said Tammy, pulling the white wig away from the head, revealing a healthy crop of blond hair. "See? Not actually decapitated.

"And he's also, David Eckstein."

"How do you know? How can you be so certain?"

"By the strawberry mark on the back of his hand," she said, pulling off the white leather gloves, revealing pure white hands with the recalled birthmark. "Remember Dexie scorned our failing to find any DNA to link him to the murders? He'd claimed to have allergic eczema. Hence the gloves. Well, there you go. Nothing there."

She'd already called for an ambulance and its siren could be heard approaching.

"I've just realised something that might have occurred to me before." She smiled grimly, her hands on her hips.

"David Eckstein shortens rather conveniently to Dexie, doesn't it?"

"God, yes! You're right. Two birds," announced Bob, heaving a huge sigh. "We could have both been killed."

"But we weren't," she sighed, overcome with weariness. "All done for now."

"All done for now," he echoed with obvious relief.

"We can deal with it from here on in," she said, as though to reassure herself. "It's what we do, isn't it."

"It's what we do," he parroted her again, still bewildered.

"Pity about the car, though," she added wistfully, looking at the remains of the Ferrari.

EPILOGUE

THE SMELL OF BAKING BREAD wafted in from the kitchen where Maria's hitherto unused culinary skills had at last been granted free rein by Tammy, whose normally tyrannical control of the area brooked no protest.

Dov, seated on the sofa with the baby on his lap, looked to be in seventh heaven. His blue jeans and T-shirt contrasting with the baby's choice of bright pink Babygro. Matty, for his part, set off gales of laughter every time the soft toy duck he banged against Dov's chest quacked.

Sprawled out beside them, in her coral silk pyjamas, Tammy looked a picture of mixed exhaustion and contentment. She'd slept for twelve hours, two nights running, and felt she could do with another twelve. Mrs Gilchrist, her PA, had hedged when Tammy had enquired about the obviously mounting backlog. "I can manage perfectly well, Miss Pierre. You won't do yourself or anyone else any good coming in before you're fully rested."

"She's as damned obstinate as I am," Tammy admitted.

"Coffee, madame," said Maria, bringing in a tray with two steaming cups and a plate of Garibaldi biscuits, which she set on one of the small side tables.

"Remind me, Maria," Tammy urged. "To change my will. Service like this must not go unrecognised."

As Maria left the living room, looking overcome with embarrassment, Tammy said to Dov, "You know, in the ambulance with Dexie, he wanted to borrow a mobile to call Eckstein."

"Schizophrenic," suggested Dov.

Easing her aching limbs, wondering if she'd ever feel normal again, she said, "Psychopathic schizophrenia, according to the ad hoc opinion of one of the senior medics I had a long chat with at the hospital."

"I've been thinking about the link between Dexie and the Dhelavi element," said Dov, reaching for a cup and chomping on a biscuit.

"So have I," agreed Tammy, following his example. Coffee had never tasted so good, she decided, wincing as she swallowed the liquid while it was far too hot.

"Anything come to mind?"

"Dexie's father, Dominic Pope, told me when I was in Belmarsh, that the family hailed from Northern Cypress."

"Ah, I see," said Dov. "A mainly Muslim community."

"Right. Explains a lot, doesn't it."

"The need to dominate women. Hatred of flaunted female sexuality. God knows what he made of the clientele at the clubs. Why would he, a wealthy businessman, bother with any of it?"

"Easy," she said. "Once he'd got the ball rolling he let Ricks source the girls, and or any more Muslim gentlemen who wanted to come here, while he sat back, did nothing, raked in his cut."

"Don't see the sense in it."

"Oh, I do," Tammy explained. "No matter how rich, the rich always want to be richer. Here was money for old rope. And remember," she added, "the Dexie, slash Eckstein, slash Pope, family that is, hailed from Northern Cyprus, meaning ...."

"Likely Muslim himself," suggested Dov. "So a warped sense of affinity with the UK Muslim community and the aims of its more dangerous elements."

"Exactly," she agreed.

"Come to think of it, God knows what brought him down from Blackburn to the clubs in the first place."

"Something we're never likely to know," she said.

"But you said he was aiming to go male with transitioning operations planned. The whole thing."

"Not something his alter ego David Eckstein would even begin to understand. Christ, he was really all man. And from Dexie's point of view, the doctor said that though he insisted he was female, he was in fact totally male. No question of mastectomies or anything else related to becoming a man. All a Dexie fantasy."

"Wow! Did you get anything else from Bob before you both left the hospital?"

"A few things."

"I'm agog. The Kerkuts?"

"Disappeared. Probably to Cypress."

"Where else." He nodded. "They'll remain a work in progress."

"Of course. The Samsonite like Jason's on the train. Still with forensics."

Then Dov asked, "Detective Constable Ricks?"

"Will turn King's evidence."

"Seems understandable. Nothing else left to him really." He waited a moment, considering the others. "The three big Muslims who brought in the girls together with the fourth, Dhelavi?"

"Bob says they'll be watched, closely."

"There's no doubt that Dhelavi will go away for a long time," said Dov.

"No doubt at all. He'll be in custody right now like the others and awaiting trial."

"Oscar?"

"We'll find what Ricks has to add to that."

"Hey," said Dov, as though a thought had just struck, "what about the girls in the East London squat? Will they be taken care of?"

"Already well in hand," she reassured him. "Daria and her boyfriend are staying. It's why they came in the first place. Some will go home. The rest will be resettled."

"All very tidy," said Dov. "Too tidy. Neat situations like this always bode trouble."

"I know. Still have loose ends. Apart from the three big men on the loose, we have two unsolved murders that have nothing in common with Dexie's killings."

"Another file to be left open."

"'Fraid so."

A long silence followed, broken only by the sound of the baby gurgling happily on Dov's lap and Maria working in the kitchen preparing lunch, the tinkle of crockery and cutlery apparent, and the couple quietly sipping their coffees.

Shifting uneasily on the sofa, Dov asked apprehensively, "Was there something else you wanted to tell me, Tammy?"

"I don't think so," she hedged, fearing his querying the baby's paternity, yet again. "Oh, yes," she brightened, "you were wondering about Hester?"

"Well ..." he countered doubtfully.

"She's over the moon. Insists I've saved her business, which I suppose I have had a part in. She's even offered to take me on a five-star holiday, all expenses paid, to the Maldives."

"Grief! Is that it, then?"

"Pretty much. Bob apologised for his panic, but after what I put him through, I don't think I'll be hearing from him again. Despite his obvious embarrassment, he'd calmed down and was considering the way forward rationally, as though nothing had actually happened. He'd already spoken with John Manus and Bill, appraised them of events. They were delighted, of course.

"I'll make a point of meeting John and Bill for a drink. Still, it'll be a pity to lose the three as professional colleagues. I shall miss them all."

"And us, Tammy?"

"Us, Dov?"

"Yes us, Tammy. You're dodging the issue. You know exactly what I mean. The baby?"

At last. She felt her heart rattle around her ribcage, and her mouth go dry. There was to be no more avoiding the issue. She'd never told Dov in as many words how much she cared for him. When she gave him the news of the child's paternity, he'd leave. Of that she was in no doubt. He'd made it clear on umpteen occasions he wanted a child of his own, a son to be a father to. Esther had let him down. Wasn't she about to do the same?

"Very well, Dov," she said quietly. "It's time I told you."

"Told me what, Tammy?"

But she held up a hand to shush him. "Let me go through everything now, my love. You have a right to know. So, let me make it clear from the start." She folded her hands in her lap. "I love you, my darling, utterly and completely. You are the best thing that ever happened to me."

"Good to know, Tammy. But …"

She held up a hand again. "But, Dov darling, know this, I will never marry you. I couldn't. You know what I'm like. Variety for me is a drug. While you were briefly away I slept with a man, Tom Volkan, I hardly knew. I'd met him in Hyde Park. Got talking about his dog. Bumped into him again a short time later, outside the pub when I was accosted by suspect Hector Binns."

She waited for a response, but getting none, she went on, "Maybe if we still know each other in twenty years and feel the same way …?"

He looked so downcast he might have been about to weep, something she'd never seen, or expected of him.

"When I was injured and in that makeshift hospital in Syria," she continued. "I was looked after by the man Nabil, head of a Free Syria group of makeshift mercenaries. Without him I would never have made it back."

"You already told me this, Tammy."

Yet again she held up a hand to quieten him. "I told you he'd raped me."

"Yes."

"But, Dov. I lied."

"Really?" Dov looked, sounded troubled.

"I don't expect you to understand. He gave me comfort. I was frightened."

"You, Tammy? Frightened?"

"I'm not Supergirl, Dov."

"Really? But I always thought ..."

"Stop it, Dov ..." she snapped. "And yes, I was frightened. Who wouldn't have been. But I wanted more than the superficial encounter he begged. I seduced him ... Properly. And totally. And here's the thing, Dov. I enjoyed it. Enjoyed it all. It gave me peace. Allowed me to rest. You know I'd been badly injured. I was a mess when I got back. He was the consolation prize. Then he got killed. Helping me escape."

The room was silent.

"Well, say something, Dov," she urged.

"What do you want me to say?" he responded sadly, shrugging.

"You seduced him. It can't have been the first time you seduced a man. It's not the end of your world or mine. You were pregnant when you went out to Syria with our boy. You needed more than just company. I can buy that."

So here it was, at last. Time for the truth, and certainly the end of her relationship with Dov.

"No, Dov. I wasn't pregnant." She paused, once again looking for some reaction on his face, in his eyes. But when he said nothing, she continued, "Dov, I thought I was. But DNA tests have shown the baby isn't yours."

"How did you get my DNA, Tammy?"

"Come on, Dov. It wasn't hard. You're here all the time."

"So, Matty isn't mine." It was a statement, not a question, and Dov looked sombre.

It was at this moment, realising she was about to lose him, that Tammy, her throat constricted, again had to fight back the tears. She looked down at her hands and said nothing. She held her breath, not daring to breathe. Waited for the end.

"So the child is a Muslim?" To Tammy he sounded furious, distinctly shifting away from her on the sofa.

She read the movement, understood it, nodded blankly, dreading his next remark. She wouldn't cry. She mustn't cry. Dammit, she was already crying. Inside.

"They read the Old Testament."

"What?" What was he talking about?

"Like Jews."

"Like Jews," she repeated dumbly, recalling Papa's comment.

"He is your son, Tammy."

"Yes, Dov."

Dov said nothing for an endless time. He looked angrier and angrier.

Then he spoke, in a soft and considered tone, "Then he will be my son too, Tammy. I will love him as my own. I already do."

"Oh," she said, tears flooding her face. "Oh, Dov." And she circled his waist with one arm, moving to sit closer to him, resting her head on his shoulder.

"Tammy." He spoke so quietly she could barely hear him. "I've never seen you cry before."

"You think I never cry? Silly boy." She warmed towards him. "I've simply never let you see it."

At that moment her mobile rang and she put it to her ear. Dov saw her concentrate hard. She seemed worried by what she was hearing.

Then, wide-eyed and gesturing in astonishment, she said, "That was Bob. He's not finished with me."

"What? What does that mean? You look as though you're in trouble?"

"No, darling. Not in trouble. Bob says he may have something for me."

END

DISCUSSION GUIDE

WHETHER YOU'RE LEADING the discussion in your monthly book club, chatting with a friend over coffee or drinks, or musing to yourself about the story you've just finished, you may find some of the questions other readers have asked since *The Black Candle Killings* was originally published in 2021 helpful.

We've also left space after each one, so you can jot any thoughts or additional questions of your own, or from your group to keep the conversation going.

Please visit the author's website, or connect with him on social media, if you'd like to get a direct response. Or invite him to speak at an event or attend a book club meeting (most often virtually, unless you're in the London area or happen to catch him travelling to your vicinity).

www.AuthorAndrewSegal.com
https://www.instagram.com/authorandrewsegal/
https://www.facebook.com/authorandrewsegal/
https://www.linkedin.com/in/randrewsegal/

What did you make of the little poem that preceded the Prologue? Who do you think "R.A." is? How does the poem relate to the story?

How did you feel about the car chase scene in the Prologue? Did Tammy's use of the PIT maneuver that she learned from "American cops" feel like scenes from movies and TV?

Did you suspect anything like what happened to the families introduced in the train scene in Chapter 1? What about how that event returned later in the book?

How many suspects did you accumulate? When did you figure out "who done it"?

If you've read any of the previous Tammy Pierre books, how would you describe the ongoing subplots? Interesting? Satisfying? Other? Which ones would you keep or discard in future books and why?

Which character, besides Tammy, do you like most and why? What flaws do you find in them and do those make them more realistic to you?

Some possibilities to discuss:

Matthew Pierre

Dov Jordan

Mrs Gilchrist

Bob Walker

Judge Roland Jeffries

Dexie

Which villain(s) do you find most challenging for Tammy? Do you like having some of them reappear across books? Do you expect to find the Kerkut brothers in future books and would you like to see their story resolved?

What do you think of the author's style of "jump cuts" from one chapter to the next? In this book, some of the gaps from one scene to its reappearance are much longer than in the prior books, like the intial car chase. Did that work for you?

Can you think of other examples of such transitions, in this book or other authors' books that you found interesting or jarring? How so?

Do the complexities of Tammy's personal and professional life make sense to you, based on the way you've seen people behave in real life, whether those you know personally or the celebrities, politicians, or others you've heard about?

If you could spend some time with the author, what would you like to ask him?

Reminder: Connect with him via —

www.AuthorAndrewSegal.com
https://www.instagram.com/authorandrewsegal/
https://www.facebook.com/authorandrewsegal/
https://www.linkedin.com/in/randrewsegal/

ABOUT THE AUTHOR

SINCE TAKING BACK CONTROL of his books, Andrew Segal has released his own Author's Editions of *The Lyme Regis Murders*, Book One in the Tammy Pierre series, and *The Black Candle Killings*, Book Two. This followed his indie publishing release of Book Three, *The Politician's Wife*, winner of the International Impact Book Award for Mystery/Thrillers.

All three are now widely acclaimed international best sellers. He also won the third prize cash award in the 2025 MTP Short Story Competition for *The Dilemma of Joseph Kaufman*.

In his "day job" professional career, handling bankruptcy and corporate liquidation matters in London's business environment, he's gained extensive experience with people and organizations pushed to the limits, including financial ruin and threats of violence.

He brings that knowledge to bear in creating his main character in this series, private detective Tammy Pierre. She's an ex-police detective, and before that, a "multi-lingual English, Spanish and French-speaking, Politics, Philosophy, and Economics, Oxford graduate, with a postgrad MBA, and more than just a smattering of Hebrew."

Tammy's work now includes both criminal and forensic accounting cases. Skills and experience from both realms, combined with her imposing physical attributes and specialized martial arts training, helped her unravel devious schemes and deal with new and resurfacing villains here in *The Clubhouse Slaughters*.

Now turn the next page for a preview from Book Five in the Tammy Pierre mystery thriller series:

A Corridor of Mirrors

Mirror mirror on the wall,
Who's naked now among them all?
Dressed yourself in tailored best,
Puffed out your futile cockerel's chest.
Perceived yourself as smug and tall,
Prince Charming heading to the ball.
But failed to spot the weir ahead,
The perils of a watery bed.

**Your lifetime spent as someone placid,
Now shrieking in a tank of acid.**

— R.A.

PROLOGUE

THE STATEMENT was barely a whisper, "He's out!" The comment came across as resolute, yet cautious.

"What! Who's out?" came the woman's alarmed rejoinder.

"Who do you think?"

"Not? Not?"

"Go on, say it, Tammy," he urged.

"Oscar Mountford?" She was incredulous. Her face flushed. She could sense the heat rise up her neck, feeling trapped, as though the room was closing in on her. And this, after all she'd done and risked putting him away.

"In one," said the other.

"Not possible," she gasped. How?"

"Clifford Lancaster KC."

"Christ, Lancaster. Of all people."

It was 6.00 am, and she was at her desk in the Bruton Street office, catching up on long neglected files, emails and telephone messages. The Art Deco dolphin ashtray atop the rosewood desk was already full of panetella stubs, despite her vow to stop smoking immediately after her son, Matty, had been born. She paused, wearily considering the unwelcome news and its implications.

"Finest King's Counsellor in the country," she enunciated, regretfully. "Hourly charge, more than twice that of New York's best. Incomparable success rate."

"The very same," came the sober reply.

"But he's hardly served any time. How can he be out already?

"Tammy, as we both know, leave to appeal against a criminal conviction has to be sought within 28 days of sentencing, which, of course, Lancaster ensured would happen. Leave was granted early with Lancaster's connections, and he's out, the Court of Appeal having quashed all his convictions.

She'd not yet recovered from the demands of her investigations into what the press had labelled, the case of, The Tilbury Ripper, the matter of a serial killer, linked to terrorism and religious extremism. Adopting male guise, her self-imposed stay in Belmarsh men's prison, seeking insight into the mind of just such a man, and the beatings she'd sustained while incarcerated, together with her run ins with COBRA, the Cabinet Office Briefing Room A, had left her depleted, demoralised and questioning her own value as a private investigator.

Mrs Florence Gilchrist, ACA, Tammy's incomparable PA, and one who insisted on the old-fashioned forms of address, due in at 9.00am, but usually at least an hour early, had not yet arrived at the office. The cigars butts would have to be flushed down the toilet, copious air freshener deployed and, if there was time, a temporary boost from a line, or maybe two, in the loo, careful to eliminate any trace. Among other things, Mrs Gilchrist was Tammy's chaperone of conscience. She would not be amused if she felt her employer had been over self-indulgent, and Tammy would not want to incur her PA's stern rebuke.

"On what grounds has the man secured a release, Bob? I thought he'd been given a whole of life tariff." Tammy absently lit up another panetella, blowing a jet of smoke ceilingward. No way, she sighed, smelling the traces, was she going to be able to rid the place of the evidence.

Detective Chief Superintendent, Bob Walker, Tammy Pierre's mentor and very nearly her nemesis when she, a budding DI, had chased after and totalled the car of a man who'd flipped her the finger when she'd remonstrated with him after being cut up. Bob had made it clear she was within a whisker of being permanently drummed out of the force. She'd not made the same mistake again, and then some six or seven years ago had established her own agency, Pierre Search and Security, in a smartly refurbished period building in Bruton Street off Mayfair's Bond Street.

"He had, Tammy," agreed, Bob. "But Lancaster argued in the Court of Appeal that the entire trial and conviction was based on unreliable hearsay evidence, albeit from a solicitor, now disgraced and imprisoned. That there was no direct evidence implicating Oscar in any of the killings and his conviction was unsafe."

So that was it. The ghost of Banquo, of which she would never be rid, gazing over her shoulder, breathing down her neck, come back to haunt her.

Except this was no ghost. She drummed her long fingernails on the rosewood desktop. This was Oscar Mountford, wealthy industrialist and murderer, who had others carry out his nefarious demands. A right-wing extremist and originator of the pseudo-political, England First, comprising a collection of white supremacists, misogynist antisemites and no good rabble rousers.

The day which had started optimistically bright now changed abruptly as a cloud portentously passing across the sun, cast the small modern Mayfair office in gloom, echoing her change of mood. Distractedly withdrawing yet another cigar from the pack, she flamed the tip with her Dunhill lighter, letting smoke drift down her throat. Then she realised she'd left the unfinished remains of her previous smoke smouldering in the large ashtray. There'd be time to do that line before her PA arrived, she decided, with the merest twinge of guilt.

CHAPTER 1 DAY 1

"I HAVE A CALL for you, Miss Pierre. She wouldn't give a name."

"Thank you, Mrs Gilchrist, do put her through."

Fiddling with an unlit cigar on the rosewood desk, for what would have been the umpteenth smoked that morning and resisting the temptation to light up yet again while her disapproving PA was in the office, she put the phone to her ear, leaving the panetella to languish temptingly in the dolphin ashtray, and announced, "Tammy Pierre. How may I help?"

"My name is, Jennifer Pascoe." The voice was nervous, uncertain.

"Yes, Ms Pascoe."

She could be heard taking a deep breath before speaking, and then, once started, she continued without pause, as though she had a train to catch.

"My husband was murdered six years ago. Tortured and killed. They put his eyes out. Literally gouged them out, according to the pathologist. They'd somehow found he liked to sketch. Can you believe it? There were traces of rust in the eye sockets. What in God's name had they used on him. An act of unimaginable depravity. Even now, it makes me sick to think of it. And it gets worse; much worse. I'll tell you about the rest in a moment," she added, galloping like a fox hunter.

"Hey, hey, hey, Ms Pascoe," the phone tucked under her chin, Tammy involuntarily raised her hands, as though she could be seen, attempting to rein in her caller. "Please, slow down for a moment, draw breath. We're not on the clock, you know."

"Yes. I'm sorry. I'm sorry."

"You don't need to apologise." Then Tammy said, "Would you feel better talking here in my office?"

An hour later they sat in the chairs in front of Tammy's desk and Tammy reassured her, "Just take your time and tell me what happened, as far as you know."

"Yes, of course. Well, drawing was his hobby; it had a calming effect on him. Stemmed some of those terrible rages he used to get. Sadly, for him, and his victims," she added, "killing had the same effect as sketching. It soothed him when he was in a state. Which was all too often.

"Whatever it was they wanted from him, his torturers, that is, information? I presume, they can't have got, so they murdered him, let him die a slow death." She sounded close to tears, even years after the event. "Time isn't always the healer it's supposed to be."

"You're making some pretty dramatic assumptions here, Ms Pascoe. Slow death?"

The woman had calmed down now, surer of herself, "No I'm not. The police know exactly what happened to him. So did the press." She waited a moment, then continued, "I said there was more, didn't I. They forced him to drink sulphuric acid."

"Christ almighty!" The revelation sent ice running through her veins and she shuddered involuntarily. She'd seen, experienced or learned about a lot of horrific acts of violence in her time on the Met, and since then as a PI, but this? This was on an unheard-of scale.

"Then as he lay dying, they dumped him into a one-thousand-gallon plastic lined tank of the stuff, but kept his head from being submerged, so when he was found most of his body had melted, but enough of his head and throat had remained intact for the pathologist to note that his vocal cords were shredded. It was said they looked like filigree; he'd screamed so hard they'd torn apart. There was barely sufficient of the rest of him left for the pathologist to make an assessment. It was considered too gruesome for the public, and the detail was largely kept from the press. I was expected to identify the body. What was left of it. Really, just the head."

"That must have been beyond horrific for you."

"It was sunken, like a deflated balloon, and skin the colour of concrete. I barely made it to the loo before vomiting. I get nausea remembering. I'll never be rid of the sight. It'll be with me for life."

"Ms Pascoe, do you happen to know where this all took place? Did the police ever mention anything?

"The Clerkenwell area was all they'd say. A derelict building was mentioned almost in passing. I wondered about the 300-year-old derelict waterworks building, now being redeveloped."

"Some killers leave a calling card, almost as though they want their so-called crimes to be the subject of accolade rather than horror. Anything you can think of?"

Jennifer paused for several seconds, then said quietly, "My cat. I couldn't take her with me when I went out that day, so Morris said, not to worry, he'd look after her. Feed her. Not to worry? That's a joke. I can't bear to think of it, how and when they got hold of Suki, who was very timid, always ran from strangers. But they disembowelled her, left her by the tank." Tammy could hear Jennifer Pascoe weeping again and said nothing further till she could hear the woman blow her nose.

Then carrying on, Tammy said, "In my few years in the police I don't think I'd ever come across or heard of anything so sinister. The act of a maniac, or group of them. Not unique of course. The acid, I mean. In 1949, John Haigh was convicted of the murder of several people, mainly to steal their valuable assets. He was hanged. Known as the acid bath killer, he disposed of his victims by immersing them in sulphuric acid. The one difference between Haigh's activities and those of your husband's killers is that Haigh's victims were dead when he submerged them. Mostly shot in the head, or else battered to death. Your husband's killing doesn't bear thinking about."

"I try not to think about it. The police have long ago given up trying to find his killers, not a trace. Not a clue."

"Not generally appreciated by the press or public, Ms Pascoe, if the police don't get a positive lead within the first twenty-four to forty-eight hours, you'd be astonished how soon the trail goes cold. For all that, from what you say, it seems they'd been thorough, though."

"As you'd expect. But the detective chief super on the case recently suggested I call you. Bob Walker. Hence, this conversation."

"An old friend, ex-boss, and mentor."

"I see. He said you might be able to help. I make no apologies for my spouse. He was a criminal and ultimately a vile individual. Vile that is, to everyone but me, and God help me, I loved him. At least, I loved the man I thought I knew. There's no accounting for it, is there. Presumably the Yorkshire Ripper's wife loved him. Though somewhere along the way I'd lost him. My husband, I mean. But, no matter, for the last ten years of his life I believe he'd tried to go straight."

"So why now, Jennifer? Why after six years are you seeking to resurrect this case if it's all gone quiet? Talk to me."

"Nothing complicated.

"I'm listening."

"Simply, once or twice I've spotted people, in the street, in a supermarket, looking at me curiously. As though they know me, though I don't know them. Am I being paranoid? Maybe. But I'd like closure, I'm not going back to Tasmania. This is my home, but I want to feel safe."

"Understood. But, Tasmania?" Tammy gazed at the woman's troubled face, then urged her on, "Tell me about your husband first."

"You see, when I married him he was a timid little nobody. Well, not little. He was around six three and should have known how to take care of himself, except he hardly ever did. I mean, he'd never stand up for himself in an argument. We struggled at first, financially, as you'd expect of most newlyweds. We wanted a mortgage but couldn't afford one, no matter how many lenders we approached; then suddenly we could. He never told me how he got the money for the deposit or how he was able to afford the monthly payments. Something had happened. He wouldn't confide. Said he didn't want me involved in any way. That's when I saw he'd changed."

She paused a moment as though considering whether to go on and reveal more. But then what did she have to lose? "I suspected it all started when he got involved in an actual fight, came home one day with badly bruised and bloodied knuckles he couldn't avoid my seeing, and from there he began to realise his own strength. Things he said to me, hints, suggestions. He was more confident. But at the same time, more troubled. I could never quite put my finger on it. I even wondered if he might have killed a man. Or men."

"What made you think that, specifically?"

"Just that nothing and no-one frightened him anymore. He became more than just self-assured, he was arrogant. Aggressive. Not with me. But with everyone else he encountered."

"And you think that makes him into a killer? Seems a bit thin, doesn't it?"

"Not just that. But, you see, within a year he'd not only paid off the original mortgage, but we'd moved from our little two bed apartment in a shabby part of Notting Hill to a four-bed detached house in Richmond, Surrey. And this is the thing, he paid for it in cash."

"So, where did you think he got the money from?"

"As I intimated to you, I'd already suspected he was doing contract work."

"Contract work? Like contract killing?"

There was a hesitation, then, softly as though afraid of being overheard, despite the privacy of Tammy's office, "That's exactly what I believed. No other way, short of winning the lottery, that anyone could make money as fast as he did and do it legitimately. I might have been wrong I wish I had been. But of course, my intuition was eventually proved correct."

"Hmm."

"On occasions, he'd leave the house early in the morning, always with something hidden under his jacket. He thought I'd seen nothing; but the bulge? Of course, it was a gun. Had to be. I'm convinced he kept it in a safe in the attic. Said he lodged the deeds of the house and other important documents there for safety's sake but never let me see inside it."

"Sounds plausible."

"What an irony he should die the way he did. As a killer ... I heard what the police learned, that he showed no mercy. But as you see, in the end, he received no mercy either." She waited a moment, emphasising her point, "Divine retribution?"

"So, what did your husband do for a living when you first met up?"

"He was a simple IFA when he started out."

"An Independent Financial Advisor."

"Correct. He was also into IT in a big way. Had a natural talent for it."

"I wonder," mused, Tammy.

"Go on."

"Your husband was murdered in 2017, a year that was the height of the crypto currency scams. Billions were made and lost as hundreds of thousands of people got caught up in the madness. Millions, in fact."

"What would that have had to do with, Morris?"

"Bear with me for a moment. You know, for anyone to have tortured your husband in the way that he was would have necessitated there being an overwhelming reason. Enough to subject him to the type of horror you've described."

"I still don't see where this is going."

"Your husband was into IT?"

"Yes."

"In a big way, you said?"

"Maybe. I, I really don't know. I think ..."

"I'm going to work on a theory. A hunch, if you will."

"What do you have in mind?"

"Before I tell you what my notion is, let me ask; did your husband ever mention anything, I mean anything at all, about crypto currencies?"

Jennifer Pascoe closed her eyes and thought for several moments, her hands nestling in her lap, "As a matter of fact, he did." She said, trying to recall what her husband had said. An idea came back to her. "Actually, now I come to think of it, he talked about them at some length, but it was all above me. I only half took note."

"Okay." Tammy was listening intently, trying to see if she could deduce anything from her tone of voice. But there was nothing.

The woman breathed, then said, "He described something called, One Coin? and then another called, Bit Connect?"

"What did he say?"

"I hardly understood, so I never really listened properly. As I said, it was all above me. He mentioned another name ..." she hesitated, thinking. Then, "Said he'd been caught up in something he wanted out of. Something huge, he'd been forced to help build? Whatever that meant. He said it was called, Coiner bIT."

"Huh! Coiner bIT," she pronounced it as one word. She said it again, "Coin a bit. How appropriate."

"Why, appropriate?"

"The three biggest crypto currency scams on the planet, involving tens of billions of dollars. Millions of so-called investors. Duped. Ripped off. Sunk without trace. I'll wager they, your husband's killers, whoever they were, wanted access to the funds of Coiner bIT, and your husband, maybe after an uncharacteristic attack of conscience, refused to give them what they wanted."

"Would an attack of conscience be sufficient for him to have gone through all he did before dying? Really?"

"No," Tammy sighed. "You're right. There'd have to have been something more. Keep talking to me, Ms Pascoe.

"I'd never thought of conscience being a factor. On the other hand, maybe he thought that by holding out he'd protect me in some way. There must have been more. I just know he used terms and words I'd never heard of before, and it seemed he wanted to unload to someone."

"What sort of terms?"

"Initial coin offers, or ICOs, as he came to call them. Crypto exchanges."

"Any names mentioned?

"Something about a BTC-e crypto exchange which he said was a Russian mega money laundering operation."

"I've heard of it. Seems your husband was involved with some pretty shady pastimes."

"He told me; he said the crypto he was involved with, Coiner bIT, was accessible only through coded passwords, known as private keys. He'd had some help in putting together the passwords needed by an Israeli IT expert called Bronstein, and that she might have had loose links to Mossad."

"You seem to be able to recall more than you imagined you would."

"You know how it is when you start talking about something you thought of as obscure. Ideas start to flow, memories to emerge."

"Don't they just. And?" asked, Tammy. "Who knew the private key?"

"From what he told me, only he knew it, in its entirety that is. Usually, they comprised twelve separate words. His was ultra safe. It was twenty-four words."

"Go on, Ms Pascoe. You're doing fine."

"I'm worked up and things keep coming back to me. Morris was concerned about the security risk if he knew the whole code, so he split it and told Sarah Bronstein to take her half and modify it so only she knew it."

"Do you recall whether he ever alluded to sums of money?"

There was a long pause, then Ms Pascoe said, "The figures seemed ridiculous at the time. but as you've mentioned it …"

"Yes?"

"Would a figure of forty billion dollars mean anything?"

"Mean anything?" Tammy erupted. "But that's it isn't it?"

"His killers wanted access to the money, and he died without giving them the pass key. Even if he'd wanted to he could only have given them his half, but that would be enough for them to start. Am I right? They'd have found his notes in the house, on his laptop wherever, regarding his liaison with Sarah Bronstein and known to approach her next?" Ms Pascoe asked. "Except they've left it dormant for six years."

"I'm surprised they didn't threaten him with a promise to kill or torture you."

"Everything gets clearer, the longer we talk about it."

"How do you mean?"

"Morris insisted I have minor surgery. A nose job. Nothing major. A bit more retroussé. Said it made my pretty face even prettier. Then he made me cut my fair hair short and dye it black. He got me a false passport and insisted I take a two-month break in Tasmania, of all places. Nothing was ever explained. But obviously, he set out to protect me, didn't he, and died because of it. He knew what was likely to happen if I wasn't spirited away."

"How soon after you left was he picked up by his torturers?"

"According to the press dates given, almost immediately I'd left."

"So he died in stalling them to give you ample time to escape. He must have loved you very much Ms Pascoe."

"I believe so," she was crying freely now.

"It rather looks like it, Ms Pascoe. Ms Pascoe? Ms Pascoe?" said Tammy, leaning forward. "Please don't cry. I'll do all I can to find your husband's killers. I promise you."

"Can we end this now? Please?"

"I won't trouble you much further, Ms Pascoe, but tell me one more thing, when you came back from Tasmania did you revert to your original name?"

"No. I kept the name Pascoe."

"Just in case."

"That's right."

"So what was, or is, your real name?"

"I was Susan Greenleaf. And to tell the truth, this conversation has left me more frightened than I was before. What if they find me and think I have knowledge of the passkey? God! What then?"

CHAPTER 2 DAY 2

SHE ALWAYS CARRIED a burner with her. If anyone tried to hack her main mobile, they'd not be able to access the disposable phone if she chose to make contacts incognito.

So it was with a jarring shock she heard the burner bleep and, extracting it from her jacket pocket found a text message awaiting her.

STAY AWAY FROM THE GREENLEAF WOMAN. YOU DON'T KNOW WHAT YOU BOTH GETTING YOUSELVES INTO.

Christ above. Whoever they were, they even knew Susan's real name. And the script surely reflected an accent. Continental? She could only draw a blank but stored it for further reference.

Tammy stopped walking. Closed her eyes, the noise of the traffic fading to an angry hum. The world tilted on its axis.

A barking dog woke her up to her surroundings.

They might be watching her now. The threat ballooned in her head till she felt it might burst.

She liked to be the one in control. Making the plans. Having people at her beck and call. She demanded it, gained people's respect because of it. That wasn't to be on the agenda here. She'd be watching her back at every moment.

Not for the first time in her professional life, instead of the hunter, she was the prey. Unconsciously, she looked over her shoulder. Any one of a dozen people walking along Bond Street might be tracking her. A tall man in an overcoat. The glamorous woman in designer bell bottoms. A young man hurrying along grasping a bunch of flowers.

What had happened to Ms Pascoe's husband? She could almost hear the screams. Not afraid to die? Tammy'd always claimed nothing scared her. But this? Her turn next? The back of her neck prickled.

Or Jennifer Pascoe?

God! Jennifer. Should she go back to Tasmania for the time being? Would anything persuade her to leave the UK, right now? Unlikely. Despite the fear she'd expressed, during their conversations, she'd still struck Tammy as being a level-headed and determined individual. Whatever happened during Tammy's investigation, Jennifer Pascoe would want to learn first-hand.

Hurrying along Bond Street, she kept her eyes open for a cab to take her to Scotland Yard on the Embankment where she'd meet up with Bob Walker and those leading the team during the initial investigation into Morris Greenleaf's murder six years ago.

She'd just hailed a taxi and was making for it when she was buffeted aside by an overweight, middle aged, track suited individual.

"Outa my way, lady." The accent was unclear.

CHAPTER 3 DAY 2

"GENTLEMEN, IT SEEMS our meddling black, Hebrew friend is looking into the circumstances surrounding the tragic death of our former IT expert, friend and fixer Mr Morris Greenleaf."

Oscar Mountford, tall, sartorially impeccable, frequently spoken of by Bob Walker to Tammy, and until recently a guest of His Majesty's, having been absolved of a raft of murders, including that of his own son, and his mistress, but paradoxically, not that of Morris Greenleaf, which killing had occurred several years earlier, was free from jail, relishing every moment of his liberty.

* * * * *

Be ready for the Spring 2026 release of
Book Five in the Tammy Pierre series:

A Corridor of Mirrors
ANDREW SEGAL

Printed in Dunstable, United Kingdom